The Sunset
Merchants

The Sunset Merchants

Harry Jordan

To order additional copies of this book, contact:
Xlibris Corporation
1-888-795-4274
www.Xlibris.com
Orders@Xlibris.com
22498

FOR PAMELA AND DANIEL, WITH MUCH LOVE

In Flanders Fields

In Flanders fields the poppies blow
Between the crosses, row on row
That mark our place; and in the sky
The larks still bravely singing, fly
Scarce heard amid the guns below.

We are the Dead. Short days ago
We lived, felt dawn, saw sunset glow,
Loved and were loved, and now we lie
In Flanders fields

Take up our quarrel with the foe:
To you from failing hands we throw
The torch, be yours to hold it high.
If you break faith with us who die
We shall not sleep, though poppies grow
In Flanders fields

John McCrae, 1872-1918

. . . . they do not sleep . . . .

Briton Shot Dead by

Russian Mafia

A British academic shot dead in Moscow was an innocent bystander caught in the crossfire of a Russian mafia shoot-out, according to police and diplomats.

Professor Beattie, from Oxford, died instantly from a gunshot wound to the head when two men burst into the £400 a night hotel and opened fire with Kalashnikov rifles, unleashing about 40 rounds.

Detectives believe the Professor, who was drinking a glass of vodka in the hotel's foyer cafe, was hit by a stray bullet after the gunmen began firing at a group of Russian men sitting at another table. Two of the group were killed and a third seriously injured. The gunmen then escaped by car, leaving behind their guns and coats.

Reports were circulating in Moscow last night that the killings involved the Razmov gang, one of a handful of competing criminal organisations that plague the Russian capital.

"We have no reason to believe that Professor Beattie was anything other than an innocent bystander," said Roger Hampbell-Davies, a spokesman for the British Embassy. He said police were compiling a report on his death that would eventually be given to Sir William Abbotts, the Ambassador.

The Independent

Prologue

ARAKAWA, TOKYO. The gunman shifted silently in the shadows, shaking the damp stiffness from his legs. His eyes remained locked onto the apartment opposite, a hawk sizing its prey, alert to the smallest sign of movement. Six thirty came and went. Now he was growing impatient.

Come on, come on!

Matsu was late. It had been a cold, uncomfortable watch. Even in the quietest corners of the night a steady flow of people had come and gone. Businessmen, party-revellers, taxis, shift workers. In the old-fashioned riverside neighbourhood of wooden houses and narrow streets, it was difficult for a solitary, waiting figure not to arouse suspicion.

A long dark limousine turned the corner. Seconds later it cruised to a halt outside the apartment. There was a brief, sharp bark from its horn. At six forty-five the door to the apartment opened. The silhouette of a man appeared, framed against the soft yellow light inside.

Now was his time. The gunman reached inside his jacket. He watched as the silhouette turned back towards the hallway to embrace an unseen figure.

'I'll see you tonight.' The words—and the sound of a kiss—carried clear and loud in the crisp, cold quiet of the dawn. There was a low female murmur in response.

The silhouette emerged into the dull yellow streetlight and walked briskly away from the apartment. There was nothing distinctive about him: a dark, double-breasted suit, dark shoes, dark tie, white shirt.

A bland businessman's uniform, cloned across the world. In his right hand he held a squat computer carry-case.

For a moment the gunman questioned whether he had the right man. Akani Matsu looked younger than his fifty-seven years and thinner than on TV. He glanced quickly up and down the street, checking for signs of a guard or escort. Nothing. Until he reached the sanctuary of his armoured limousine, Matsu was alone. It was time to move. A few more steps and Matsu would be inside his armour-plated car, out of range.

The gunman stepped out, the gun thrust forward in a double-handed grip. Fifty metres to go. He started to run. Matsu opened the car door. Forty metres. Matsu placed his computer case on the passenger seat. Thirty. Matsu removed his jacket, hung it inside the car, said something to the driver. Twenty. Matsu started to turn as if sensing the gunman's silent approach.

At ten metres and closing the gunman fired, the heavy gun bucking angrily in his hands. One, two, three, four. Done. He turned and moved swiftly towards his moped. In Tokyo's seamless traffic, two-wheeled transport is the only way to move. The moped barked into life and moments later he had vanished into the twilight dawn.

The bullets hit Akani Matsu, head of Japan's National Police Agency, as he was midway into the car. Three of the .38 calibre bullets passed straight through him, penetrating his back, chest, leg, stomach and pancreas. The fourth shattered his spinal cord. By the time the driver and his wife reached him, he was already dead.

The assassination headlined the international news. Media-friendly rent-a-quotes blamed revenge by the *Yakuza*, Japan's organised crime syndicates. Matsu had played a key role in drafting legislation to restrict their activities. His office was long accustomed to receiving, and discounting, death threats. Until now they were just that—threats. Some speculated that the shooting was revenge. Others blamed an obscure religious cult.

But none of the so-called 'experts' were right: the attacks were simply a demonstration—a small sideshow. An opening skirmish in a battle that was only now about to begin.

1

MOSCOW, RUSSIA. It was early evening, shortly after six. Tourists stood idly on street corners trying to make sense of their maps. Muscovites and army soldiers sauntered leisurely along the streets, talking and laughing in small groups. A tiny, coiffured dog ran alongside a woman and yapped at her ankles, ignoring her efforts to shoo it away. A wind gusted from the north and for the first time there was a hint of the cruel Russian winter in the air.

Peter Brewer sprinted up the steps from the Metro three at a time. He stopped at the top to take his bearings and then turned and walked briskly along *Prospekt Marksa* towards the *National*. He failed to notice the large figure who had been waiting opposite the Metro entrance and who now carefully folded his newspaper into quarters and moved purposefully towards him.

Brewer moved quickly along the street, oblivious to the gunman drawing closer behind him. His thoughts were elsewhere, dwelling on the unlucky hand that London had dealt him. There could be nothing more routine, more dull, to him than this: an uneventful investigation into the death of an ageing British academic. This new Russia was different to the Russia he had once known: the whole country, in its post-Communist euphoria, was like a young, stumbling child trying to take its first uncertain steps. He was not so sure he liked the changes he saw: there had been something distinctive about the Russia he had known under Brezhnev, Andropov and Chernenko.

It was only a child's chance playful shout that made Brewer

turn. Now luck was with him. As he turned, his eyes locked momentarily on the gunman's. He caught the glint of metal, sensed rather than saw the weapon held loosely at his side. Brewer's response was pure instinct: there was no time to think, no time to reason. He ducked, turned and ran.

Now was the gunman's chance. He accelerated, his arm raised, the gun steady in his grip. Shots rang out. One, two, three. Suddenly the mood changed. Tourists and Muscovites turned to stare in disbelief at this new and unexpected street theatre. Brewer rushed past their blank, uncomprehending faces, shouting at them to move, to clear out of the way. The yapping dog scampered away whining. Somewhere a woman screamed. Brewer stumbled, twisted and recovered.

The gunman edged closer, fitter and faster than his prey.

He fired again as Brewer reached the foyer of the *National.* An invisible hand jerked violently at Brewer's sleeve. Chips of sharp, stinging paint and concrete flew into his face. His breath came in short, panting gasps. God, he was out of condition. Too many years of easy living had taken their toll. A second volley of shots, dull metallic *thump thumps*, erupted as he ducked behind the hotel's interior staircase.

He needed something to defend himself with and fast. But there was nothing. Hurried footsteps hammered across the cold marble flooring. One more step and the gunman would see him. Even a blind man with a burlap sack over his head could not fail at this range. Brewer remembered the automatic pistol hidden inside the suitcase in his room. Why the hell had he left it *there?* He was stale, had forgotten the ground rules, the first basic laws of an agent abroad:

Know the territory; always be prepared.

The footsteps halted. Brewer froze, catching his breath. There was a glimpse of a man muffled in an overcoat and scarf, the stale, warm smell of his breath, and then just as quickly the man was gone, his hurrying steps echoing around the foyer.

Brewer stepped out and into the street. He looked quickly one way, then another, his restless eyes scanning every doorway, every window, anxious not to be caught unawares a second time. Nothing. A typical Moscow street scene. The whole episode could have been a dream, a moment of crazed insanity. Even the irritating, yapping dog had reappeared. Crowds milled aimlessly around as if nothing had happened.

Perhaps it was for the best. Brewer was not in the mood to chase an armed maniac with nothing more threatening than a used handkerchief. Hotel staff were already gathering by the door and cluck-clucking with familiarity at the bullet holes scarring the hotel's pre-revolutionary facia. They had seen it all before.

'Mafia,' one confided wisely, chewing slowly on imported American gum.

'Maybe,' Brewer nodded and went up to his room, unconvinced.

The following afternoon, refreshed and re-energised, Brewer found himself negotiating hard with a receptionist at the former KGB archives, who in return was examining him with outright disdain.

'This is a simple matter. The state archives are open only to accredited researchers.' The man shrugged and raised his arms in the air. 'You do not have the accreditation, so I regret access is not possible.'

'Whatever happened to *Perestroika*?' Brewer asked. 'You know, openness, democracy, all that brave new world bullshit?'

Bureaucracy was a nagging thorn snagged right in the middle of Brewer's life. It was not the first time his enquiries had been blocked by a small, balding man in a borrowed suit. And it would not be the last. The same breed of obstructive official exist the world over. Somewhere a very successful business, *Jobsworth International Inc.*, turns out petty-minded officials to order, nationality, race, age, gender no obstacle. Brewer knew: he had met them all.

The curator shook his head again at Brewer's persistent questions.

'*Perestroika*? A matter for the President. What is a man to do? I have my instructions.'

'Nothing changes, does it?' Brewer responded sharply and turned away.

Welcome to the new Russia, Brewer thought bitterly as he stepped outside. The spots had changed, but he still recognised the animal lurking inside. One thing was certain. He was never going to secure access to the former KGB archives without serious high-level pressure. London, in that suave, blithe way of theirs, had assured him that gaining access to the archives was not an issue.

'Don't worry, Brewer,' they had promised him before his trip. 'It's all very different in Russia these days. No need for all that quintuplicate paperwork and bundles of used dollars for backhanders. Russia's one of us these days, back in the fold.'

So it was London's screw-up, not his. Which somehow came as no surprise: screw-ups had long since become London's trademark. His pre-mission lecture on the 'new' Russia came courtesy of a so-called Civil Service 'fast-streamer', a spotty Oxbridge type whose closest encounter with Russia was probably a *Sunday Telegraph* review of the fifty best places to buy a cappuccino on the Black Sea coast. The whole operation stank and Brewer had better things to do with his life than run London's dead-end errands. The idea that the former KGB archives were public property rang about as true as the inebriated marriage vows of a groom dressed as Elvis in downtown Vegas meeting his bride for the first time.

Brewer could almost have stomached the aggravation if it wasn't for one unfortunate fact: it was not the Russians who were responsible for blocking access to the KGB's innermost secrets— it was the West. The threat of the former KGB's confidential internal papers becoming public had made the West's security and political echelons swallow hard and reach for their wallets. If the KGB had dared to carry out its original promise of throwing its archives open to the great unwashed, far too many of the West's own dark and miserable secrets would also have been exposed for all the world to see. It could all have turned very ugly indeed.

Of course, the KGB knew this very well. The whole idea had

only ever been a negotiating tactic. The result of the KGB's threat to open their archives was a flurry of diplomatic activity. Anxious men in dark suits and dark glasses had scuttled to Moscow from London and Washington to reach an 'accommodation' that certain 'sensitive' papers would be withheld under cover of a humanitarian aid and assistance programme: the Russians sat back and named their price. And now the archive's key papers were buried deeper than under the communists—up to a point, that is. Like anything else in Moscow, access could still be arranged: for a price. The only problem being London has not played that game since the Stalinist bureaucracy and penny-pinching brought in by the Thatcher administration. Even after Al Qaeda's attacks on America, money remained tight. Any new money that did come into the service soon disappeared into signals intelligence, head office staff, middle-management processes and external management consultants: rarely did it find its way through to the field agent. And Brewer was not about to start volunteering his own small change on London's half-baked schemes.

He stood quietly on the street and lit up a small *Romeo y Julieta*. It looked like there was no alternative: he would have to request assistance from Captain Sarkovsky. The thought did not excite him. Worse than that: the thought positively depressed him. Leonid Sarkovsky of the Russian Federal Security Agency, the KGB's successor following the USSR's demise in 1991, resented the outbreak of East-West co-operation deals and made no effort to hide it. And Sarkovsky was far from alone.

Most Russians had long since come to a cold and unpleasant conclusion: they had been sold a pup by the West, a mirage of a promised land of milk and honey that vanished as soon as they signed the loan agreements. Only too late had they noticed the financial small print. The transition from a centralised totalitarian state to an egalitarian democracy was not proving an easy journey, and as usual, those at the bottom of the heap were suffering most.

Despite its problems, Brewer still had a deep, strong affection for Russia. It had long been his home ground, his turf under the Firm's former Russian Controller before his transfer to the

European section. The old Russia, with all its warts and faults, he had at least known and understood. Times had changed—and quickly too. Brewer was beginning to miss the Cold War, miss the contrast and electric energy that once existed in the antagonism between East and West. There was little interest for him in the wall-to-wall instant gratification, big business sponsored pop-youth culture that was slowly infecting every country. It was local customs and culture that made a country distinctive, which lent it character and interest. And everywhere these qualities were in retreat, ebbing rapidly across the sands.

Yet, thought Brewer, as he walked slowly back towards the Metro station, even anti-Western cynicism didn't prevent the very same Russians who complained bitterly about the West from queuing for Big Macs, drinking Coke and watching Hollywood movies. Perhaps it was just a time of transition, difficult days that would pass only when a new regime had been constructed from the ashes of the old. Or perhaps it was just the same old bullshit the politicos spouted in every country and he was getting too old and cynical—and should find himself some new glasses without the rose tints.

Pre-occupied with his problems, the unmarked khaki Lada parked on the opposite side of the street went unnoticed. Its occupant watched Brewer's progress with close interest. Yesterday Brewer had been lucky. *Prospekt Marksa* had been too busy, the *National* too full of witnesses. Today would be different.

The man took the AKM from the rear seat and rested it on the open window. The AKM, a successor to the highly successful AK-47, is not a subtle weapon: but with a rate of fire around 800 rounds per minute, frankly who cares. It has the compensation of being deadly effective. And violence is too commonplace on Moscow's streets for subtlety to matter any more.

He adjusted the crude sights until Brewer's head filled them. His finger edged towards the trigger. One more step and his assignment would be fulfilled. Brewer would be removed. And then only the Professor's girlfriend would remain: Anastasia. She would be simple. And he intended to have fun with her. He smiled in anticipation, impatient to finish Brewer.

The man missed the sound of the car's passenger door being opened behind him. Big mistake. The first sound he heard was the silencer as it snapped sharply into the barrel of the small automatic. By then it was too late. As he turned, his mouth wide with surprise, the first two bullets shattered his skull. The AKM fell from the window sticky with blood.

His killer hesitated for a moment, as if surprised at the results of his own handiwork. He appeared an unlikely murderer: smartly dressed, with gold-framed glasses and short ginger hair, he looked like a nervous accountant.

'And that, in case you were wondering, was for the Professor,' he said quietly and turned away, pushing the car door shut. He turned to look across the street.

Brewer, oblivious to the short and violent drama that had been played out behind him, reached the steps to the Metro and disappeared from sight.

The man smiled. 'Goodbye, Mr Brewer,' he whispered. 'Safe journey.'

2

'Ah. Mr Brewer.' Captain Sarkovsky failed to hide his obvious disappointment at seeing Brewer again. 'I presume this is not a social visit, so what is it you want of me?'

Brewer lowered himself into the worn wooden chair in front of Sarkovsky's desk.

'Your assistance. To be precise, access to the restricted section of the KGB archives.'

Sarkovsky raised his eyebrows. 'Access to the restricted archives? Interesting.' He sat for a moment without speaking. 'Perhaps I can ask you why?'

'I'm continuing my inquiry into the late Professor's line of research. Following through on a few leads first hand. You know how it is.'

Sarkovsky swivelled slowly from side to side in his chair, generating a teeth-jarring atonal melody of metal grinding against metal. He did not look like Brewer's idea of a Russian. He was tall and balding, a lanky figure with the appearance of a retired second league baseball player. His clothes hung on him with all the elegance of a well-worn 1970's suit draped around a mannequin in a second-rank charity shop. Sergei Sarkovsky looked like the type of cop who would be at home out on the streets pursuing an investigation—not stuck behind his desk.

On the wall behind him several framed certificates of commendation gathered dust. They had been issued in the heyday of the old Communist regimes. It was all a lifetime ago, a world that must have existed in a parallel universe—it all seemed so remote and unbelievable now. Names out of history books. Brezhnev, Andropov, Chernenko, Gorbachev.

Sarkovsky was evidently no disciple of clear desk policies. His desk was invisible beneath layers of yellowing files and papers. In front of him lurked an old manual typewriter, an orphan prop from a bit part in a 1930's movie. Around him his colleagues sat silently at their desks, scribbling with blunt pencils on discoloured grey paper, lost in the cavernous space of the high-ceilinged, smoke-stained room. In the corner, a bakelite telephone with a rotary dial and fabric flex rang unanswered.

'Ah, Mr Brewer, Mr Brewer. You are wasting your time. There is nothing of any interest to you in the archives. You are an intelligent man. Why do you bother so with the Professor?' Sarkovsky sighed. 'I have lost no sleep over the matter. It was an accident. Wrong place, wrong time. Like so many other victims of chance crime, the Professor was killed purely by accident. Such a dull man too. A sad lonely academic with a hyperactive libido. Nothing out of the ordinary. But perhaps you can tell me, what brings so many of your dull academic Westerns professors here? Have they nothing better to do? Something more productive, something more profitable?' He spat out the last word as if it choked him.

'Professor Beattie was murdered. No accident. All I want is to know why. I don't like mysteries. Then I will go home.'

'Ah! *You* say he was murdered.' Sarkovsky leaned forward. 'But *I* say it was an accident. He was an innocent caught up in a street crime. That is all. Nothing more. Nothing less. It is all so simple, but not it seems to your mind. You interest me, Mr Brewer. What makes you so sure he was killed? Perhaps, for example, you know something I do not.' He thought a moment. 'Was he working for London?'

Brewer smiled. 'Is that what you think?'

Sarkovsky sighed again. 'I do hope that it was not the case. It would be against our agreement. East, West, friends is best. And we must, must we not, be so very careful with the archives. The Professor was given full access as an academic. He should not have misused that position.'

'I never said he did.' Brewer removed his glasses and polished them slowly with the corner of his shirt. Sarkovsky became a blur. 'Let's just say his interests and ours were developing along conveniently similar lines. We hoped that Professor Beattie might save us the trouble of doing unnecessary footwork ourselves.'

'And now he is dead.'

'And now, as you so correctly observe, his state of health has declined irrecoverably.'

'Then perhaps you can tell me. What was this work you hoped he would do?'

Good. Sarkovsky was biting.

Brewer put his glasses back on. Sarkovsky jumped into focus. Brewer was not sure he liked the improvement.

'I'm hungry. Let's eat.'

Sarkovsky chose something the restaurant menu called 'veal', but which had all the colour and freshness of a discarded cardboard toilet roll. Brewer opted for a double *oeuf Russe*, which was more *oeuf* than *Russe*. After several all-night sessions spent examining the former contents of his stomach Brewer was now careful to avoid 'meat' in the restaurants of the new Russia. His suspicion was that most of the 'meat' had until recently been scuttling around the sewers squeaking and dragging its tail behind it.

Brewer remembered visiting the same restaurant in the seventies, a time when it had been a glitzy Party showpiece, a Westernised retreat for diplomats and their boyfriends, trade delegations and wealthy tourists. Now someone had waved a wand and instead of relaxing in First World decadence, Brewer was back in the Third; flies and peeling wallpaper, rotating ceiling fans that threatened to fall and decapitate the diners, waiters in stained, discoloured uniforms. It was somehow typical of Sarkovsky's stubbornness that he should continue to frequent the restaurant long after it had ceased to have anything to recommend it: clearly, old habits died hard. A fly-spotted sign declared the restaurant was scheduled for demolition, an act of benevolent euthanasia long overdue.

Brewer lifted his glass of over-priced, diluted wine. 'To the new Russia.'

Sarkovsky scowled at Brewer's disrespect and continued eating, apparently eager to get the better of his grilled toilet roll. 'Why don't you share with me what is happening, what your real mission is? It would be easier for us both.'

'Since when did we make things easy for you?' Brewer asked and knocked back his drink in one, like a cheap sherry. Only it wasn't that good.

'You want help,' Sarkovsky shrugged. 'You do as I ask. Is that so much?'

Brewer didn't reply. He took two *Romeo y Julieta's* from his pocket and offered one to Sarkovsky. 'Here. A present, Sergei. On one condition. You have to smoke it now,' he insisted. 'I'm not subsidising your black market barters.'

Sarkovsky looked at the offered cigar with a sad expression and shook his head.

'Did you not see the sign? *Nikurit!* No Smoking!'

Brewer shrugged, took one for himself, cut it and lit up. 'Health fascism. That's another Western import you could do without. Whatever happened to Russian pride? Anyhow, smoking these helps your Cuban comrades, the only ones who have stayed true to the cause.'

Sarkovsky did not rise to the bait. Instead, he finally abandoned his futile attempt to eat the contents of his plate and sat back in his chair. He wiped the corners of his mouth slowly with a yellow-stained napkin. 'Let me tell you something,' he said. 'The Professor requested certain files from the archive that he could never have known about without inside information. Was that you?'

'That all rather depends. Which files are you talking about?'

He sighed. 'You want to play games? You can do better than that, Mr Brewer.'

'Except I'm not playing games. And that's the truth. Which files?'

Sarkovsky thought for a moment and topped up his glass. 'It

is not right that you hold things back like this. We are both policemen of a kind are we not, with an interest in doing the right thing? If we would put our two parts of the jigsaw together, we should see the whole picture.'

'Co-operate you mean? Blasphemy. What brave new world is this? *Perestroika? Glasnost?* Phrases for the bourgeois, Sergei. And you would tell me everything of course,' Brewer commented sardonically. 'You're wasting my time.' He stood and pushed away his plate, interrupting the flies at their feast.

Sarkovsky stayed seated, a smile breaking across his face. 'You are always so impatient, Mr Peter Brewer. Here.' He pulled a small grey envelope from his pocket. 'Sit down and stop making a spectacle of yourself.'

Brewer sat down and opened the envelope. Inside was a slip of paper with a hand-written number. Brewer looked up, puzzled.

'What is this Sergei? An inside tip for the state lottery? A locker full of secret files hidden at the airport? My own private Swiss bank account?'

Sarkovsky shook his head. 'Just another tiny fragment of our puzzle. The number of a file. Or, to be more precise, the number of a file now missing. Whether the Professor took it, or someone else took it from him, we do not know. Perhaps you can tell me where it fits?'

Brewer leant back in his chair and drew deeply on his cigar. 'I know the Professor's general area of interest, as I'm sure you do.'

'No. Not an interest. An obsession, I think, with the Third Reich. A repulsive subject somehow made particularly dull by the Professor's dry academic approach. Always the trouble with these people, don't you find?'

'Come on, Sergei. There was more to it than that,' Brewer said. 'Beattie's real interest was the papers stolen from Berlin by your lot at the end of the war. A right flock of magpies, old Uncle Joe's boys. And like Hitler's old bones, all you've done is sit on them all these years, waiting for something to hatch. Perhaps it finally has. Have you considered that?'

'Stole is such an ugly word. I prefer 'appropriated',' Sarkovsky commented. 'And don't be so hard. They were different times. Russia nearly died at Nazi hands. Stalin had his reasons. The right man at the right time, as you say. Not a good man, no. But let's be honest, Brewer, Churchill was no teetotal saint. Coffee?'

Brewer nodded and let Sarkovsky order. They waited while the waiters took the used plates and serving dishes towards the kitchen.

'This number.' Brewer fingered the scrap of paper. 'It must mean something. Its sequence, some sort of correlation with surrounding files. Doesn't that tell us anything?'

'Unfortunately not. The files are numbered arbitrarily, not in sequence. The Nazis had them in perfect order, as you would expect. But by the time they were brought back to Moscow and emptied out from the crates.' Sarkovsky shrugged. 'You know how it is when you move house, well it was just the same but magnified on a gigantic scale. No-one was interested at the time. The war was over, after all and we had won. Who was going to care about putting Nazi papers in order?

'After the Professor's death we found the note and sent ten clerks into the archive. For a week they worked their way outwards from that missing file in all possible directions.' He shook his head. 'Nothing. Unless you have an interest in Bavarian railway timetables from July 1941. Whatever it is that may or may not have brought about the Professor's death, find those missing files and I suspect you will have your answer.'

The waiter brought their coffees and they fell silent until he was safely out of earshot. Sarkovsky poured three large tablespoons of dark brown sugar into his cup. When Brewer sampled the coffee, he could taste why.

'So what now Mr Brewer?' Sarkovsky asked.

Brewer shrugged. 'One dead academic and a file that's disappeared? No other clues? It's not promising. I'll have to run this by London.'

'Just one thing,' Sarkovsky asked. 'The man who used you

for target practice outside your hotel. Do you know why we should now find him dead?'

Brewer looked at him with genuine surprise.

'Oh. Come, come, Mr Brewer. You did not know? Yes. Dead. Deceased. And please, before you say anything, I would like to help. That really is the truth. Oh, it's not that I care particularly about you,' he explained, smiling. 'But these things happening here on the streets of Moscow are so bad for tourism you see. And we must protect the tourist dollar.'

Brewer stood. 'Thanks Sergei. But you're on your own on this one. I'll stick to handling the dead Professor. Dead Russians are your problem, not mine.'

He walked briskly out of the restaurant, leaving Sarkovsky to pick up the bill.

While Brewer and Sarkovsky sparred over the significance of the missing file and Professor Beattie's death, three men were busy drinking in the rather more sedate surroundings of private dining room B in the House of Commons refreshment corridor. The mock gothic atmosphere of the Palace of Westminster provides a convenient rendezvous for discreet private meetings. Conspiracy and adultery, revolution and revelation have all been plotted in its corridors and rooms. Long regarded as London's most exclusive club, the men had dined well, generous helpings of wine from the sommelier's cellar adding to their general good mood.

Sitting at the head of the table was an MP. Mark Hamilton was in his mid forties, elegantly handsome with swept-back dark hair and a permanent tanned complexion—gained not from a sun-bed, but from frequent sojourns abroad. His double-breasted dark grey suit was Saville Row, his silk tie Italian, his shoes hand-made from supple black leather. He radiated that innate sense of confidence and purpose that remains the exclusive preserve of those who inherit wealth. Even before he spoke, it was clear that he was the product of a private school: the air of indifference, detachment and disdain signalled it as clearly as a flashing neon sign outside a tattoo parlour.

But Hamilton was far more than an elegant dresser. He came from a politically active, Liberal background. His father, a former local councillor and highly successful lawyer, stood twice for election to Westminster, and twice failed. Whilst at University, Hamilton outraged his father by turning his back on the Liberal Party and becoming chair of the Young Conservatives. His incisive, ruthless debating skills did not pass unnoticed. Even before his graduation there were rumours he would be offered the opportunity to stand for Parliament. His political approach was simple: to shoot from the hip, to say it how it was. Or, more accurately, to *appear* to say it how it was. In truth, appearing simple and direct in politics requires the most cunning and duplicitous of minds. Hamilton possessed just such a mind.

Surrounded by a generation of media-conscious performers, by those who struggled endlessly to reconcile the impossible— of expressing firm convictions without alienating potential voters—he appeared sharp and lucid. Even his opponents, who detested his political opinions, confessed their admiration of his style. It was only those who took the trouble to listen closely who saw beyond the rhetoric. Like the opinionated drunk propped up at the bar of a pub, on the surface Hamilton's views were simple and self-evident: common sense. But beneath their apparent reason was a carefully contrived mix of popular bigotry and intolerance, masked by Hamilton's suave manner and easy smile: Hamilton was a uniquely dangerous man.

Hamilton earned his spurs in the traditional way, playing the Party rules by the book. He stood in two general elections, running for seats the Conservatives knew they would never win. They were two of the dirtiest campaigns ever recorded. After surprisingly strong results proved beyond doubt that demonising personalities, rather than focusing on policies, can sway voters, Hamilton was finally offered a safe seat. He succeeded where his father had failed and entered Parliament in 1983, part of the second wave of Thatcherites, keen to do service for a leader he considered Britain's best since the inspired wartime leadership of Winston Churchill. It was not long before his outspoken views and strongly loyal support brought him reward in the shape of a junior ministerial position, first in the then Department of Health and Social Security and later in the Ministry of Defence. Finally after the Conservative's surprise election win of 1992 he arrived: Secretary of State for Defence.

But all this was a small footnote in history. As he sipped at the wine and smiled at his companions, he found himself pre-occupied with the ugly truth that his whole world was turned inside out. And it was likely to be for a long time to come. The Conservatives, after eighteen years at the helm, had been ejected from power in a humiliating electoral wipeout. Not once, but twice. His own seat held solid in both general election defeats thanks only to a high personal vote. But he still found himself unable to adjust to the relentless humiliation and hopelessness of Opposition. Worse still, there were those in the Party who were beginning to believe it would never be able to hold power again. He did not share that view—but he was still keen to make plans to ensure that if that did happen, he and his Party would still be in a position to wield considerable influence.

Opposite Hamilton sat Eric Cham, one of the Deputy Chiefs of the Secret Intelligence Service—better known as MI6. Cham was in his early fifties, a sharp-eyed man with a carefully nurtured strip of grey hair stretched across his otherwise prematurely bald head. He wore a mundane high-street pinstripe suit, a kipper tie in clashing bright colours of the type popular in the 1970's and a pair of brown suede shoes. Beneath his portly figure it was still possible, with a suitable stretch of the imagination, to discern the build of a one-time athlete. Only in the last few years, as he had become tied increasingly to his desk and the tedious committee meetings that dominate the day of so many in public service, had his figure begun to dissolve.

In contrast to the head of the Service, the 'Chief', who was now public property, Cham maintained a low profile. He was still part of the world that believed certain things should not be discussed in public. The idea that the Service had become more open, more accountable, made him uncomfortable. Hamilton was the sort of Member of Parliament whose company and friendship he appreciated: they shared many of the same opinions, possessed similar privileged backgrounds. This was the preferred way to conduct business: over a quiet dinner, behind closed doors. There were too many matters of real importance that could never be expressed in public. No written agenda or minutes existed of their meetings: their subject matter was too important to risk the dangerous luxury of formal records.

Cham was lucky. During the so-called Christmas Massacre of 1992-3, when the Firm cleaned out the old boys from its top ranks and swept in a new generation, Cham was amongst those men—and they were overwhelmingly men—in their forties who suddenly found themselves in power. It was an opportunity that Cham had seized upon. From there he had risen rapidly and was now at the pinnacle of his career.

He raised his glass in a toast. 'To success.'

'One moment,' interrupted Hamilton.

He took the wine from the table and replenished the glasses, although only his own was empty. Hamilton turned to their other companion, who had remained silent for the last few minutes, content to let Hamilton and Cham do all the talking.

Lieutenant Commander Graham Parke was until recently an important member of the Royal Navy's specialist procurement executive. At one time a key player in the Trident missile programme, since leaving the Navy a few years before he had joined the board of a small defence consultancy.

Parke was the same age as Cham, but looked ten years younger. His dark hair was carefully cut and groomed to look fuller than it was, thickened with a gel that left a slight shine. His clothes sat awkwardly on his lanky frame: civvies were not his style and he preferred his uniformed days. His deep blue jacket was slightly too large, his matching slacks too short in the leg, riding up to expose his socks whenever he was seated. But most people did not notice his clothes: Parke had a commanding presence; a sharp, incisive bearing that helped him dominate his surroundings.

His career had been slow and steady: Parke was no high flier. Whereas others from his intake rose through the ranks more rapidly and took senior positions earlier in their careers, Parke had been content to work through at his own pace. His record was exemplary: his methodical approach, his ability to make sound decisions under pressure, were exactly the skills the Royal Navy valued. During the Falklands war, Parke proved himself a superb field officer. In the heat of an Argentinean aerial attack against their frigate, his senior officer sustained a minor head injury. Parke took command and ensured prompt and effective defensive action.

His decision was believed to have saved not only his own ship, but several others, at a moment in time when the Navy was experiencing some of its worst losses since the Second World War. In reward, Parke's senior officer had been 'volunteered' for a package of notional promotion and early retirement and Parke was promoted into his shoes.

Despite his performance during the Falklands war, Parke still regretted the war's necessity. He regarded the loss of men and materiel as totally unacceptable, the result of a failure of political will and a stain on the record of the intelligence services. His views, however, he kept carefully guarded to himself and those few around him whom he knew he could trust. The Royal Navy might have misunderstood his clinical analysis for pacifism, or worse, as criticism of the British Government.

In truth, Parke held no animosity for the former Prime Minister. Thatcher's first administration he regarded as one of the most inspired of recent years: a view held in common with his companions. He laid the blame on the weakness of those who had surrounded her, the lack of backbone of those who ultimately conspired to bring her down to replace her with a straw-headed puppet. The quality of Members arriving at the House was in long-term decline, amongst whom Hamilton stood out as a remarkable exception. Time and the tide of political events were running against them. It was important that they acted soon, before the situation became irrecoverable: Hamilton was the key. And now their plans were nearly complete. The long years of waiting were coming to an end.

'Now gentlemen, to success,' Hamilton said, smiling as he raised his drink.

The three glasses chimed briefly against each other and the men enjoyed long leisurely sips. Hamilton was pleased with the way the meeting had progressed.

Soon it would be time to put their ambitious plans to the test.

3

Anastasia's flat was located on the outskirts of Moscow, tucked away in an ugly high-rise concrete block of the type inflicted across Europe in the post-war years. It lay beyond the *Sadoveye Koltso*, Moscow's unofficial breakwater between the elegance of the old city and the slums and industrial defecation of the suburbs.

As Brewer approached the apartment block, a gang of shorthaired teenagers in torn jeans ran forwards, hassling him for Levis, dollars or dope. He ignored them and stepped into the foyer where a Grand Canyon of a crack zigzagged through the concrete wall alongside the lift, large enough to stick a finger into. Brewer resisted the temptation and waited for the lift to descend, its tortured metallic groans resonating from the lift shaft like the dying shrieks of a mortally wounded animal. Using the lift probably qualified as a dangerous sport and invalidated his travel insurance, but Anastasia's flat was on the fourteenth floor and Brewer had never been a keep-fit freak. When he pressed the button marked '14' the lift moved, which was good enough for him: even if the odour in the lift suggested it also doubled-up as a mobile urinal.

The door to her flat was ajar. Old habits die hard in Moscow. In the Communist era crime was virtually unknown, the streets safe for the average citizen. Only the enemies of the state had anything to fear. But it was a time rapidly being forgotten. Now everyone had to be careful. Brewer entered unannounced and closed the door behind him, shutting out the drab green linoleum floors of the communal hallway. There was the sound of crockery in the kitchen and he found Anastasia washing up. The smell of burnt toast hung in the air.

'How are you?' she asked.

Her accent was stronger than Sarkovsky's, a rough Moscow cockney. Her long hair was tied back. Without her shoes she looked shorter than he remembered. She had put rouge on her high cheekbones and picked out her deep-set eyes with a mascara that was too strong. Brewer guessed she had been painting the same face since she was a teenager. Perhaps then it had looked attractive. Now it was too strong. But clearly she was still proud of her appearance. Her slight build was fuller and more feminine than the pouting androgynous stick insects with angular faces who postured uneasily in the pages of Russian fashion magazines.

Brewer sat at the table and took a swig from a bottle of mineral water.

'I have glasses,' she said, fetching one from a cupboard. She wiped the neck of the bottle clean and poured him a glass.

A former colleague of Professor Beattie's had given her name to Brewer. Professor Beattie and Anastasia worked closely together on his projects in the KGB archives. It did not take a Sherlock Holmes to realise their relationship was more than purely professional. There was a slim chance she could give him a lead: business or pleasure, Brewer was not fussy. Any lead was better than staring mutely at the lint in his navel.

Brewer first contacted Anastasia via her Moscow college. She had reacted with unease. Despite *Perestroika*, despite *Glasnost* and all the political hot air spouted by the neo-reformists, most Russians still looked over their shoulders with an all too familiar mixture of fear and apprehension, still believed the apparatus of the secret state police continued to monitor their activities. And not without reason. Everyone had pet stories of private market traders whose front doors were kicked down at four in the morning and their supplies seized; of protection rackets run by former KGB officers, embittered and yet still powerful in the turbulent post-Gorbachev, post-Yeltsin era. Anastasia was no exception.

They agreed to meet at her apartment: this was his second visit. On the first, she was awkward and reticent. Today she appeared relaxed.

Brewer took a *Romeo y Julieta* from his pocket.

'Not in here, please!'

Before he could clip it, Anastasia flipped it from his hand and into the sink. He gave her a sharp look, decided from the look in her eyes that this was one argument he would not win and slipped the cigar cutter back into his pocket.

'So you have found his killers?' She sat opposite him and leant her elbows on the table, resting her head in her hands.

Brewer took a drink from the glass and wished it was something stronger. 'I have a number.' He handed her the note on which Sarkovsky had written details of the mystery file.

She looked at it for a moment. Brewer expected her to hand it back and ask what it meant. Instead she left the table and fetched a bottle of vodka and two glasses from under the sink. She slopped out two generous measures, sat down and took a long drink.

He gave her a moment and then said: '*Spasyba*. But what have I done to deserve this?'

She looked down and prodded at the paper on the table. 'This is the first lead, the first breakthrough, *da*? You are a good detective. To find this. It is progress, *nyet*?'

'It is?' Brewer somehow neglected to mention that the note came from Sarkovsky: compliments were a rare commodity.

'Of course. I recognise this number. But this is not the only one. There are others.'

'Others?' She was full of surprises. 'What are they?'

'Someone telephoned the Professor.'

Brewer sighed. 'Anastasia, you're not making sense. Take it from the beginning and keep it slow.'

'There was a caller, on the telephone. To the Professor, like I say. And a note pushed under his door at the *Hotel Ukraina*, a note with a number just like this.' She tapped at the piece of paper on the table. 'And then this person kept calling him, providing him with more numbers. He wanted the Professor to bring out the files, to steal them from the archive.'

'And did he?'

She shook her head. 'No. But he did locate them, these files in the archive. Of course he did. Anyone in his position would have done. And he told me they were very important, that he had never seen such files before.'

Brewer could smell the vodka on her breath: he liked it. And sometimes when she spoke she hugged herself, as if she were cold. But the room was warm, so it had to be something else: maybe she was missing the Professor, maybe it was his absence that made her cold. Although she appeared strong, there was still something of the child about her.

He tried to get more. Days, times—details of the contacts. Anything that might give him a fresh lead. But she did not know anything else—or if she did she was not telling. She just kept repeating what the Professor told her: he tracked down the files, studied them himself but refused to bring them out for the mysterious caller.

'He was so excited. I had never seen him like it before. You know, like a little boy with a new toy, his eyes sparkled. He said it was the biggest find of his life, the biggest story since the war. It would make him famous.'

'Famous?' Brewer's question came out flat and cynical.

'Yes, famous.' She sounded hurt, offended by his scepticism.

Brewer pushed hard, but she stuck firmly to her story: the Professor never spoke in detail about the papers, never explained the nature of his find. All very neat, very precise. Brewer felt as if he was sitting in a theatre, watching a rehearsal. The words came too easily to her. She was lying, he was sure of it. But why? What was there to hide?

'How do you know he never brought the files out?'

Her eyes flashed bright with anger. 'He told me everything. Everything.' She glared at him, daring him to doubt it.

'So if it wasn't the Professor who brought the file out, it must have been someone else.' Brewer shrugged. 'This file has gone. And from what you've told me, I doubt it's the only one.'

She thought for a moment and then slowly shook her head. 'Perhaps. It is true I did not see him for several days before his . . . death. I had much work to do, you know, for college. Perhaps he found something else in that time, something more important.' She placed a hand on Brewer's arm. 'Please understand I am just telling you what he told me. He was very principled. He would keep much to himself until he was sure. I do not understand why anyone would kill him, what these files were.'

Very principled, Brewer thought. He wondered if Anastasia knew about the Professor's wife and family at home, his illegitimate child in Canada courtesy of another overseas sabbatical, his sordid reputation amongst former students. The Professor's Moscow sabbatical was not a reward for good work. Far from it. It had provided a welcome opportunity for his Oxford College to send him abroad, neatly postponing an investigation into serious allegations made against him by a succession of female undergraduates. But now was probably not a diplomatic time to raise the subject of the Professor's infidelities. Not if he wanted Anastasia's co-operation. God knows what lies the Professor had told her, what wild and unfounded promises he had made to bed her and bring her under his spell. In photographs the Professor appeared a small, nondescript man. Brewer had difficulty picturing Anastasia with him.

'Tell me,' Brewer said quietly. He placed a hand on top of hers, surprised by how cold she was. 'Who do you think killed him?' It was a question Brewer had asked before, but he wanted to dig deeper, to keep pushing her. She was an amateur at this game. The more she talked, the more chance there was of her tripping up, of contradicting herself. 'The police still claim it was the mafia. A simple gang killing. Mistaken identity. A mistake full stop. Another chance victim of Moscow crime.'

She snatched her hand away and gave him the look he deserved. And an answer he did not want. 'It was the Nazis.'

She had given the same stubborn, absurd answer before. Brewer smiled. Bad idea. She slammed her glass down hard, leaving an indent in the table. For a moment Brewer thought she was about to introduce the base of the bottle to the top of his head with similar effect.

'You think it's funny? Why! Why! This is not funny.'

'These rumours about the Nazis,' Brewer said, gently shaking his head. 'I find stories of their survival much exaggerated. The Professor's obsession with them was insane. Comic book stuff. You must know that. The war ended over fifty years ago. It's all dead and in the past.'

'You have so much to learn, don't you?' she said coldly. 'You English are all the same. The Professor told me. Tight-assed, stuck-up, patronising.'

Brewer shook his head. He was growing weary of her allegations, the same crazy obsessions that had driven the Professor. There was nothing for him here, nothing for him in Moscow. The trail was long cold, maybe even dead. Whatever she knew, she would not talk, would not make sense. Moscow was a cul-de-sac. Perhaps Sarkovsky was right. Perhaps the Professor's death was just a chance killing after all. They were common enough in Moscow these days.

It was time to report to London and get the case declared closed.

Iyas Qalwyr, editor of the *London Arab News*, was late leaving his office. Earlier that afternoon a lengthy and unexpected fax had spewed out of the machine and curled onto the cheap carpet in a confusion of paper. When he scooped it up to read it, a delighted smile flickered across his face. This was important news—and from a trusted source. A quick call confirmed the basic facts. Qalwyr replaced the phone with a shaking hand, his eyes a bright mix of excitement edged with fear.

The decision to replace the front page had been easy.

For the next few hours Qalwyr busied himself with revising the paper, using a mix of computer paste-up and the old-fashioned manual cut and paste methods learnt during his apprenticeship in Baghdad. Now, as he left and locked the door, he clutched tightly at his briefcase. Inside was the final master.

Qalwyr could barely disguise his mood. Every editor dreams of a scoop: and now, finally, his time had come. This would be big. It would put the *London Arab News* on the international media map. There was the possibility he would be invited to appear on TV, perhaps even *Newsnight*. Wait until his wife heard about this. It was everything he had ever worked for. And now he had made it. His name would be known and spoken of with respect amongst his peers in the media world. This was his day and he would exploit it to the full, would embarrass the corrupt and traitorous regime as best he could.

He checked his watch. If he was quick, he would still be in time to reach the printers and have the print run completed overnight for distribution the following day. At just 1,000 copies, the *News* did not have a large circulation, but as the leading opposition paper to the dictatorships of the Middle East and their links with organised crime and heretical militia groups it was widely read and appreciated by the dissident movement in Europe.

This scoop would cause great excitement amongst the dissidents and Qalwyr was keen to release it quickly. He knew the old regime well: if they learned of this leak, they would not hesitate to kill the story. Despite their fall from power, they remained a dangerous group to cross. The premises of several dissident publications had already been firebombed in 'mystery' arson attacks.

London has an unfortunate, but well-deserved reputation, as the easiest European city for foreign secret services to operate in. Most of the Middle East's political assassinations, bombings and campaigns of intimidation have been planned or executed here. London has also long been an international centre for those international terrorist movements who hide behind an artificial allegiance to Islam. In reality, true adherents of Islam, such as Qalwyr and the other dissidents, are the genuine voice of the

Middle East. Terrorists and dictators have long hijacked Islam and the poor of the Arab world for their personal gain.

He smiled to himself. This time, whatever they did, it would be too late: the *News* was ready to print. And when the story broke, demand would be intense. He would ask the printers to produce an extra 500 copies.

Qalwyr was surprised by the sudden warmth of the winter's evening as he stepped outside. His small office was damp and poorly decorated, situated above a plastic-fronted burger bar in the Kilburn High Road. He smiled through the dusty downstairs window at Oz, the bar's owner, who was busy serving a tramp. It was not an ideal location, but funding was difficult and London was an expensive city. One day he would return home to his native country, one day when the present unrest had eased and some semblance of decent, honest government had been established. Every night he prayed for that day to come soon. Enforced exile from one's homeland is a cruel and inhuman experience.

The unseasonably good weather made Qalwyr think of his home and his wife. He wished he had called her earlier, made arrangements. It would be a pleasant evening to go out, perhaps have something to eat at a local restaurant. After a day spent cutting and pasting and cursing the computer he just felt like talking. But it was too late now to arrange a baby-sitter. Perhaps if he was swift at the printers there might still be time to organise his evening. And if his neighbours, his good friend Ali and his wife, were home, he could invite them round instead. It would be good to have company tonight, a time to celebrate and relax.

He turned and started walking. He had taken just three steps when the gunman stepped out, put the gun to his head and shot. One, two. Qalwyr was dead before he hit the ground. By then the gunman was gone and so was Qalwyr's briefcase.

It took several minutes before someone stopped to find out what was wrong with the well-dressed man sprawled on the north London pavement that warm winter's evening.

4

Stoke Newington Church Street, London, eight-thirty pm. Outside—dull, dark and grey. Inside—the Anglo Asia restaurant was hot and noisy. Its large windows glistened with diamonds of condensation as uniformed waiters moved briskly in and out of the kitchen, trays of drinks and food balanced on cluttered trays. The seductive smell of fresh coriander and other spices filled the restaurant like some strange exotic perfume. A young couple wrapped in thick coats and scarves stood awkwardly inside the front door, momentarily lost and purposeless while they waited in limbo for service and a table.

Brewer was sitting at the bar. He downed his glass of beer in one, gestured for another and started talking about local news with the manager. He relit his cigar and changed position on the stool, enjoying the intense and hectic atmosphere: it was the perfect antidote to the sterility of Moscow.

It was only a few hours since he had returned to his flat in nearby Gibson Gardens to find it cold and silent. A pile of post had boomeranged the front door back at him. Once inside, the answer machine had winked irritably at him with an angry red eye: three messages. One wrong number. Then a bland, coded message from the Firm.

And finally a message from Jane.

Jane. That shocked him. He had not seen her for months, had not even thought about her. He shook his head: *impossible.* Amongst the women he had known in his life, Jane was the one who had really moved him. Jane had married too young and found herself prematurely middle-aged in a dull relationship. Instead of just accepting the situation, as her parents wanted, she divorced her husband in her mid twenties and committed herself to recovering all those years lost in the tedium of her marriage. She threw herself into her work, rapidly becoming manager of a large West End store.

A strong, confident woman, Brewer had taken to her immediately. Their affair was passionate and sensual. And then work drifted them apart and in Brewer's long absences she became involved with Gary, Brewer's closest friend. It was not an easy time for any of them.

Gary and Brewer's friendship had been forged in the smithy of the local schools. They shared an attitude of independence, a natural inclination to tease and buck the system. And both were suspended on several occasions—nothing serious, just the minor misdemeanours that always seemed to upset head teachers: smoking cigarettes, gambling, indiscretions with girls, talking back to teachers on level terms. The usual currency of youth. They were good years, years spent on the streets of Hackney, Dalston and Stoke Newington. Truant afternoons spent in the cover of the sprawling undergrowth and crumbling Victorian tombstones of Abney Park Cemetery.

Even now, when Brewer could afford to move elsewhere, to more fashionable, more 'comfortable' parts of London, he chose to stay in the area he had always known. There was a life and vitality to it, a dynamic, buzzing edge, a unique melting pot of immigrants and east-enders, of wealthy and poor living side by side. Through all the changes, the growing gentrification rippling up from Islington, and even now his parents were dead, it still retained strong bonds of friendship and community. If there was anywhere Brewer could truly call home, this was it.

Gary and Brewer left school together at sixteen to join the army, keen to escape the unemployment and poverty that had plagued their parents' lives. But their career paths soon divided. After long years of graft, both gained promotions through hard work and aptitude. Brewer transferred to Intelligence. Gary went into the SAS: he had always been the fitter of the two.

And then came the first Gulf War. Gary was signed up for one last tour of service: a tour that took place in Iraq, a mission deep inside the interior. He never returned. Somewhere behind enemy lines he had been intercepted, taken prisoner, tortured and beaten. He was finally put out of his misery with a merciful shot through the back of the head. Saddam Hussein's Republican Guard stuck his skull on a stick for a month and dragged his headless corpse through the streets. Someone sent his regiment a photo and an anonymous low-life from a tabloid paper later forwarded a copy to Jane and asked her 'how she felt about it.'

Gary and Brewer had promised each other to keep an eye on Jane if anything ever happened to either of them. But it was not so easy. Brewer's job was no nine-to-five: there was no guarantee of being around to offer a shoulder to cry on.

Brewer returned her call. But she was out—or not taking calls. He left a return message on her answer phone, promising to call back later and then dialled into work on a secure line to pick up his messages. There was a meeting request for the following morning with Pendleton, Controller of the Firm's European sector—his boss. The other messages were minor: brief updates on assignments, projects placed on hold awaiting his return from Moscow.

Brewer was growing tired of wasting time on a sideshow while others landed the plums. Whatever the Professor might have found in the KGB archives, it was not important. Not a fifty-year-old file about Hitler's Germany. It might have been exciting enough to send ripples through the colostomy bag of an ageing academic, but Brewer was desperate for a real assignment.

Yet the hard reality was that he stood as much chance of getting a decent assignment as of becoming Archbishop of Canterbury. The new management did not like the old methods of operation—or the old operatives. The signals were clear: they wanted the old crowd put out to grass, wanted their loyal, unquestioning clones in post. They adored the young blood who spouted their vacant management-speak—and who, Brewer noticed with some pleasure, usually screwed up. But at least they screwed up within budget and that was all that mattered to the new breed of manager. Balanced books and contrived mission statements had become the new objective—not delivery of an effective, efficient service. If you duck down low enough, keep your head below the parapet, it will not get shot off: it is a law the Civil Service have followed for years. Mediocrity rules.

Brewer's food arrived in two large brown paper bags with carry handles. The manager walked him to the door, chatting busily about his plans to expand and seeking Brewer's advice. After more than twenty years as a customer, Brewer was regarded as much a part of the business as the kitchen staff. As a connoisseur of Indian cuisine, he rated the Anglo Asia amongst the best in the UK.

Back in his flat, Brewer emptied the take-away foils onto a chipped willow-pattern plate and switched on the small black and white TV in the kitchen. As the subtle, fragrant sauce dribbled down his chin, his eyes noticed Anastasia's package beside the door. Damn. He had intended to post it earlier.

After scoffing the meal with more haste than the food deserved, he picked up the parcel. He prodded it and put it to his ear, shaking it gently. Not for the first time, he resisted the temptation to open it. He had given his word. He shook it. Nothing. It was probably just a gift for a friend. Anastasia was too suspicious to trust him with anything important. He placed it back by the front door and made a mental note to post it in the morning.

He was about to turn in when the phone rang.

'Peter? It's Jane. Remember me? You said you'd call me back, you maggot.'

Her voice awoke memories long forgotten, emotions he would have preferred not to rekindle. They spoke for over an hour, nothing in particular. She just wanted to talk. By the time she rang off, Brewer was wide awake. He was surprised by the strong emotions Jane still aroused. And it wasn't just emotions. Tomorrow he would call her, arrange a rendezvous in the pub he still thought of as the Tanners Arms, although it had long since been re-branded in the collective madness of themed pub makeovers that had rippled through the city.

He took a couple of beers from the fridge and fell asleep in front of an old schlock horror movie on TV, trying to put memories of Gary and Jane and the past from his mind.

Brewer woke early with a stiff neck and the stale odour of the previous night's food wrapping itself around him. He freshened up with a cold shower and change of clothes. Outside the sleepy morning light was dull and grey. At the entrance gates to Gibson Gardens he cursed and doubled back to fetch Anastasia's package. He stuck on several first class stamps and forced it roughly into a post box on the corner of Church Street.

A 73 Routemaster took him into town. A hyperactive, singing conductor tried to chivvy the early morning commuters: she would have been more successful raising the dead. From Victoria station it was a short walk through the backstreets and their eighteenth century homes to the dull office block on Millbank. It was an anonymous building squeezed between media studios and a Parliamentary outbuilding, one of the few remaining satellite operations since the Service concentrated staff into its Vauxhall Cross extravagance.

Within the next month his part of the European section house on Millbank was scheduled to move, a move repeatedly delayed by a succession of internal politics—there were those who thought consolidation into a single building was complete madness: and after 9/11 there was a growing number who thought they were probably right.

By the time Brewer reached Millbank, the grey dawn showed signs of cracking. A few hesitant fingers of blue poked uncertainly between the clouds. The wide pavement was littered with the recent by-product of pigeons perched together for warmth in the bare branches of the trees above.

No-one responded to his first press on the buzzer. On the second, a uniformed security officer opened it, checked his ID without a word and waved him in. It was still early. Apart from the night shift on the duty desk, Brewer was first in. He usually was. The building was cluttered with bright orange packing crates in preparation for their move, but no-one appeared to have started packing. Not that it was easy to tell: his part of the European section had a long and jealously guarded reputation for being the most untidy, a reputation it maintained without any apparent effort.

He checked his desk on the fourth floor: the usual circulars, memos about tea-making facilities, warnings about the misuse of stamped envelopes for personal purposes, details of a branch Christian Union prayer fest. The usual office chaff. And several files he had requested, files he wanted to see urgently before his trip to Moscow. They had arrived with their usual sense of timing— days after his departure. Brewer ticked 'For return' on the transit slips, scribbled an obscenity below and put them into the 'Out' tray. There were several phone messages, nothing important other than a couple of requests from Pendleton to see him as soon as he returned.

He phoned Pendleton's office. No reply. Not that he expected one: not this early. Pendleton followed a strict routine that ensured he would never see the dawn. Brewer replaced the receiver and cleared the papers from his desk into the waste bin. Monroe arrived and boiled a kettle.

'Coffee, thanks,' Brewer called.

Monroe grunted. 'Good trip?'

'About as productive as a eunuch in fertility ward.'

He nodded. 'Aren't they all? Milk-run jobs. It's all they give us old hands.' He stirred instant coffee into two mugs, his ambitious beer gut gyrating in sympathy in a cruel parody of a belly dancer's routine. 'Have you heard the latest?'

'What now?'

Monroe drew a line across his throat. 'Cuts,' he rasped.

Brewer stood and went over to him. 'We had enough of them under the last lot. What about all this new money sloshing about since September 11?'

'Rumour has it there still isn't enough room to have us in Vauxhall. Particularly since September 11 and the new people brought on board. And we're the easy ones to squeeze—Europe isn't seen as the problem area right now. Middle East is getting all the attention since 9/11. Story is, Pendleton's going to get the shove. Too grey on top. Here.' He handed over a mug. 'Talking of which, the old man wants to see you.'

Pendleton had managed to avoid the shock of the last major shake-up, but both he and everyone else knew that he was surviving on borrowed time. The Service operates a strict retirement age of fifty-five, an age Brewer suspected that Pendleton had long since passed.

'If he graces us with his presence.'

Monroe looked at his watch. 'Give him a few hours. You might just catch the old bugger between breakfast and lunch. Old civil service habits die hard.'

Brewer took a sip of scalding coffee. 'Guess who called me last night?'

'The pope?'

'Jane.'

'Jane? Christ. How is the darling girl?' There was a time—a time that seemed long ago now, almost in another life—when Monroe had been close to Gary and Jane.

'Lonely.' Brewer sipped at the scalding coffee.

Monroe looked at him slyly. 'And what are you planning to do about that?'

Brewer shook his head with an angelic expression. 'Nothing.'

'Bullshit.' Monroe leaned towards him. Too late, Brewer remembered his acute halitosis. 'Mark my words, there's more to this than meets the eye.'

'Not this time, Monroe,' Brewer assured him, retreating to the safety of his desk and a pocket of breathable air.

He located his computer hidden beneath a library of box files, powered up and logged into the network for the first time in weeks. Several hundred e-mails screamed at him to be read, some of them flashing an urgent and insistent red. He deleted them: nothing urgent ever came by e-mail. He fired up his search system to check what it had found in his absence. It had been sniffing on the Parliamentary Data and Video Network, Parliament's internal computer network, during his absence. Although snooping on Parliament was really MI5's and Special Branch's turf, Brewer was keen to test the system. There were a few interesting messages between an MP and his male secretary and the Secret draft of a Defence Committee report, but nothing to take his fancy.

He called Moscow to check on Anastasia: no reply. Brewer guessed she must be busy in the archives continuing the Professor's work. The Professor's college had commissioned her to wrap up the loose ends and another academic was due to fly out in a week or two's time to pick up where the Professor left off. Brewer made a note to call later, early evening Moscow time.

Although there was little of substance to include in his field report, it took several hours to complete. One line of terse text, even a solitary question mark, would have exaggerated the success of his Moscow investigation, but it needed sufficient detail to give it credibility or the back-room analysts and accountants would send it back. More importantly, without a report his expenses would not be cleared. Field reports had to qualify against a set of cost-effective measures established by the Finance Committee. He padded it with minor observations, the dead-ends he had constantly explored. But he held back on a couple of items: he wanted time to follow them up in his own way.

By the time he was finished, the office was humming. Brewer had never been a missionary for open plan: a concept designed by work-shy gossips to slow everyone to the speed of the office snail and for egotists to hold loud, tedious phone calls to establish their own self-importance.

He decided to leave. But the phone rang and it was Pendleton's secretary instructing him to go to his office immediately, do not pass Go, do not collect £200.

Brewer walked down the service stairs to the third floor. Unlike the open plan offices of other floors, the third was a designer warren of individual offices, lined with half-oak panelling and fittings apparently poached from an eighteenth century house. Walls were hung with etchings and paintings of distinguished, but anonymous figures, on loan from one national collection or another. There was no open plan for Pendleton or any of the upper management echelons. But the accommodation in the Vauxhall building promised something different, a complex of individual offices designed for 'delivery of maximal human resource ergonomics'. Brewer would believe it as soon as he saw a Gloucester Old Spot on final approach into Heathrow.

Pendleton's secretary was busy gossiping on the phone to someone called Agatha when Brewer entered. Not wishing to disturb her important social commitments, he walked straight past and into Pendleton's room without knocking. Pendleton was seated behind his desk, the microphone for his Dictaphone in one hand.

'Do you mind?' he asked. 'I haven't finished.'

'When you're ready,' Brewer replied and took a seat. He picked up a financial magazine from the table and skimmed through it, feigning interest in the predictions of the City astrologists.

He felt Pendleton staring at him for a time and wondered if he had overstepped the mark. Finally Pendleton sighed and set down the microphone.

'Very well, Brewer. I'm ready.'

Brewer dropped the dull magazine onto the table and pulled up a worn padded chair in front of Pendleton's desk. Pendleton was looking older. His last few grey hairs had surrendered to the onslaught of his shining bald dome. Dark, thick veins were clearly visible on the back of his hands and Brewer thought he detected a hint of arthritis. His dark suit was worn, like something found in a second rate charity shop. There was more than a little of the Wilfred Hyde-White about him.

Maybe Monroe and the office gossip were right: maybe Pendleton was on the way out. He had never made any effort to hide his distaste for the new regime, the Alice in Wonderland nonsense that accountants should run everything, that cost control was the only meaningful measure, not quality. The accountants mistook efficiency for effectiveness, and measurement for achievement: fundamental errors. In Pendleton's day attention was sharply focused on ability and initiative, not the processing of expense claims and the monitoring of self-evident and tangential statistics. The Age of Aquarius had quickly given way to the Age of Accountancy.

'I asked you to contact me urgently,' Pendleton complained, lighting one of the cheap unfiltered French cigarettes that he favoured.

Brewer shrugged. 'I called you earlier. No reply.'

'What time?' Pendleton looked at his watch.

'About seven.'

'Last night?' he frowned.

'This morning.'

Pendleton arrived at ten past ten sharp every day: everyone knew that. Something to do with leaves on the track, wrong type of train, scheduling difficulties, invaders from Mars. Something like that. Pendleton sniffed and took another puff on the cigarette. In a moment of impulsive generosity, Brewer had once given him a box of Davidoff cigars, but he had never seen Pendleton light one: he was too much a creature of habit to smoke a good cigar. Sometimes Brewer wondered whether he should risk asking to have them back. He hated to see good cigars go to waste.

'I understand Moscow was quiet?'

'Very,' Brewer confirmed. 'A waste of time and money. I don't understand why you sent me.'

'That's for us to know,' he replied archly. 'But you agree the Professor was murdered?'

'The locals aren't so sure. Could have been local mafia, a chance killing. Just like the papers said.'

'And you believe that do you?' Pendleton's eyes locked onto Brewer's without blinking.

'No,' Brewer said. 'But I can't tell you why. The locals are frosty. They don't understand why we can't co-operate fully, fill them in on the details.'

'And what's your line on this? You agree, I take it?'

'It's their patch,' he conceded. 'I'd be the same.'

Pendleton narrowed his eyes. 'What about the girl?'

'Anastasia? She won't change her story. Still claims the Professor was killed by Nazis.'

Pendleton did not react. 'Interesting. Suffering from the same delusions as the Professor, is she? If they are delusions, of course. What makes her think that?'

'Paranoia,' Brewer said, only he did not believe it.

'She gave you a package.'

It was not a question: it was a statement. It took Brewer by surprise.

'She didn't give me anything. I agreed to post a package for her.'

'We'd like to see it.'

Brewer moved uneasily in his chair. 'We?' Brewer waited but Pendleton did not rise to the bait.

Instead Pendleton leaned forwards, his eyes widening in disbelief. 'Good god, Brewer. Don't tell me you posted it?'

Brewer wondered who had provided Pendleton's information: he had not mentioned the package to anyone.

'And what about its contents?' He waited. When Brewer did not react, Pendleton angrily stubbed his cigarette into an ashtray the landlord of the nearby *Marquis of Granby* had been missing for months. 'Bloody fool. You didn't even look, did you?'

'There was no reason to snoop. It was just a favour.'

Pendleton stood and paced up and down. Brewer did not need a postgraduate qualification in psychology to detect he was angry.

'You'll have to return to Moscow,' he snapped.

Brewer was astonished. 'For what? You're not thinking straight. Look at the facts: some files went missing, the Professor's dead, Anastasia gives me a parcel to post. Big deal.' He stopped. 'You can't possibly be thinking the Professor's mysterious files were in the parcel. Or are you?'

'What do you think?' Pendleton demanded shortly. 'That is, I presume you do think, do you Brewer?'

'It wasn't the files,' Brewer replied. 'Anastasia isn't stupid, she wouldn't have trusted me. Not with something that important. She's far too cunning for that. She knows I would have looked at them, brought them straight here.'

'But you didn't, did you? Who was this parcel addressed to? I take it you can read, Brewer?'

Brewer stayed silent. If Pendleton was right, Brewer had been played for a complete fool. Goddamit. He felt like a pupil in front of the headmaster. He closed his eyes and tried to picture the writing on the parcel. A few words came to mind. 'It was a hotel.'

'UK?'

'North West London.'

Pendleton thought a moment and then slumped back behind his desk with a resigned air. 'You're on the next flight to Moscow. Put pressure on her. Whatever it takes. You know your clearance. I want to know what was in that package. I want you to retrieve that package. And I want this case closed. Clear?'

'Yes, sir.'

And when Brewer had done that he would pull a white rabbit out of a hat and dance like Fred Astaire.

Mark Hamilton entered the Parliamentary building at 7 Millbank without producing a security pass. It was a point of principle for him never to carry a pass. Although Parliament's security system was introduced specifically to protect Members in response to several terrorist attacks, including an IRA bomb that detonated in Westminster Hall and the car-bomb killing of Airey Neave in the Commons car park, Hamilton refused to comply with the House's security requirements. And he was in good company: more than a third of Members of Parliament did not have passes and an even higher proportion never showed them. After all, they were important people, weren't they? Only cleaners and waiters, the lower orders, carried such things. So far as Hamilton was concerned, his face was his pass.

The security guard recognised the former Minister and allowed him through without comment. Hamilton was not popular amongst staff of the House. The only occasions when he condescended to speak with them were when he wanted to complain. Outside, Hamilton's Special Branch minders watched him disappear into the building and then moved their black Rover round to Dean Stanley Street and waited, bored by the tedium of their hand-holding role. Former Prime Ministers, Northern Ireland and Defence Secretaries receive state protection for their rest of their lives, guaranteeing a whole host of protection officers boredom for life.

Hamilton entered his office on the first floor. Emily, his secretary, sat hunched over her desk, busy with constituency correspondence. One of his most detested tasks was handling the boring, tedious grind of constituency business. Sometimes he wished they could return to the days of restricting the right to vote to a select elite. No wonder Parliament had trouble attracting men of ability when they had to deal daily with the stupidity and fickleness of the general public. Hamilton had certainly not entered Parliament to waste his time answering letters about noisy neighbours or dog shit in the park. They were local administrative matters: and they should be dealt with at local level. Unlike so many of his colleagues, Hamilton had no intention of playing nanny to inadequate, nappy-wetting constituents: his sights were set on the international stage.

Emily handled the constituency side of his office, prepared exactly the sort of letters that his constituents liked. She was always careful to include something personal: it was important that Hamilton appeared to care. Despite his loathing of those who elected him to office, his reputation remained excellent in his constituency, a reputation that owed everything to Emily and little to his own endeavours. Those constituents who wrote regularly (referred to in Parliamentary jargon as 'Exlax'—precisely because of the regularity and the content of their communications) were logged into a database: Emily was careful to ensure the same stock phrases and paragraphs were never written to them more than once. Each letter appeared individual, the work of an MP who cared. In truth, it was generated by Emily's database, but his constituents would never know. Hamilton had long ago realised that image was everything.

Emily looked up and smiled as he entered. He motioned her into his office. Before she could close the joining door, he pulled her tight against him and closed his lips around hers. They kissed for several seconds, Hamilton lost in the scent and softness of her presence.

'I needed that,' he said. 'You can't believe what a bloody bore of a day I've had.'

She smiled. Emily had worked for him since he entered Parliament. Their affair started within weeks and although Hamilton's wife was openly suspicious of their relationship, she was never able to prove anything. Hamilton was no fool: he knew how much his Parliamentary success depended upon Emily's handling of his constituency work and his wife's public support at the endless grind of fetes and local events. The recent general election had demonstrated that. At a time when most of his Conservative colleagues' majorities were slashed, or lost, Hamilton's share of the vote held up well. He knew the political and electoral importance of appearing to be a reliable family man as well as promoting an image of an effective constituency MP. It was a fine balance between wife and mistress.

He squeezed gently at Emily's left breast through her jumper, felt her nipple hardening through the supple fabric of her bra. He moved her onto the desk, sitting her on its edge. His hand moved along the top of her thighs and between her legs. Her mouth dropped open, her lips moistening, her head moved backwards.

Half an hour later, Hamilton appeared at the side entrance to Millbank House and climbed into his waiting car.

'Just had to check a few things,' Hamilton announced dryly. 'Sign a few papers, make a few calls. Usual bullshit.'

His Special Branch detectives exchanged a look and said nothing: Hamilton had forgotten to zip up his trousers.

As the car gathered speed, Hamilton sat back in the soft leather upholstery and decided to call Cham. It was finally time to put their plans into action.

5

The Nazi submarine that was once U-534 lay slumped like a beached and bloated whale, a dark brooding presence behind a curtain of mist. Powerful hoses played jets of water across its hull twenty-four hours a day, slowing the salvaged wreck's decay after more than fifty years at the ocean's depths. Every now and then the spray of water caught the light of the bright arc lamps overhead, twisting it into brief flashes of broken rainbow.

Larsen Lak, head of the Danish salvage operation, led Brewer across the pitted concrete concourse of the massive dry dock and pointed at the hulk of the U-Boat.

'Look closely and you can see where parts have broken. Some from the original aerial assault, but some also from erosion and damage over the years. Still, it is in a very good condition for its age.'

The submarine had been sunk in May 1945 as it attempted to flee Germany through the Kattegat, the stretch of water between Denmark and Sweden. Two allied Liberator planes strafed it, believing it to contain high-ranking Third Reich executives attempting to flee to South America. Their attack was successful: U-534 sank, taking its secrets with it to the bottom. And then in August 1993 a Danish crew salvaged it amid press speculation of gold hidden in special secret compartments allegedly added at Stettin during a refit shortly before its final, fatal voyage. After its recovery, it was brought to Hirtshals in Denmark and kept well away from the glare of media attention. Only after a long, painful legal wrangle about ownership had restoration work finally been allowed to commence.

The excited press speculation about forgotten Nazi gold had some legitimacy: U-534 belonged to the infamous 33rd flotilla. Formed in October 1944, its original brief was to transport vital raw materials required for the Nazi war effort from the Far East. But by the closing stages of the war it was carrying a new and very different cargo: senior Nazi officials on the run. By that time in the war it was only Hitler, isolated in his madness, who still believed Germany could win. Those around him had long since recognized the warning sign and were busy preparing their escape and a comfortable future for themselves in South America after the war.

Since Brewer's meeting with Pendleton, two hectic and frustrating weeks had passed. There had been numerous failed attempts to contact Anastasia. Finally he made contact with her on an appalling phone line to Moscow. The day afterwards she had vanished. It worried him. He did not like to have that effect on people. And in their last conversation she was frightened and anxious.

'Did you post the parcel?'

That was her first and most insistent question. The question seemed to confirm Pendleton's suspicions and made Brewer even more uneasy that he had made a terrible blunder. Brewer countered by asking directly what it contained, but she remained evasive.

'It is dangerous. They killed the Professor before they had everything.'

One important lead came out of their disjointed conversation: it was Anastasia who first mentioned the U-Boat. Brewer initially assumed that it was just another of her crazy Nazi stories, a fantasy created by her obsessive imagination. He listened impatiently as she claimed the submarine contained something they were after. When pressed, she refused to say where her information came from. Brewer assumed 'they' referred to the fantasy Nazis—the same fantasy Nazis that Anastasia also claimed killed the Professor. If, that is, they were a fantasy.

Brewer did not take her seriously, despite the panic in her

voice. He had heard her wild stories before and long since grown bored with them. She sounded absurd, another sad victim of the same paranoia that obsessed Professor Beatty. But Anastasia remained resolute, unshakeable in her conviction. She claimed that the Professor's killers were after her now, that they wanted to silence her. As permanently as the Professor. Yet when he asked Anastasia if she knew what it was they were hoping to find, the line went abruptly dead. Attempts to re-establish contact with her failed.

A few days later, Brewer reluctantly called Captain Sarkovsky. Sergei was well aware of Anastasia's disappearance: her flat had been ransacked. He sounded amused that Brewer should call him over such a minor matter.

'Events have moved quickly in Moscow since your departure,' Sarkovsky commented. 'It is perhaps just as well that you are no longer here. I might even have suspected you, Mr Peter Brewer.'

Brewer neglected to inform Sarkovsky that he was fighting a major rearguard action to prevent Pendleton returning him to Moscow. And it was clear Sarkovsky knew more, but was not telling. Brewer guessed that went for both of them. Sarkovsky was right, had always been right. It would be much simpler if they exchanged the information each of them knew, but that simple idea lay well outside the rules of the game.

Brewer took some comfort from the call—at least no-one had found Anastasia's body. Not yet anyhow. Brewer hoped she had just gone to ground and was not about to surface in the same unhealthy condition as Professor Beatty.

Brewer saw this as an opportunity to ditch the assignment. If Anastasia was not in Moscow, there was little sense returning there. It took a few more days of hard wrangling and then Pendleton finally gave ground and instructed Brewer to tidy up his other cases. The Professor's disappearance was officially downgraded. Brewer forgot all about Anastasia's wild claims about Nazis and a U-Boat until a small filler in the British press caught his attention:

COPENHAGEN, Denmark (Reuters). Danish police revealed last night that earlier this week an intruder attempted to enter the Hirtshals dockyards where the salvaged German submarine U-534 is being restored. The intruder, whose identity is unknown, was pursued by security officials, but escaped without trace. Security at the docks has already been increased following an earlier and unexplained request by the German government for the Nazi U-boat to be returned.

The piece intrigued Brewer. Was it just coincidence that the attempted break-in had happened so soon after Anastasia had mentioned the U-boat? Possible, but unlikely. In his experience, genuinely significant coincidences were less commonplace than conspiracies.

He called Information Services to request copies of all material relating to the U-534 project. When the official file arrived on his desk, it contained nothing but a handful of press cuttings. After the initial burst of excited media publicity there was almost no further published information. Intrigued, Brewer made his own enquiries and soon found out the truth: the submarine salvage operation was covered by the Danish equivalent of a D-notice. Further media coverage was expressly forbidden. That indicated only one interpretation: something important *had* been discovered. Anastasia's claims suddenly looked a little less wild. Perhaps it was time to give her the benefit of the doubt.

Brewer mentioned his suspicions to Pendleton and the possible link with the Professor's death in Moscow. Pendleton feigned disinterest, but a few hours later a file arrived on Brewer's desk with stories about the U-boat the media were barred from running. For the first time Brewer wondered whether Anastasia's stories of Nazi involvement in the Professor's death and the link with the U-boat might be true. Cynicism and scepticism are two key qualities that a good field agent rapidly acquires. Surrounded by a world of conspiracy theorists and shady make-believe characters who want nothing more than to gain entry to the world of intelligence, Brewer had long since refused to believe anything that did not come with a guarantee of at least one hundred percent proof—including his drinks. But equally, sometimes professional cynicism needed to give way to pragmatism. Now might be just such a moment.

After some initial hesitation, the Danes agreed to Brewer's request to visit Hirtshals. Relations with London were good and Larsen Lak was happy to co-operate: he was a great Anglophile. His father had been active in the resistance during the war, working closely alongside Special Operations Executive agents.

The night of his arrival, Brewer dined with Lak's family. Their hospitality was faultless, his wife amusing and talkative, their two young children noisy and fascinated by their overseas visitor, refusing to go to bed long after their normal curfew.

For the first time in months, Brewer relaxed. He had forgotten—or, more accurately, had forced himself to forget—how enjoyable good family company could be. Much of an agent's work requires the ability to shut down emotions, to wipe out sensations and feelings that most people take for granted on a daily basis. It was good to be reminded of why he did his job, how important the dull and sometimes cruel world he lived in could be.

Now, as they approached the salvaged U-boat, the damp and chill of the morning air cut through him. What he would have given for a warming flask of *arkavit*.

'There was a German reporter here last week,' Larsen informed him as they crossed behind the keel. 'Everyone still seems so fascinated with the Nazis, do they not, even after all this time. Evil seems to hold an incredible attraction for people.'

'A reporter? What did he want?'

Larsen shrugged. 'He was interested in what we had found.' He smiled. 'But unlike you, he did not have clearance. We sent him away.' He stopped alongside the hull where a section had been removed. 'So, Peter. What do you know about submarines?'

Brewer wiped some spray from his glasses. 'They go under the sea. And if they're lucky, they come back to the surface again.'

'Top of the class.' He turned and thumped the hull. 'We were fortunate. This was not a war grave. Most of the crew survived. Unusual, in fact. Most U-boat crews in the Second World War lost their lives.'

'How many crew would it carry?'

'Fifty-two was standard. But this one, she was carrying around four extra tons of provisions than was usual. Would you like to see inside?'

Brewer glanced along the ominous dark shape of her two hundred and fifty foot hull. There was a presence, a sense of foreboding that made him uncomfortable. It was the same sensation that had come over him in Watten when he visited the vast V-weapon bunker at Eperleques: a tangible, haunting sensation of evil.

'Not unless I have to.'

Larsen looked disappointed, but made no comment. Evidently he had been looking forward to his role as a tour guide. Instead, he beckoned Brewer to follow him up a metal staircase to an office overlooking the covered dry dock. The unpainted steel handrail was cold to the touch, almost freezing Brewer's flesh to the metal as he gripped it. At the top they entered a small pre-fabricated cabin. The door swung shut behind them, dulling the ceaseless hiss of the hoses and the sounds of work being done on the boat.

The office was decorated plain cream. A few yellowing maps were pasted on pin boards and a scuffed wooden desk was pushed back against the end wall. A row of old grey filing cabinets and a safe stood to one side. A small electric fire with one bar gave out a dry, dusty smell and no heat.

Larsen moved over to the window and looked down at the boat.

'Soon she will go on public display.' He turned and smiled, rubbing his hands together for warmth. 'Minus her interesting artefacts, of course. I think it will be a good, how you say it, money spinner. Something for the tourists. Drink?'

Brewer sensed he meant something stronger than tea. He

suggested a Scotch and was gratified when Larsen produced a Highland Park and poured two large glasses. Brewer downed a generous gulp, enjoying the glow of warmth inside. They stood for a time watching work progress on the boat. The flash of the arc welding equipment cast an erratic, blue-ish, flickering light along the dark hulk of the boat and sent eerie shadows dancing along its side. Parts of the hull and conning tower had been stripped away to reveal a Meccano-kit skeletal framework inside. Several workers were clustered around a foreman, consulting a plan and pointing at the foredeck.

'And so to business.' Larsen opened the safe and took out a bundle of papers. 'You understand, these are only copies. The originals are too delicate to handle. They are with our restoration experts.'

Brewer nodded and moved over to the desk. Larsen spread out page after page of neat, tidy handwriting, almost too small to discern the characters.

'You read German?' Larsen asked.

Brewer shook his head and Larsen laughed.

'I forget. The English. Not great linguists.' He looked down at the page. 'My German is fairly good, but I do not understand this. It is evidently some kind of list, possibly the manifest. The occasional word I recognise, but much of it does not make sense.'

'Some sort of code?' Brewer asked.

He nodded. 'We thought at first it might be Enigma, but it is not. Neither is it the post-Enigma code. It is not a code we know. To be frank, no-one has yet broken it. Even our best people, even our computer boffins. We think the higher echelon Nazis were using an entirely new cipher right at the close of the war. It has been suspected for some time that the inner core of the SS had developed a more secure code for their own personal use.'

'But why all the secrecy? It could just be Hitler's laundry list.'

'It could be, yes,' Larsen responded and topped up both their glasses. 'But I don't think so. They would surely not be interested in smuggling Hitler's laundry list in the last days of the war? And certainly not in code. I believe they had more important matters on their mind, such as self-preservation. No, it has to be something more. Something they felt essential to preserve for what was to come after the war. It would be interesting to know.'

Brewer looked down and flicked through the papers. The pages were narrow-lined, the writing so small that it left a large gap between each row of text. At the top of each page was stamped a neat black swastika and eagle. The photocopies were grey, an indication the originals were discoloured. The writing became distorted where it approached the central binding. Despite what he had said, he read German fluently, but the words meant nothing to him. It was a job for the crypto-analysts back at GCHQ and their fancy computer equipment. Or what was left of them.

In 1995, the Hurn Report, the result of a Committee appointed by the former Conservative Prime Minister, severely damaged GCHQ's operational efficiency by guillotining a massive thirty percent from its budget. In the confusion that followed, not only did its most highly skilled staff depart, but some of its most delicate intelligence gathering operations were aborted mid-programme, forcing both the SIS and the Security Service to turn to America's National Security Agency to fill the gap. The irony was that the Aspin Commission in the States repeated the same mistake by cutting the NSA, believing that the British experience had been a success. Such was the narrow-minded attitude of the bureaucrats on both sides of the Atlantic before Al Qaeda struck America. That assault had signalled the end of the so-called 'peace dividend' and the belief that men carrying calculators knew more about intelligence than the specialists in their field. It was a lesson learned at a very high price.

'Are these for me?' Brewer asked, indicating the papers on the desk.

'Copies will be made available. Subject to the usual security arrangements.'

'Of course,' Brewer confirmed. 'I'll request London to organise a reliable courier.'

'Could you tell me what is it you are looking for? Perhaps I could help.'

Brewer sipped at the malt. 'Thanks for the offer. But to be honest, it's just a hazy jigsaw of loose pieces to me right now.'

Larsen looked out of the office window and put his drink down with a thump, visibly annoyed. Brewer moved over to stand beside him and followed his gaze through the wire-meshed glass.

A tall man in a knee-length, sand-coloured leather overcoat stood beside the keel of the U-boat, talking with one of the workmen. It was difficult to make out his features, but as they watched the workman pointed up at the office and the man turned to look at them.

'We have a visitor,' Larsen whispered. 'The German journalist I was telling you about. I did not expect to see him again.'

6

The German visitor stooped low to come through the doorway. When he straightened, Brewer saw a long-faced, tall man. He had striking pale blue eyes and fading straw-coloured hair, swept back from a receding hairline. Brewer guessed the man was in his late sixties—a youthful late sixties. Beneath the flaps of his overcoat he wore a dark suit, pale shirt and burgundy tie. Only one thing was certain: this was no journalist.

And they had a problem: the documents that Larsen had taken from the safe were still on full view. As Larsen stepped towards the desk, the German intercepted him and extended his hand.

'Good afternoon, Mr Lak.'

He spoke in English with an accent Brewer could not place.

'You have the better of me,' Larsen replied uneasily, his eyes darting nervously towards the papers. 'I seem to have forgotten your name.'

'Straker, Ernst Straker, Mr Lak.'

Straker turned to face Brewer and released Larsen's hand. 'And your name also?'

'I never share names on a first date, Herr Straker.'

The man stared at Brewer for a moment, a hard uncomfortable scrutiny. Behind him, Larsen swiftly gathered up the photocopied papers. He was about to secure them in the safe when Straker turned sharply.

'One moment. I should like to see those.'

Larsen shook his head. 'I'm afraid that will not be possible.'

'Hümmler.'

Straker spoke softly. The office door swung open and a Luger appeared pointed at Larsen. Its owner was a thuggish dark-haired man in his forties wearing a leather jacket and jeans. Without the gun, he would have been a nondescript jerk. With it, they gave him their undivided attention. Brewer had not seen or heard him arrive, but unless he was a member of the Magic Circle he must have been listening outside the door waiting to stage his entrance.

'Please, there is no need for this.' Larsen asked. 'Now put that gun away. I shall call security.'

Larsen was midway between the desk and the safe. Brewer guessed he was calculating how quickly he could get the papers into the safe and lock it. But their visitors guessed it too.

'Please. Don't do anything foolish,' said the man with the Luger, shaking his head.

It was not the sort of command you ignored. Not with a gun to back it up.

'Good,' said Straker. He beckoned to Larsen with his forefinger. 'I should like to see those papers, please.'

'Herr Straker. Perhaps you would be kind enough to tell us what you've done with Anastasia?'

It was a wild shot: but Brewer's question clearly hit the target. Straker looked at Brewer sharply. 'Anastasia? An interesting question from the anonymous Englishman. What do you know about this?'

'I asked first.'

There was a moment's silence. Hümmler looked like he was itching for any excuse to use his vintage toy. But instead of issuing instructions to make Hümmler's day, Straker smiled instead.

'I remember now. How remiss of me. I usually have a better memory for faces. You were in Moscow, weren't you?' he asked.

Brewer said nothing: it did not sound like the type of question that required a reply.

'And you were not very successful, I understand. For that you should be grateful.'

'Did you kill Professor Beatty?'

Straker laughed. 'What a ridiculous question. Why should I have any interest in killing some sad, perverted Professor? You have the wrong idea about me, entirely the wrong idea.'

'I'm not so sure,' Brewer commented. He looked more closely at Straker's sidekick. Was it Hümmler who had chased him through Moscow's streets firing off shots? He did not think so. Hümmler's build was different. And if Sarkovsky was to be believed, someone had already taken care of that particular stalker—permanently. That meant there was more then one gunman in circulation. So maybe he owed Anastasia an apology after all. Maybe her crazy sounding ideas had not been such fantasy after all.

Hümmler smiled with his mouth, but his eyes remained cold. He squeezed the trigger just once. A single, tiny, deadly movement. The shot was explosive in the small office.

Larsen was dead before he hit the floor. A thin trail of blood trickled down the wall behind him. It was all very quick, very cold.

'He moved,' Hümmler observed dryly.

Brewer's reaction was pure instinct. He stepped forwards, intent on snatching Hümmler's Luger away from him and emptying its entire magazine into his oafish features. And then just as suddenly his professional instincts brought the shutters slamming down. He turned off a part of himself as easily as turning off water running from a tap. He stopped. Now was not the time for emotion. Larsen was dead. It was time to look after himself.

Straker's smile dropped as he stepped towards Brewer. 'You disappoint me. And you now have the death of a man on your conscience. It would be better for you to listen when I talk.'

Hümmler fixed the Luger on Brewer. Brewer watched in silence as Straker retrieved the photocopied papers from where they had fallen and flicked briefly through them. He nodded.

'What do you want with those? They're only photocopies for Chrissake,' Brewer said, his voice hoarse. He cleared his throat. 'The originals are safe. We can run off a thousand more copies if we need to.' He turned to Hümmler. 'You didn't have to kill a man for that.'

Straker looked at Brewer with disdain. 'Do you really hold such a low opinion of me?' He came closer. 'Let me make this absolutely clear. You cannot run off a thousand more copies. You cannot even run off one more copy.' He looked over at Hümmler and smiled. 'Why? Because we possess the originals too. Isn't that right Hümmler?'

Hümmler nodded, as if the mental effort involved in speaking would prove too much for his Neanderthal abilities.

'What strikes me as particularly sad, however, is that I don't believe you comprehend what these papers are, do you?' Straker demanded.

'Perhaps you could enlighten me,' Brewer suggested.

Straker shook his head. 'No. It is better for all of us if you don't waste any more of your time trying to find out. Not unless you want to end up like your friend. This is best forgotten. Let the past be. It was all, I'm sad to say, a very long time ago.'

He hesitated a moment, as if about to add something else, and then turned and was gone, his footsteps clattering into silence on the metal staircase outside. Several minutes passed. Hümmler stood motionless with the gun, watching Brewer and showing no signs of following Straker's example.

He was waiting for something and Brewer had a nasty feeling about what it might be.

7

From the early days of the fight to establish a Jewish homeland in Palestine, to the hunt for Nazi war criminals and undercover operations against terrorists abroad, the Mossad has played a key role in the security and protection of Israeli interests. With the possible exception of the UK's Secret Intelligence Service, which is itself a small operation by other countries standards, the Mossad is often rated as producing the best product of any intelligence service. At its best it has managed to combine the ruthlessness and regimentation of the Russians, the imagination of the old pre-war British intelligence service and the bravado and lawlessness of the French. At its worst, it has been riven by the schisms and polemics that have affected the state of Israel itself.

Despite its many alliances, the Mossad never really relies upon anyone but its own agents. It will co-operate where it can and accept intelligence where it can, but it never trusts anyone. It has learnt the cost of doing so.

The news of the assassination of Akani Matsu came as no surprise to the Mossad. For some time they had been tracking the actions of the group responsible. They had first encountered their activities in Europe, commencing with the small-scale direct actions against immigrants and refugees that were both feeble and yet also unpleasantly reminiscent of the early Nazi attacks of the late 1920s. Plans by the group to develop similar actions in the Far East initially came as a surprise: it was not their traditional theatre. As soon as the Mossad was convinced the group was about to commit a serious action, they had contacted the Japanese intelligence services through an intermediary 'friendly' agency and given them a clear and unambiguous warning about an impending poison gas attack. The Japanese were uncertain how to react. Terrorism and anti-State groups were virtually unknown in Japan: it was difficult to comprehend the reality of the potential threat. In the end the authorities compromised and purchased gas masks for the police and emergency services.

Then they made their fatal mistake: they sat and waited to see if the intelligence was accurate.

When the gas attack ripped through the Tokyo underground system exactly as the Mossad had predicted, the Japanese police experienced difficulty explaining their sudden purchase of anti-gas equipment shortly before the attack took place. Then came the assassination of Akani Matsu as he left his home for work. The Mossad had provided a warning too of the presence in Japan of Ahmed Rami, an Iraqi suspected of close involvement in numerous terrorist actions. The warning did not reach the right department until it was too late. By that time, Rami was already half way round the world on a flight to Frankfurt. In any case, he knew better than to travel under his own name and was adept at adopting disguises.

Following the shooting of Matsu, a hurried meeting of senior executives took place in the offices of General Isser Dayan, Head of the Mossad, in the Hadar Dafna Building on King Saul Boulevard. Since the Israeli spy Jonathan Pollard was imprisoned in America for acting as a double agent whilst in the employ of US Naval Intelligence, the Mossad's relationship with its American colleagues has never been as comfortable as it once was. But whatever the diplomatic cost, the Mossad continues to base agents in the States.

At the meeting, the General played host to an American visitor and did his best to make him welcome. Arthur Dole, the CIA's Head of Mid-East Division, was visiting Tel Aviv to talk with the Agency's local Head of Station when the Tokyo gassings and then Matsu's assassination took place. The unscheduled meeting with Israeli intelligence was hurriedly arranged at the Mossad's request.

For a time they exchanged pleasantries. There was some discussion of chemical and biological weapons programmes being developed in the Middle East and the extent to which organisations such as Al Qaeda were involved. In private, military analysts have understood for at least the last decade that the next major conflict will not be nuclear: it will be conducted with either traditional weaponry, probably in a third world theatre— or it will involve the use of tactical biological and chemical weapons. And future wars will not take place on the remote fields of a foreign country, but on the streets and in the houses of home. In general, governments have been reluctant to heed their warnings: defence against chemical and biological warfare is prohibitively expensive and far less glamorous than new fighters and submarine missile systems. And in any case, talk of chemical and biological weapons frightens the horses. Best not to mention them at all. At least, until September 11 that had been the case. Now the whole landscape had changed.

General Dayan handed Dole a flimsy file. 'Accept this as a gift. You may find it useful.'

Dole opened the file and flicked through its meagre contents. He saw several names he recognised. One of them was very familiar: Helmut Schengel. The Agency had first encountered Schengel during his involvement with secret poison gas projects in Libya, in the days when Libya had directly supported terrorism. In Tarhuna, forty miles south of Tripoli, and Rabta, hundreds of tonnes of sarin had been produced. Schengel, originally a German scientist, had been closely involved with its production. Later there had been more substantial proof of his links with 'undesirable' regimes. The Agency had identified his involvement with Iraq's former bio-chemical weapons development. According to the Mossad, he had been in Japan six months before the Tokyo sarin incident.

Dole looked up. 'What do our Japanese friends know about this?'

General Dayan shook his head. 'Nothing. We provided them with early information, but they were too slow to act. Unlike us, they are not used to being under siege; they do not have the right mentality to act quickly. How pleasant it would be to live in such a country. You will of course understand our problem. If we continue to help them, we fear revealing something of our own operations.'

Dole appreciated the problem. The Mossad evidently had well-placed sources operating within Japan. In common with most countries, Japan would not be pleased to learn that it was being spied upon by a so-called 'friendly' country. America certainly hadn't been delighted when the fallout from the Pollard case had hit the fan.

'Where is Schengel now?'

The General looked at Dole and smiled. 'That is what I felt I should tell you.' He waited and then dropped the word with maximum effect. 'America.'

Dole went cold. The terrorist attacks on the World Trade Center and the Pentagon, and the earlier bomb attacks on the Atlanta Olympics and the federal government building in Oklahoma City, had turned the prospect of terrorism in America itself into a blunt, brutal and bloody reality. In response to the problem, the Agency was operating under special instructions to focus intelligence resources on international threats to America's domestic security. With the big, bad threat of the Warsaw Block and the Cold War dissipated and fragmented since the demise of the Soviet Union, America has for some time been painfully aware of the threat it faces from overseas and domestic infiltration by extremist movements. It was only recently that such threats had started to become a reality.

'Do you know what he's doing there?'

The General shrugged. 'But of course not. As you know, since Pollard we have not operated researchers within the borders of the United States.'

'Bullshit,' Dole replied and found himself smiling. They both knew the Mossad was as active in America as it had always been, but the two intelligence services understood the public games they had to play to keep their political masters happy.

General Dayan leant back in his chair. 'That document tells you enough. You should be able to find him. That is,' he said, lighting a Cohiba which he took from a desktop humidor. 'If the Agency will be dealing with it. Perhaps this is more of an FBI matter?'

Dole let that one pass. General Dayan was well aware of the running battle between the CIA and the FBI. The FBI was making serious attempts behind the scenes in Washington to have the Agency dissolved and assume the CIA's role. It had been a vision of the late J Edgar Hoover's that the FBI would eventually become a single agency responsible for domestic and foreign intelligence alike. What worried Dole was that the FBI had several leading politicians batting on their side and Hoover's vision was closer to being realised than ever before. The new Department of Homeland Security had already started things moving down a path where all intelligence work was co-ordinated through a central body.

'What do I owe you for this?' Dole waved the document briefly in the air.

The General waved his cigar. 'Nothing, of course. Just two old friends helping each other.'

'Okay,' Dole said, pushing back his chair to stand. 'I'll let you know of any developments.' He understood the deal on the table: the General would call in the favour when he needed one. With interest, if past evidence was anything to go on.

'Good luck,' the General said, rising and stretching out his hand. 'I would not like to see the Tokyo incident repeated on the New York subway. New York—which, incidentally, is my favourite city—has suffered enough.'

The thought turned Dole's stomach. But what was Schengel doing in the States? More importantly, who was he working for? With previous employers that included General Ghadaffi of Libya and Saddam Hussein of Iraq, they were questions that made Dole feel distinctly uneasy.

He hurried away to catch his flight.

Hamilton was late. Emily paced the kitchen with increasing impatience. Sometimes he could be such a selfish shit. Two and a half hours earlier she had arrived at his house in West London happy and relaxed and cooked him a special meal. His favourite: a steak casserole cooked in a rich Burgundy and green peppercorn sauce. And now it was thick, dry and rubbery.

There was the sound of a key in the front door. She ran towards it.

'About time too, you bastard!' she exclaimed and despite her irritation gave him a hug.

He kissed her briefly and pushed her aside. 'Sorry. Something came up at the House.'

'Did it?' she said with a mischievous look in her eyes. 'I like it when something comes up.'

He ignored her innuendo and brushed past her into the kitchen. 'That smells good.'

She followed him like a lap dog and hated herself for doing it. She had never been so submissive with other men, so willing to put up with being treated like an accessory rather than a person. But there was something about Hamilton that held her in awe. He was the only person she had ever known with a real presence, a palpable aura of power, drive and ambition that turned heads and silenced conversations when he entered a room.

'That's about all that can be said for it,' she commented. 'It's burnt.'

He peered into the oven. 'Ah. I see what you mean. Sorry. I wanted to be here.'

'Your wife called,' she said.

Hamilton swung round sharply to look at her. 'Did you speak to her?'

'Of course not,' Emily replied. 'It's on the answer phone. I was here when she called, but I left it when I heard her voice.'

'Good girl,' Hamilton commented. 'Shall we go out to eat?'

'I'd rather stay in,' she replied slyly, pushing her tongue against her cheek.

'Good idea. How about we get a home delivery?'

She nodded. 'That'd be nice.' She moved closer to him and ran her hands through his hair. 'When are you going to tell her about us? When can we be together, properly together I mean?'

'Soon,' Hamilton replied, looking down into her sky-blue eyes. He ran his hands along her spine and over the gentle curve of her hips, slowly massaging her soft, pliant skin. 'Do you want to eat first? Or did you have something else in mind?'

She looked up at him and smiled. 'Something else.'

Brewer learned the lesson a long time ago: always take the first chance. Most people caught in a trap sit and wait, never sure whether *this* is the time to take action. Bad idea. There is nothing worth waiting for: act as soon as you can, or you never will. So when there was an explosion in the dry dock downstairs, when Hümmler was distracted for that first split-second, that's when Brewer moved.

His fist cracked sharply into Hümmler's chin, the surprise knocking the gun from Hümmler's grasp. As Hümmler tripped backwards, grabbing for the weapon as it fell, Brewer took the chance and ran out of the office. The whole place was a confusion of light, heat and sound. No time to think. He jumped down the stairs, taking them five at a time and using the handrail to maintain balance. The metal stairs echoed and bounced in time with his movements. Suddenly a sheet of flame and heat burst across the dry dock, robbing the air of oxygen. He gasped for breath. Thick, oily smoke caught in his throat. It was the submarine: exploding. God knows what was happening here.

Brewer hit ground level and raced breathlessly towards the exit. By the time Hümmler appeared at the office doorway, it was too late. There was the brief sound of gunfire, the hint of a ghostly hand at his shoulder as a bullet winged close and then Brewer was out in the dockyards and lost amongst the cranes, sidings and dry docks.

He took refuge in an old goods carriage that stank of rotten cabbage and was covered in bird excrement. Through a crack in the rotten wood of the carriage, he watched as wild plumes of demonic orange and yellow flame consumed the dry dock and its temporary cover. Salvage workers and firefighters ran around in the dust, flames and smoke, shouting contradictory instructions at each other in the chaos. Amongst the fire trucks and ambulances, Brewer saw a long dark limousine and thought he recognised Straker's figure. And then Hümmler joined him and he knew for sure. They spoke for a moment, looked briefly around as if they half-expected to see Brewer, then climbed into the car and were gone.

Brewer emerged from the carriage and walked calmly towards the centre of activity, brushing himself down. The fire continued to rage with an intense, bright red fury, the attempts of the fire fighters a futile gesture. By the time it was under control, the fire had left the U-boat a warped, peeling dark hulk. Brewer stood and watched with a mix of anger and sadness. He shivered in the biting chill of the air and wished they had left the sub at the bottom of the Kattegat, back in the past where it belonged.

Later, in his hotel, he filed London an update. They were not happy: they never were. He spoke with his contacts in the Danish service and asked them to convey his regrets to Larsen's family. He meant it. Larsen did not deserve what happened. He had been caught in the wrong place at the wrong time with the wrong people. Brewer told them everything he knew. If the Danes could catch Straker and Hümmler, so far as Brewer was concerned that was good news: it would save him the trouble. And if London didn't like it, that was their problem. Turf wars were outside Brewer's sphere of interest. All he ever wanted was results. The means were irrelevant.

He switched on MTV as a backdrop while he sat at the table in his room and thought. He had assembled a motley collection of pieces, but he just wasn't seeing the picture. Two things were clear: London knew something they weren't telling him. And Moscow knew something and they certainly weren't telling him.

He lit up a *Romeo y Julieta* and took off his glasses. Every year it became harder. When the Cold War went, so too did the routine, the certainty. No-one knew any more what they were looking for, what the next problem would be. Before, all that you needed was patience, persistence, and a bit of luck. Now you needed brains, persistence, and a heck of a lot of luck. But the Firm was always too slow to change and adapt: it was still stuck in its cosy private school ways, run by clubby young men in suits who had about as much experience of the real world as Daffy Duck. And they spoke about as much sense too.

If Brewer was honest, he had enjoyed working behind the Iron Curtain. Most of them had. It had been another world. Now when he came off a plane, he never knew where he was: London, New York, Moscow, Peking. They all looked the same, all had their McDonalds and their ersatz cosmopolitan feel, all spoke a language of 'efficiency' and 'market forces', the same hollow mantra the world over.

He sighed. This was getting him no-where. Once upon a time London would have trusted him with everything they knew. Not any longer. Now everything was 'team-based': some sort of new management theory about a 'team discipline ethic'. Loners were to be avoided: they were unpredictable, dangerous. Field agents were even being sent on outward-bound courses to encourage tighter team bonding. Well, maybe that was right when you were cooking hamburgers, singing lewd sea shanties, and breaking wind round the campfire, but successful intelligence has always been a loner's game. High tech gadgetry has its place, but so too does human intelligence—yet that takes hard work, often years of sheer unremitting graft undercover, and cannot guarantee such easy results. So the spotty-faced new management have ignored it. And now they were paying the price. So too were those whom they were there to protect.

The Firm has never been as good as it was before and during the Second World War. Then it had revelled in the individual, recognised the true nature of intelligence work. Since then it had lost direction, been haunted by disaster and misjudgement. The supply of specialist and lethal advice to Pol Pot's Khmer Rouge in Cambodia by both the Firm and the SAS was one of the lowest points in its history. The new guys in suits didn't seem to understand that: Brewer guessed they had forgotten to opt for the module on their MBA course—one of the least useful pieces of bureaucratic confetti handed out by the "revenue-generation" arms of the cynical higher education establishment. A tired and emotional senior lecturer had once confessed to Brewer at a Foreign Office party that the whole MBA industry was, to use his phrase, 'a load of bollocks designed to bring in the fat cat mugs and their money'.

He found himself thinking about Jane. They had met when she was in her mid twenties and Brewer was thirty-two—and still ignorant of long-term relationships: something to do with never being in the same place for more than a few months. It started with an unlikely encounter in a launderette. A mundane conversation about what change the machines required and then a loan of washing powder. A few minutes later they were both in the pub and talking about so many things they missed the launderette's closing time and only collected their laundry the following day. That was their first rendezvous. Within weeks they were living together.

And then work intervened and Brewer was back overseas on assignment for six months. Jane had claimed she didn't mind. She had enough interests to keep her occupied. And it was true. When he returned from his assignment it was as if he had never been away. He had introduced her to his friend Gary soon after, while Gary was in London on leave. There was something even in that first meeting that made him uneasy, a feeling that some sort of unspoken biological signal had passed between Gary and Jane.

The next time Brewer returned from assignment it was to discover Jane living with Gary. Or she would have been, except by then Gary was on a posting overseas. Brewer and Jane arranged to meet in the same pub as their first encounter. It was a tense rendezvous, their conversation forced and stilted. He did not see her again until Gary returned from his overseas tour of duty and dragged them all out together to patch things up. By then Brewer was over it and suddenly everything snapped into place and Jane became just a good friend like Gary.

Shortly before Gary's death, Jane and Gary had talked of little else but their plans for what they would do when he left the forces. Brewer had never thought of him as a family man before, but under Jane's influence he saw another side. Shortly before Gary's final posting, there was a hurried wedding. And then the disaster of the first Gulf War happened and Gary went and got himself killed over someone else's oil in someone else's back yard.

Brewer guessed he should have comforted Jane more than he did. But he had known Gary since school and his death hit him just as hard. He made a resolution with himself: next time he was back in London, he would make the effort to take her out for an evening. He didn't know what he would say, what he wanted. It had always been the way: at work he could cope with any situation, make instant decisions, find a way through. In his personal life, nothing ever seemed so clear-cut, so easy to decide.

Before he went to bed, he wrote a short letter to Larsen's widow and children: and enclosed the balance of his cash expenses. That would give London's army of desk accountants something to write memos about.

A hot, dry wind blew sent a dancing plume of desert sand through the middle of the military display stands. From the comfort of the air-conditioned observation tower, Parke noted with satisfaction the professional approach of the event's organisers. Of course, it was to be expected. The majority of them were ex-service men. Since the end of the Cold War, a massive pool of highly trained military talent has become available for those with the resources and inclination to fund them. And there has been no shortage of wars to keep them occupied. Some have found work with mercenary armies in third world trouble zones. Others have applied themselves to relief agencies such as UNICEF and voluntary organisations involved with refugee assistance programmes, often helping in those very same trouble zones where some of their former comrades in arms are fighting. And others have been re-employed in various military forces, working for organisations that are not recognisable nation states.

Parke was a happy man. The test results were impressive. All the omens were good that the deal he wanted, the deal they all wanted, was going to happen. Outside, the desert air made the displays shimmer and wobble like a mirage, the shape of the missile launchers and missiles themselves slipping in and out of focus.

A variety of missiles were being showcased. The majority were of the command-guided variety. Tracking beams from ground radar were used to monitor both the target and the missiles launched towards it. At the computerised command centre, advanced trajectory systems analysed the radar beams and sent a constant stream of messages back to hold the missiles steady on their path. Several rusting Russian T34's were destroyed by the first fusillade of missiles, the flash and boom of sound rolling across the empty desert sands.

Also on display were guided missiles, utilising a refined heat-seeking mechanism that enabled the missiles to home in on the heat trail left by their target. The row of ex-US Army armoured personnel carriers vanished in a mountainous fireball.

And the final category on show was ordinary ballistic missiles: less sophisticated and less expensive than the others, the ballistic missiles followed a simple trajectory determined by the angle at which they were fired. But even they could cause extensive damage, as the evidence of wrecked remains of the Jeeps clearly demonstrated.

The variety of weapons was typical of such displays. So too was the audience: Parke had noted with interest the variety of potential clients and their proxies attending the event. The more prosperous would purchase the most sophisticated missiles, those with less purchasing power would settle for the ballistics. Nobody asked what such weapons would be used for. Vague diplomatic terms like 'domestic and foreign issues of security' were employed.

There was one omission from the display, however. None of the missiles with the specially developed warheads in which he was most interested could be displayed: the risk was too great. That demonstration would come later under strict control conditions, held underground, away from the prying lenses of the spy satellites that doubtless hovered somewhere overhead.

Parke sipped at his flute of *Moet et Chandon* and turned to the man beside him.

'Very impressive,' he commented, nodding towards the displays outside the observation window.

The man smiled. 'We aim to please. But as you will appreciate, these missiles are so crude. There is nothing new here. Doubtless a man of your background has seen it all before. I gather your interest lies elsewhere?'

Parke nodded. 'These missile systems are all very well for conventional battles, but I think we have passed that stage. The Gulf Wars, the World Trade Center, Kenya, all showed us that.'

The man nodded. 'I agree. For third world countries squabbling amongst themselves, perhaps these weapons are still relevant. And for the economies that build them for trade, there too they remain important. But for other types of battle on, let us call them, more advanced and more complex territories, other more appropriate means must be found.'

'Exactly.' Parke turned to look briefly over the desert scene outside. Technicians were busy dismantling the missile launching systems and returning them to their camouflaged hangers.

'Did you enjoy our Tokyo demonstration?'

The question was asked quietly, very matter-of-fact. Parke turned back to look at the man, trying to discern his features behind the dark glasses. 'Very impressive. And quite convincing.'

The man waved a hand. 'That was nothing. A little taster. I believe you are considering more ambitious projects?'

Parke looked around uneasily, but none of the other observers were close enough to overhear. 'I would rather we spoke somewhere more private.'

The man smiled. 'Naturally. Let us wait until after this evening's demonstration.'

Parke concurred and sat back in his chair. Everything was going well. But at the back of his mind something nagged him: fear. Fear of discovery before they were ready. Fear that someone might start to dig, to unravel things. There was too much time and money invested now to run that risk. The answer was quite simple: if someone started to dig, they would have to be removed. Using whatever force was appropriate.

It was too late to get cold feet now.

8

Simon Gilbert was the only witness to the murder of Iyas Qalwyr, editor of the *London Arab News*. But he had little intention of phoning Crimebusters to claim his reward. Instead he followed the assassin to a small hotel and then sat in a café opposite from where he could watch comfortably without drawing attention to himself.

A smartly dressed man in his early thirties, Gilbert looked like a minor banking official, perhaps a solicitor's clerk. He wore gold-framed glasses and his ginger hair was clipped short. Even to the most highly trained observer there was nothing to suggest that Gilbert was one of the Mossad's top operatives. Since saving Brewer's life in Moscow, he had been kept busy.

Gilbert had followed the assassin for two weeks after intercepting him in Frankfurt on transit between flights. He knew everything about the assassin's moves over the last fortnight and would have welcomed the instruction from Tel Aviv to remove him. But for the moment his instructions were merely to follow and observe, not to intervene.

Ahmed Rami, the assassin who had ended Qalwyr's life, provoked both hate and a certain degree of professional respect in Gilbert. Rami was deeply involved with extremist causes in both radical mid-Eastern regimes and in Europe. But he was a smart and intelligent operator, no mere puppet boot solider mindlessly following the orders of others. Rami believed passionately in a cause: the creation of a pan-Arabic state. He had become the leading assassin hired by a group of several loosely affiliated organisations who worked mainly under the pretext of religious movements, but who resorted to direct action when power eluded them—as it generally did. The close alliance between Nazi organisations and extremist mid-Eastern dictatorships was forged in the years before the Second World War. It was nurtured when leading Nazi party officials fled to friendly extremist regimes at the end of the war, united in their common desire to continue working on a so-called "final solution" to the Jewish "problem".

The assassination of Qalwyr meant nothing to Gilbert. He knew nothing about the story the outcast editor had been about to publish, did not understand the significance of his removal. That intelligence was reserved for others based in the Hadar Dafna Building on King Saul Boulevard. The Mossad has always been the most careful of organisations in applying the 'need to know' maxim. From experience it knows that its enemies will use any method to extract information from those of its members unfortunate enough to be captured. Every risk has to be contained, every operative provided with only a single instruction. Gilbert knew only that he was to follow and report.

It was two hours before Rami emerged from the hotel and flagged down a taxi. He had changed into a loose fitting casual outfit and was carrying a small leather suitcase. Gilbert watched as the taxi pulled away and then stepped out onto the pavement. Another taxi was already approaching. He waved it down, directing the driver to Heathrow. It was a guess, a guess based on experience.

Half an hour later his guess was confirmed. Rami was ahead of him, walking towards a British Airways check-in counter. Gilbert approached close enough to confirm Rami's destination, ticket type (First, of course—the preferred class of terrorists) and flight and then headed for a nearby pay phone.

It was time to file an update.

Pendleton was standing looking out of the window when Brewer entered his office. He turned and waved impatiently for Brewer to sit down.

'Look at these damned pigeons,' he commented. 'I can barely see my window sill. Perhaps I should make a living as a guano trader. God knows why anyone feeds the damned things anything other than poison.' Pendleton sat behind his desk. 'We don't seem to be making much headway on this one, do we Brewer? And what a bloody mess you left behind in Denmark. What were you playing at? The accountants are screaming blue murder.'

Brewer nodded. 'Music to my ears. But it did confirm one thing.'

Pendleton raised his eyebrows. 'That perhaps I never should let you out in the field again without a minder?'

Brewer did not rise to the bait. 'No. That the Professor certainly wasn't the victim of a chance mafia killing.'

'I think we knew that already,' Pendleton responded dryly. 'Your mission was to find out who did kill him and more importantly why. And do you have any news on that?'

'Not exactly what I would call 'news',' Brewer hedged.

'I'll take that as a no.' Pendleton sighed. 'I'll be blunt, Brewer. Our new lords and masters are not patient people. They need to see progress, weekly, on their project management charts. They have colourful GANTT charts to track and update. They don't like to see them turning red.'

Brewer understood the difficulties facing Pendleton. The ability to manage had long since been taken out of the hands of the very people in the Firm who best knew how to do it. Every day the Service was becoming more bureaucratic, more constrained by sub-committees and working parties, assessment reviews and accountants. In the early 1990's, the Service had been badly damaged by a cut in its overseas operations. Stations in Africa, the Far East and Central and South America were closed. Resident agencies were out, field agents in: cost-cutting was the name of the game, or 'multi-operational dynamics through flexibility' as the new breed of managers preferred to call it. The emphasis moved to signals intelligence and away from human intelligence. The result was a sharp drop in the quality of product and a weakness in precisely those regions that were becoming economically and politically more significant on the world scene. That was always the problem with accountants: they never have been any good at staring into crystal balls. If they were, they certainly wouldn't be accountants.

As European Controller, Pendleton reported through Cham, who in turn reported to C, the head of the Secret Intelligence Services. As part of the Foreign and Commonwealth Office, operational decisions were approved by not only the Foreign Secretary and sometimes the PM and Cabinet, but also by the Permanent Secretaries Committee on the Intelligence Services (PSIS), the Intelligence Co-Ordinator and the jaw-aching talking shop of the Joint Intelligence Committee (JIC), with its endless sub-committees, assessments staff and secretariat. It was no wonder the SIS's recent track record had become a bland list of committee-approved compromises. The mess and controversy around the second Gulf War and the overthrowing of Saddam Hussein's regime in Iraq had shown all too clearly just what a muddle the chain of command and intelligence gathering was in.

There still remained a deep smouldering resentment in the SIS that their detailed and prophetic warnings in advance of the attack on Saddam's regime had not reached the right people in time. A failure caused by the Civil Service committee system that oversaw every aspect of their operations—except perhaps which type of biscuits to serve with afternoon tea. And even that, Brewer suspected, was on the list of items to be investigated by a relevant JIC sub-committee on "refreshment department logistics and the delegated taxonomy of confectionary and allied trades as applied to office-based intelligence operations".

'What sort of 'progress'?' Brewer asked quietly.

Pendleton looked away, avoiding his gaze. 'You need to be reassigned.'

'Re-assigned? Their decision or yours?'

'Does it matter?'

'It does to me.'

'Theirs of course, you bloody fool. You know me better than that.' Pendleton sighed. 'But I can sympathise with their reasons.'

'Can you? That's very noble of you. And do you mind telling me what exactly it is that I'm being reassigned to?'

Pendleton coughed. 'Duty desk rota.'

Brewer exploded. 'Bloody hell Pendleton! You know I can't accept that. How can you even suggest it?'

'Politics. I have a little local difficulty with the other Controllers,' Pendleton explained. 'You wandered out of territory.'

'On your bloody instructions.' Brewer shook his head in disbelief. 'So now what? Every time we have to extend beyond Europe we're meant to involve the CIS and Western Hemisphere Controllers too? That's crazy. I thought you said these guys wanted results.'

Pendleton smiled. As European Controller his sphere of operations was clearly defined, but an operation like Brewer's spanned several spheres of control. Normally the Liaison group would handle the complex of interrelationships, but the whole concept was misguided and both of them knew it. Criminals and terrorists have always taken advantage of the silo'd nature of police and security agencies. Pendleton did his best to shield his agents from the nightmare bureaucracy that bound the Service in a straightjacket and made it so ineffective. His days were filled with committee meetings, strategy meetings, liaison meetings and working lunches.

In the past, when the Firm was at its peak, individuals had been trusted to make their own decisions, to act and react quickly. The technique worked. But after the war, the vines of the committee system had crept in from Whitehall and slowly strangled the Service. Prevarication, power-play and ossification became the order of the day. International terrorists have long played such hopeless bureaucracy to their own benefit. Like the split between the police, SIS and Security Service, which for years played into the hands of the IRA, Pendleton never understood the reason for segmenting responsibilities by arbitrary geographical area rather than by interest. Occasionally when COBRA—Cabinet Office Briefing Room A—was in operation to oversee a national crisis, the mandarins would be forced to relent and they and politicians alike would finally let the Service call the shots. But those occasions were the exception: it took something such as 9/11 to break through the bureaucracy and shock the mainstream establishment into understanding the cruel realities of the world they lived in.

'We have to give these new boys and their new ideas time,' Pendleton commented, sounding as if he was trying to convince himself. 'Changes always cause a certain disruption before they settle in.'

'Bullshit,' Brewer responded, rising from his chair and leaning across the desk. 'If this lot of overgrown schoolboys carry on like this, the Firm won't even exist in five years time. We're a bloody laughing stock.'

'Maybe. But that doesn't change the facts. Your new assignment starts with immediate effect.'

'Thanks. That's just what I need.' Brewer sank back into his seat.

'Count yourself lucky,' Pendleton continued. 'Poor old Monroe's out on his rather substantial backside.'

'Monroe?' Brewer was shocked.

'And Mortimer and Powell.'

'Jesus. They're some of the best we have.'

Pendleton shrugged. 'Our MBA action men think otherwise. We're all being sent on a "behaviours workshop". And there are new cost centres, new efficiency models, team-based networking, and quantative performance indicators. All sounds very impressive doesn't it?'

'About as impressive as a dog turd on the pavement,' Brewer responded. 'Only I'd rather step in that than the ideas these losers come up with.'

'The trouble with you Brewer is that you're an unreformed socialist. You see someone in a suit and take an instant dislike to them.'

'Not at all Pendleton,' Brewer replied, standing. 'The word you want is communist. Didn't you know? I'm the missing sixth man.'

'Oh. And I thought that was me,' Pendleton whispered as Brewer walked towards the door.

When Arthur Dole, the CIA's Head of Mid-East Division, returned from Tel Aviv to his office in the CIA's headquarters at McLean, Virginia—more commonly known as Langley—he arranged an urgent meeting with Frank Vogel, the head of the Agency.

Vogel and his Head of Divisions had been anxious to turn the Agency around in the wake of disasters such as 9/11 and the Ames affair, acutely aware of the threat presented by the FBI's predatory attitude and the Agency's own lack-lustre performance. Ames—the most successful mole in the Agency's history—was generally attributed with causing the death of at least ten Agency operatives during his covert operations, as well as agents of other friendly powers compromised by his revelations. And now the political noise and threats from Capitol Hill were becoming more transparent, particularly since the terrorist destruction of the World Trade Center and the damage to the Pentagon: the Agency was living on borrowed time. Either it would prove itself, or it would cease to exist in its current form.

When Vogel read the information about the scientist Helmut Schengel that Dole brought with him from Israel, he quickly appreciated its importance. But there was just one problem.

'This is T-BAR turf,' Vogel commented, looking across the broad table to where Dole was seated and using the Agency's vernacular for the FBI. 'It's domestic.'

They were the only occupants of the meeting room. There were no secretaries taking minutes, no recordings. The room was secure, reserved for the exclusive use of the Agency's directors amidst their suite of offices in the old building. Only they would know what was discussed in here.

'I think we both appreciate that,' Dole replied. 'The question is how we handle it. Do we hand it over, or do we undertake some preliminary work ourselves? This could be big and God knows we need a breakthrough, something to give us real kudos. Helmut Schengel has been on our list for a long time. The fact that he's temporarily in the US does not mean we can't continue to investigate. The international perspective is clear enough.'

'But it could lead to complications,' Vogel returned. 'And not just with the FBI.'

'What other complications?' Dole enquired. 'Rounding up a covert operation like this would be a real plus right now. God knows we need to pull something off and damn soon too. The politicos have been breathing down our necks since 9/11 for not handling things well in the past, the Iraqi weapons of mass destruction fuck-up, dropping the ball between us and the Bureau. So this time, why not make sure we've got everything cracked first?'

Vogel waved impatiently. 'That all sounds very good, but what troubles me is where this one might lead.'

Dole frowned. 'You think there's another dimension?'

'I *know* there's another dimension,' Vogel replied shortly. 'Sorry Arthur. This is one we're not going to touch.'

'I don't believe I'm hearing this. We have a clear and legitimate interest. Schengel's work in Libya and Iraq alone would be sufficient reason to reel him in. He's in clear violation of the 1925 and 1972 conventions, let alone the right we have now to drag deadbeats like him straight off the street. I say we go ahead, act on this information ourselves.'

'Tough,' Vogel countered. 'I'm telling you now, Arthur. Leave it alone. Give it to the Bureau as quickly as you can.' He rose and moved over the window, looking out over the Langley complex. 'Goddamit. Why do the Mossad always have to stick their nose in? You'd think they had enough problems of their own to focus on right now instead of butting into our business.'

Dole studied his boss's back for a time before replying. Vogel's reaction was a surprise. He had been sure this would be one the Agency would want to run with, one that it could take credit for. Why did Vogel want to hand it on a plate to the Bureau?

'It's solid information. They were being helpful.'

'You sure about that?' Vogel turned from the window and stared at him. 'I wonder. The Mossad are a nightmare to read. When they get helpful like this, it's a damn sure sign they expect something in return. It wouldn't be the first time they've sold us a dummy. No, just do as I say. Get rid of it. I don't want the Agency involved. And not a word of this to anyone.'

Dole shrugged. 'Whatever you want.' He moved over to the door and waited for Vogel to say something, but Vogel ignored him and stood staring out the window. Dole shook his head and closed the door gently behind him.

Vogel waited until Dole was gone and then snatched up the blue telephone on his desk and pressed one of its programmed buttons. It was a scrambled direct line, bypassing the sophisticated Agency switchboard—and more importantly, also bypassing its elaborate monitoring systems. He spoke as soon as he heard the voice at the other end.

'The Mossad's uncovered something. They've given Dole a whole dossier of material.' He paused and listened. 'Yeah, it's good quality. They've fingered Schengel. And they've gotta know more than they've told Dole. No. I don't know. I've told him to give it to the Bureau.' A pause. Then: 'I don't see we have much choice. We can't just bury it.' Another pause. 'Okay, okay. I'll give it a try.'

He replaced the phone and sat at his desk. This operation was not going how he had foreseen it. On paper and in discussions with his co-conspirators, it had seemed elegant and easy to accomplish. But now there were too many loose cannons. If the Mossad knew so much, so might others. It was not a happy thought.

Hamilton met Parke in the Boardroom of GDM, the specialist security company with which they had both long been involved. The rule that government Ministers must resign from the boards of the companies of which they are directors is nothing more than an irritating technicality: in the past, many have 'resigned' their boardroom seats, yet remained closely involved and continued to obtain benefits from such companies, including financial. In the case of GDM, Hamilton retained close contact throughout his time in office and had effortlessly slipped back into his old role as soon as he lost the post of Secretary of State for Defence. The company had more than made up for the loss of benefits he had experienced during his time in Ministerial office with a generous 'golden hello' compensation payment.

In order to ensure complete privacy during his meeting, Hamilton dismissed his Special Branch minders. Parke poured two large glasses of malt as they settled down around the large oak table.

'So how are things with you, Hamilton?'

Hamilton took a generous sip from his drink before replying.

'These should interest you.' He took a pile of documents from his briefcase and passed them to Parke.

'Excellent.' Parke looked through the papers. The information was first rate, classified documents relating to the letting of defence contracts. Details of procurement plans and budgets. It would place GDM in a strong position to bid successfully. 'I'll see it reaches the right people.'

Hamilton stood and moved over to the window. 'We need to accelerate our plans.'

Parke shrugged. 'I share your concern. But we can't risk moving too soon, too fast. These things take time to arrange.'

Hamilton looked thoughtful and then asked: 'I presume the demonstrations in the desert were satisfactory?'

'Very,' Parke replied. 'The hosts proved the effectiveness of their new catalogue very well. I don't think we need doubt that the products will sell well and attract a very particular type of customer.'

Parke did not think now was the appropriate time to go into detail. He had attended the special evening demonstrations of biological and chemical weapons in a massive concrete underground bunker. There he had been surprised to learn that they intended to use human victims for the demonstration. But his hosts were very relaxed.

'Just political prisoners and violent criminals,' they explained. 'Sentenced to death in any case. We might as well get some value from their executions.'

The nerve gasses were quick and effective, but they had left unpleasant images in Parke's memory. They were not quite so clean and clinical as he had imagined they would be. There had been screaming and blood. All very unpleasant. Parke preferred long range weapons where one didn't need to worry about the consequences. To him, war meant the press of a button, the monitoring of a blip that disappeared from radar screens, the increasing value of key stocks and shares: he did not associate it with visible flesh and blood. And visible death.

'Tokyo was an excellent sales sampler,' Hamilton commented. 'Inspired. They must have people beating a path to their door by now, clamouring for their product. How did the discussions about our potential role in exclusive representation go?'

'Very well,' Parke purred. 'I think it's in the bag.'

'Really?' Hamilton was visibly impressed. 'Are you sure?'

'Ninety percent. We're just going through some of the small print now. I'm very positive about this one. I think they're prepared to make GDM sole worldwide agents for their entire chemical and biological warfare catalogue. This could be the biggest contract we've ever secured.'

Hamilton finished his scotch in one gulp and stood, his face flushed red. 'If this is true, this is excellent news, Parke. You've done an excellent job. An excellent job.'

9

Pendleton's view that Monroe was a man on the way out of the Service clearly was not shared by Monroe. Brewer found him still seated at his desk, his head buried in a pile of paperwork. Despite the best efforts of the training department, Monroe continued with a vigilant one-man crusade against the onslaught of computers. His proud claim was that his computer was used for nothing more important than as a repository for Post-It notes. An attempt to scupper his Luddite stand by removing his old IBM golf ball typewriter had failed: within two days of its disappearance it just as suddenly reappeared in pride of place on his desk. Instead of forcing Monroe into the hands of modern technology as had been intended, without his typewriter the management soon discovered to their horror that Monroe no longer bothered to send them their beloved reports. Faced with the imminent collapse of their bureaucracy, Monroe's typewriter was duly returned, post haste. That was the last attempt to drag Monroe into the twenty-first century.

'Haven't you gone yet? The old man promised everyone you'd been booted out,' Brewer commented, slipping behind his desk and moving a pile of unread memos from the *In* tray to *Pending*.

Monroe looked up and smiled, slipping a pencil behind his ear. 'Apparently they have a personnel issue. Some sort of contractual difficulty.'

Brewer smiled. He wasn't surprised. Monroe possessed the mental and legal agility of the country's best libel lawyers. If Monroe could find a method of tying up the Firm in its own red tape whilst simultaneously holding onto his job, he would. Monroe was a fixture and fitting. He had seen more new men and new ideas come and go than he could remember. Beating them at their own game was an intellectual challenge. And Monroe rarely lost intellectual challenges.

'So what about you, Brewer? Word is you're being sent down.'

Brewer slipped a paper knife through the seal of an envelope. 'Duty desk.'

'Now I know you're joking!' Monroe's mouth gaped open.

'I am, but I don't think they are. No, they can't be. No sense of humour. No such module on their MBA course.'

Monroe stood and moved over to Brewer's desk, allowing his stomach to rest along its edge. He looked furtively over his shoulder as if anxious not to be overheard and then leaned closer and whispered.

'But why now? Surely you've heard the news?'

Brewer pulled back, reluctant to share the experience of what appeared to be a unique combination of raw mackerel and garlic lingering on Monroe's breath.

'What news?'

'You really don't know, do you?' Monroe sighed. 'I tell you, this place is turning into a nut house. I was sure they'd tell you. It's that woman. The Russian one. What's-her-name.'

'Anastasia?' Brewer sat up. 'What about her?'

'We know where she is. Here. In London.'

'We know what!' Brewer jumped to his feet, ignoring the looks of surprise from occupants at the other desks.

'Keep it down, will you!' whispered Monroe, his face flushing with embarrassment. 'For Chrissake, my neck's on the line on this one.'

Brewer nodded. 'Sorry. Of all the things you could have told me, I didn't expect it to be something about Anastasia. What have you heard?'

Monroe's eyes sparkled. 'How would the address suit you?'

'The address? That would suit me just fine, Monroe. Just fine.'

The orders from Tel Aviv were clear and unambiguous. Simon Gilbert followed Ahmed Rami from Heathrow airport to New York's JFK. There, Rami made a brief phone call and boarded an internal flight. Gilbert was becoming uneasy. It was only a question of time before Rami would spot him. It's possible to follow a man for only a limited period before he gets wise to the fact, particularly someone of Rami's class. But without backup, Gilbert had to take the chance and boarded the domestic flight early. Nothing attracts attention so much as the last few people to board. When the flight landed in Lincoln, Nebraska, Gilbert made another quick call. He needed support and fast. He was given the name of a hotel where he would be contacted.

He took a taxi from the airport and trailed Rami's limousine to a high-walled, guarded compound on the city precincts. Rami's car disappeared swiftly from view behind a large metal gate which shuddered noisily shut behind him. On either side of the gate imposing metal fences ringed with razor wire made clear that unauthorised access was not encouraged. A watch tower stood alongside the gate. Gilbert could just make out two men on observation duty, binoculars strung around their necks. He couldn't be sure, but it looked as if they were armed.

'Nice place,' he commented under his breath. Walled compounds with razor wire and lookout towers made him uneasy. They evoked images of other camps, of a time and a world that could never be forgotten.

'You know this joint?' the cabbie turned to him, his mouth gaping open to reveal the gum he had been chewing ever since Gilbert flagged him down.

Gilbert shook his head.

'Cuckoo-World, that's what.'

Gilbert frowned. 'And what does that mean?'

'It's full of cranks and nutcases, real fruit cakes. You know, they dress up in uniform, strut all over the place, see. You must've heard of them, one of our all-American home-grown militia. Claim to be patriots. Biggest bunch of losers you ever saw.'

Gilbert leaned back in the seat and watched the compound for a time. 'And what else happens in there?'

'Believe me buddy, you don't wanna know. So long as we don't get another Waco on our hands, I don't care, see. You with the Bureau?'

Gilbert ignored the question and instead gave the cabbie instructions to a hotel in town. It was not the hotel where he would be staying. There was a chance he had been seen, might be traced. And cab drivers were not the most discreet of people. There was no point making it too easy. By the time the cabbie dropped him and he had hurried across town on foot and reached his hotel room, the support he wanted had already arrived and made themselves at home in his room watching BBC World.

Gilbert was grateful to be back amongst friends.

Brewer found the address, a small end of terrace council house near Hatton Cross. The strained, irritating whine of planes taxiing and preparing for take-off at Heathrow airport was close enough to be a nuisance. The pungent smell of jet aviation fuel hung in the air like the penetrating scent of a cheap perfume.

He watched the house in silence, wondering whether Monroe's information was correct. The news was so unexpected that he had overlooked the most basic questions. Like how come Monroe knew about it? And what was Anastasia doing in London? He found it hard to imagine her outside of Moscow. If this was Anastasia's first taste of the delights of the West she was in for a surprise. She had left one carbuncle of post-war crumbling council housing for another, a rude shook if she had been expecting a quaint country cottage and a bed of roses. *Plus ca change . . .*

There was only one way to check Monroe's information. Brewer crossed the road, walked across the short strip of grass in front of the house and rang the doorbell. He waited. The house was silent. He rang again. Still nothing. He walked round the side of the house to peer over the fence into the back garden. Everything was quiet. At an upstairs window the thin, faded yellow curtains were drawn. A small metal gate opened to his touch and he walked through. A dried-out pond and a burnt-out motorbike populated the back garden, fighting a losing battle with wild seeding grass and thistles.

Brewer hesitated. If Monroe had given him rogue information, he was not only trespassing but he was now about to break and enter as well. And if the house turned out to be nothing more than home to Mr and Mrs Law Abiding Briton he was going to have a lot of explaining to do.

Mind you, so was Monroe.

Inside the security of the compound, Rami showered and changed into an elegant, hand-made silk suit. In his late forties, Rami was an outwardly attractive man. If instead of terrorism he had chosen to turn his abilities to the more respected, if less exciting, vocations of banking or finance, he would have been equally as successful as he was in his chosen profession—and probably at least as wealthy. Like the late and unfortunate editor of the *London Arab News*, Iyas Qalwyr, Rami was born in Iraq and also spent much of his adult life in Europe. But unlike Qalwyr, Rami had enjoyed far closer and more cordial relations with the late head of the Iraqi state. In fact, Rami endeavoured to keep on good relations with precisely those governments, regimes and movements with which the West felt least comfortable. It was a very profitable niche vocation.

In his time he had given advice to such unlikely bed-fellows as the IRA, the PLO, some of the extreme nationalist groups operating under the banner of 'anti-globalisation' and even the extremist fringe of the Animal Liberation Front. Any movement that Rami believed would advance his agenda and undermine that of his opponents. It was not that Rami was against the state of Israel itself: what drove his cold ambition and strategy was the duplicitous nature of the treatment of Arab states and their peoples. Whereas Israel repeatedly broke UN mandates, refusing for example to withdraw from illegally occupied Palestinian lands, whenever an Arab state likewise broke UN mandates they were punished—either through economic sanctions or bombs. Rami's first ambition was to ensure Israel returned to the borders the UN had originally created for it. Beyond that, he wanted to see many of the existing Arab states changed—their often brutal dictators removed and replaced with genuinely representative leaders. Of course, he did not share his vision with anyone. For the moment, he worked with many who in the long run he would prefer to see eradicated. When his time came, he would remove the dictators and movements that funded him as quickly as he now dispatched their enemies. Heretical anti-Muslim movements such as Al Qaeda would be removed quickly and efficiently. And with the changes he aimed to bring about in the nature of the Israeli state and the structure of the Middle East, the whole fuel of desperation that drove so many to such drastic measures as suicide bombing would be gone. His people—by which he meant the whole Arab diaspora—deserved better. It was this mission that fuelled and guided him. He would use anything and anyone to achieve the objectives he sought.

He reached the second floor, nodded briefly at the uniformed armed guard and entered the elegant wooden office without knocking. Another uniformed man sat working behind a desk, his lapels decorated with small silver skull and crossbones. He looked up as Rami entered and gave a brief smile of recognition. Unless he had already known the man's age, Rami would never have guessed that Walter Stronik was in his late eighties. His skin was healthy, with none of the telltale signs of wrinkling or liver spots that many ten years his younger displayed. His hair was thinning, but at least it was still his own. Only a touch of arthritis in his hands and legs suggested his true age. And only a hint of an accent gave away the fact that he had once not been an American at all.

'Good afternoon, Ahmed. You have done good work.'

Few people, of whom Rami was one exception, knew that Walter Stronik had once been a Ukrainian from Mosty Wielkie. He had a good reason for assuming a new identity: during the Second World War, he had been responsible for the deaths of many gypsies and Jews. But 'Walter' had always been lucky.

At the end of the war, he was arrested for his war crimes, but within days was released by the Americans after spinning a tale that persuaded them he was a useful source for their intelligence services. Stronik still remembered with gratitude the actions and support of the US Major who released and protected him, believing that he really did have inside knowledge of value. After a shady career of little merit to his saviours, he was finally provided with a new identity and resettled in the States during the 1950's.

Stronik had done well for himself in his new homeland for one very good reason: as well as manipulating the Americans, Stronik had also continued his work for the Nazis and their post-war network. From 1945 onwards, he directed every effort into ensuring that as many former Nazis as possible evaded the 'persecution' unleashed by the Nuremberg trials and were 'rehabilitated' into respectable positions of authority in the new Europe. He was very successful in his chosen task, convincing the Americans that senior Nazi officials were in fact highly valuable double agents who could provide inside information on the Russians' true intentions.

Since the Nazis of the Third Reich were as much thieves as murderers, finance in the post-war years was not a problem. During their reign, the Nazis stole from those they detested, from those they arrested and drove from the countries they occupied and, of course, from those they butchered to death. It was not only slave labour that enabled Hitler's war machine to be built: it was the billions plundered from those the Third Reich bullied, robbed and slaughtered. Gold and money plundered from banks across Europe that fell to the Nazi war machine. Gold and money stolen from the accounts of those the Nazis killed. And gold taken from wedding rings, jewellery and fillings of the millions of men, women and children sent to the Nazi death camps. Hitler's 'economic success', the envy of many other Western leaders, aristocrats and diplomats at the time, was easy to fund. Hitler's army did not march on its stomach: it marched on the bones of the millions of dead. World War II created more millionaires within the space of a few years than any time in history before or since.

When the war in Europe ended, the bankers were more than willing to fund the Ukrainian's new alter ego, Walter Stronik. Those few bankers who had the misfortune to be tried in the post-war mood of justice were rapidly acquitted, or received only token prison sentences: most were released in a matter of months. It was of course fortunate that Göring and Himmler, who were amongst the few Nazi leaders involved with the bank's attempts to prepare for Nazi funding after the war, both committed suicide without revealing anything of the bank's role or its massive reserves of stolen gold and money. Even Roosevelt's wartime commitment to dismantle the IG Farben poison gas plants was cancelled by those who took power after his death: the installations and communications systems of Auschwitz were not destroyed.

The attitude towards IG Farben was symptomatic of the Allies' approach by the end of the war: at the close of 1946, hardly any Nazi industrialists were in custody. The Nazi network and their whole support structure, and of course their finances, survived: as the Nazis always intended. And Walter Stronik was one of the greatest beneficiaries. Stronik used his new found status to establish the NSDAP-AO in the States. The NSDAP was the original name of Hitler's party (*Nationalsozialistische Deutsche Arbeiterpertei* or National Socialist German Workers' Party). AO stands for *Auslands und Aufbau Organisation*, or Foreign and Development Organisation. It was the NSDAP-AO compound that Gilbert's taxi driver had referred to as 'Cuckoo World' and where Rami was now resident. The NSDAP-AO soon became the key umbrella organisation for the continuation of the Nazi ideal and inherited substantial funding from the Bank of International Settlement and interim organisations such as ODESSA (the organisation of former SS officers), which helped leading Nazis escape from Europe and establish new identities.

After years of research, planning and infiltration, the NSDAP-AO was beginning to involve itself in an increasing number of displays of direct action. Rami intended to play a key role in their plans: at least for as long as they continued to serve his own objectives.

'Come here, Ahmed,' Stronik beckoned him closer. 'I have a couple of visitors I would like you to meet.'

He turned and opened the door leading to the adjacent conference room.

The kitchen showed signs of recent occupancy. There was a dirty teacup beside the sink and the smell of fried food hung in the air. The dull odour of stale tobacco permeated the furnishings. Brewer felt the kettle. There was no hint of warmth. But someone had definitely been here. He hoped he was not too late.

He explored the ground floor. The furnishings were basic, the type of cheap veneered and cup-stained furniture that landlords favour for bed sits. There were no pictures, no photographs, no ornaments. None of the usual personal effects that go to make up a home. That made him more confident. This was definitely not a normal residential home. He knew exactly what it was: a safe house. But whose? If Monroe was aware of its existence, that suggested it was the Firm's. But what were they doing shielding Anastasia and why hadn't Pendleton told him? Did Pendleton know? And if he didn't, how did Monroe? It looked like the department was still playing games, still keeping him out of the complete picture. Was Anastasia's arrival in London the reason why he was being reassigned to administrative duties?

Brewer stopped at the foot of the stairs. There was a sound outside, a footstep on gravel. He waited. The sound was not repeated. Imagination. Moving quickly, he climbed the stairs and entered the main bedroom. He stopped. The bed was made, the room perfectly tidy. On top of the bed was Anastasia. One glance was enough to confirm the obvious. She wasn't sleeping: she was dead. A small bullet hole in her temple and her eyes staring blankly at the ceiling were more than enough evidence of that. And she was still wearing too much mascara, Brewer thought idly—only he guessed it didn't matter too much to her right now. He touched her. Cold. She had been dead for some time.

There was a crash of glass downstairs. The front door had been thrown open, shaking the house with the force. Brewer spun round.

It was a trap.

Brewer moved quickly across the bedroom. There had to be somewhere to hide. But it was already too late. There were loud shouts. Multiple footsteps pounded up the stairs. Downstairs another window was broken. There was a kick at the bedroom door. Two uniformed and armed policemen in bulletproof vests and a third man in a plain grey suit burst into the room.

'Good afternoon,' Brewer started, but the man in the suit waved at him to be quiet. The coppers grabbed Brewer and pinned his arms back behind him.

'I have to inform you, sir, that you are under arrest. Anything you say will be taken down and may be used in evidence against you.'

Someone had set him up like a rotten maggot on a hook. Monroe had some serious explaining to do.

The slide projector cast a dazzling image across the darkened room and onto the pull-down screen. Seated to one side, Mark Hamilton could see the drifting dust caught in the projector's beam. The room was becoming too hot for comfort. Around the table were five men, one of them shuffling noisily and coughing.

Hamilton continued his presentation: 'The yield if we invest now could offer a ratio of as much as one hundred to one within a twelve month time frame.'

Now he had their interest. The shuffling and restlessness stopped.

'Twelve months?' It was a French accent. Either the Frenchman or the Belgian. He strained to see which in the subdued light.

'Twelve months,' confirmed Hamilton. 'At one hundred to one. And these are conservative estimates of the likely profitability curve.'

'What about the chemical and biological warfare conventions? We are not permitted to deal in such things, isn't that true?'

Hamilton smiled. 'Given the outbreak of gas attacks in Japan, the assault on America and elsewhere, surely countries have the right to defend themselves? In any case, we know the conventions are nothing more than diplomatic sentiments. Russia, America, France. They all have CBW capacity. We are in a new era gentlemen. A new era that demands new tactics.'

There was silence. Outside, the ceaseless rumble of the Strasbourg traffic could be heard. Here, inside a committee room of the European Parliament, Hamilton was hosting what he hoped would be the final meeting of his alliance. A cross-party team of highly influential Euro-MPs keen to ensure that the West was better prepared to defend itself against chemical and biological warfare. And if that meant breaking the Conventions prohibiting involvement in handling and storing chemical and biological weapons, that was too bad. Terrorists did not play by some unwritten rulebook: so why should they?

'One thing: I need a decision. Today.'

Hamilton flicked off the projector and plunged the room into total darkness. He waited a moment before switching on the overhead lights. The middle-aged, suited men who were gathered around the table blinked as their eyes adjusted. Hamilton crossed to the blinds and opened them. Late afternoon sun came shafting into the room between the slats, reminding them of the unlikely reality that it was still daytime outside.

'Today?' It was the German who broke the silence. 'But that is impossible. To make a decision so soon. So quickly. You ask too much of us.'

'Time is an extravagant luxury,' Hamilton returned. 'This is quite simple. Either you're in or you're out. We have to decide now. We could see a repeat of the Tokyo attack at any moment, an assault that makes the outrage against the World Trade Center trivial by comparison, an attack right here in the heart of Europe. We must be ready to defend ourselves.'

One of the men stood up and walked slowly round the room, his hands plunged deep into his trouser pockets. 'I do not see how this will work.'

Hamilton shrugged. 'That is my problem. I've laid out the costs, the projected return.' He leaned forwards across the table.

'And remember this. It is not if, but when. Somewhere in Europe there will be a biological or chemical attack. It may come tomorrow, or not for a week, maybe a month or a year. But it will come. No-one can deny that. Tokyo has demonstrated that all too clearly. The terrorist threat is real: there are too many examples now for me to detail. We are vulnerable. We have been too busy looking for the reds coming over the wall, but now the wall is down. The enemy is within and can strike at any time. Will strike at any time. It's not missiles and bombs we should fear now. They are nothing alongside these new technologies. We must arm ourselves too. Only GDM can do that. Only GDM can provide you with the deterrents you need. You must seize this opportunity.'

The man stopped pacing. Hamilton recognised the Euro-MP for a large urban seat in Spain.

'There are rumours I have heard,' he said in his uncertain English. 'That Tokyo was deliberate, a demonstration rather than, let us say, an actualité.'

Hamilton did not react. 'A demonstration? In its way I suppose it was. A demonstration of the dangers we all face from cranks and nutcases. God forbid if European or Arab extremists get hold of this technology.'

There was a murmur of assent from around the table. While the world worried about nuclear weapons proliferation, the real danger came from the growth of biological and chemical weapons, which have the distinct advantage of being cheaper and easier to produce. And far more lethal. Biological and chemical weapons are rapidly becoming the terrorists' and guerrillas' weapon of choice: they remove humans simply and efficiently, but leave infrastructure standing.

'I did not mean that,' the Spanish MEP continued. 'I meant that it was a set-up, a provocation if you like, not a terrorist outrage at all but a cold-blooded demonstration.'

There was silence. It was a serious allegation, a clear suggestion that Hamilton was in some way implicated. The other MEPs looked to Hamilton for a response.

'An interesting notion. What makes you think that?'

The MEP smiled. 'Why does a manufacturer advertise his product? Why, to attract buyers.'

'Are you suggesting,' Hamilton asked, injecting a deliberate hint of anger into his voice. 'That the Tokyo tragedy was nothing more than a massive marketing ploy?'

'Perhaps,' the Spaniard shrugged. 'A big advertisement to the world. Come and bid for this if you want it for yourselves. And if you don't, someone else will.' He smiled at Hamilton. 'Very similar, you will agree, to the arguments you have put to us today.'

Hamilton returned his smile, but inside he was cold. Cham's intelligence had suggested the Spanish MEP was the most likely to break ranks. The MEP was known to have close contacts with the Spanish intelligence service. Someone had been talking. Was the man just suspicious or did he have hard evidence? Hamilton had not expected him to say something now, at this critical stage. And not in front of the other potential investors. He needed to turn this round. And fast.

'I have heard these rumours,' Hamilton said quietly. 'But they are wrong. They have their origins in the Middle East. From parties that dearly wish us not to make moves to protect ourselves. We must beware false prophets. If we do not move quickly we shall be too late.'

For a moment it was in the balance. And then there was a ripple of agreement from around the table. Good. He had not lost them. The fear of a repeat of the Tokyo events in Europe, the images of the World Trade Center were too great. And the potential for an easy return on their investment too good. The Spaniard was isolated. It would be easy to pick him off.

'So, gentlemen, shall we discuss terms?' Hamilton asked, taking papers from his case.

Four of the men came and gathered around him, eager to sign the contracts that would make them wealthy. If they were lucky, it would also boost their political careers. When Europe came under attack as Tokyo and New York had done, they could show they were ready, that only they had anticipated and prepared for such an event. They would be lauded for their foresight, able to meet terror with terror. After all, isn't that how nuclear weapons had worked? A balance of fear, a balance of terror? And with that could come peace. History was their evidence, their proof.

The other man stood alone at the end of the room. Hamilton looked at him and smiled. If he knew the danger he was in, his expression did not show it. The Spanish politician had just signed his own death warrant and had less than thirty-six hours left to live.

Arthur Dole, the CIA's Head of Mid-East Division, kept going back over his meeting with Vogel like an alcoholic returning to a favourite bar. Something wasn't right. His instincts were never wrong. What was it Vogel had said?

'I know there's another dimension. This is one we're not going to touch.'

Vogel was holding something back, almost as if he already known about Schengel.

'It could lead to complications. And not just with the FBI.'

What complications? And since when did complicated cases mean that the Company wouldn't touch them? The intelligence world is rooted in complication and complexity. Dole sat deep in thought at his desk in the Langley complex and wondered what he should do. In theory the answer was simple: he should forget the whole affair. Vogel's instructions were clear enough. The case had already been passed to the Bureau, who had been only too keen to take it.

But it was not like Vogel to turn his back on such a high profile investigation. Like most heads of the CIA, Vogel was primarily a politician and an ambitious one at that. A case like this offered the potential for a publicity coup, a chance for career advancement. And if the reasons for leaving the Schengel affair alone were not practical, that meant Vogel was avoiding the case for political reasons. But what reasons? There was only one way to find out, only one person who might know the full story.

Dole picked up the phone and selected a secure line. And

then he placed a call to General Isser Dayan in the Hadar Dafna Building on King Saul Boulevard. The Mossad official who took the call was evasive. The General was not available, but the official could take a message and pass it on.

Dole hesitated. This was not the way the Company worked. There were strict procedures, carefully constructed rules of etiquette for the conduct of operations and inter-agency liaisons. If anyone discovered that he was calling the Mossad directly about something as specific as this he would face a severe reprimand, possibly disciplinary action, even dismissal. He swallowed hard and repeated to himself, like a lucky chant, that his instincts had never been wrong before.

'Can you tell him to call Dole? He has my number.'

The man repeated the message and then hung up. Dole left his office and took the elevator down to the parking lot, leaving via the turnstiles at the exit to the new building and its statue of William J Donovan. Nearby was the inscription from John 8:32: *And ye shall know the truth and the truth shall make you free.* There was something about the phrase that always made Dole uneasy: an unfortunate resonance between it and the infamous Nazi phrase at Auschwitz about *work shall make you free.*

His Oldsmobile was parked at the far end of a long row of cars. As he approached it he glanced up at the sky, surprised to see that the weather was turning milder, the angry hint of winter that had lurked in the air chased away by a bright sun and cloudless blue sky.

He climbed in, reversed the car from its parking place and turned towards the main gate off Dolley Madison Boulevard. The radio was playing a Rolling Stones hit. It took him back to his college days. Suddenly work and the politics of the Agency seemed less important. The weather was good, the music was good. He would pick up some beers and maybe a take-out. For once he would be home early. For once he and his wife could have some time together. He mimed the words to the song, his fingers beating out the rhythm on the steering wheel.

At the main gate, the armed guard gave him a wave of

recognition and then he was pulling out and accelerating towards the main road. Busy with his thoughts, Dole did not see the motorcyclist, did not notice the glint of metal until it was too late. His windscreen exploded in a thousand shards, the 700 rounds per minute firepower of the Colt Commando making short work of Dole. Dead at the wheel, his car swung wildly across the road, smashed into an oncoming lorry and burst into a fireball.

By the time the guards at the main gate reacted, the motorbike was already a dot on the horizon.

Rami did not know either of the two men waiting in the compound's conference room. He followed behind Stronik and noted the respect they showed towards him.

'Please,' Stronik said. 'Let me introduce you. This is Ahmed Rami, our most excellent international ambassador.'

The tall blonde man nodded towards Rami.

'Your reputation is well known.'

'And allow me to introduce Ernst Straker and Erich Hümmler, two of our key European partners.'

Rami knew Straker's name. He was an important figure in the NSDAP's European organisation. From the little he knew, Straker was a Nazi believer who had risen to prominence as a successful businessman in post-war West Germany.

'As you may have guessed,' Stronik continued, taking an opened bottle of red wine from an engraved silver platter. 'This is not merely to be a social gathering. We have important matters to discuss.' He poured the drink into four large glasses. 'I trust the little local problem in Russia has been resolved?'

Straker nodded and put a hand on Hümmler's shoulder.

'Hümmler has again proved his worth. All the documents have been reclaimed.'

'And the Englishman?'

Straker smiled and consulted his watch.

'By now both he and the Professor's Russian assistant will be helping the authorities with their enquiries. But I do not think the Russian will be talking much, will she Hümmler? How the mighty can so easily fall from grace. Romance and passion can be such troublesome emotions, bring forth such violence.'

'Ah, an affair of the heart. Romance, envy, murder. The English are a very repressed people. Such emotions are always the most dangerous,' Stronik commented wryly. 'Please, gentlemen. Take your drinks.'

They did as he instructed. He raised his glass.

'To success.'

'To success,' they repeated.

The police were polite, but firm. They were, as might be expected, suspicious about Brewer, openly sceptical of his story. Not that he could blame them. Being found in a house with a dead woman and the murder weapon nearby was not on the face of it a good case for his defence. The house had filled with SOCO (Scene Of Crime Officers), every surface was being examined and dusted, photographed and sampled.

The Inspector in charge sat beside Brewer in a Rover outside the house and searched through Brewer's papers. He puzzled over the mix of identity papers Brewer carried and then came across his official SIS ID card, sandwiched between a UK Press Card and a CID card.

'Shit,' he said, looking up and staring at Brewer. 'That's all I need. A spook.'

Brewer shrugged. 'I gave your officers the story.'

'Sure,' the Inspector said. 'You were just visiting and found her.'

'That's exactly how it happened. And someone must have tipped you off. I don't suppose you'd like to tell me who, would you?'

The Inspector shook his head. 'We can't compromise a source. I'm sure you understand that.'

'She's Russian you know,' Brewer added. 'And if I know anything about her, I'd say that she was killed by Nazis.'

'Nazis?' The Inspector looked at Brewer as if he were a Care in the Community patient.

'She had an obsession with them. She claimed her lover was killed by Nazis.'

'Her lover?' The Inspector was looking confused. 'Do you want to tell me about her lover's murder as well?'

'Inspector,' Brewer replied. 'You must understand. Nothing is as simple as it appears.'

'So I gather,' the Inspector sighed.

'Here it is in a nutshell. I did not kill her lover. I was trying to find out who did. Then she disappeared.'

'Disappeared? Very convenient,' the Inspector remarked, scepticism evident in both his voice and his face.

'Not really,' Brewer replied. 'And by the way, you should be thanking me. If the Firm knew how much I'd already told you, there'd have me out on my ear in a matter of seconds.'

The Inspector looked at him for a while and then said: 'Okay. If I go along with your crazy theory for just a minute, and I'm not saying I do, who do you think killed her?'

Brewer smiled. 'At a guess, I'd say a short ugly German with a gun. And he probably had a taller man with him, another German, his real boss.' Brewer gave him detailed descriptions of Straker and Hümmler. The Inspector gave no reaction as he covered several pages of his notebook with shorthand.

A uniformed constable called the officer away. They spoke for a time and several glances were shot in Brewer's direction. His future was being decided. This was the critical time. Either he was about to be taken down to the police station and held for further questioning as the prime suspect, or the police were going to believe him.

The Inspector came back and directed him to climb out of the car. Brewer stepped out into a hint of icy rain.

'For the moment, we're not going to take you in. Just make sure you don't disappear.' The Inspector leaned closer and for the first time there was a hint of warmth. 'Seems like you're lucky. Two men answering the descriptions you gave were seen in the neighbourhood behaving suspiciously late yesterday afternoon. And someone in your office has vouched for you, said you were on special assignment.'

That had to be either Monroe or Pendleton. He owed them one. It was good to know someone was batting on the same side for once.

Before their meeting began, a fifth man, older than the others, joined Stronik's gathering in the compound. Edward Thielstrom was a difficult man to miss. A deep indentation—the result of a war wound—on the bridge of his nose between his eyes and a protruding left eyelid gave him a distinctive appearance. With a long face and a half-bald scalp, he wore a hat and glasses to hide the worst of his defects. Rami noticed that whenever he spoke or laughed, a corner of his mouth turned down. When Stronik introduced Thielstrom as head of the European NSDAP-AO operation, he also mentioned Thielstrom's role as a former SS officer at Auschwitz.

Thielstrom's autobiography, which denied the holocaust, had been banned in Germany. A German reporter who managed to provoke Thielstrom into revealing that his autobiography was false and that Auschwitz had indeed been a death camp was later found murdered, his body badly mutilated. Despite their suspicions, the police were never able to establish a firm case against Thielstrom. For some reason, no other journalists had challenged Thielstrom's distasteful views since. Violence and intimidation have always been one of the Nazis' most effective weapons. Thielstrom moved frequently around Europe without challenge. His current residence was England, but if their plans worked as they hoped, that would soon change. Finally he would return to his fatherland. Permanently—and in style. His demands were reasonable: he wanted to be able to die in peace in his homeland. It was not so much for an old man to ask for.

'It is time,' Stronik stated. 'For us to start our operation.'

'Are we ready?' Straker's question hung in the air like a direct insult.

Stronik smiled. 'It is time to seize the moment. Everything has slipped into place. I think it is time to discuss the details.'

Jane opened the door before he was halfway down the path. Brewer embraced her as she hugged him tight and kissed him.

'Peter. Thank god you're safe.'

They went inside and up the flight of stairs to her first floor flat. She had dyed her hair blonde and Brewer was surprised to see that it suited her.

'Tea?' she asked.

He nodded and went through to the living room. It was exactly as he remembered. He walked over to the TV and picked up the photo on top of it. It showed Gary and Jane arm in arm, standing in front of a Channel ferry. He put it down as Jane came into the room with the tea.

She looked good. Her figure was still that of a woman ten years younger and she knew it, wearing leggings that hugged her figure and a tight top that emphasised her hourglass shape and revealed a span of tightly muscled abdomen. Her hazel eyes were bright and she smiled at him, nodding at the picture.

'It was always my favourite.'

'It's good of you both.' He took the offered mug and sipped at the scalding tea.

'What's happening with the police?' She slipped down onto the sofa and tucked her legs beneath herself, her tea cupped in both hands.

Brewer had called her from Hatton Cross station and given her the briefest sketch of his brush with the law. He did not want to return to his own flat and needed somewhere else to stay. He wanted time to think things over, to work out what was happening.

'Their enquiries continue.' Brewer sat opposite her in a sagging armchair. 'Fortunately for me, strings were pulled.'

'Someone dropped you in it?'

He nodded. 'That's my guess, yes.'

'What have you been up to, Peter?'

'You know better than to ask,' he replied. 'But if it helps, it makes no sense to me either.'

She shook her head. 'You're so like Gary. I've never understood either of you. What makes you stay in such shitty jobs?'

'One shitty job's much like another,' Brewer responded. 'Anyhow, I used to enjoy it.'

She sighed. 'But you don't any more, do you? And now look what's happening. Can't you see they're just using you, that they'll do whatever they can to get rid of you?'

'So what do you think I should do? Take my P45 and move on? Maybe join a security company, offer advice on burglar alarms and Chubb locks?' He shook his head. 'I can't see it. No, I have to see this through. There's something happening and I want to find out what. Then I might, just might, think about leaving.'

'Peter, read my lips. It's not your job. You told me that yourself. I can only say I'm pleased.' She moved and came over to sit on the arm of his chair. 'It'd be good to see more of you.' She rested her head against his arm. 'I miss you when you're not around.'

He took the mug from her hands and put it on the small table beside the chair. She moved over to sit on his lap. For a moment their eyes locked and then they kissed. Her perfume enveloped him as he pushed back her long hair. Lifting her in his arms, he placed her on the deep pile rug, his hands loosening her clothing. Her back arched as he touched her, her breath coming faster.

Tonight, he thought as he looked down into her warm hazel eyes, was going to be a good night after all.

After their meeting, Stronik took Rami on a brief tour of the compound. Everywhere Rami looked, he saw the results of millions of dollars of investment. He had no hesitation in supporting the NSDAP-AO's objectives. They were prosperous and careful men with clear objectives. If they were successful, then he would see his own dream fulfilled. There could be the creation of one democratic, Arabic nation stretching from the Atlantic coast to Persia: Israel would be contained to its UN borders. And if they failed, he could bide his time, find other groups with whom to align himself. He had a vision that one day there would be peace and justice for his people: but the road to that goal was filled with pain and sacrifice.

The compound was heavily guarded. Men in the black uniform of elite SS squads stood by every door, lined every corridor. The NSDAP-AO's was a serious operation, a more impressive control centre and military command than many small nations possess. But Rami knew that he had not seen everything, had not been told everything. Stronik was a key man, but was he the top man? Rami doubted it. Somewhere behind the public face of the movement there were hidden players. Men with real power. He wanted to meet them, to find out precisely what their long-term agenda was, but he knew it was unlikely.

They continued through the processing plants while Stronik provided technical details beyond Rami's grasp. Large metal containers and vats and the smell of chlorine filled the air. Men and women in white suits and helmets moved slowly around, carrying or pushing small metal barrels. The scale of the operation worried him. The compound covered many acres. It was inconceivable that the American authorities were not aware of its existence. The movement of lorries and personnel alone would be enough to draw attention to it. And from the air, the full size and complexity of the compound would immediately be apparent. He voiced his concerns to Stronik and was surprised when he laughed.

'Do not worry. Let us say we have an understanding. Besides, it is too late now. We have already produced more than we need. Even now, we are starting to wind down production. Just a few more weeks. Now come, there is someone I should like you to meet,' Stronik said.

He turned and waved towards a man dressed in a white lab coat and long gloves. As the man approached, Rami guessed he was in his late fifties. He wore thick-rimmed metal glasses with lenses as thick as the base of a wine bottle.

'Allow me to introduce Helmut Schengel,' Stronik said.

Rami and Schengel shook hands.

'Pleased to meet you,' Schengel said in English heavily fractured by a German accent.

'Helmut is the scientific genius behind our movement,' Stronik added, placing an arm around his shoulders. 'He has an excellent track record.'

Rami had heard the name before, was aware of Schengel's involvement in Tarhuna and Rabta, Libya's poison gas factories where thousands of tons of sarin gas had been produced. Those stockpiles of sarin gas were amongst the supplies of weapons that had been monopolised by Parke on behalf of GDM and were shortly to be distributed around Europe courtesy of Hamilton's agreement with the MEPs. But that formed only part of their arsenal. The market price had become too high, so the NSDAP-AO had bought Schengel instead and now manufactured its own raw materials.

'Helmut is a model worker. Every hour of every day he devotes to the furtherance of our cause.'

'*Wahrheit macht frei,*' Schengel commented.

Stronik laughed and clapped him hard on the back.

'Helmut is our most valuable asset. Whatever else happens, Rami, you must ensure he is safe.'

Rami smiled. 'It will be a pleasure.'

'Behind these different windows,' Schengel explained, waving them towards a set of thick glass panes beyond which workers in protective clothing could be seen working. 'We are developing our new materials. Ethyl NN-dimethylphosphoramide cyanidate, iso-propyl-methylphosphoroflouridate, ethyl S-2-diisoprophylaminoethyl methylphosphorothiolate.' He turned to them and grinned. 'If you know them at all you will know them as tabun, sarin and VX.'

Stronik nodded. 'Tabun and sarin. Good German weapons.' He smiled. 'Tell us Schengel.'

'Naturally,' Schengel murmured. 'It was the great Gerhard Schrader, working for the IG Farben chemical company, who made the breakthrough. In 1936 he developed tabun. It was an interesting discovery. Unlike other poison gases, tabun enters the skin through absorption. It disrupts the functioning of the nervous system. And of course, its effects are irreversible.'

'Of course,' murmured Rami, peering through the glass and trusting that the laboratories were secure.

'Tabun is up to one thousand times more toxic than chlorine. An amount the size of a pinhead will prove fatal, causing death by asphyxiation. And then in 1937, Schrader developed a compound ten times more toxic which he named sarin after himself, Ambros, Rudriger and van der Linde, the other scientists involved in the research.'

'Ah.' Rami turned to Stronik. 'Sarin. The Tokyo experiment.'

Stronik nodded. 'Our little test bed. Very effective, don't you agree?'

'Sarin is a light brown, odourless liquid,' Schengel continued, moving them on to peer through another of the secure lab windows. 'It evaporates quickly, a bit like gasoline, and its effects are toxic. A concentration of just 100 milligrams per cubic metre is sufficient. It starts by attacking the eyes. Vision blurs. Breathing becomes difficult and the chest tightens. Then comes the vomiting and headaches. Finally the body convulses as the heart and lungs cease to function.'

They stood for a moment and watched the technicians busy with their work.

'Schrader went on to develop soman in 1944.'

'So far as we know,' Stronik added. 'None of these chemicals were deployed intentionally during the war.'

'If they had been,' Schengel said quietly. 'The outcome would have been different. Hitler was poorly advised. VX is different, developed in the 1950's. It is the most toxic nerve gas ever produced. Ten times more effective than soman. It has very interesting characteristics. An oily liquid, it is very resistant, remaining for up to three weeks in warm weather. And up to sixteen weeks at minus ten centigrade.' Schengel looked at them, as if hoping for a reaction. 'Of course. That is just the chemicals. The other labs are working on bacteriological devices. Derivatives of the Yersinia pestis, bacillus anthracis and pseudomonas pseudomallei.'

'Thank you Herr Schengel. Let us not detain you any further from your work.'

Stronik's curt dismissal sent Schengel scuttling back to his laboratories.

'A peculiar man in many ways. But useful. For the moment. We need many different players in our orchestra. And we have made the necessary arrangements to avoid any problems with our operation here,' Stronik continued. 'Everything has become so much easier since Waco. The authorities have become very sensitive about violating the rights of citizens and militia groups under the Constitution. Thank god for loudmouth liberals. Where would we be without them? We have an agreement: they leave us alone and we leave them alone.' He stopped and looked at Rami. 'Believe me, we have friends in places you wouldn't even begin to suspect.'

Rami wondered again who the real power brokers were behind the movement—and just how highly placed its backers might be.

10

The Federal Bureau of Investigation's Mission Statement states that it will uphold the law through the investigation of violations of federal criminal statutes; protect the United States from hostile intelligence efforts; provide assistance to other federal, state and local law enforcement agencies; and perform these responsibilities in a manner faithful to the Constitution and laws of the United States. Both the CIA and the FBI, along with other agencies, such as the NSA, have been given enhanced powers since September 11.

But neither the FBI nor the CIA have managed to maintain a great reputation. The discovery of long-term spies inside both organisations, troubled field operations like Waco and poor human intelligence (with an over-reliance on signals intelligence) together with mistimed cutbacks in critical field operations during the 1990's has caused voices to be raised calling for both to be abolished and for a unified agency to take over. The creation of the Department of Homeland Security has helped to some extent by consolidating 22 separate organisations under one umbrella.

Although the FBI handled the original bombing of the World Trade Center and the bombing in Oklahoma City with acceptable professionalism, September 11 changed everything. It brought into the open the often bitter conflict between the Bureau and the Agency. And the separation of roles remains blurred: the FBI is empowered to send agents overseas not merely to gather forensic evidence, but also to pursue investigations and assist local police forces. Then again, neither agency is particularly happy about many in the political establishment: the leak of classified information from a congressional probe of September 11 intelligence failures is one obvious reason why.

The information about Schengel passed on by the CIA to the Bureau was discussed at the highest level at a meeting that included the Director of the FBI. Since America's painful experiences of terrorism on its own territory, the issue has rocketed to first place on the security agenda. The possibility that Schengel was inside the country, with his wider involvement with hostile Middle-Eastern countries, was enough to justify a high-level investigation. The Bureau decided to assign one of their best special agents: Paul Yellow Hawk.

Yellow Hawk was unusual in the ranks of the FBI. US Government agencies do not have a good historical track record in the employment of Native Americans at senior grade. But then the US Government historically does not have a good track record in its treatment of Native Americans, period. Out of the 370 treaties signed between Native Americans and the US Government during the occupation of the North American continent, nearly all were broken by the colonists: the Native Americans never breached a single one.

Yellow Hawk was a direct descendent of the Pawnee whose villages once spread along the rivers of what is now Nebraska. But like so many Native Americans, Yellow Hawk's life bore no resemblance to that of his ancestors. He was born on the outskirts of Columbus, Nebraska, within spitting distance of the Platte river. His father worked as a farm labourer, his mother in part-time waitressing. As one of five children, Yellow Hawk's childhood was never easy. But he had been quicker than the other children his age and larger in build. His success in both the classroom and on the sports field ensured him a good education, an education he used well, escaping from the poverty and decline that his parents and grandparents generations had known. For him, the aspiration of the American dream had become a reality.

There were, of course, those who criticised him, who regarded him as selling-out and joining the white man's society instead of continuing to observe his own traditions and ancestors. The criticism hurt. Yellow Hawk was proud of his heritage. But he was also a realist: the world of his ancestors was gone. Forever. Unlike others, Yellow Hawk was able to observe the past objectively, to understand that Americans today bore no more guilt for events that happened before their time than young Germans did for Hitler and the Nazis.

After an initial career in academia, Yellow Hawk took an abrupt and unexpected change of direction: he joined the FBI. His intelligence and fitness had put him amongst the highest of his intake. Yellow Hawk was a large man, over six and a half feet tall and with a strong, unmistakably Native American face. His long dark hair he clipped short, or sometimes grew and tied into a simple pony tail. His career progressed rapidly and he soon became one of the Bureau's most successful and respected special agents. Most of his work was not undercover: Yellow Hawk was the sort of person everyone noticed when he walked into a bar. But his success was not without its detractors even inside the Bureau: American militia groups are not the only organisations with bigots and paranoids amongst their members. Every police and intelligence service has its own rednecks and Yellow Hawk encountered his own share of prejudice and problems. But Yellow Hawk was quick enough and strong enough to handle his difficulties: those who chose to cross and challenge him did so only once.

Yellow Hawk listened to the detailed briefing on Schengel in silence. His trip to the counter-terrorism unit in Washington DC came hard on the heels of a refresher course at Quantico. There he had spent days in Hogan's Alley, running through a covert surveillance and raid routine as part of his counter-terrorism refresher instruction. Hogan's Alley provides a simulated American town in the grounds of the FBI's Quantico base, populated with amateur and professional actors working to the Bureau's scenarios and scripts. It was built in 1986 after a disastrous shoot-out in Miami left two special agents dead and five other people injured. Hogan's Alley enables both rookies and experienced agents alike to refine their street abilities in a realistic atmosphere in the hope they will be prepared for any crisis encountered in the field. Yellow Hawk had also taken the opportunity to sharpen his abilities on FATS—the firearms automated training system, a sort of Halo video game shoot-out on steroids.

Yellow Hawk was not a fan of Washington's bustle, noise and traffic and was impatient to return to the field office in Omaha, his normal base of operations. The dull uniformity of the fort-like J Edgar Hoover building on Pennsylvania Avenue and its corridors of endless suited bureaucrats and administrators made him uneasy. Although the FBI's Director and his predecessors had initiated changes to root out the Hoover legacy of stifling initiative and punishing agents who became too successful (and who therefore threatened Hoover's image of himself as the only true G-Man), it would continue to take time to force significant change through the system.

Yellow Hawk concentrated on the fuzzy photographs of Schengel. As he listened to the allegations of involvement in illicit CBW production in Libya and Iraq, he took brief notes in shorthand. Schengel had flown into Omaha two months before and gone underground. His movements since were not known: the first priority was to locate him.

The Washington briefing went into fine detail about the likely effects of biological and chemical weapons. Yellow Hawk fidgeted uncomfortably in his chair as slides of animals on which CBW had been tested were displayed on the screen. Worse followed: shots from Halabja, where Saddam Hussein used chemical weapons against his own people. Men, women and children lay dead in the streets: a ghost town with corpses. Those few who had survived had then been shot by Saddam's men. The use of 'insecticides against insects' was how one of Saddam's officers had described it.

He wondered where the information on Schengel originated. It was detailed and precise, particularly strong on Schengel's role in the near- and Middle-East. There were few security operations in that part of the world that co-operated with America. Egypt was a possibility, or perhaps a leak from inside Libya or the Yemen from disaffected elements. But it was Israel that was the most logical source. He wondered what the Israelis had to gain by providing the US with this information. If the product came via a third party such as the Mossad, there was also a strong likelihood that not all of the relevant details had been placed at the FBI's disposal. He wondered what they might have left out, what dangers he might face from this man Schengel and his secret financiers.

One thing he could guarantee: men like Schengel always have protection. And whoever his protectors might be, they would think nothing of removing unwelcome Federal attention.

General Dayan was not surprised to see the message from Dole on his desk when he returned late that evening to his office. Mossad sources in the States were already indicating problems with the Schengel case. He selected a secure line and placed the call, a direct line to Dole that bypassed the CIA's main switchboard.

The phone rang. He waited a minute and then glanced at his watch, calculating the time of day in Langley.

The phone was answered.

'Dole?' the General asked.

There was silence and then: 'Who is this?'

'A friend,' Dayan replied carefully. 'Is it possible to speak with Mr Dole please?'

There was the sound of the mouthpiece being switched into mute, a short break and then another voice. He guessed the call was being taped and probably a trace run, but that did not concern him. A voice modifier attached to his phone ensured that no-one could identify his voiceprint. And the call was untraceable: the Americans had kindly provided Mossad with the appropriate technology.

'I understand you want to talk with Mr Dole. Can you please state your business?'

Dayan did not recognise the voice.

'I am calling on a confidential matter. I must speak with Mr Dole personally.'

There was another pause and then: 'I'm afraid that will not be possible. Mr Dole died earlier this afternoon. Perhaps I can help you?'

Dayan hung up and sat quietly for a moment. Dole's death could not be an accident: it would be too great a coincidence. So he had been killed. And that lead to another, unpleasant conclusion. The penetration of America's intelligence services ran far deeper than they had realised.

Parke was shown into Cham's Vauxhall Cross office at exactly ten a.m. Despite its glamorous exterior, the building has that dull hand of the Civil Service indelibly imprinted upon it. Outside it might look stylish and modern: inside it was typically public sector, with office furniture and clutter straight from the civil service suppliers' catalogues.

Cham looked up from his desk and smiled.

'Parke. Good to see you.'

They shook hands formally and sat facing each other across Cham's desk. The desk was entirely empty of paperwork, decorated with just a small telephone, and a computer screen and keyboard in an angled recess. The view from the window looked across the river and towards the other bank of the Thames. Outside was a wide terrace. The quality and positioning of the room reflected Cham's seniority.

'I trust everything is going well?' Parke asked.

'Very well indeed,' responded Cham. 'Just heard from the RG. A tip-off about Hamilton's Strasbourg meeting.'

RG was the *Resiegnments Generaux*—the French secret service

Parke frowned and looked concerned. 'The RG? Doesn't that worry us?'

Cham shook his head. 'Not at all. It's part of their routine surveillance of the Euro crowd. They won't be digging any deeper—it's our turf. Naturally I assured them I would pass the information on to other appropriate agencies.'

'But of course,' Parke smiled. Cham would, of course, do no such thing. 'More importantly, the man from Madrid has become the problem we predicted.'

Cham sighed. 'The problem is under control. Through very unofficial channels, of course. The question is whether he might already have talked.'

'Surely a man in your position would know that.'

'Hmm. Not necessarily. Making enquiries can reveal more than staying silent. But Hamilton performed well I gather.'

'Quite so. With the exception of the Spaniard, they all signed.'

'GDM shares must be doing well. I shall find the time to increase my holding,' Cham commented. 'I hear you also secured a sole distributor deal with the manufacturers?'

'Absolutely,' Parke replied, wondering when Cham would offer him a drink. And not just a coffee or a tea: something stronger. His life in the Navy had given him a taste for alcohol. 'GDM does indeed have sole distribution rights to the products.'

Cham nodded. 'Excellent news. And what news of further demonstrations?'

'Not necessary. At least, not for the moment,' Parke responded. 'The spate of copycat gassings and the fuss about that cult in Japan will ensure the news maintains its headline status for some time to come. There's always a nutter somewhere who'll take the credit for someone else's handiwork. Of course, it may be necessary to remind people if memories fade. Something on the streets of London for example.'

'Good God, are you mad?' Cham replied angrily. Parke was surprised. He had not seen Cham angry before. 'Paris, Rome, New York. Never London. Do you understand me? Never shit on your own front doorstep.'

'Of course, of course,' Parke replied quickly, realising his mistake. 'I wasn't thinking.'

'Quite so. Well, is there anything else we need to discuss now or can it wait for our regular meetings?'

'I don't think there's anything.' Parke rose. Cham was making it obvious that he had overstayed his welcome. And there was little chance of that drink now.

After Parke's departure, Cham sat at his desk for a time deep in thought. Parke and Hamilton were important elements in delivering his plans. For the moment. But a time would come when he would need to decide what to do with them. The speed of current developments meant that day was drawing rapidly closer. But Parke and Hamilton were not stupid men. Eventually they would realise there was more to Cham's plan than they knew, that their role in it was only bit players in a larger production.

Cham sighed. He would need to choose his moment carefully. And when that moment came, Parke and Hamilton would be quietly and efficiently removed.

Brewer left Jane's flat at six thirty the following morning. It took just two minutes before he knew he was being followed. The man was good. Someone with less experience than Brewer would never have noticed him. Brewer wondered whose tail it was: the choice was wide. It could be the Firm, or one of their subcontractors, or the police. Or, despite his removal, someone involved with the Russian case. Nice to be so popular, he thought ironically.

Despite his uninvited shadow, Brewer saw no reason to change his plan. Anyone interested enough to tail him could easily find out where he lived. It was hardly an Official Secret. At half-past seven he reached the front door of his flat in Gibson Gardens. Inside, he switched on the radio and made himself breakfast. He saw his anonymous tail through the slits of the Venetian blinds checking out the rear of the block. His shadow would soon realise the flat had only one door. A few moments later, Brewer saw him return to the front of the building and take up position in a recessed entrance in the next block to the right.

Brewer finished his breakfast—some lightly burnt toast, one of his specialities—took some rope from a cupboard and placed it on the living room floor. Moving quickly, he put the front door on the latch, opened the rear window to the flat and slipped out. Surveillance by a single person ensures the least likelihood of discovery, but it does leave fatal weaknesses. Absolutely critical is the need to avoid being observed by your target: particularly when the subject of the surveillance is trained in counter-surveillance tactics. Brewer's skills had been acquired in a variety of theatres, many of them hostile territory. Working quite literally in his own back yard was a piece of cake by comparison.

Brewer scrambled over the wall surrounding the flats, around the back, along the railway embankment and over another wall until he was positioned directly behind his target. Only a few yards separated them. The man was big, with that distinctive overweight caused by years of excessive drinking. It was always simpler to kill a man silently than to capture him. But right now he could do without the complication of another corpse: Anastasia's was proving troublesome enough. Brewer wanted information: he needed to persuade the man to talk. There were questions he wanted answered. Who had sent him? Why was he being followed?

His mind made up, he darted forward. One hand squeezed the man's throat and held his neck in a lock, preventing him from uttering a sound. The other he pushed forcibly into the small of his back to thrust him forwards. Taken by surprise, the man's resistance collapsed before it could begin. They ran like two insane and unnaturally intimate joggers across the open space. Brewer glanced round, praying no-one had seen them. All looked quiet. As they reached the front door of Brewer's flat the man started to struggle. He slipped an elbow free and swung it back, aiming for Brewer's stomach. But Brewer ducked to one side, pushed him up the couple of steps to the front door and jerked him into the flat.

The man fell face-forward onto the floor and Brewer was instantly on his back.

'Keep quiet or you're dead.'

The man wasn't listening and struggled and cursed beneath him. Brewer gripped his head and smashed it twice into the floor. Underneath the thin carpet was a layer of reinforced concrete.

'This is your last warning.'

This time the man listened. His movements stopped abruptly. Brewer took the rope and bound the man's legs and arms before spinning him round onto his back. He reached forward and searched the man's pockets. He found a Derringer High Standard tucked inside a discreet inside pocket.

'Very colourful,' Brewer commented, standing and drawing his breath. 'Quite the cowboy aren't we? Can't remember the last time I saw one of these.' He snapped the gun open. 'Point two-two long, two rounds. Fancy yourself as a gambler, do you?' There was no reaction. Brewer snapped the gun shut. 'No? Well allow me to introduce myself. Peter Brewer, but I expect you already know that. And you are?'

'Screw you.'

The man had an accent Brewer couldn't place precisely, but it was definitely East European.

'What I really want to know is what you're doing. Perhaps you might care to enlighten me?'

The man smiled. 'Forget it.'

'Well,' Brewer continued, speaking in a slow, laboured voice like a teacher explaining something to an especially slow pupil. 'Let's consider the facts, shall we? You follow me and you're armed. Perhaps you want to kill me?'

'You would already be dead if I wanted to shoot you. I know my job.'

'So tell me, is there any particular reason why you're taking such an interest in my affairs?'

The man stayed silent.

'Obviously,' Brewer resumed. 'It has something to do with the death of Professor Beatty, the sad death of Anastasia. Such a pretty girl, didn't you think? And the murder of Larsen Lak. Now that,' Brewer said, leaning close to the man. 'Does annoy me. Larsen was a good man.'

The gunman spat in Brewer's face. He did not react. The

warm, unpleasant spittle ran down his face and dripped back onto the gunman's own.

'And that,' said Brewer. 'Also annoys me.'

Brewer whipped the Derringer sharply across the man's face. The man screamed. A deep cut sent blood flowing across his face, stinging his eyes.

'Your choice. You don't want to do this in a civilised way, so we won't do it in a civilised way.'

The man moaned, one eye shut against the flowing, stinging blood.

'Let me make it clear. I want to know who sent you. And I want to know why they sent you. If you're very lucky, I might settle just for knowing who sent you. With details of where I can find them, of course.'

The man stared up at him with his one open eye with unmistakable loathing. 'You will learn nothing.'

'Ah. So you're planning to play the hero. By the rules of the game, I can only assume in that case that you want me to play the villain.'

Brewer struck again with the Derringer. This time the man passed out. After a couple of minutes, Brewer fetched a jug of water from the kitchen and threw it over the unconscious figure.

'I'm not very happy. Just look at the state of this carpet,' Brewer complained. 'I expect you to reimburse me for the dry-cleaning, preferably cash before you leave. Now, enough polite conversation. Let's get down to business, shall we?'

Scotland Yard's SO12 ('SO' stands for Specialist Operations) is more familiarly known as Special Branch. Since the progress towards peace in Northern Ireland, it has been locked in a running battle with the Security Service (better known as MI5) for anti-terrorist and other domestic security issues in the United Kingdom. Anyone familiar with the petty rivalries and politics of the public sector will not be surprised to learn that the same bitchy point-scoring, bureaucracy and pointless committee meetings that occupy and waste so much time in other parts of the Civil Service spread their cancer into areas of policing and security as well.

Special Branch has always been viewed with deep suspicion by the civil rights lobby, who like to portray Scotland Yard's SO12 as a sinister force that persecutes harmless citizens for political reasons, acts in underhand ways to assist the security services and is accountable to no-one. Scotland Yard, naturally, does not agree with this view: they regard their Special Branch as a part of the police force that has a necessary and important job to do and which is as accountable as any other part of that police force.

What is perhaps not so well realised is that each police force in Britain has its own Special Branch, responsible to its own Chief Constable, unlike other European countries where every Special Branch equivalent is part of a national structure. This fragmentation of the British Special Branch, and indeed the British police, has been of no particular benefit to anyone, other than criminals and terrorists of course—and, some cynics have argued, politicians with shady backgrounds. It has long been recognised by both Scotland Yard and the Security Service that in order to be effective, a counter-terrorist unit requires the skills of police officers and the Security Service. Both the head of the Security Service and the Commissioner of the Metropolitan Police have made clear their views: that there should be a national, co-ordinated structure. This battle has now largely been won by the Security Service, who lobbied hard under the patronage of their then Director General, Stella Rimmington, to be handed control of all anti-terrorist measures.

Scotland Yard's Special Branch has constructed itself around several specialist units. 'A Squad' provides personal protection services and is responsible for the personal safety of ex-Prime Ministers, such as Margaret Thatcher, as well as special protection for those believed to be at risk such as the writer Salman Rushdie and former Northern Ireland Ministers. The Special Branch officers assigned to the former Defence Secretary, Mark Hamilton, were members of A Squad. Only two foreign ambassadors in Britain routinely have Special Branch Protection Officers assigned to them: the American and the Israeli. A Squad carefully assesses the risks into various categories before deciding whether protection is appropriate and at what level such protection should operate.

'B Squad' was formerly pre-occupied with anti-IRA terrorism activities, a role that since October 1992 the Security Service has now largely absorbed as part of their post Cold War re-alignment. Its relationship with the Security Service is becoming stronger year on year, but has yet to be fully stabilised.

Special Branch's 'P Squad' organises surveillance at ports of entry into the UK. With the reduction of internal borders in Europe, its role in detecting the movement of 'undesirables' has become more important. Of particular concern are those known to be active in European terrorist movements and those of extremes from both right and left. As well as the obvious entry points, P Squad maintains a roving presence at less obvious locations, such as Biggin Hill airfield in Kent. In particular, P Squad keeps an eye open on behalf of other agencies that have requested assistance. Sometimes their instructions are purely to watch: at other times, they also apprehend and arrest.

It is, however, Special Branch's 'CE Squad' that has perhaps the most demanding duties, its name coming from an amalgamation of two former squads. Whereas the Security Service studies subversion as it effects the state, CE Squad studies it as it affects public order on the streets of London. They concentrate their activities on three main areas of responsibility: International Terrorism, Public Order, and Investigation. CE Squad has an ill-defined, but generally friendly, relationship with the Security Service. It organises its work into three basic categories: right wing groups, left-wing groups and international terrorism (although sometimes deciding which category to drop any one particular suspect individual or group into can be a relatively arbitrary process).

CE Squad maintains a list of recent terrorist incidents and those it believes to be responsible: it reads like an international

'Who's Wanted'. Incidents listed identify the following as responsible: Abu Nidal, Libya, the Seychelles, Iran, Afghanistan, the PLO/Force 17, Al Qaeda, Israel and Sikhs. Its biggest breakthroughs generally come either from the occasional disillusionment of former members of extremist groups, or covert placement: the infiltration either of someone co-operating with Special Branch, or, more dangerously, the undercover placement of a Special Branch officer. With some of the extremist groups, this type of human intelligence operation can prove exceptionally difficult to achieve.

Detective Inspector David Howarth of Special Branch's CE Squad had himself acted on occasion as an undercover agent. It was not a role that he would repeat. In 1989, he was infiltrated into the Socialist Workers' Party prior to the events that culminated in the Poll Tax Riot in Trafalgar Square in March 1990. It was his controversial evidence that proved the SWP were not responsible for organising the high levels of violence and intimidation during the Riots. Despite protests from right-wing politicians, who wanted a simple solution and someone like the SWP on whom to pin the blame, DI Howarth established the uncomfortable political truth: the major part of the Riots was a spontaneous eruption from elements of London's 'underclass' who were not affiliated to anyone, but saw the opportunity to take part and express themselves—an expression that was not entirely uninfluenced by alcohol and other less socially acceptable drugs. At most, the SWP had been guilty of promoting political unrest by capitalising on the already unpopular Poll Tax legislation. But holding public meetings and printing protest leaflets does not rate as unlawful behaviour in Britain: at least in theory.

DI Howarth was sitting at his desk in New Scotland Yard making notes in the margin of an intelligence memo when he received the phone call. It came from one of his highest placed and most reliable sources.

'Put him through.'

As his secretary transferred the call, Howarth tried to remember the last time he had spoken with the contact: three, four years ago maybe? On that occasion however the information had not proved reliable.

'Howarth speaking.'

The contact was brief. He wanted to meet urgently at a local rendezvous. The information was of such importance that he could not risk imparting it over the phone. Howarth sighed. It was a familiar tactic, often used by sources simply to obtain free food and drink. He looked at his watch. He had a full day mapped out ahead of him, but the contact repeated that it was urgent. Very urgent. Given the choice between losing part of his day or losing what might be a critical lead, Howarth only had one real choice.

'Seven-thirty this evening,' Howarth suggested. 'It's the best I can do.'

'The usual place?'

For a moment Howarth had to think where that was.

'Yes. That'll be fine.'

He put down the phone and sighed. His wife would not be pleased. She had made him promise to avoid after-work meetings and in particular to avoid after-work drinking.

And now he had just agreed to do both.

Brewer made the call from a public phone box in the Euston Road, using 141 to block his number. Although issued with a mobile phone, he declined to use it. Mobile phones are one of the best tracking devices available. So long as a mobile phone is switched on, its position can be pinpointed to within fifty feet, deduced from the triangulation strength of its signal relative to the various relay transmitters that carry mobile phone calls. It was a widely used technique in tracking suspected drug dealers and traffickers, who have a dangerous fascination for mobile phones, although, for obvious reasons, they generally prefer the anonymity of the pay-as-you-go variety. Brewer had no intention of giving away his current position.

'Monroe? It's Brewer.'

Monroe sounded surprised. And possibly guilty. 'Look.

Brewer, you have to believe me. That info I gave you about the Russian girl. I had no idea it was a—'

'Stop fretting, Monroe,' Brewer assured him, his eyes resting briefly on the wall-to-wall business cards for 'discreet massage services'. 'I'm not ringing to pass judgement on you. That particular misunderstanding is sorted. I just want to know who supplied that information to you in the first place.'

There was silence. And then: 'I'd like to help, Brewer. All I will say is that it came from high up. There's something going on here that I don't understand.'

'You're not the only one, Monroe. Look. I'm going to need your help.'

He sensed Monroe's hesitation.

'Oh come on Monroe. I think you owe me one.'

'Maybe.' Monroe did not sound convinced. 'It all depends what kind of help you had in mind.'

'Quite simple. Someone put a tail on me.'

'So what? You think it was the Firm?'

'No.' Brewer scowled at an impatient-looking woman who was pacing up and down outside. 'Something to do with our Russian friend.'

'I'm not sure I want to have this conversation. What have you stepped into, Brewer? Don't you ever look where you're walking?'

'Listen Monroe. I interviewed the tail. And he sang. After a little initial reluctance.'

'Jesus Brewer. Tell me it was nothing too messy.'

'He gave me a name.' Brewer read from his notebook. 'Some guy called Thielstrom.' He spelt it out.

'Thielstrom? Sounds Danish or something. Did you get a first name?'

'Edward.'

'Edward?' Monroe laughed. 'So maybe he isn't Danish. You want me to run a search I take it?'

'Please.'

'Any middle name?'

'Not that I know.'

'Okay. Edward Thielstrom it is. Is there a number I can call you? Are you at your flat? I don't suppose you have your mobile, do you?'

'No.' He looked at his watch. 'How about I call back at twelve?'

'Twelve? That's cutting it tight.'

'Monroe, it's urgent.'

'Okay. But after this we're quits.'

'Sure, sure. After this we're quits.' Brewer replaced the phone. As he did so, his hand dislodged one of the lurid 'business' cards placed there by local pimps and sent it spinning to the ground. He bent down to pick it up.

The woman waiting outside pushed roughly past him and into the phone box as he straightened with the card in his hand. She looked down at it, her face flushing crimson.

'Dirty old sod,' she muttered.

In Gibson Gardens, the gunman Brewer had 'interviewed' sat recovering in the communal laundry yard behind the paddle steamer block. His fingers gingerly explored the dried blood and injuries to his face. He did not resent Brewer: he would have done the same if the situation were reversed. Although he probably would not have been so gentle. At least Brewer had spared his life. But now he was unarmed. And when he reported, Thielstrom would not receive this news well. There was also the problem of his appearance. The average pedestrian does not react well to bloodstained figures staggering along the pavement.

He rose slowly to his feet and steadied himself against the nearby wall, still dizzy. There was the sound of footsteps and before he could move, two men appeared around the corner of the block. He squinted at them through swollen eyelids. He caught a few details: dark suits, hand-made leather shoes. As he recognised them, a flutter of terror ran through him.

'I lost him,' he blurted.

'We know,' one of the men responded.

They each took one of his arms and guided him slowly around the corner. Their grip was firm. Too firm.

'What's going to happen to me?'

They did not reply. Only when they reached the car parked outside on the main road and placed him on the back seat did one of them speak.

'Thielstrom would like a word with you.'

The car shot away from the pavement with a screech and the stench of hot rubber.

In his Langley office, Vogel's fingers stabbed at the telephone number pad, his anger barely under control. He waited just four rings, slammed down the phone and dialled again. This time it was answered at the second ring.

'It's Vogel,' he said, his voice a tense, tetchy rasp.

'Yes?'

'What the hell are you playing at?' he demanded, his breath coming in short, tense gulps. 'You killed him, you killed Dole.'

The voice at the far end was calm, detached. 'We could not risk him making enquiries.'

'Bullshit!' Vogel screamed. 'He was one of the best men we had. Don't you understand? He knew the Middle-East better than anyone.'

'Precisely,' the voice purred. 'He had to be removed.'

'Removed? Removed?' Vogel laughed, his voice close to hysteria. 'You could ruin everything. Have you any idea what's going to happen now, hey? Do you seriously think everyone's going to shrug their shoulders and say 'Too bad, old Dole's dead?' Bullshit they will! There's going to be an inquiry, that's what. We have the police and Company people crawling over the place. How the hell is that going to help us? Who knows what they might come up with?'

The voice became harder. 'Listen to me, Vogel. Everyone is dispensable. Everyone.'

Vogel stopped short, the threat behind the quiet words penetrating his anger.

'Within an hour, an extremist Middle Eastern group will contact the *Washington Post* and claim responsibility for the shooting. They will state that it was revenge for ongoing CIA assistance to Israel and American intransigence about settlers on the West Bank. The matter will end there.'

'The hell it will,' Vogel replied weakly, his anger ebbing.

'Trust me,' the voice said.

The line went dead. Vogel sat listening to the dull clicking hum, his eyes staring blankly at his office wall. For the first time he understood how serious they were, how strong they were. For the first time he had doubts, began to question his own judgment.

But it was too late to change his mind now. Far too late.

Jane opened the window. Something moved in the street below. But not fast enough. She briefly saw a man duck into a doorway. It was obvious that he had been watching her flat from the end of the road. She drew a long breath and shivered. Who was he? What did he want?

She moved away from the window and over to her computer humming on the table. Brewer never told her much about his work, but she knew who he worked for, the dangers he faced. That was more than she was meant to know. Maybe she was being over-anxious: perhaps it was just the police outside. Following up on the incident that Brewer had sketched only briefly. The idea it was the police loitering in the street and watching her flat was more comforting than some of the other possibilities that came to mind.

She found herself unable to concentrate on the work in front of her. The spreadsheets, the cash forecasts she was developing for the small engineering company swam before her in a tumble of cascading numbers. She switched off the computer, went back to the window, and stared out. Nothing. Perhaps she had imagined it. Only she was not fooling anyone, least of all herself.

Jane took Gary's photo from the top of the TV set and ran her fingers along the line of his face. Why were the men she loved such fools? Why did they work for people they disliked, in careers where no one gave a damn for them? She tried to block the images of those other photos from her mind, the photos of the remains of what the mystery correspondent claimed was Gary. Brewer was good to her then, but she knew the loss had shaken him as much as her. Possibly more. Gary and Brewer had been close, as close as two friends can ever be.

And now Brewer was in trouble. She drew a deep breath, frightened by a dark world she did not understand, by the thought that Brewer too was in danger. She would share her fears with him when he called again, let him know about the man watching her flat. But he would only laugh, make light of her concerns. Try as she might, she could not reconcile the relaxed, amusing man she knew with the other world she knew he inhabited. Gary had been the same. A big hulk of a man who was every inch the cliché of the gentle giant. She had seen him sworn at in pubs, pushed around by men half his height and frame. But he merely shrugged away such challenges, turned his back on his would-be tormentors. The same man who thought nothing of killing in his work would avoid confrontation whenever and wherever he could in his own private life.

She could not lose Peter. Not after Gary. It would break her, tear her apart. Even if he laughed, even if he accused her of imagination, she would tell him about the man watching her. If his life was in danger, she would do everything she could to help. Never again did she want to carry the guilt and hurt that she now carried, the sense that it was her fault that Gary had died. If only she had done this, if only she had done that. Perhaps Gary would be here now, her whole life would be as she once imagined it could be.

She sat and cried. Gary's picture slipped unnoticed from her fingers and into the soft, deep pile of the rug.

'Sorry. Haven't been able to find very much.' Monroe's opening comment when Brewer phoned again was a disappointment. 'But there's definitely something odd about this guy. I'd guess Edward Thielstrom's not his real name. Started using it some time in the fifties. Before that, who knows? Looks like he might have been some kind of refugee.'

'Refugee? From what?' Brewer fed another coin into the pay phone.

'I don't know. Anything before that's inaccessible. Classified. Seems to have been very active travelling round Europe.'

Brewer thought for a moment. 'Was he working for the Firm?'

'It's possible. Might explain the gaps, the constant travel. Oh, and he seems to have written a book.'

'A book? Odd. What about?'

'World war two. Sorry, couldn't get any more on it than that. I think it was only published in German.'

'German? Interesting. Suggests it must be his native language. I don't suppose you came up with an address, did you?'

'Brewer,' Monroe sighed. 'Don't you think I might have told you up front if there'd been anything so bloody obvious as an address? Sure, I've got that, a semen sample and his DNA profile too.'

Brewer hung up. If Thielstrom had written a book there was one obvious place to find a copy.

Inside the British Library students and academics sat pouring over texts, taking notes on paper and small notebook computers. Brewer noted that most of the users seemed to be young students, or older, retired men—and generally they were men. The atmosphere was less quiet and reverential than in the old British Library, which had been more like the interior of a church than a library. Brewer found the new building a welcome change. To him the purpose of a library was to find what he wanted as quickly and efficiently as possible.

He flicked quickly through online catalogues until he found what he was looking for: Thielstrom's name and the title of a book. He requested a copy and occupied his time while he waited by sketching in his notebook, attempting to connect the different strands of the case. The picture soon resembled a spider's web, too complicated to be of any use, except possibly to a psychoanalyst.

'Excuse me, sir.'

He turned to find a thin, middle-aged man standing beside him.

'You requested the Thielstrom book?'

Brewer nodded. 'Is there a problem?'

'I'm afraid it has been withdrawn from general availability, sir. It requires special clearance to obtain access.'

'Special clearance? What does that mean? Is that unusual?' Brewer was not a frequent user of the Library, despite holding a reader's card for more than twenty years. These days he was accustomed to conducting most of his research on-line using the Firm's computer network.

'Very,' the man advised. 'But then so is the book.'

'Is it?' Now Brewer was most definitely interested. 'And why do you say that?'

'It's been banned in Germany. Completely banned. And even here it's almost impossible to obtain permission to see our copy.'

Brewer leaned closer, falling in with the air of conspiracy. 'That's all very interesting. What else do you know about this book? It's very important.'

The man hesitated. 'The book is about Auschwitz. I suppose I can tell you that much. The author was a camp commander there.'

'This chap Thielstrom?' Brewer was startled by the revelation. 'He was at Auschwitz?'

'But Thielstrom was not his name at the time. He's changed it several times, like many of the former SS and Nazi officials. The main thing about his book is that he refutes all the claims about Auschwitz being a death camp.'

'But everyone knows what Auschwitz was.'

'Yes. That's why the Germans have banned it. Denial of the Holocaust is an offence under German law.'

'Yes, yes,' said Brewer impatiently. 'But why would that make it so difficult to see a copy here?'

'I don't know. After all, there are many other revisionist texts. This is no different to many others. I can't tell you why it was been restricted, who decided it was necessary.'

'Thanks anyway. You've been very helpful.'

Brewer left the Library, his mind racing. There had to be

something else in the book, something far less obvious than the stupid denial about Auschwitz. But his real question now was: what was a major league Nazi war criminal doing at large in Europe? He had a good idea of where he could find the answer.

Brewer reached the Public Record Office at Kew an hour later. The PRO maintains the national archives of the United Kingdom, preserving the records of central government and the courts of law. It is a unique institution, with records spanning an unbroken period from the 11th century to the present day. If Brewer was going to find what he was looking for anywhere, he would find it here.

He spoke with one of the staff about his requirements and for another hour there was a succession of indexes and catalogues to be consulted before a pile of files was eventually retrieved from the archives. Brewer lifted them onto the tiny reading room desk and started to flick through them.

Most had been classified and kept locked away for thirty years after the war and bore the stamps of their original classification and a later stamp, approving them for de-classification. Page after page dealt with the Nuremberg trials. There were lists of papers prepared at Church House in Westminster prior to the end of the war when it had already been decided that war crimes trials would be conducted after the defeat of Hitler's Reich. Lists of names and verdicts. Lists of names never brought to trial—a much longer list, Brewer noted, than those who were.

Brewer opened his notebook and jotted briefly as he worked. Somewhere here had to be a record of Thielstrom's real name, a record of what happened to him at Nuremberg, whether he was caught and if so, what action was taken against him. Brewer started work on the second file. The pages depressed him. The myth that it was only a handful of people, an inner circle of Nazis that had mislead and betrayed the German people, was given the lie by these documents. There were thousands of names, thousands of acts of individual and collective brutality. No wonder Nuremberg had become bogged down with detail and bureaucracy and finally been abandoned in the late 1940's.

It was only slowly that Brewer noticed a pattern emerging. Certain pages that were missing from the files, certain absent documents that broke the flow of the paperwork and left holes in the accounts of the preparation and workings of the trials. At first he thought it was merely coincidence, perhaps a few pages that had been misplaced over the years. But some of the files contained small yellow slips and a few words:

> Under the terms of the Official Secrets Act, certain documentation from this section has been withheld on grounds of national security.

Brewer called the clerk back over and pointed at it.

'What does this mean? I thought these documents were fully de-classified.'

She looked at it without surprise. 'I'll check for you.'

She was gone about ten minutes and when she returned, one look at her expression was enough to convince Brewer he was in for a re-run of his British Library experiences.

'I'm sorry,' she started. 'The missing papers are still restricted. They're subject to a hundred-year ruling.'

'A hundred years? What the hell is in them?'

'Most papers of a sensitive nature are subject to thirty or fifty-year rulings before they can be de-classified. The one hundred years embargo is unusual, but we do have other papers in that category, including some from the First World War as well.'

'Can you tell me why these particular papers are barred for so long?'

She shook her head. 'There is no requirement to provide any form of explanation. The only unusual thing in this case is that fact that the classification order was made only recently.'

Brewer leaned forwards. 'How recently?'

She checked some handwritten notes. 'Six months ago.'

'Six months!' Brewer was confused. 'Does this make sense to you? It certainly doesn't to me.'

'It does happen from time to time. Papers that were given

thirty- or fifty-year rulings are reviewed by committee as they come up for general release. Occasionally that review leads to an extension.'

'I'll send my grandchildren to read them,' Brewer responded.

'If you want to get more information about Nuremberg, there is one person who may be able to help.' She wrote down a name and address and handed it to him. 'He comes in here from time to time. I believe he's working on his memoirs.'

Brewer looked at the note. It was the name of a peer and a London telephone number.

'The name seems familiar to me.'

'He was there, at Nuremberg.'

Now Brewer realised where he had seen the name before. It was dotted throughout the papers he had been examining, a name associated with the prosecuting council. Brewer thanked her and left. It was drawing near to the end of the afternoon. Suited commuters were already beginning to make their way home. He stopped at a telephone box near Kew station and made a call, reading from the note the assistant at the PRO had given him. After two rings it was answered.

'Northwood.'

The voice was old but firm. Brewer spoke briefly. There was uncertainty at first, and then agreement. Lord Northwood lived nearby, just a few stops from Kew. Brewer caught the District Line to Turnham Green, walked along South Parade and up into Bedford Park, stopping to ask directions just once.

His destination was a large arts and crafts detached house set back from the road behind a curved white wooden fence. The house was decorated with balconies and terraces, a mix of red bricks and Flemish influence. Wisteria had spread its arthritic fingers across the front and tangled itself around an old cast-iron down pipe.

He tugged on the old-fashioned bell-pull and heard chimes from deep inside the house. It was at least a minute before a shadow appeared behind the glass of the front door. A moment later it opened. Brewer found himself facing an elderly man in his eighties. His once tall frame was now stooped, his back arched. His hair was grey, but thick, his eyes a sharp blue. He wore a graph-paper pattern shirt and a plain brown tie: the universal uniform of the retired brigade who fought in world war two.

'Lord Northwood?' Brewer enquired. 'Peter Brewer.'

'Come inside.'

Brewer followed the peer through to a rear dining room with views over a small, landscaped garden. With the exception of the ticking of a giant long case clock in the hallway, the house was silent. It was furnished in keeping with the outside, the walls a riot of rich William Morris wallpapers and the rooms filled with the elegant wooden lines of arts and crafts furniture. Brewer had the impression of a man who lived alone, that the woman's touch here had long grown cold.

They sat and Brewer waited while Northwood poured him a cup of tea from a chipped china teapot.

'I have something stronger for after if you'd like,' the peer said and smiled. 'Now, how can I help?'

Brewer briefly explained his problem: that he wanted to track down Thielstrom. He did not explain why and the peer did not ask. He detailed the problems he had encountered at both the British Library and at the PRO and the little information he had already gathered. Northwood leant back in his chair and took a long drink from his tea before replying.

'You've probably thought of this yourself,' Northwood commented. 'But it sounds to me as if this man might be involved in some way with the intelligence services. I can see little reason otherwise why the facts surrounding him should be held back in the way you describe.'

'Yes, the thought had crossed my mind,' Brewer responded.

'Unfortunately, if that is the case, I really don't see how I can help,' Northwood continued. His eyes rested on Brewer's. Despite their age, his eyes cut through him. Northwood had been one of the most formidable prosecuting counsels at Nuremberg.

'I wondered if the name meant anything to you, whether you had any details to add about Thielstrom?'

'Should it? After all these years?' He shook his head. 'There were so many Nazis, you really can't imagine. It wasn't just a question of hundreds. It was thousands and tens of thousands. They organised the biggest, most efficient, most calculated killing machine the world has ever seen.' He stopped and finished his tea. 'And they came closer to winning than you and I shall ever realise. But those files will be harder to find than Thielstrom's. I dare say they've long since been destroyed. Most of the truly embarrassing material was pulped at the end of Nuremberg. Sherry?'

'I'd prefer a malt.'

The peer smiled. 'Good man. I'll have one myself.'

Northwood rose with difficulty from his seat and crossed to a small drinks cabinet. While he filled the two glasses, Brewer rose and looked out of the windows.

'Do you like it? The garden I mean.'

'I'm not much of a gardener myself,' Brewer replied quietly.

The back of the house was a combination of order and variety centred around a lawn dotted with shrubs and trees. A narrow path wound down its middle, looped around two crooked apple trees and disappeared beyond a hedge about one third of the way down. In the border a mix of evergreen and annuals blended with roses and herbs.

'My boss would appreciate it more than me,' Brewer added.

'Keen gardener is he?' Northwood handed him a generous glass of whisky.

'Very. In another life he would have been one.'

'Wouldn't we all?' Northwood sighed, and turned away to sink down into his chair. 'But it's only in retirement that one at last finds the time to pursue one's true interests.'

Brewer turned to face him. 'Have you any idea how I could find Thielstrom?'

'I could have a word with the All Party War Crimes Group, if you like. There's also the War Crimes investigation team. You might find it worthwhile talking to them.'

'I thought they'd been wound up.'

The peer shook his head. 'No, just in Scotland. So far. Might be worth asking if anything they've uncovered has mentioned Thielstrom.' He sighed. 'Trouble is, you see, you're hitting the same problem the Scottish lot ran into. Many of these Nazi types worked for the West after the war. Makes it very difficult to bring a prosecution now. Runs the risk of being accused of double-standards.'

'A justified accusation.'

'Quite.' The peer's voice was firm. 'What do you know about Nuremberg?'

'Only as much as most people. That it brought key Nazi war criminals to justice.'

'Oh, it was certainly meant to.'

'Are you suggesting it didn't?"

'I know what I'm saying. Somehow drawing closer to death makes one see things so much more clearly. Things that were grey and blurred around the edges suddenly slip into focus and one realises they weren't ever grey at all, but black and white. It's just in the midst of our careers we judge things differently, compromise on our core moral values. Only later, with time do we reflect, do we come to understand and reject those earlier behaviours. Do you understand me?'

Brewer sat down on the sofa and took a sip from his glass. 'And you believe that this chap Thielstrom was one of the Nazis that someone in the West was prepared to overlook?'

The peer stopped and looked up at him, his eyes glistening. 'That would seem a likely supposition, don't you agree?'

Brewer nodded slowly. 'It might also explain one or two other things that have been happening.'

Northwood struggled to rise from his seat. Brewer motioned him to stay put and refilled his whisky glass for him.

'It's good malt,' he said.

'Highland Park,' Northwood replied. 'Not that you would know it to listen to me now, but my mother's family came from Orkney once upon a time.' He took a sip and then set down his glass and looked at Brewer. 'And what will you do now?'

'I think,' said Brewer. 'That it's time to pick up where the Nuremberg trials left off, don't you Lord Northwood?'

The peer raised his glass.

'A little word of caution. Trust no-one. They never fight a clean fight and they still have influential friends. I once thought we'd conquered them, but I realise now you can never eliminate poisonous ideas. At best you can just contain them.' He smiled. 'I wish you every success. Although dare I say it, I fear you are too late. Most like me are old men now, or dead.'

Brewer smiled and chimed his glass against Northwood's. He wished the old man was right: but he had an uneasy feeling that the Nazi movement was going to prove far from old—and far from dead.

11

Howarth left New Scotland Yard and arrived at the *Paviours Arms* in Page Street near the Houses of Parliament just before eight o'clock. His contact was already seated in the corner, nursing a pint of lager. Howarth nodded towards him and went up to the bar. It was midweek and the pub was quiet, the office workers already departed after their post-work pints. The Paviours' interior was a masterpiece of art deco doctored in the more recent past with chromium furniture, a brutal reminder of just how bad decor had been in the 1970's. Howarth bought himself a pint and went over to join his contact.

'Sorry to keep you.'

'No problem. What's that you've got?' The contact motioned at Howarth's pint.

Howarth smiled. 'Fuller's ESB,' he replied. 'Don't tell the missus.'

They exchanged pleasantries for a few minutes and then the contact handed over a copy of a document.

'I thought your lot might be interested in this.'

DI Howarth looked at the cover briefly and flicked through it.

'Can I ask you where you acquired this?'

'Sure,' the contact smiled, lighting up a fresh cigarette. 'The tooth fairy brought it.'

Howarth smiled and shook his head. 'Thanks all the same. If this is as good as it looks, payment will be made in the normal way.'

It was the contact's turn to smile. 'I'd be disappointed if you told me any different.'

'Lights.'

At Stronik's command, the lights in the conference room dimmed. There was the hum of an electric motor as a wooden panel dropped down to reveal a projector screen. Overhead the red, blue and green lights of a video projection system clicked into life. Horizontal flickering lines appeared across the screen and then assorted TV images of the aftermath of the Tokyo sarin attack.

There was footage of unrest in Europe: neo-Nazi burnings of refugee hostels in Germany; the attack on the World Trade Center and the Pentagon; street violence including Britain's Poll Tax riots and the success of the National Front in France; trouble on the streets of Belfast; unrest in Indonesia; violent protests at meetings of the World Bank and G8; car-bombings in Israel; headlines of political scandals affecting politicians in Britain, Belgium, France and Italy. The presentation continued.

The impression was of a world in upheaval, of unstable societies ill at ease with themselves, left rudderless by a generation of inadequate politicians concerned more with personal ambition than tackling fundamental political problems. It was powerful, hard-hitting propaganda.

The video stopped. The lights were switched back on.

'Perhaps you are wondering why I have shown you these things.'

'It is like Weimar,' Thielstrom muttered under his breath. 'Weak leadership, moral drift.'

'Precisely so,' Stronik said. 'We have used these problems before. We can do so again.'

Straker stirred in his seat. 'You think the time we have waited for has come?'

Stronik nodded enthusiastically. 'Yes, the time is now. Democracy is failing again. We must use all the methods that democracy provides in order to eliminate it. As the Führer himself wrote, a movement like ours will never die. The correctness of our ideas, the purity of our will, our supporters' spirit of self-sacrifice, will always enable us to rise from repression stronger then ever. Our purity shall overcome the decay and corruption.'

Rami noticed that Hümmler appeared disinterested by the discussion around him. Hümmler, he guessed, was most like himself of all the men assembled in the room: a man with a preference for action. Hümmler appeared happy to let Straker do his talking for him. Of course, plans and theories are always necessary, but it is direct action that achieves true results. No war has been won with words, no peace brought about through negotiation—other than negotiation backed up by the hard threat and reality of violence.

'Three pre-conditions are key,' Stronik continued. 'One, the indoctrination of youth. Two, the escalation of hate. Three, a hard core sworn in for street battles. Gentlemen, we have precisely such conditions today, particularly in the Middle East where we have focused so much of our effort. Now those same conditions are spreading here to Europe. All that is required is for us to provide the trigger. And we already have that trigger. We have tried it in the field and proved that it will work. And once our supporters are free and can rise again, we shall give them direction, shall channel their energy of destruction to overthrow the failed systems, the failed leaders that bind us.'

'More importantly perhaps,' Thielstrom commented quietly. 'We now have the Maastricht Treaty.'

Straker smiled. 'Yes, Versailles without a war. Gentlemen, Europe is ours for the taking. And once we have Europe . . . '

The Mossad agent had lived in London for years, a small but expensive apartment on the second floor of an elaborate terrace close to Regent's Park. He liked the city, enjoyed its anonymity, its variety, its history and its warmth. Everyone knew the reality of his attachment as a 'special advisor' at the Israeli embassy and everyone turned a blind eye. Such attachments are the established, and accepted, standard cover for spies. His love of

London life was so great that long gone was the slim young man who had once filled the post. In its place was the portly middle-aged man who arrived late for his meeting at Vauxhall Cross and stamped his feet in the foyer to shake off the cold. Only one thing had not been changed by the passing years: the brilliance of his mind. He was still rated amongst the most effective and perceptive of the Mossad's field agents. With London functioning as a place of exile for so many different Middle-Eastern groups and interests, Israel's need for good agents capable of producing valuable product had never been greater.

The British Intelligence Service's Vauxhall Cross building never ceased to amaze him. It was an extravagance he found ironic in view of the cuts in the Service's field operations. Designed by the post-modern architect Terry Farrell, the building had run severely over budget, clocking up a total bill well hidden from their political masters. Inside it was a dull, Whitehall-inspired dungeon with all the charisma of a bus shelter. From examining the Mossad's detailed architectural plans of the building, freely available on the intelligence circuit, he knew that lurking elsewhere inside it were a sports hall, computer rooms, library, restaurant, covered parking and archive stores. It was certainly a change from the old headquarters at Century House, a building that had generally been referred to as Gloom Hall because of its chronic lack of maintenance and facilities. It was somehow typical of the British that they should go from one extreme to another.

Cham was pacing up and down when the Mossad man was shown into his room. They exchanged brief, courteous greetings and then turned to a general discussion. The meeting was largely a formality, a routine long established. Occasionally useful details of mutual self-interest passed between them, but mostly there was little of any consequence. Today however the Mossad man brought with him information that he knew would interest Cham. After their coffee arrived, he took out two thin sheets of A4 paper and passed them over without a word.

Cham looked at them. The Mossad man watched him closely, sensitive to every reaction. Cham read the papers a second time before looking up. His manner was very controlled, his thoughts difficult to read.

'Interesting. What provenance are these?'

The Mossad man smiled. 'A1T.'

A1T (or 'A1 Trusted') meant it was regarded as a verified and trusted source of the highest calibre.

The SIS Deputy Chief nodded and placed the papers on his desk.

'I'll have our people look into this.'

'You understand,' the Mossad man said, leaning forward. 'The importance we attach to this matter? The events of recent European history are with us still.'

'Of course I understand,' Cham reassured him. 'But you must know that reports of this nature reach us frequently. If I believed every report that crossed this desk, fanatical groups that threaten the very foundation stones of democracy are all around us. On investigation such things often turn out to be a handful of cranks, a lonely old man and his dog, or a couple of crack-crazed teenagers, not the organised conspiracy that we feared.'

'But I offer you my personal assurance that this is different.' The Mossad man was like a hawk, Cham's every word, his every intonation was inspected and analysed. There was something in Cham's manner, in his response, that made him suspicious. 'There is no doubt about this information.'

Cham smiled. 'If that is true, why have you brought this to me? Doubtless, your own organisation is already active. Whilst we can look into this, you must understand we have many other active projects of longer standing. And in any case, this one is political.'

'Our whole business is political,' the Mossad man murmured.

'Oh, of course, of course,' Cham accepted. 'Leave this with me. Next time we meet, I shall update you on developments.'

'As you wish.' The Mossad man was now convinced. His true purpose in visiting Cham had been to test him, to find out if the indications that Cham himself was involved were true. There was no longer any doubt: Cham *was* involved. The Mossad man would report his findings. What happened after that was not a matter for him.

After the Mossad man's departure, Cham took the documents and shredded them. He was beginning to worry. Too many people were asking awkward questions. Hamilton's inclinations were sound: they would need to accelerate their plan.

And some of these dangerous loose ends would have to be sorted out before they threatened to unravel the entire project.

'Mr Brewer?'

The tall man in the light grey suit was waiting for him outside his flat. Brewer did not notice him until it was too late. Now he stood between Brewer and the front door. He was a gaunt figure, his face long and angular with a jutting triangular chin. His hair was dark and clipped short. A thin scar ran from below his right eye to the edge of his lip, the memento of a knife wound, but it suited his face.

'Correct,' Brewer replied. 'And you're in my way.'

'I won't be long.'

'That's right,' said Brewer and moved to push past him. The man raised his arm and blocked him.

'I want a word,' the man said.

'You've had several already,' Brewer said. He struck quickly and dislodged the man's arm. Before the man reacted, Brewer stepped past him and opened the front door. He waved casually towards it and smiled.

'Please. Why don't you step inside?'

Now it was the man's turn to hesitate. He had lost control of the situation, lost the advantage. After a moment, he moved forwards and into the flat. Brewer followed him.

'Now what is all this?' Brewer demanded. 'I would offer you a cup of tea, but I only offer tea to my friends. I may be wrong, but I get the distinct impression you are not now and will never be a friend. Therefore, no tea.'

Brewer crossed into the kitchen and filled the kettle, ignoring the bloodstain on the floor where he had interviewed his previous tail. The man followed him.

'You must stop your current line of enquiry.'

The plug snapped into the socket. Brewer flicked it on and took a tin of tea from the cupboard.

'Earl Grey,' he said, holding it up. 'My favourite.'

He popped a teabag into a mug and replaced the tin on the shelf.

'You have been lucky so far, Mr Brewer.' The man stepped closer. 'But your luck has run out.'

'Do you think so? I'm not so sure.' Brewer checked the milk in the fridge. It was a bit high but it would do. 'I know the purists don't approve,' he said. 'Milk in Earl Grey. Very English, don't you think? How is Mr Thielstrom?'

'I'm not playing games, Mr Brewer. The man who followed you before made too many mistakes. They will not be repeated.'

'Ah, I remember him,' Brewer said. 'How is he?'

'Dead, Mr Brewer.'

The noise of the boiling kettle and the click of its shut-off filled the silence. The mood had suddenly changed and Brewer sensed it. This man and the people who worked with him were not playing.

Brewer stepped forwards and jabbed a pointing finger into the man's chest. 'Tell Thielstrom that he's wasting his time. He can threaten all he likes, but it doesn't work with me. You may have a big organisation behind you, but so do I.'

The man smiled. 'Do you really, Mr Brewer?' He leaned closer. 'You're alone, Mr Brewer. And we can pick you off any time we like. Take a look at the paper. Page seven.'

The man pulled a copy of the *Evening Standard* from his pocket and left it on the table.

'I hope we don't need to meet again.'

'The feeling's mutual,' Brewer said.

He watched while the man turned and left and then poured the boiling water onto the teabag before reaching out to look at the paper.

It was on page seven. A photo of a man found dead in the Thames. Brewer recognised the face: his shadow from the previous day. Whoever they were, Brewer had a nasty feeling the man was right: they could pick off anyone, anytime they liked. Now he had been warned. If his guess was right, there would be no more warnings.

The next time they would kill him.

Four hours after passing over the document provided by his contact, together with a note requesting verification, DI Howarth was instructed to report to Deputy Assistant Commissioner John Buckley. DAC Buckley was in overall charge of SO12 and Howarth was surprised to receive the unusual request.

He entered Buckley's office directly from the corridor rather than through the secretary's office. Buckley was seated behind the desk leafing through a file. He indicated to Howarth to sit opposite him. Having risen through the ranks, Buckley was no stickler for pointless formalities.

'How are things in CE, Inspector? Keeping busy?'

'Have you ever known it any other way?'

Despite the London Mayor's best efforts, financial constraints on Scotland Yard's budget at a time of rapidly escalating workloads were a rumbling complaint across all levels of staff. Buckley smiled and looked down at the file in front of him.

'Interesting material you've come up with.'

Howarth shrugged. 'I assumed it was a fabrication despite the quality of the source.'

Buckley leaned across the desk. 'And who is the source?'

Howarth hesitated. 'Is the document true?'

'It contains interesting information, some of which we can authenticate.' He sighed and leant back in his chair. 'I take it you don't want to reveal the source?'

'He came to me in confidence.'

'And what did you promise him?'

'The usual payment if the information was true. If not, nothing.' Howarth replied.

'And he was happy with that?'

'I've worked with him before. He's reliable more often than not.'

'I expect he is. I certainly wouldn't want some wild-tongued fool running around with material like this.' Buckley sat and thought for a time. 'I'm going to have to refer this one higher. If it is accurate, we shall need to be careful. And I think they're going to want to know where it originated.'

Howarth bit his lower lip. 'I'm not sure I can do that, sir.'

Buckley was not happy to be called 'sir'. He took it as the snub it was intended to be: a sign that Howarth was distancing himself, resented the probing at his source. Informants were always to be guaranteed anonymity except in very exceptional circumstances.

'Don't take it like that. You've seen the report. If it is true, what action do you think we should take?'

Howarth had anticipated the question. 'We don't have any choice. We'll need a full-scale surveillance, maybe even to run someone undercover.'

'Exactly my thoughts.' Buckley tapped a finger thoughtfully on the desk. 'I'll discuss this with the Commissioner or one of the Assistant Commissioners to make sure we've covered our backs. But you'd better prepare yourself for some flack. I think we're going to have to run with it. Make sure you handle yourself properly on this one, won't you? I think it's going to be big.'

That would turn out to be the greatest understatement of the year.

12

Simon Gilbert and his colleagues from the Mossad spent several days discussing options at their three-star hotel in Lincoln, Nebraska. The support team was a tight-knit and highly accomplished group of snatch and run experts more accustomed to rescuing hostages and eliminating terrorists than playing a game of wait and see. They were impatient to move in on the compound and found little pleasure in the routine drag of surveillance work. In five days of intensive observation, Rami had not once left the compound. But there was a stream of other temporary visitors: they were photographed and the digital images transmitted securely to Tel Aviv via encrypted satellite phone. Food supplies and other unmarked lorries arrived, unloaded and departed. The compound was a fully functional miniature village.

And then Gilbert received new instructions: they were to infiltrate the compound, to discover what was happening inside and report back as a matter of priority. This was no trivial request. They could not go in overtly: that would reveal their hand, reveal that they were monitoring the compound. That would only drive the Nazis underground and make them more difficult to penetrate. No, it meant running someone undercover, someone who was prepared to take the risk of being discovered and shot. Or worse.

The new instructions made it clear that Tel Aviv believed something of major significance was happening. But none of the immediate support team were suited to penetrating the compound. It required someone of unquestionable background and authenticity. Someone the Nazis would believe was one of their own. Missions of this kind were normally years in planning and execution: this time they had no such luxury.

Gilbert contacted Tel Aviv. He told them his requirements: until Tel Aviv identified a suitable agent, the surveillance operation would continue.

While Yellow Hawk was busy being briefed in Washington, things started to roll on the ground. The special agent in charge at Omaha moved quickly to raise a crack team and establish an initial surveillance operation in Lincoln, where there had been a positive ID of Schengel following a routine check on the compound.

The Bureau employs a highly devolved field structure. Each field office is run largely autonomously by a special agent in charge (SAC), generally with the assistance of several deputies, supervisors and unit chiefs. The SAC is the most important figure to most special agents. It is him (and almost all are male) who makes a decision on which operations to pursue and which to drop, and which agents to use. There are from time to time important exceptions: the Waco operation was conceived and run by Washington. The Lincoln compound operation was similar: Washington had identified its role, linked it with the arrival of Helmut Schengel and briefed local agents on the possible problem, but the local SAC was given autonomy to run the operation itself.

Yellow Hawk was selected by his SAC to run the operation. Control was now largely devolved to him. If he conducted it well, he knew it would increase his chances of promotion to SAC. Becoming an SAC is the goal of most ambitious Bureau agents: it offers a high degree of personal control and discretion which is rare in almost any organisation, perhaps most similar to a battle commander given carte blanche in a war.

On his return from Washington, Yellow Hawk collected his car from the airport parking lot. Before he climbed in, he conducted a careful ritual. With the aid of a mirror, he checked the underside. It would not be the first time an agent had found his car rigged with explosives. It looked clean. He unlocked the trunk and retrieved his Heckler and Koch HK54, the model with the telescopic stock, from the locked, armoured compartment. He checked it, pumping through a few rounds. The HK54 uses 9mm Parabellum ammunition, weighs in at just over two and a half kilos and can deliver six hundred and fifty rounds per minute, although its standard magazine holds only thirty rounds.

He placed the HK54 on the passenger seat in the front and then checked his 9mm Colt Commander automatic and slipped it into a holster on his hip. Several other items from the trunk he placed on the rear seat, including a bullet proof vest. Finally he climbed inside and keyed the ignition. From the outside, the Cadillac looked like any other car, although the careful observer might wonder why so many aerials were necessary alongside the roof and the top of the trunk. Inside the car was an assortment of mobile phones, pagers and GPS equipment, and two receivers— one homed on the FBI despatch network, the other to the local police department.

He drove out from the airport and past the hotels, heading towards downtown Omaha. During Yellow Hawk's absence in Washington, good progress had already been made by the local field office. Schengel had been positively identified in Lincoln. Yellow Hawk's SAC had already laid the groundwork and established a suitable base of operations since Lincoln only operated a small resident agency. Within twenty-four hours of Washington notifying its interest, a small team moved in and started to watch the compound. Lincoln was only a short distance away, but it was likely Yellow Hawk would not see Omaha again for months.

He turned and drove past the expensive apartments on the western outskirts and once again wished he did not live alone. The problem was the Bureau had become more than a job. It occupied almost every moment of his week. On the occasional weekend he managed to meet up with old friends or family, to have a few drinks and wind down. But finding personal time became more and more difficult. The more involved and more successful he became at the Bureau, the harder it was to continue with any kind of private life. He knew several agents who were once married, but who were now separated or divorced. It was not an easy balance, particularly when there was the prospect of being called away at short notice to work on the other side of the country, often undercover. Some undercover operations continued for years and one successful agent had worked with the mafia for nearly six years and not seen his wife or children in all that time.

The following morning he drove to Lincoln and made an interesting discovery: the Bureau were not the only ones watching the compound. For a few days, Yellow Hawk wondered who the others were. The photographs transmitted to the Bureau revealed nothing: none of the unknown team observing the compound could be identified. No record could be found among the 75 million that the Bureau holds on file. That meant either they were very good, and had not previously been identified, or that they were not American. There was something about them, Yellow Hawk decided, that made him support the latter option.

He assigned a couple of agents to follow and identify them. The signals that came from time to time from their radio equipment proved impossible to decipher. Only one thing was for certain: these were no amateurs. He wondered for a time whether they might be from the Agency. Despite the fact that it has no remit to operate within the US itself, the CIA has from time to time done so. Details of the unidentified second surveillance team were sent to Interpol and overseas friendly agencies to see whether they could provide any positive identification. Under powers introduced after 9/11, Yellow Hawk could choose to have them arrested and held for the duration of the operation. But he would rather know who he was dealing with before he moved in.

The Bureau surveillance team turned their attention instead to the compound and its occupants. Which was when things started to become really interesting.

13

The tall, wrought-iron gates were closed. Beyond them a long gravel driveway was flanked by a series of mature oak trees. At the end of the driveway a large half-timbered house was visible, set back in its own grounds: the Hamilton residence. Brewer paid the taxi fare and waited until the driver was gone. The silence was a surprise, the only sounds the occasional drone of traffic passing on the road behind him and a lone singing blackbird. There was no-one to be seen.

The journey from London had been uneventful, but somewhere during that journey Brewer had entered another world. The rolling Sussex downs, the small wooden copses, the isolated villages and solitary residences were an alien world, a million miles from the crowded, closed-in streets of London. Brewer felt uncomfortable. At best he found the countryside a diversion, a momentary relaxation from the buzz of city life. At worst, it made him feel ill at ease. London was his city, his country, his home. Somewhere he always felt comfortable. Everywhere else was a foreign land. It had always seemed to him that the countryside, the isolation of its houses with no neighbours, was for loners, for the less social: those who liked the company of their fellow men always tended to live in the cities and towns.

He pushed at the gate and went through. The loose gravel crunched angrily beneath his feet. The day was unusually warm, one of those indulgent wintry days that like to masquerade as summer. As he walked slowly towards the house he saw a movement at an upstairs window. His arrival had not passed unnoticed.

The visit was Lord Northwood's suggestion. Benjamin Hamilton was once a highly respected lawyer and a noted Liberal councillor. More importantly, he had worked alongside Northwood during the Nuremberg trials as an assistant prosecutor. There were increasingly few of that generation alive and Brewer knew he was running against time. With all the official sources effectively blocked, he desperately needed information from first-hand witnesses. He was already convinced that the documents the Professor had seen in Moscow and the documents in the U-boat in Denmark were in some way connected with the post-war survival of the Nazi regime. But either the papers had been destroyed or they were being kept well out of his way. Anastasia's once-crazy stories were beginning to become more believable. All he needed now was some hard evidence, something more than speculation and theory. Without forensic, rock-solid proof he stood no chance of convincing Pendleton.

A single step led up to a covered wooden porch and a large, unpainted door. Before he had the chance to knock, the door opened to reveal a man in his late eighties. He was bald, with a large discolouration across his scalp, as if red wine had been spilled across it. His glasses were thick and heavy, their bifocal lenses distorting his pale grey eyes. The light cotton shirt with a scarf tied beneath an open collar and his light grey slacks and sandals were apparently designed to make him look or feel younger. Instead they merely made him appear eccentric.

'Mr Hamilton?' Brewer enquired. 'My name's Brewer. Lord Northwood called you.'

'Come in.' Benjamin Hamilton's voice was still firm and incisive, honed by years of public presentations in courtrooms. 'Funny old weather we're having, I thought we could sit outside. Enjoy it while it lasts.'

They went through the house, past its hallway furnished with original oil paintings and antique *objects d'arts* and into the rear garden. A long rolling lawn stretched away as far as the eye could see, merging into the nearby farm fields dark with the regular pinstripe furrows of recently ploughed soil. A pot of tea and delicate china teacups were already set up on a white garden table. They sat on either side of the table and Brewer waited while Hamilton poured Darjeeling from the pot.

'So,' Hamilton said, sitting back in his chair and fixing his gaze on Brewer. 'I understand from my old chum Northwood that you're digging into the past.'

Brewer nodded. 'Except that not all of it seems to have stayed put in the past. One or two people who should have stayed there seem to have a nasty habit of popping up.'

'It doesn't surprise me,' Hamilton commented. 'You can't kill an idea. People don't understand that. The Americans thought they could kill communism by killing communists. Nonsense. Once an idea exists it's here to stay. Al Qaeda demonstrate the same thing. However crazy an idea may be, there will always be someone to believe it, to follow it. It's the same with the Nazis. Nuremberg did what it was meant to. It was never meant to bring all the Nazis to justice. Just enough to get the message over, to demonstrate the world's disapproval.'

'And what about the banks?' Brewer enquired, sipping at the luke-warm tea.

Hamilton looked at him with a curious expression. 'The banks? Why should they concern you?'

Brewer shrugged. 'From what I understand, they kept the spoils of the Nazis' war, didn't they? It looks as if that money is still being used to support extremist movements and regimes, anything that will further the Nazi cause. That's rumoured to be why the Swiss banks have taken so long to make amends.'

There were two shots from the woodland to the side of the house. Birds rose startled and noisy into the air. A moment later there two more shots. Hamilton looked towards the noise.

'That'll be Mark.' He turned back to Brewer. 'Mark's my son. Come down to visit his old man for a few days. He's a Member of Parliament, you know. Tried to run for Parliament a couple of times myself. Never succeeded.' He sighed. 'Probably just as well.'

Hamilton fell silent and appeared to be thinking. Brewer was about to prompt him about the banks, when he suddenly spoke again.

'Northwood mentioned a name. Thielstrom, wasn't it?' His eyes locked firmly onto Brewer's.

'That's right.'

'Why him? Out of all the thousands of wretched old men you could choose from.'

Brewer smiled. 'That's difficult for me to answer, Mr Hamilton. Let's just say I have a personal interest. Do you know him?'

'Of him,' Hamilton replied slowly. 'And his book, of course. Caused a bit of a storm with its denial of the final solution. Personally I don't know why he bothered. Eichmann himself wrote in 1944 that the number of Jews killed amounted to nearly six million. It is not a matter to be questioned, it is a matter of regret.'

'Regret?' Brewer thought it a strange term to use for the systematic slaughter of millions of people.

'I'm afraid there's not much else I can tell you. For all I know Thielstrom's long been dead and buried.'

At that moment a man appeared around the corner of the house, a double-barrelled Purdey shotgun broken and resting over an arm. In the other hand he carried two wood pigeons. As he came closer Brewer recognised Mark Hamilton, Benjamin Hamilton's son. He was in his mid forties, his dark hair flicked back and his skin well-tanned. He wore casual country clothing of the type that only Saville Row can provide. There was an air of arrogance and certainty about him that Brewer instantly disliked.

'Afternoon, father.' He slapped the two pigeons down onto the ground and rested his gun beside them. 'Poor fare today, nothing but a pair of beastly pigeons. You didn't say you were expecting visitors.' He leaned forwards and thrust out his hand. 'Mark Hamilton.'

Brewer rose. 'Peter Brewer.'

'Still on the tea, father? Thought you'd have the stronger stuff out by now. Been boring you with his dull old anecdotes has he?'

'Not at all,' Brewer replied.

Mark Hamilton pulled up a chair and sat between them. 'So what's happening?'

'We were talking,' his father replied. 'About the past.'

'History you mean?' Mark Hamilton laughed. 'A pet hobby of my father's. I'm sorry. I didn't quite catch who you were. Not your name I mean. What you're doing here.'

'I'm a friend of Lord Northwood,' Brewer replied, exaggerating the truth.

'Northwood sent him here to pick my brains.'

Mark Hamilton frowned. 'About what?'

'Nuremberg. The Nazis.' Brewer hesitated. 'Thielstrom.'

There was no glimmer of recognition in the MP's face. He noticed that Hamilton senior was watching them both carefully. These two men knew something, but it was not about Thielstrom. So what were they hiding? Or was he just becoming overly suspicious and seeing shadows where there were none?

Mark Hamilton smiled. 'Rather a dull topic for a splendid day like this, surely? I never think there's much point digging up the past. No good ever comes of it. Can't change the way things were. Look forward, that's the key. Let's talk about the weather instead. Much more interesting, don't you think?'

The conversation had not been promising before Mark Hamilton's arrival. With his presence, Brewer sensed the conversation was going nowhere, that he was going to learn nothing.

'Well, perhaps Mr Hamilton,' Brewer said, addressing Hamilton senior. 'If you do recall anything that you think might interest me, you'd be good enough to call?'

'Of course, of course,' the old man responded, taking the offered piece of paper on which Brewer had written a contact number.

Brewer finished his tea and made his excuses. He called a taxi from the house and left.

After his departure both Hamiltons sat for a time without speaking to each other. Finally Mark Hamilton stirred.

'I have to make a call,' he said.

He went into the house and looked up a number on a piece of paper pasted inside his diary. It was a direct line, answered before the end of the first ring. Hamilton recognised the voice at the far end.

'Cham. We have a problem. There's some guy been snooping around here. Name of Peter Brewer. Not sure who he works for. Could be police, security service or just a journalist out of his league. He knows something, keeps going on about some guy called Thielstrom. Mean anything to you? No, me neither. But if he is digging around he may stumble across other items, if you understand me.'

They spoke for a few more minutes and then Hamilton hung up. One thing about dealing with Cham: he was deadly efficient. And right now that's exactly what he needed to be—deadly.

When Brewer called Lord Northwood and told him about his abortive visit to Sussex, the peer was puzzled that Benjamin Hamilton had not been more forthcoming.

'Very odd. Not like him at all. Let me think.' A pause. Then— 'There is someone else you could try.'

He suggested that Brewer make contact with a man called Jonny Miller. Miller was a former National Front member who finally turned against them, in the process revealing to the anti-fascist movement a wealth of detail about the NF's membership and operating methods, including its links with the wider fascist movement around the world. His infiltration had ultimately destroyed the NF.

'Nuremberg was a long time ago,' Northwood commented. 'But the same ideas still keep circulating.'

It was an almost exact echo of Benjamin Hamilton's sentiments.

'Jonny Miller may know something more current about Thielstrom. He's still in touch with sympathisers inside the movement, what's happening now, not back in the past.'

Miller's flat was in walking distance of Gibson Gardens, tucked away in a Dalston council block. The morning was damp, a fine, opaque drizzle in the air that flicked specks onto Brewer's glasses and cast a chill in the bones. The flat was in a 1940s brick-built four-storey block, the type with external balconies and communal washing lines. Outside, a car with its wheels removed rested on bricks, its guts burnt out. Sickly pigeons with club feet sat picking at the festering, putrid contents of a bin. The staircase smelt of urine, and graffiti covered the peeling white paint with exposed cheap brickwork beneath. As Brewer reached the second floor, a pack of children raced past him, spraying an aerosol of paint in all directions and screaming and knocking on front doors. He ducked back in time to miss the paint and watched as they hurtled down the staircase, swearing and cursing in loud, excited voices, a trail of smoke and dope left in their wake. Things had certainly changed since his childhood: parents had cared about their kids then.

Flat 24 had a bright orange door and a rusting knocker, which he rapped twice. Somewhere overhead a hi-fi played loud reggae music, with only its repetitive base line audible. The door opened.

'Yeah?'

'Jonny Miller?'

'Yeah.'

'Lord Northwood gave me your name.'

Miller stared at him suspiciously. Miller was older than Brewer had expected, somewhere in his early fifties. His greying hair was clipped back close to the scalp, making him look bald and probably older than he was. He wore a baggy pair of jeans, walking boots and a T-shirt that was small enough to emphasise a pronounced beer gut.

'Press, are you?'

'Just looking for some facts. Northwood thought you could be the man I'm looking for.'

Miller scowled and went back inside the flat. Brewer followed. The hallway had a bare concrete floor painted blue, the walls plain white emulsion. Thin wooden doors led off in various directions. Beyond one of them Brewer just had time to catch a glimpse of a stained mattress on the floor and a sleeping bag before his glasses steamed up from the central heating. He took them off and wiped them on his shirt, moving into the living room with its thin grey carpet, a sofa with foam bursting from its seat and a veneered wooden table with four mismatched chairs. A small black and white TV sat on the floor in the corner beside a metal framed door that opened out onto a small balcony where laundry flapped listlessly in the damp autumnal air.

'You want a drink?'

Brewer shook his head.

Miller grunted and left the room. Brewer watched him enter the tiny kitchen across the hallway and fill a glass from a duty-free litre bottle of blue label Smirnoff. When he returned, he motioned Brewer to sit opposite him at the table. Miller sat and sipped at the glass, staring without blinking. The bass beat of the reggae came thumping through the ceiling.

'So what is it you want?'

'I'm after some background on the Nazi movement and one person in particular. I think you may be able to help me.'

'Maybe I will,' Miller replied, his eyes unmoving. 'Maybe I won't. Depends on motives, see. What you doing it for?'

'It's probably best if we don't discuss that.'

Miller grunted. Brewer felt uncomfortable. Miller's glass was already nearly empty, his eyes still fixed unmoving on his face. Brewer had seen the same look before, in the faces of soldiers suffering from shell shock. But in Miller's case it had to be something else: probably alcohol, possibly something stronger.

For the first time Miller looked away, his eyes staring towards the window, but not focused on anything. 'You won't change anything, you know. Whatever it is you're up to.' He stood up and looked back at Brewer. 'You sure you don't want something to drink?'

Brewer shook his head. Miller fetched himself another vodka, talking as he went.

'Thing is with these people, the only way to make them sit up and take notice is direct action.'

'Which people?' Brewer was confused.

'The Nazis, of course. Who do you think? We're not talking about the flaming cats' protection league are we?'

'Northwood said you'd been with the NF.'

'Northwood is old and talks too much for his own good,' Miller said shortly and returned to his chair. 'That was a long time ago. I was young, didn't think about what I was doing. It was easy to blame someone else for my problems. They gave me easy answers. Blame the Jews and the pakis and the niggers, they said. Hitler wrote all that about the Jews. Blame them for everything, eradicate the vermin. It's in *Mein Kampf* plain as day.' He sipped from the vodka and laughed. 'Bullshit. The only problem with this country is the type of people that support the NF, the English Nationalists. It's them we gotta tame, them we gotta sort out. Thick as shit. But you can't underestimate them. They're nasty, and I mean real nasty. And there's more sympathise with them than you'd think. The boot boys are just the front line, just the visible face. Scratch the surface of half the people round here and somewhere you'll find they sympathise. Maybe not with everything they stand for, but with a hell of a lot.'

There was a look in Miller's eyes that Brewer distrusted. He had seen the look before: in the eyes of religious zealots, in the eyes of fanatical businessmen and corrupt politicians. It was a look approaching madness, a sure belief that only your own views were right, that everyone else was wrong and you had to prove to them they were wrong. It was a danger signal, a red flag. Miller was a powerfully built man and Brewer had no doubt he was accustomed to using physical force to win an argument when words failed.

'So how do they operate? How do you prevent them operating?'

Miller looked at Brewer for a time without speaking. 'You know nothing, don't you? Just another dopey bystander.'

Miller finished his second glass. He rose to fetch another and when he returned, crossed over to the balcony door and stood staring at a woman in a bra hanging out her laundry on the high-rise block opposite. Brewer slipped a cigar from his pocket, clipped it and lit up.

'They're clever,' Miller said quietly. 'You don't know how clever. They know what they're doing, the men behind them. The thugs you see on the football terraces, they're just the foot soldiers, puppets following orders. They print *John Bulldog* for them. You seen that?'

Brewer shook his head. Miller looked at him scornfully, his opinion confirmed.

'They make it like the *Sun*, nice and easy to read. Only they fill it full of spite, sort of like the *Daily Mail*, although even more spiteful, it that's possible. That's what they give them on the terraces. Keep the lads happy with tales of Asians attacking 'English' people, blacks getting jobs just because they're black. But they produce other stuff too, real clever stuff. Stuff you can't knock so easily. Stuff that appears to be straight history, praising the greatness of the Anglo-Saxons. Tributes to great European thinkers. Only not the Jews of course. Marx and people. They're denigrated for being corrupt. The collapse of the Soviet Union and the behaviour of the Israeli state have made that easier for them. Now they point and say 'See what the ideas of a Jew do for you.' They know what they're doing.' For the first time since arriving, Miller seemed calm and thoughtful. 'They've got some crafty people working for them. They're re-writing history and you know why?'

Brewer shook his head. Miller was clearly on his favourite hobbyhorse now. He needed to get the conversation round to the subject of Thielstrom. Miller moved away from the window and came and sat opposite him, leaning close, his breath reminding Brewer of the old copying machines at his school: a smell of pure alcohol.

'It's like Hitler said, propaganda is the key. Drip, drip, drip. Pollute the waters of society with your own ideas, slowly at first. Repeat it time and again. Like arsenic, it's a slow poison, but you gently increase the dose, start to see its effects. People always want someone else to blame, someone to scapegoat. And it's working. More and more people are drifting to the right. Not just in this country, but across Europe, the States, the Pacific. And the Nazis know more would join their movement, that many support their views. But they have a problem. They have a real problem persuading people to support them. At least, out in the open.' He stopped a moment to drink from his glass. 'There's the Holocaust. It's a real stain on their past. So what they're doing is making out it never happened, that it was a conspiracy to condemn the Nazis at the end of the war, to justify what the Allies had done with the bombing of Europe.'

Something clicked. Miller had just answered a question: the significance of Thielstrom's book. Denying the Holocaust was exactly what it did. So maybe that was its purpose: laying the groundwork to cleanse the Nazi ideology of the main accusation thrown at it. Without the Holocaust, Nazi ideology could be rehabilitated, presented as just another political creed alongside all the others: and one that had worked, or so its supporters claimed—at least in its early days.

'You say the people behind them are intelligent, that they know what they're doing. The ones who pull the strings. Who are they? Who do they answer to?'

Miller stared at him. 'I told you. They're clever. You don't think they're gonna let the boot soldiers know who's running them do you?' He shook his head and stared hard at Brewer. 'Why don't you come on an action?'

'An action?' Brewer had an unpleasant premonition of what that might mean.

'Yeah, an action,' Miller said. 'We're planning to do over the English Nationalists place. Sometime soon.' He smiled unexpectedly, revealing a row of broken and stained teeth. He leaned close to Brewer and grabbed hold of his jacket. 'You tell that to anyone, you're dead. I can see from the look in your eyes, you don't even begin to understand, do you? Another bleeding heart liberal. The only way to deal with this scum is to tackle them head on. Kick them where it hurts, smash them up. I know what I'm talking about, believe me. You fight fire with fire.'

He let go of Brewer and stood again, pacing restlessly up and down. 'We've gotta stop them before they get strong again.

And they will, you gotta believe that. They're growing all the time.'

'But how does it help?' Brewer asked slowly. 'Tackling the front line's not going to remove the generals, is it?'

Miller stopped as if Brewer had slapped him. He reached out a wavering hand and pointed at Brewer, his eyes black with anger and hatred.

'Don't you come here telling me what to do. You get that? What are you doing here anyway? Writing stupid words, is that it? Think that's going to change their fucking minds, do you?'

He stood there waiting. Brewer shifted uneasily in his seat and puffed slowly at his cigar, wondering how best to handle Miller. Finally he spoke.

'I just want some names or places. Somewhere I can get to meet these people.'

Miller continued to stare at him without saying a word. The music upstairs stopped and a pair of footsteps crossed noisily above. A moment later and the music started again. The clogs returned across the ceiling. Suddenly Miller snapped out of it, as if someone had jerked on the strings of a marionette.

'Yeah, yeah. You want to meet them.'

He snatched the glass from the table and downed its contents in one. As soon as it was finished, he fetched another from the kitchen, sat opposite Brewer and looked at him thoughtfully.

'So what is it you're after?'

The change in mood was sudden and disconcerting.

'Any background you have on the present-day Nazi operation. How it organises and finances itself. And anything you know about Thielstrom.'

'Edward Thielstrom?' Miller spat out the words. 'You and a million others.'

'He's hard to find?'

'Always on the move. He's on Israel's hit list.'

'You can't know that,' Brewer protested.

Miller smiled. 'I know the man's form. Believe me, he's on

their list.' He took a more moderate sip of his vodka. 'You know about ODESSA?'

Brewer nodded. It was the organisation responsible for smuggling former Nazis out of Europe at the end of the war.

'It was only one of many organisations that were set up. You want to know about the others?'

Brewer nodded. 'If that would be useful.'

Miller smiled. 'You'd better hold on tight because you're not going to believe it. These guys are organised, and I mean really organised. All these different cover groups all the way across the world. They're slowly coming together.' He stopped and shuddered. 'One day, someone's going to trigger them and then they're going to be ready. They're going to be back out there in the streets, smashing windows, killing, taking their creed of hatred and death into every household once again. You can see it in little pockets already. And their numbers are growing. One day soon there's going to be enough of them, they'll overwhelm the police. Worse than that, they'll become the police. They've done if before. They can do it again. We're mad it we don't understand that, if we don't learn from the past. The more these extremist groups such as Al Qaeda frighten and intimidate people, the more rightwards our politics will drift. People don't like uncertainty and fear. And that's when they'll start to turn back to the fascists for easy answers.'

Brewer thought back to Northwood's words about the Nazi's survival after the war. With Miller's gloomy picture, for the first time Brewer began to believe that Anastasia had been right, that the Nazis were still very much alive and kicking. The only question now was: what were they planning to do next? And how soon?

Brewer sighed and looked up at Miller. 'I think I might have that drink now.'

14

Pendleton did not look pleased when Brewer came through his office door and slammed it shut behind him.

'We need to talk,' Brewer advanced on Pendleton's desk and leant over it.

'Brewer? What are you doing here? You're supposed to be on leave, to avoid any embarrassment over this police enquiry. And before you start to argue, the instruction came from the top. The very top. Even if I wanted to, there's nothing I can do.'

Brewer slumped into the seat beside the desk. 'I'm not here to argue.'

Pendleton grunted. 'That'll be a refreshing change. But what is it you do want? You know damn well we have to wait for the police to finish their investigation.'

'Don't tell me you believe I killed Anastasia?' Brewer mocked him. 'I can see the headlines now, can't you? Desk Duty Boy Kills Russian Beauty.'

'I believe nothing, good or bad,' Pendleton murmured. 'Until I see the evidence. However, I still don't understand what you were doing there.'

'Neither do I,' said Brewer. 'I was a damn fool. Someone set me up, that's all I know.'

'Well it wasn't anyone here. No-one knew she was in our safe house.'

Brewer raised his eyebrows in surprise. 'So it *was* ours?'

Pendleton fell silent. It was a bad slip and he knew it.

'For god's sake, Pendleton. It's hardly a state secret now, is it? Someone knew she was there. That's why they sent me there. Find out who fingered me and you might start to crack this case.'

Brewer sat back in the chair. 'Anyhow, that's not what I came about. I wondered what you knew about GDM?'

'GDM? Is that a company?'

'Oh come on, don't bullshit me Pendleton. GDM Matériels. It's a defence consultancy business.'

Pendleton shrugged. 'And why would you expect me to know about that?'

'It's a front of some kind. It has to be.

Pendleton examined Brewer before replying. 'You've been pursuing this case, haven't you?'

'That's my job,' Brewer responded.

Pendleton shook his head. 'No. Your job is what I tell you it is. And right now you're meant to be sitting at home with slippers on your feet and a cup of hot cocoa in your hand watching Kilroy.'

'What I do when I'm on leave is my own business, isn't it?'

There was a knock at the door. A security guard opened it and looked in.

'Do you need assistance, sir?'

Pendleton looked at Brewer and for a moment it was in the balance. Finally he sighed and shook his head.

'No thank you. This is purely social.'

The door closed. Pendleton looked at Brewer.

'Aren't you going to say thank you?'

'You owe me that,' Brewer replied. 'And a lot more besides.'

Pendleton shrugged. 'Perhaps. Now what's all this about?'

Brewer briefed Pendleton on recent developments, his meetings with Northwood, Hamilton and Miller. It was hard to gauge Pendleton's reaction. His face showed no emotion as Brewer spoke about the trail he was pursuing. But his right hand drummed slowly on the desk, a sure sign he was interested. When Brewer finished, Pendleton sat back in his chair and pressed the fingertips of his hands together.

'Brewer,' Pendleton spoke softly. 'Why are you such a pain in the backside?'

Brewer smiled. 'It's in the genes, sir.'

Pendleton sniffed. 'Not only do you insist on disobeying orders, but you're working well out of territory. If the other lot get to hear about this, they're not going to be happy.'

'I thought we were part of Europe now,' Brewer responded. 'Therefore under the jurisdiction of the European Controller. Which just happens to be you.'

'A naïve mistake, I suppose, to think Britain is anything to do with Europe,' Pendleton commented. 'So what do you want from me?'

'I keep running into brick walls.'

'It hasn't stopped you before.'

'I'd like to know more about Professor Beatty, the significance of the files. It's all part of this.' Brewer leaned forwards. 'Am I in this alone, sir? Or are others working on it?'

Pendleton sighed. 'What do you think? You know how tightly stretched we are.'

'But what about the Professor's murder? You can't tell me that it's been sorted.'

'No, it hasn't,' Pendleton confirmed. 'But the case is closed.'

'Tell me you're joking.'

'I gather it was not proving itself to be a profitable cost centre,' Pendleton commented. 'Some accountancy issue like that. The word came down from God to concentrate on cases that could be solved. Something about hitting our chartermark for projected caseload resolution and public sector benchmarking.'

'Sir. This case needs a whole team assigned to it. I can't do it alone'

'You know the way it works, Brewer. Bring me evidence, not idle speculation and accounts of conversations. What is it our cousins say: 'show me the money?' Anyway, I have already made it clear. You're not officially working on anything at the moment.'

'Meaning you don't mind if I pull something off myself, but if it goes wrong you'll leave me sitting in shit?'

'You do have such a wonderful way with words, Brewer,' Pendleton replied. 'Have you never thought of the Diplomatic

Corps? Anyhow, I dare say you are worrying unnecessarily. I'll speak with the other lot. I'm sure they'll have it covered.'

'You can't mean that, sir,' Brewer said. 'You'd do better speaking with the Yard.'

'Brewer. When will you understand that there are certain rules of diplomacy and etiquette that one has to follow in my position? We have to work firstly with our sister service, not with the Yard whatever we may think of their respective abilities. It's up to Thames House to co-ordinate with the Yard, not us.'

'And will you believe a word they say?' Brewer asked.

A half-smile hovered around the corners of Pendleton's lips. 'I shall let others do the talking. I think someone more senior than me might elicit the best answers.'

'Just promise me one thing,' Brewer said, rising from his seat and moving towards the door. 'You won't leave it to one of the accountancy boys, will you? They couldn't spot a problem if I thrust it down their throat and pulled it out their backside.'

'That, Brewer, is a particularly unpleasant image,' Pendleton remarked with distaste.

He watched as Brewer left and then picked up the telephone on the right side of his desk. 'Pendleton speaking. I wondered if I might have a moment of your time? Later this afternoon would be fine. Five thirty. Your office. Yes, goodbye, sir.'

Pendleton replaced the phone. He would hand the problem over to Cham. If Brewer was right, Pendleton did not want to be involved. He was getting too old to cope with the stress of uncertainty these days. Time to let his boss shoulder some of the burden. After all, what else is a manager for? Cham would know what to do with Brewer's information.

DI Howarth was kept waiting for forty-five minutes in Central Lobby at the House of Commons before Mark Hamilton condescended to meet him.

'We'll go to a colleague's office. More discreet,' Hamilton commented and lead him away along a warren of corridors lined with library shelving and into a small area packed with tiny offices.

'Take a seat.'

Hamilton waved him to a large green chair. Howarth briefly surveyed the office. The desk was piled high with Order Papers and back copies of Hansard. Several filing cabinets lined the edge of the room and shelves of books held the usual fare: Vachers, Dodds and a few other reference volumes. In the corner of the room were a couple of mugs and a steaming kettle. The view from the window showed the top of the inner courtyards, a ramshackle run of roofs, buildings and portacabins. The wind lashed the fine drizzle against the window, blurring the scene.

'Drink, Inspector?'

Howarth shook his head. 'No thank you.'

'As you wish.' Hamilton poured himself a tea and then sat down beside his desk. 'So what can I do for you Inspector? I trust I haven't overlooked any parking tickets?'

'Not my department,' Howarth responded. 'Something of more substance than that.'

Hamilton watched him closely, his eyes fixed on the Inspector's face trying to gauge his mood.

'I'm Special Branch,' Howarth continued.

'Ah,' Hamilton leaned back in his chair. 'Come to check up on my minders, have you?'

'No. Your protection squad are part of A. I'm CE.'

'It's all letters of the alphabet to me. That means . . . ?'

Howarth smiled. 'My area of interest is international terrorism, public order and investigation.'

'Ah. Must keep you busy in these troubled times,' Hamilton replied. 'But I must say, I had always thought that was the Thames House crowd.'

'There's a certain degree of overlap with the Security Service, that's no secret,' Howarth responded.

'Perhaps our Committee should start looking over your shoulder as well?'

Howarth smiled at the suggestion and hoped Hamilton was not serious. The 1994 Intelligence Services Act established the Parliamentary Intelligence and Security Committee to oversee the Security Service, the Secret Intelligence Service and GCHQ. Hamilton was a member of the Committee. The PISC was unusual: it did not report to Parliament as other Committees do, but met within the privacy of the Cabinet Office and reported directly to the Prime Minister, who was also responsible for appointing its members. The word on the rumour-mill was that the Committee had become a pain in the backside, constantly interfering and politicking.

To overcome the problem of the Committee, which they regarded as an unacceptable security risk given some of its members, the services had an understanding that they would work together in an unusual spirit of co-operation. It was felt important that the Committee should have little involvement in operational matters. This was achieved by diluting its effectiveness in a charm offensive that flattered the MP's egos and filled their heads with irrelevant and somewhat suspect 'inside' information. Not that the MPs' complained: they made too much money writing books about the intelligence services full of the nonsense and false histories that were given to them by the services' spin-doctors.

'We have received certain intelligence,' Howarth said, deliberately maintaining a neutral tone. 'That we are currently assessing with a view to an investigation. This information relates to the illegal movement and sales of armaments.'

Hamilton did not react, but Howarth sensed that he was consciously controlling himself.

'And what relevance does this matter have to me? Are you informing me in my capacity as a member of the Committee or for some other reason?'

Howarth paused a moment and watched a pigeon land on the window sill outside, seeking shelter from the rain. He needed to be careful. Whether Hamilton was involved or not, the way he handled this could affect the whole course of his investigation. The wrong word now could destroy the investigation before it had properly begun.

'There appears to be a possibility, and at the moment it is

only a possibility, that someone has been using a certain company, namely GDM Matériels, to deal in illegal shipments.'

Hamilton frowned. 'Are you certain?'

'No,' Howarth said. 'As I say, the information is new. However, I thought it would only be a courtesy to inform you of these accusations as soon as possible.'

'Thank you. I appreciate that,' Hamilton responded. 'You obviously understand how sensitive such matters can be.'

'Exactly,' Howarth replied. 'One word in the newspapers and the whole story could easily become distorted, blown out of all proportion. That would be most unfortunate.'

Hamilton leaned forwards, perhaps noticing the veiled threat in Howard's words. 'Do you have anything specific?'

His question was the first sign that the news meant more to him than it should. It looked as if the information was right. Hamilton wanted to know exactly what it was that the police had on him.

'Not really,' Howarth lied. 'And please be aware that GDM is only one of several companies mentioned in the information.'

In fact the information from Howarth's informant was very specific and very precise: and only mentioned GDM. Howarth wanted to rattle Hamilton enough to see where he ran, who he contacted, without frightening him off. Contrary to the impression Howarth had given, a full investigation was already under way involving a squad of ten highly experienced officers. Hamilton's phone was being monitored, his mail intercepted, his movements watched.

The idea that placing a phone tap requires the permission of the Home Secretary has long been an irrelevance. With modern methods of telecommunications interception, a "tap" is no longer required. An appropriate software configuration within the public telephone network's digital switchboards is enough to ensure that details of all calls are automatically tracked and recorded without any specialised device being required. Calls intercepted in this fashion by the police, security services and GCHQ number in the thousands on a regular basis. All mobile phone calls in the

UK are routinely intercepted for sampling and tracking by GCHQ, with some the target of prolonged surveillance. This information is generally freely exchanged with the NSA in America, part of the close partnership between the UK and the USA in all matters of intelligence and mutual self-interest.

The Special Branch operation would ensure that if Hamilton was directly involved with the illegal trading at GDM, it would be discovered. His A Squad minders had been briefed to report anything unusual. And it had already paid dividends. The fact that Hamilton was conducting an affair with his secretary could be useful information if Howarth needed to step up pressure on the former Minister.

'So do you think it will be necessary to investigate my company?' Hamilton enquired. His attempt to make it appear a casual question was contradicted by the intense scrutiny of his eyes.

Howarth shrugged. 'We're investigating a few other organisations at the top of the list first. If we find anything there, obviously we'll need to dig deeper. If we don't, then the whole case is likely to be dropped.'

Hamilton nodded, his relief evident. 'Good, good. That makes sense. But you will let me know if you're going to take things any further, won't you?'

Howarth stood. 'Of course I will, Mr Hamilton. Thank you for your time.'

'And thank you Inspector. You've been most helpful.'

As soon as Howarth left, Hamilton picked up the phone and dialled the direct line to Parke at GDM.

'Parke? I've had a visitor. PC Plod. There are suspicions about GDM.'

'Rubbish. It's watertight.' There was alarm in Parke's voice.

'Don't say anything on this line,' Hamilton warned. 'We need to talk. We also need to tell our friend. And soon. He may be able to pull levers.'

'I'll do that immediately,' Parke replied.

Good. Parke had understood the reference to contacting Cham.

'They won't find anything. There isn't anything to find.' Parke was trying hard to convince himself.

'I know that,' Hamilton responded, with less confidence. He did not share Parke's conviction that they had covered their tracks sufficiently well to withstand a detailed police investigation. And Howarth had been keeping something back, he was sure of that. They would need to be careful from now on.

Very careful.

By chance, Brewer arrived at GDM's head office within half an hour of Hamilton's call to Parke.

His meeting with Jonny Miller had provided enough information for Brewer to jump-start his investigation. It was a chance connection of facts that lead him to GDM's door. Brewer knew from his own research that Mark Hamilton was a director. And when Jonny Miller had mentioned GDM as well, claiming it had trading links with some of the regimes known to be harbouring former Nazis and sympathetic to the Nazi cause, Brewer's interest had been further stoked.

GDM's UK head office was situated above a bank near Piccadilly, within earshot of its ceaseless traffic and congestion. A cold wind blew from the north and specks of rain nibbled at Brewer's face and smeared his glasses as he stood outside the door and looked at the small collection of obscure plaques and company names. A group of damp and miserable pedestrians queued alongside him, waiting for access to the automatic teller. At that moment, a motorbike courier came out of the door. Brewer stepped smartly forwards and caught the door before it closed.

Inside was a flight of stairs covered in pale blue lino and walls painted a thick cream gloss. The door on the first floor was for a travel company. He moved on up to the second floor.

The decor changed from thickly painted gloss to half-boarded walls. The lighting was more discreet and a thick carpet lined the stairs. Instead of a cheap wooden fire door, there was a heavy oak door. This was GDM. He admired its subtle combination of luxury and security: the impressive oak was not only for show, it would also hold back a serious attempt to break through it.

Brewer tried the door. It was locked. He pressed the security buzzer and took the opportunity to examine the CCTV camera that had turned to follow his progress up the last flight of stairs. There was a delay, the buzz of a relay and the door opened an inch. He pushed it open and stepped through.

A wash of air-conditioning struck him, sending a shiver down his spine. He found himself standing on a thick pile carpet, the beige walls tastefully hung with framed pictures of armaments and weaponry. The lighting was atmospheric, provided by a mix of floor lamps and wall-mounted up-lighters. Ahead of him a young woman sat behind a desk, busy working on a computer recessed into its top. Beside it was a small telephone switchboard suitable for about eight extensions. It was a smaller operation than he had expected. Behind the desk and to the right was a half-glass door which he guessed led to the main offices.

The woman stopped for a moment, looked up at him and smiled.

'Can I help you?'

'I'd like to have a word with Mr Hamilton, please,' Brewer said, advancing on the desk. 'The name's Brewer, Peter Brewer.'

'Is he expecting you?' There was a tinge of a cockney accent in her voice, masked by several intensive, and doubtless expensive, elocution lessons. Her hair was dyed blonde, the roots visible. Her eyes were a bright green, possibly from coloured contact lenses. Brewer guessed she was in her early twenties, with a deep tan that had certainly not come from the sun.

'We've met before,' Brewer replied, which was true.

'I'm afraid Mr Hamilton is rarely in the office. He's very busy at the House of Commons. Perhaps you would like to make an appointment?'

'Not really,' Brewer insisted. 'Is there no-one else I could speak with?'

'Possibly,' she replied. 'In connection with what?'

'Certain transactions, shipments if you like.'

'That sounds very vague. Can you be more specific?'

Brewer smiled. He could see why they had employed her as their secretary. She was a very effective front line of defence.

'I'll be more than happy to speak,' he replied. 'To the right person.'

She smiled at him, but her eyes flashed something less attractive. 'And you don't think I'm the right person, is that it?'

'No offence, but I only deal with directors,' Brewer responded. 'Now are you going to let me speak with one of them or not? I have a very busy schedule and you're wasting my time.'

Her smile vanished. 'I'll see if Mr Parke is free. One moment.'

She stood, pressed a button under the desk and went through the door behind it. Brewer leaned forward to see what she was typing on the screen. It was a letter. He moved round the desk and slipped into the chair. He flicked quickly through the documents on disk. There was nothing unusual: the customary quotes and invoices that he would expect to see in any small company. If GDM were up to anything underhand, then it looked possible the secretary genuinely knew nothing about it.

'I trust you found something interesting?'

The secretary had re-appeared behind him. He rose from the chair.

'You should upgrade. There's a newer version of Word, much better features,' he said.

'Mr Parke will see you. But he doesn't have much time. An important client is due to arrive any moment now.'

'That's fine,' Brewer responded. 'It won't take long.'

She showed him through to Parke's office. He found himself in a large room decorated with wood panelling and oil paintings of dull-looking bald men looking smug in suits. A small desk stood at one end, but the room was dominated by a long window and filled by a large mahogany meeting table around which stood at least a dozen chairs.

'Mr Parke, this is Mr Brewer.'

She gave Brewer a look evidently intended to shorten his natural life expectancy and closed the door a touch too loudly.

'You must ignore Miss Rilla,' Parke said, rising and moving around his desk. 'A very capable woman, but she has a short temper and is quick to judgement.'

Brewer recognised the posture and vocal characteristics of an ex-military officer as soon as Parke spoke. He had a powerful presence, a body language that conveyed authority without a word being spoken. Parke's black hair was gelled and cut short. He was wearing a blazer and tie instead of a suit.

'I apologise for arriving without an appointment,' Brewer said. 'I didn't intend to upset Miss Rilla.'

'Of course not.' Parke shook his hand, a firm handshake that made its presence felt long after it had finished.

Parke waved him to sit at one of the chairs clustered around the meeting table and seated himself a few chairs away.

'I understand you know Mark?' Parke enquired.

'Only informally,' Brewer said. 'It's his father I know better.'

'Is that so?' Parke was clearly curious about his new visitor. He appeared slightly nervous and fidgeted from time to time with his shirt collar. 'And how can we help you?'

'I'll come straight to the point,' said Brewer. 'I understand that you deal in, let me say, armament logistics. You can provide a certain service for those who request it.'

Parke smiled briefly. 'You make it sound very obscure. In fact it's quite simple. We buy and sell munitions, Mr Brewer. For example, if you own a rifle club, we can certainly offer very competitive rates on both the weapons and the ammunition. What exactly is your interest?'

'You also act as a broker in other areas. With regard to armaments on a much larger scale. Is that right?'

Parke shifted in his chair. 'What do you want, Mr Brewer? I think you neglected to tell me your business.'

'And you also deal with regimes that the West publicly denounces. Or has somebody been misinforming me?'

'This is wearisome, Mr Brewer. I take it you are not a policeman, or you would have extended me the courtesy of showing me your ID. And if that is the case, I see no reason to answer your questions.'

'You are correct in your assumption, Mr Parke. I am not a policeman.' Brewer took a UK Press card from his pocket and showed it to Parke. 'I'm doing a major feature for one of the Sundays, you see, about illegal arms trading. And in that context, GDM has been mentioned to me. I thought it best to check the facts first-hand. After all, I wouldn't want to print something if it was just hearsay.'

'I see.' Parke fingered the Press card for a moment and then handed it back. 'It would indeed be unfortunate if GDM were quoted in such an unflattering context. I can assure you that everything is well above board in this organisation.'

'In that case,' Brewer smiled. 'Is it possible for you to answer my questions?'

The meeting continued for a further ten minutes until Parke's visitor arrived. Parke's answers were quick and straight. Either Jonny Miller's facts were seriously wrong or Parke was a well-practised liar. Even mention of Tarhuna and Rabta in Libya, where hundreds of tonnes of sarin had been produced, provoked no response. If GDM was acting as an agent for those supplies, Parke was an effective PR man. GDM, according to Parke's account, dealt only in small-scale and light calibre armaments. It stayed strictly within government guidelines and never dealt with suspect regimes. From the way Parke described it, Brewer could expect to find Snow White and Bambi working as his co-directors.

When Brewer left, Parke excused himself briefly from his new visitor to make a quick telephone call. Cham did not take Parke's news well. He had met with Pendleton only the previous afternoon and learnt with some alarm of the undercover operation already in progress—and now to find Brewer sniffing around GDM was too much too soon.

He drew in a deep breath. It was time for executive action.

'Don't worry,' Cham assured Parke. 'It will be settled. Just one thing. Not a word of this to Hamilton. The less he knows, the better. He's already had one visit from Special Branch.'

'Special Branch!' Parke was alarmed. 'What on earth did they want?'

'Nothing,' Cham assured him. 'They're just floating a few ideas to see what shakes out. I'm meeting with one of the AC's to ensure they back off.'

'I don't like this,' Parke reacted. 'It's beginning to look like they're onto us. This guy today, Special Branch probing Hamilton. Someone's talked.'

'Not at all,' Cham responded. 'It's a few loners. We can pick them off. Forget it, Parke. I'm handling it. There won't be any more problems.'

Cham put the phone down. His only worry was Parke and Hamilton, not the investigations around them. They were weak links. With Brewer probing Parke and the Inspector from Special Branch probing Hamilton there was a danger something would give. He would have to keep a close eye on them. Any sign of weakness and he would need to take quick action. He could not risk his own position being compromised. First he would attend to Brewer and Pendleton. With them out of the way, Special Branch would be easy to pick off. And if things did not quieten down after that, he would have to take the logical next step—and remove the scents they were following.

When Brewer left GDM's offices, he noted the short man who peeled away from the queue of customers at the cash machine and followed him round the corner and along Jermyn Street. After a few turns and changes of direction, there could be no doubt: the man was following him. And he was a professional. Several times Brewer lost sight of him only to spot him ahead, or on the other side of the street. The question was: had someone at GDM arranged the tail while he was busy talking with Parke, or had he been there earlier? Brewer had not been looking for another tail.

Brewer headed northwards, up through Bond Street, across Oxford Street and up into Marylebone. The man stuck to him like a limpet as he took a left turn off Marylebone High Street and along one of the side roads. Moving quickly, he ducked through a set of gates into a small cluster of private flats and flattened himself alongside a wall.

He didn't have long to wait. The man announced himself with running feet and short snatches of breath. The next moment a gun appeared. Brewer snapped his arm out, snatching at the gun. He felt the cold of the barrel, wrenched it free from the man's grip, and half pushed, half tripped him to the ground. The man fell, grabbing at Brewer's jacket. For a moment Brewer lost his footing. The man kicked out, catching him in the groin. The pain shot through him like a cut from a broken bottle. Winded, Brewer dropped to the floor. Now the man was on his feet and delivering a double-handed blow to the back of his neck. A black shutter came down across his eyes. His neck felt ready to snap and Brewer crashed forward, scraping his head against the tarmac. He kicked out backwards and was lucky. He caught the man square in the stomach and sent him crashing back into the wall, his head snapping backwards with a whiplash and bringing him tumbling to the ground. Brewer fought back against the pain and stood and reached down, landing a high speed blow on the man's chin. There was a snapping noise and suddenly the man was still, his eyes staring unfocused at the sky. He was nearly unconscious.

Brewer slapped his face and forced him into a sitting position.

'Who the hell are you working for?'

The man's head rolled, a thin vein of blood dripping from one corner of his mouth. Brewer looked at the gun on the ground. It was not police or service issue. The man had to be working for the same team as his previous tail.

'How about Thielstrom?'

For the first time the man reacted. He tried to shake his head, but it was too late. Brewer had the information he wanted.

He stood and let the man slump back to the ground. He took the gun and emptied its magazine, putting the rounds in his pocket. He looked around one last time. The man would not be going anywhere, at least not for a few hours.

Brewer hurried away, dropping the gun in a pile of black sacks outside a nearby restaurant. He did not notice the two men who watched him leave. Neither did he see them enter the block of flats, find the injured man and put a single, fatal bullet through his head.

15

Something was nagging at Brewer. Something related to his meeting with Parke. He had a growing unease that the answers to his questions had come a little too quickly, the wording been a little too perfect. He should have pushed harder, used his questioning and interrogation skills to penetrate Parke's calm and disarming manner.

He needed to dig deeper into GDM's background. It was dull, routine work. But there was a good payback. Buried amongst GDM's company details in its recent statutory filings at Companies House he located a list of its directors. And directly below the entries for M Hamilton, MP and G Parke (Lt-Cmdr retired) was a third: E Thielstrom. The information he had been chasing like some crazed, steroid-enhanced athlete was sitting there, publicly available all the time.

Brewer cursed his own stupidity. It was the sort of mistake that he should not be making, not now. He knew the value of solid leg work, solid research. A good agent spends as much time ploughing through routine paperwork and archives as he does in the field. It was the same sort of stupid slip he had made with Anastasia and her parcel. He was getting slow. Time was, he would never have made such elementary errors. Maybe Jane was right, maybe it was time to hang up his ageing ego and break out the carpet slippers and the pipe.

So Jonny Miller had been right. GDM was acting as a front for something. But how much did Parke and Hamilton know? Possibly Thielstrom was acting without Parke or Hamilton's knowledge, but Brewer found that difficult to believe. In such a small company it was highly unlikely that Parke and Hamilton did not know everything. In which case, Parke had lied to him the previous day. And it was equally likely that the tail had been put in place while he was sitting in Parke's office.

Brewer considered this fresh information. He would have to tread carefully. The idea that a former Secretary of State for Defence was involved in illicit arms trading and possible right-wing extremist movements was a hot story. If Brewer had been a genuine journalist, this story would have made his name, and probably his fortune. But Parke and Hamilton were not stupid. And neither was Thielstrom. The man who had tailed him had not been doing so for sport: the gun indicated a more deadly intention.

But Brewer still lacked enough hard evidence to convince Pendleton. Worse—what he had discovered was all domestic material: Pendleton would merely tell him to hand it over to the Security Service as he had done before, or possibly Special Branch. Brewer needed hard facts. He needed to establish an international dimension to ensure the Firm kept hold of the operation. In which case, he thought, as he returned the company papers to the desk clerk, he would need to take a closer look at the files held in GDM's offices.

Simon Gilbert greeted the man sent by Tel Aviv with surprise and mixed emotions. For years he had hated the man, detested him as one of the new wave of Nazis, one of the revisionists with enough education to fool the simple and politically naive. Gilbert had lost count of the times he had wished the Mossad would remove the man. He had stirred up right-wing extremists in both Europe and South Africa, had published books of revisionist history. His ambition was to write the reality of the Holocaust out of the history books and rehabilitate the Third Reich. In the 1980's the man sent by Tel Aviv was associated with race riots in Britain; in the early 1990's, with race riots in Los Angeles. He was an arch manipulator of crowds, a man whose rhetoric could move them to action and violence.

It had come as something of a shock for Gilbert to discover that the man—the same man that many in Israel openly hated and said they wished were dead—was a staunch and loyal Zionist, a Jew whose family were wiped-out in the Nazi death camps of the second world war and who had long been on Mossad's payroll. He was an agent provocateur worthy of the name, a deep undercover mole with a public profile at the opposite extreme of the political spectrum. He ran the ultimate risk: of supping with the devil and believing he could stay sane, could win against the extremists.

As all agencies have discovered who have run agents deep undercover—be they the Firm, the security service, Special Branch, the FBI, the CIA—the risk is enormous of a man turning. The rewards on offer from drugs cartels, from the well-funded neo-Nazi movements, have turned even the hardest, most loyal agent. The opportunity to earn in weeks what most will never earn in a lifetime can make even the most committed turn in the blink of an eye. The line between the criminal, and law and order officials is all too frequently the face of a mirror: in a moment, it is possible to flip from one side to the other. On both sides, the sense of excitement, the rush of adrenalin is the same. But on one side the rewards are higher. For many, it is a simple choice to make.

But Gilbert sensed this man was different. This man was a chameleon with a firm moral root at his core: from the outside his views floated and changed. Yet inside was an unchanging kernel that knew what was wrong, what was right. Gilbert's opinion changed within moments of meeting him. This man would never truly be known, never be worshipped by respectful admirers, never be featured in fawning magazine articles, interviewed in documentaries: this man was too important and absolute secrecy, absolute deception were key to his success.

For the first time, Gilbert understood the true difference between a good agent and the specialist. This man would risk everything, would be killed by the opposition as thoughtlessly as a child swats a wasp. He would live as one of the enemy, not just infiltrate them: he would become one of them, would stay deep undercover for years. They would take him into their own. From the sketchy background provided by Tel Aviv, Gilbert knew that this man had once been on the brink of becoming a Mafia wiseguy. If that particular operation had not been prematurely terminated as a result of precipitate action by the American authorities, he could have brought down a whole web of Mafia families. Now it was hoped that he could do the same with the Lincoln compound—without the luxury of time on their side. It was a mad and highly risky enterprise: but they both knew that risk had to be taken.

They spent a week together: Gilbert, the other Mossad agents and the man sent by Tel Aviv. It was meant to be a training exercise for him, but the reverse was true: by the end of the week, they were all better agents. The man's experience was deep and unparalleled. For agents who had assumed they were the best and knew most of what there was to know, it was a humbling experience.

It was a painful and unpleasant vocation fixing the scenario that would ensure the man from Tel Aviv penetrated the compound. But the man's right-wing credentials were well-known. It did not take long to persuade the compound's occupants of his value to their cause. He spoke at a public meeting in Lincoln, gained coverage in the local papers and on other local media. In the end it was they who came to him, they who made the approach and suggested that he join them.

Gilbert watched with a sense of foreboding as the man finally achieved his initial objective and accepted an invitation inside the compound, accompanied by Straker and Hümmler. He saw them smile and joke in the back of their Mercedes, but no smile crossed Gilbert's face. He wondered whether he would see the agent again, whether anyone else understood the price the man had paid and continued to pay. And all for a motherland he never saw—would probably never see.

He turned away and headed back to the hotel.

Brewer broke into GDM's offices shortly before two in the

morning. The front door to the building was easy, a simple Yale with worn cylinders and an alarm that he silenced before it could sound with a quick snip of a knife. So much for the sophistication of the 'defence specialists'.

The door to GDM's offices presented a greater problem. Working in the limited light of a slim pencil torch, he was almost upon them before he saw the red-eyed laser detectors at the side of the stairs. Simple but effective: breaking the beams would trigger the alarm. He eased forward, wondering how best to slip past them and nearly missed the pressure sensor hidden beneath the carpet. It was good. Often with such devices there is a telltale distortion of the carpet, a change of colour, a slight bump. Not this time: it was invisible to the naked eye, the work of a professional. He quickly revised his opinion of how serious GDM were.

He stopped and ran his fingers under the rough edge of the carpet, tracing the outline of the sensor, the delicate electrical wires that linked it to a central alarm. Taking a small pair of scissors from his pocket, he gently eased them until their angled blades were wrapped tightly around the cable. It was a fifty-fifty chance. If it had fail-safe wiring the act of cutting would itself trigger the alarm. But he had no choice. With both the pressure sensor and the laser-beams there was no way to move any further forward.

He cut the cables in one quick movement.

Silence. He waited. There was no alarm, but he knew that might mean nothing: the alarm could be silent. Somewhere in another building a light might be flashing, a bell ringing. He would have to move quickly. He slithered forwards on his chest, his back barely below the level of the lasers. At the door he took in the two Chubb mortices and the cylinder. No problem. He removed a set of masters from his pocket and made short work of them.

Brewer knew that as soon as he opened the door he would have at most 60 seconds to locate and disable the alarm. During his visit to Parke, he had memorised the office layout. The most likely location for the alarm control system was behind or under the secretary's desk. He breathed deeply. It was several years since he had undertaken an operation like this, but the senses and skills came back quickly. Despite the sounds of night-time London from outside, it was easy to imagine himself once again behind the Iron Curtain. The risks were much the same—but at least discovery here would not result in death. Not unless he was very unlucky.

He jerked the door open and dashed across the room. A loud warning tone came from a wall alarm as a bright amber light flickered a regular and accelerating pattern. The narrow shaft of torchlight revealed the desk in front of the far wall. Brewer reached it within seconds. Its drawers were locked, no switches or keyholes visible. He cursed and swung quickly to examine the alcove behind him. A coat rack, an old umbrella and a worn paperback. Nothing else. He turned, running the pencil beam of light over the walls. Just the light fitting, a wall switch, up-lighters, and the glossy promotional photographs. The photographs. They were an obvious possibility. He checked his watch. Twenty seconds since he had opened the door. The amber light was becoming faster, like an increasingly demented disco strobe. The noise was louder. Any moment now and the warning tone would turn into the full alarm.

He wrenched at the first photo. The frame was fixed firmly to the wall. He tried the next, and a third. None of them budged. He found it behind the fifth. A small steel unit recessed deep into the wall.

By now the room was bathed in an almost continuous dull orange glow. The noise from the countdown to the alarm throbbed inside his head. He checked his watch. Fifty seconds. He brushed his sleeve across his brow to wipe away the sweat. The keys clattered in his hands, the metal slipping in his fingers. Two keys. Neither fitted. He tried a third and then the fourth. None of them worked. Impossible: the set was guaranteed to fit all known alarm systems. He tried them again. This time the first key worked.

A click and the room fell silent. The orange glow faded into blackness. Only the light from the pencil torch illuminated the room. Brewer sighed. It should have been easier. He had been clumsy. Fifty-eight seconds. Two seconds from disaster. Under thirty or better was standard. The alarm could have been set to thirty. This time he had been lucky.

He directed the torch towards Parke's office and walked through. The door opened to his touch: no lock, no further alarms. It was unlikely any secure papers would be kept by the secretary—they had to be in one of the directors' rooms: Parke's office was the most logical place to start. The desk was clear, its drawers open, full of nothing more exciting than headed paper and business cards. Brewer helped himself to a handful. Such items often come in useful.

He checked the rest of the room and found a small safe hidden behind a painting in one corner. He smiled. Whoever installed GDM's security had a limited imagination. Pictures, photographs and books are the most obvious covers for safes. The best security companies use the unexpected: false electrical sockets with cavities behind, hidden panels in office equipment such as photocopiers. The safe was small, the type designed to hold a few documents, petty cash and jewellery. The type of safe intended to delay or prevent a casual burglary. It would have been more at home in a house, not in the offices of a dubious defence consultancy.

Brewer took a small device from his pocket the size of a Sony Walkman and attached pressure pads to the front of the safe. He clicked a button on the side of the unit and spun the tumbler on the safe door. After a few minutes a dull green display flashed a series of numbers and directions at him. He spun the tumbler to clear it and entered the numbers on the display. The lock clicked.

He replaced the unit in his pocket and opened the safe door. It was nearly empty. There were a few papers bound together in a folder and a sealed envelope. He took out the papers and examined them in the pinpoint light of his torch. Although the papers were few, the information on them was dense: it had been reduced from larger sheets, probably on a photocopier. He slipped them into the large pouch inside his coat. The envelope was heavy for its size. He cut it open with a paperknife taken from the desk.

He whistled. Inside were photographs and technical data sheets. The technical data he did not understand, but he didn't need to: the photographs were clear enough. They had been taken somewhere in a desert. They showed missiles being launched and targets being hit. And they also showed several chained men in the final stages of death, their figures twisted and broken, their flesh eaten away.

'Bingo,' Brewer whispered.

It was time to leave.

DI Howarth had a set of photos of his own to examine the following morning. They had been taken with a mix of ultra-fast and infra-red film and printed a few minutes before his arrival. The paper was still sticky to the touch. As he looked through them he left his fingerprints embossed in the gloss of their surface. It had been a busy night for the surveillance crew. GDM had been burgled by a professional. The intruder's description and early copies of the photos had already been run through the central identification system. So far it had come up with nothing.

'No previous form,' Howarth thought aloud as he leafed through the pictures in the Ops Room. Members of the Special Branch surveillance task-force were busy around him chasing up other potential leads on GDM, Hamilton and any others aspects of their investigation which had become known. At this stage, no lead was too small to pursue. The first stage of an investigation is always to gather as much information as possible: the theorising and thinking can come later, when the facts are to hand.

One thing Howarth did not understand: no-one from GDM had reported the burglary to the police. Instead, soon after his arrival at GDM earlier that morning, Parke had placed one call and reported the burglary, but not to the police. The number Parke called caused Howarth to raise his eyebrows.

'Since when,' he asked the night supervisor. 'Has MI6 been

the place to call when you discover a burglary? Whatever happened to good old 999?'

The Sergeant had not answered, presuming, correctly, that it was a rhetorical question. The real problem facing the Special Branch team was identifying who the call had been routed to within MI6. The Secret Intelligence Service has a sophisticated switchboard with facilities that the standard call monitoring software running in BT's switches was unable to analyse. Parke's call had vanished into a black hole. No identifiable names or references had been made during that short, scrambled phone call.

Howarth studied the photos of GDM's night intruder. Whoever he might be, GDM clearly did not want to go public on the burglary. And the intruder had certainly taken something. One of the photos had been enlarged to reveal the corner of an envelope protruding from an inside pocket as the burglar left the building. But this was no casual burglar: security at GDM was tight. Howarth had spoken with the company responsible for its installation, run by a former Metropolitan Police Inspector. It was good enough to hold or deter most casual burglars. So the intruder was a professional, but he was either so successful that he had never been caught, or he was not the normal run of burglars that break into offices during the small hours of the night. Howarth's money was on the latter.

'MI6 and a burglar, Jeffreys,' Howarth commented to the Sergeant. 'What an interesting night.'

The Sergeant was having difficulty staying awake. It had been a long, tiring night and he wanted nothing more than to return home and collapse into bed. Instead, he drew himself up to his full height, tried to look interested by opening his sleepy eyes wide and made what he hoped would be an intelligent contribution.

'It's possible there's a connection, sir. Particularly with GDM's background. It's the sort of world they move in. Professional job.'

Howarth nodded. 'But then why did Parke call them? If MI6 took the files, it doesn't make sense. You think he'd just leg it if something's gone wrong.'

'Maybe he doesn't know it's them who broke in. Don't you have any inside tracks at Vauxhall Cross, sir?'

'Hardly,' Howarth commented. 'We're not exactly members of the same club. Anyhow, if MI6 are involved in this, they won't play straight with us, will they?' He shook his head. 'We're going to have to play this one carefully. If the intelligence boys are involved, this could get nasty.' He picked up the photographs. 'I think the secret's going to be tracking down this fellow. Any word on that?'

The Sergeant shook his head. 'Not yet, sir. But we've still had no report from Hobson. If we're lucky, his tail might have scored.'

'I doubt it somehow,' Howarth remarked. 'If this guy's as professional as he looks, he's not going to have any problem throwing off a tail.'

'Hobson's very good sir.'

'I'm not questioning that. I'm just saying this burglar is an unknown quantity. I think we need to tread carefully.'

'Softly, softly sir?' whispered the Sergeant and smiled.

Brewer took the documents and photographs to Jane's flat: his own was becoming too hot. She took five minutes to answer the door and cursed him for arriving at a time of night she had not seen for years.

'You mean there's a four o'clock in the morning as well?' she asked.

He followed her upstairs to her flat, his eyes taking in her figure outlined beneath the sheer silk of the dressing gown wrapped tightly around her. She made them both a thick black coffee and then sat beside Brewer on the sofa as he flicked through the documents.

'You shouldn't be seeing these,' he commented.

'Afraid I'm a Mata Hari?' she asked and smiled. 'What are you up to Peter?'

He did not reply. Not all of the papers were clear to him, but they were forming a picture. There were dates and names he could identify: Tokyo, Tripoli, New York, Baghdad, Oklahoma City, Washington, Lincoln. He took out the photographs.

'Jesus!' Jane turned away.

'Not exactly holiday snaps are they,' Brewer observed coldly.

The photos were gruesome: shots of the after-effects of biological and chemical weapons. Some of them were clearly 'clinical trials', conducted under test conditions. Others appeared to be live trials in the field. Brewer had seen similar pictures before, in the wake of the first Gulf War. Pictures of allied and Iraqi soldiers, their bodies twisted and wracked in death. Saddam had been keen to test his chemical and biological weapons arsenal and had done so with deadly effect. In the bottom right-hand corner of the photos were reference numbers. They appeared to correspond with paragraphs in the documents. Brewer needed these documents analysed by a specialist: the text was too small to read and possibly encrypted.

He sat back. One thing was certain: GDM was trading or somehow otherwise involved in illicit weapons. And that placed Mark Hamilton in an interesting position. Not only was he an MP, but as a former Secretary of State for Defence, this was politically explosive material. If the media picked up one hint of this, the scandal would rock not only Hamilton but his Party and possibly the whole political system. There were always rumours of MPs being involved in illegal arms trading, but nothing as significant or compelling as this. Even Pendleton would have to admit this was hard enough evidence to widen the investigation. The only concern Brewer had was that all of this might be happening with some kind of official sanction: in which case it was not Hamilton who would be in trouble, but himself. He had long since known that there was an inner cabal, a kind of inner state within a state that held the true reins of power in Britain: if this was one of their projects, then he was on very dangerous quicksand indeed.

He became aware of Jane massaging his neck. He put down the photos and turned to her.

'Sleeping in your make-up?' he enquired, noting the smudges around her eyes.

'What a tart,' she confessed.

They kissed, gently at first, then stronger, increasingly passionate. Her tongue explored his lips, then deeper. He reached out and pulled gently at the cord of her gown until it slipped down over her shoulders and he helped it fall silently to the floor. Her fingers loosened his clothes and together they sank down. In the first dim shadows of the dawn, they lost themselves in the passion of their embrace, the rhythm of their movements.

Outside, the man watching Jane's flat cursed at the cold and stomped his feet to keep warm.

16

The gate to the Hamilton residence was already open when Brewer arrived. One of Hamilton's Special Branch minders was loitering nearby and spoke briefly to Brewer as he entered. He was expected. Brewer walked quickly down the drive and up to the house. He did not notice the Special Branch man take out his mobile phone and make a call.

The front door was open. He hesitated a moment, knocked twice and then stepped inside. Somewhere he could hear a radio or CD, the sound of opera: Wagner, Ride of the Valkyrie.

'Mr Hamilton?' Brewer's calls were deadened by the rich furnishings of the hallway. 'Mr Hamilton?'

He moved on through the house, towards the rear. The music grew louder. Somewhere upstairs a door slammed shut. He stopped and looked upwards. Nobody appeared, but he caught the scent of perfume. As he stepped into the rear living room, he saw Mark Hamilton slumped in the leather sofa, his eyes shut, the music swelling to fill the room. Brewer hesitated.

'Mr Hamilton?' he called.

Hamilton opened his eyes and stared blankly for a moment before he reacted. Then he stood up, smoothed down his hair and stepped towards him.

'Mr Brewer,' his voice carried over the music. 'I didn't hear you.'

'I'm not surprised,' Brewer replied, trying to make himself heard as he nodded towards the loudspeakers.

Hamilton smiled. 'I've a passion for Wagner.' He crossed the room and lowered the volume. He turned and waved him to a chair and they both sat and faced each other across the marble coffee table.

'So how can I help you? Still on the trail of missing Nazis?'

Brewer shook his head. 'No. A slight change of plan.'

'Really?' Hamilton stood. 'I must apologise. I should have offered you a drink. Or is it too early for you?'

'It's never too early for a drink,' Brewer responded. 'A beer if you have one.'

'A beer?' Hamilton appeared surprised. 'I had you down for a wine man myself.'

'I can drink that too,' Brewer said. 'When there's no beer.'

'One moment.'

Hamilton exited and was gone for several minutes. Brewer took the opportunity to study the room. It was furnished in Edwardian style, a reminder of a forgotten age of elegance and formality. A massive mirror above the fireplace caught the light from the French windows and illuminated the darkest corner. A series of original paintings hung from the picture rail. On a bureau stood a range of photographs, many black and white: family groupings and individual portraits of young men in uniform.

'Here,' Hamilton returned and handed him a pint glass filled to the brim. 'No idea what it's like.'

Hamilton carried a large glass of deep red wine. He sat and looked at Brewer. 'So what is this mysterious change of direction? Not going to tell me my father's really a spy, are you?'

Brewer smiled. 'Not your father.'

Hamilton's smile slipped. 'And what exactly does that mean, Brewer?'

'Your company,' Brewer said. 'GDM Matériels.'

'What about it?'

'Are you fully conversant with its business interests?'

'Of course I am, man,' Hamilton exclaimed. 'I'm a bloody director.'

'So you know about everything that goes on at GDM, Mr Hamilton? Are you sure about that?'

'Brewer. You have something on your mind. Would you mind having the courtesy of telling me? I'm not one for these games of cat and mouse. I like straight talking.'

'As you wish, Mr Hamilton.' Brewer took a couple of photos from his pocket and laid them on the table.

Hamilton looked down at the photos, his lip puckering in distaste. 'Good God, man. What the hell are these? Don't tell me you're peddling obscene photos.'

'They came from GDM. From a safe in Parke's office to be precise.'

Hamilton did not respond. He stared directly back at Brewer without the slightest emotion, his face set rigid as a mask.

'Brewer, what are you playing at? Is this some kind of sting? Ah, I see. You're after money, aren't you, that's what this is. God damn you.'

Brewer shook his head. 'I want to find out how much you know. How far you are involved.'

'Involved in what, for God's sake?' Hamilton responded. 'These mean nothing.'

'Not on their own, I admit that,' Brewer said. 'But there are papers as well. Isn't it true that Parke recently attended a technology fair in a certain North African country? And didn't he see a demonstration there of certain weapons. Not just the usual run of things. Something much more lethal. Biological and chemical weapons perhaps?'

Hamilton drew in his breath. 'That's enough. I don't think we should talk any more, Mr Brewer.'

'No?' Brewer raised his eyebrows in surprise. 'I think you should, Mr Hamilton. I may be your only lifeline.' He leaned forwards. 'Tell me what's going on, Mr Hamilton. If I can find all this, so can others. They may not be far behind. And they may be less patient, less sympathetic.'

'I told you, this means nothing to me. GDM operates in the same way as any defence consultancy company, there's nothing unusual going on.'

'I disagree,' Brewer replied, taking a sip from his beer. It was a thin weak lager, not his sort of thing at all.

Hamilton watched him thoughtfully, drinking slowly from his wine. 'It's very kind of you to worry about me, Brewer. But I do already have several lines of defence.'

Brewer nodded. 'I met one of them by the gate. But that won't stop the sort of people I have in mind. I know the way they operate.'

He watched as Hamilton stood and moved over to the fireplace, his wine glass in hand. Hamilton looked at himself in the mirror for a while and then turned to face him.

'Just how much do you think you know, Brewer?'

Brewer smiled and shook his head. 'That isn't the way these things work. But I can tell you now, you're in deep. It looks to me like GDM is involved in illegal trading of biological and chemical weapons. That it may have been involved in the Tokyo sarin attack. Further, that a board member of GDM is a former high-ranking Nazi still wanted for war crimes.' He paused. 'This is serious stuff. It doesn't look good for a former Defence Secretary does it, Mr Hamilton? The media would have a field day.'

Hamilton sipped thoughtfully at his wine. 'And what do you want out of this, Brewer? Money, is that it? Blackmail? How high is your price?'

'You're not listening to me,' Brewer replied coldly. 'I want your co-operation. It's the only way to save yourself. You're already running against the clock. When the authorities—or someone else—catch up with you, it's not going to be pretty.'

'And you're not the authorities?' Hamilton asked. 'I presume you must be Mr Nice. Does Mr Nasty come next?'

'If you knew me, Mr Hamilton, you'd know for sure that I'm no Mr Nice,' Brewer said quietly. 'Who or what comes after me is entirely in your hands, Mr Hamilton. '

'Brewer, you're not a naive man. You must know that the world of armaments trading and defence procurement and consultancy is not the profession of angels. GDM is no different to its competitors. And before you go around making wild accusations and stomping with your hob-nailed boots, I think you ought to look a little closer to home.'

The beer was too warm. Brewer took a long sip and wished

he'd tried the wine. 'Are you suggesting that GDM is operating on behalf of an official agency?'

Hamilton adopted a look of feigned surprise. 'Did I say that?'

'It's what you're implying,' Brewer said softly.

'You're out of your league, Brewer,' Hamilton said, his eyes cold. 'Back off.'

There was a sound at the door. Brewer turned. It was Hamilton senior.

'You really are becoming something of a nuisance, aren't you Mr Brewer?'

The old man stood in the doorway. In his right hand he held an old army-issue Enfield revolver. It was fixed unwaveringly on Brewer.

'Is this man troubling you, Mark?'

'You might say that.' Hamilton finished his wine and smiled at Brewer. 'Can you keep an eye on him for me? There's one or two items I have to tidy up.'

'What about Emily? She's hovering upstairs like a motherless foal.'

'I'll take her with me.' Mark Hamilton stopped and turned towards Brewer. 'Thanks for the warning, Brewer. I'll make good use of it.'

And with that he was gone. Hamilton senior stood in the door and watched Brewer closely.

'Don't think you can try anything, Mr Brewer. I'm a good shot.'

'I'm sure you are, Mr Hamilton,' Brewer replied, taking a sip from his drink. 'Although I can't say much for your choice of beers.'

There was the sound of a woman's voice, anxious and confused, then Mark Hamilton's and then footsteps on the staircase. A moment later the front door slammed. A car started, stalled and revved. There was a kick of gravel and then it was gone. Silence.

'Now what?' Brewer asked.

Hamilton senior came further into the room and leaned against the chair opposite him.

'How much did you hear of what we were talking about?' Brewer asked.

'Enough to know Mark was in trouble, Mr Brewer. I don't like everything my son has done, but he is my son after all and I don't want him brought down now.'

'But you know what he's done, don't you?'

Hamilton shrugged. 'Trading in armaments is no crime, Mr Brewer. It's a big employer, a big money-earner. Our government sanctions it, all governments sanction it.'

'Not biological and chemical weapons, Mr Hamilton.'

'I don't believe you.' He eased himself carefully into the chair. The gun remained firmly fixed, pointing steadfastly at Brewer's head.

'Do you also know that your son is involved with Thielstrom, the Nazi?'

Hamilton nodded.

'And that doesn't bother you?' Brewer continued. 'After your war experiences, after the death camps, after Nuremberg?'

'Mr Brewer,' Hamilton sighed. 'That was all a long time ago. There comes a time when we must forgive and forget, a time when we must move on. That's a lesson more people could do with learning. Most of our problems today, wars and terrorism, are caused by those who live in the past.'

'And you think Thielstrom's agenda has changed, do you?'

Hamilton shrugged. 'I've never met the man. Neither has Mark. He's very much a sleeping partner.'

'You don't expect me to believe that, do you?' Brewer asked. 'You must know he's still very active on the neo-Nazi scene?'

'What Mr Thielstrom does is his concern.' Hamilton sighed. 'One thing you must understand, Mr Hamilton, is that not all of us subscribe to the simplistic view of history that currently prevails, the idea that the Nazis were all evil and wrong, that the Allies were gilded saints who came gallantly to the rescue. You're an intelligent man. You know that nothing is that black and white. Hitler achieved many remarkable things. One need only look around to realise that our system does not work well at every level. Look at the state this country is in now. Where are the visionaries, the men of insight and thought? They do not exist. We have a generation of weak-minded men, unable to make decisions, unable to express a vision for our future.'

Brewer watched the man carefully, waiting for a moment to take his chance. The old man's grip was sure, but occasionally his attention wavered. Brewer would have to choose his moment carefully: there would be no second chance.

'And you, Mr Brewer, you do not understand these things. You see only the shadows on the wall, not the events themselves. GDM is working to protect this country, Mr Brewer. You must understand that. We are at the mercy of lunatic groups, groups who will deploy sarin and other gasses as they did in Tokyo. We have to prepare to defend ourselves. GDM sees that, GDM is providing the protection we need. No-one will complain that it is illegal when the threat comes to the streets of this country, when thousands die in terrorist incidents as they did in New York. The next wars will be fought within our countries just like the former Yugoslavia, not one nation pitted against another, but a single nation pitted against itself, against the hatred of pan-national extremists in our midst and those who believe in a better world. The real battles now are for ideas and position, for supremacy over other internal viewpoints.'

'So what will you do with me, Mr Hamilton?' Brewer asked quietly.

Hamilton smiled and raised the gun. 'I am going to kill you, Mr Brewer.'

There was a single shot, a loud explosion of sound in the room. Brewer recoiled, flinging himself onto the floor. The old man had missed. He seized hold of the side table, swung it left and aimed it at Hamilton's head. A hand grabbed hold of his arm before the blow landed, leaving the table to crash to the floor. He spun round. Two men with automatics stood staring at him. Brewer froze. He had no chance, had not even heard the men arrive.

'Well,' he said, catching his breath. 'Aren't you going to finish me off?'

'Not at all Mr Brewer,' one of them replied. 'Didn't you hear the bugle? We're the cavalry.'

The other man stepped past him and over to Benjamin Hamilton. He stood and stared at him, and then stretched out a finger and poked him gently. The old man toppled backwards. For the first time Brewer saw the small entry wound in Hamilton's temple.

'It looks like,' said Brewer as he turned back to the stranger holding his arm. 'You arrived just in time. Now would you like to explain to me just who the hell you are?'

Howarth was not surprised to receive the summons to see Buckley: it was something he had been expecting for days. He hurried down the back staircase of New Scotland Yard and along the corridor. Deputy Assistant Commissioner John Buckley was seated behind his desk with the fingers of both hands pressed tightly together to form a steeple. He looked up sharply as Howarth entered him and waved him to the seat opposite.

'Thanks for finding the time Dave.' Buckley pressed the *Do Not Disturb* button on his telephone. 'I hear you've been a busy lad.'

'This case is proving more interesting than either of us imagined,' Howarth replied evenly, wondering whether this was it. Was he about to get an A1 bollocking? Buckley looked uneasy and impatient. Was he just going to be pulled from the investigation, replaced by someone more politically acceptable? Had orders come from above to bury it, as they had done in the past?

Part of the reason for Special Branch's difficult relationship with the Security Service was that in the past the police have been forced to abandon enquiries because of issues of 'state security'. The only problem was that in reality too many of those reasons of 'state security' were little more than the prospect of severe political embarrassment to leading members of the government. It all came down to different definitions of 'State'. There was always a tension in the relationship between Special

Branch and the Security Service: Special Branch officers regarded themselves as ordinary men and women from the ranks who had worked their way up through sheer hard work and ability. The agents from Thames House, however, were viewed as spoilt private school dimwits who had walked into their positions merely because of background and who were more concerned about which clubs to join and wine-tasting societies than in operating a professional service.

In reality, neither stereotype was accurate. It was the politicians who were to blame. For years they had dithered, too frightened to take the decision that would unify both operations under a common command structure. Politicians feared only one thing more than a free press: an effective intelligence service. Too many on the right and left worry about laying the groundwork for what could become a police state in the wrong hands. In the meantime, organised crime and terrorism had grown. Britain was rapidly becoming the back door into Europe, the first location of choice for the new syndicates operating illegal drugs, illegal immigration and gun-running rackets. Several times both the head of the Security Service and the Commissioner of the Met had come as close as they could to calling publicly for a British equivalent of the FBI. And too often their requests had been declined and ignored.

'I gather you've been sniffing around Hamilton.'

'I'm only investigating the papers that we inherited,' Howarth stated flatly. 'Has someone been complaining?'

'The Commissioner has indeed had certain representations made to him,' Buckley said quietly.

'By whom?'

Buckley shook his head. 'He wouldn't tell me. In any case, it doesn't matter. The Commissioner rebutted the approach. Said he had absolute confidence in you.'

Howarth did not know how to respond, so he stayed silent.

'However,' Buckley continued, his bright intelligent eyes scrutinising Howarth. 'You do understand the delicacy of this situation.'

'Of course.' Howarth felt offended. 'But there's something you need to know.'

Buckley frowned. 'What's that?'

'This goes beyond Hamilton,' Howarth said. 'Possibly a long way beyond. It looks like we have intelligence involvement.' He outlined briefly the break-in at GDM's offices.

'Christ. Here we go again,' Buckley sighed. He slammed a fist down onto the desk, venting his frustration. 'When will they learn? I thought they'd put their house in order, stopped spinning their little webs of lies and deception. They said they'd cleared the cowboys out.'

'I hoped so too,' Howarth agreed. 'Only this time I don't think it's the Thames House boys. It's the lot over the other side of the river.'

Buckley closed his eyes in disbelief. 'I trust, David, that you are not saying this merely to give an old man a hard time?'

Howarth grinned. 'You're hardly old.'

'I'm getting older every minute,' Buckley sighed and leaned forwards across the desk. 'Please Dave. Tread carefully. I'll square it with the Commissioner, but there's only so much we can do with a case like this.'

'I know,' Howarth said. 'You're not going to like it, but I have the nasty feeling this is going to become far more complicated and unpleasant before it gets better.'

'I thought you might say that,' Buckley said, shaking his head wearily. 'Now go away will you? Please? I feel a migraine coming on.'

The first two weeks of the Mossad's surveillance and penetration of the Lincoln compound had been tense. The normal day to day movement of supplies continued, interrupted only by the occasional unmarked lorry, or the arrival and departure of other identified figures. Photos were taken and relayed to Tel Aviv for further analysis. But there was no sign and no word from their man inside.

Gilbert was not unduly worried. Not yet. The agent's silence meant nothing. A week or two was insignificant. The agent would be building his cover, establishing himself as reliable and trustworthy, someone who could be depended upon. The compound's inhabitants would be watching his every move, alert to the possibility of deception, that he might be a cuckoo in their midst. They would challenge him to complete minor tasks to prove his commitment. The agent was authorised to use personal discretion in any situation.

Whereas agencies like the FBI have strict guidelines that prevent them transgressing the law in any major way when operating undercover, the Mossad agent operated under no such limitations. If required, he would kill someone to prove his loyalty to the Nazi cause. The bigger picture was more important than the life of any one individual: if those inside the compound were to succeed, the cost would be far higher than a single life. Whereas most agencies work from the principle that they are basically at peace and can afford the luxury of rulebooks and chains of paper-bound accountability, the Mossad works on the assumption that Israel is a country at war, threatened by known and unknown enemies. It operates accordingly.

The Mossad agent would even now be working his way into the confidence of the senior officers within the compound. He would continue his work until he had moved to the very centre of their operation. It was essential that when they moved in, every part of the neo-Nazi control and command structure was understood: it had to be destroyed. Not just damaged: destroyed. Their agent would be busy collecting every small piece of data and information that he could.

Either that or his cover was already blown and he was dead: if he was lucky.

17

When Brewer and his two new companions left the Hamilton residence, their departure was closely monitored. Three men moved into the house as soon as their car had departed. They found Benjamin Hamilton's body in the living room, his revolver at his side. It had not been fired. They searched quickly through the rest of the house, checking whether anything had been taken. Nothing was disturbed. They opened the safe in the upstairs study and removed certain papers. It was only then that their leader made a telephone call.

'Hamilton B is dead. Single shot. Hamilton M is absent, destination unknown. We'll find him. Our friend from the Firm was here. Two others with him, origin unknown. Yes, yes.'

He replaced the phone and turned to his companions.

'Clean this place up. Remove the body to safe keeping. Hamilton B died of a heart attack. Everything must fit the scenario.'

They moved the glasses around, made it look like Hamilton had been on his own. They worked patiently at the blood traces on the sofa until nothing was visible. They returned Hamilton's gun to the safe. Everything had to look as normal as possible. If anyone else came digging it had to be good enough to fool them.

They burned the papers taken from the safe on a bonfire in the back garden. Hamilton's body was placed in a body bag fetched from their car and his body placed in the boot. By the time they were finished, the casual observer would have noticed nothing out of the ordinary at the Hamilton residence. It would take painstaking work by a forensic team to identify what had really happened here. And no-one had any intention of sending in such a team.

The leader locked the door and joined his companions in his car.

'Now we have to find Hamilton M.'

The car screeched away, kicking out a wave of gravel in its wake.

Brewer arrived back at Jane's flat with his two new companions beside him. He knew as soon as he stepped out of the car that something was wrong. Jane's front door was splintered around the lock, the door hanging ajar. He felt a sense of shock. Nothing had prepared him for this, not for Jane to be put in danger.

He spoke quietly to his companions. They nodded and one of them moved away to find a back entrance into the flat. Brewer and the other man moved slowly forwards, one of them watching the front door, the other the windows upstairs for any sign of movement. Nothing.

Brewer's heart pounded. He could think of only one thing: Jane. If anything had happened to her . . . They reached the door and listened. Silence. Brewer stepped forwards and pushed gingerly at the door. It moved slowly and silently. He stepped inside and waited. There were no sounds from upstairs. He looked back at his companion and motioned him forwards. As soon as the man was beside him, Brewer started up the stairs.

He kept close to the edge, anxious to avoid the danger of creaks. Every few steps he stopped again and listened. Still nothing. He looked down at the man at the base of the stairs. He stood covering him, a gun in hand. Not for the first time, Brewer was grateful that the Mossad men were with him. Brewer continued upwards. Part of him wanted to turn and run, worried what he might find. Images of the dead women and children in Iraq flooded through his mind. An image of Larsen Lak dead in the U-boat shed. He fought to stop them. He needed every sense alert: it could be a trap, a spider's web. There were echoes of the way in which he had been led to find Anastasia. He must be careful.

He reached the first floor. Ahead of him was the bedroom, to his right the bathroom. A few stairs led upwards towards the kitchen and the living room at the front of the house. He stepped forwards. There was a sound behind him. He swung round and ducked. Nothing. But there had definitely been a noise. From the front room.

He turned and moved slowly up the remaining short flight. His companion reached the landing behind him and watched him closely, his gun at the ready. Brewer put his eyes to the gap in the living room door hinges. It was difficult to see anything. There was a noise again, a muffled sort of sound. He frowned. He could see something moving, but couldn't make sense of it. He watched for a moment. Suddenly everything fell into place.

'Jane!' he shouted.

He pushed open the door and raced into the room, his years of training forgotten. Jane was on her side on the floor, her arms and legs tied around a kitchen chair. He reached her and pulled at the cords that held her, loosening them. She was conscious, but only just. Her eyes were blackened, her face streaked with blood, her clothes dishevelled.

'Jane!' he repeated, unable to think of anything else.

His companion burst into the room, his gun held ready in a double-handed grip. He stopped short at the scene. Brewer cradled Jane in his arms, close to tears. Jane sobbed, her body heaving with released emotion. The second agent came into the room.

'No-one at the back. The place is clean.'

'I couldn't stop them,' Jane sobbed. 'They hit me and beat me. I thought it would never stop, I thought I was going to die. They said they were going to cut my throat.'

'It's okay,' Brewer reassured her. 'Everything's okay.'

'They took the documents and the photos, they've taken everything Peter. I'm sorry, I'm so sorry.'

Brewer pulled her closer. 'Look. All that matters is that you're okay, yes?'

He looked over at the two men. 'Don't worry. I made copies,' he said. 'Sent them to a safe place.'

They put away their weapons and stood looking awkward.

'Don't just stand there,' Brewer shouted at them. 'Get some water and soap, something to clean her with.'

'I'm sorry, I'm so sorry,' Jane repeated.

'It's okay, everything's okay,' Brewer whispered in her ear.

His mind switched into a higher gear. Now he was angry. Until now it had been professional: suddenly it had just got personal.

Very personal.

As she left the tube station, Emily glanced at her watch. She was late. It had taken longer to get into town, collect Mark Hamilton's papers from Millbank and return on the tube than she had expected. She accelerated her pace, her new high heels clicking along the pavement like the tap-tapping of a blind man's guide stick. Mark would not be pleased. He liked her to be punctual. She gripped her document case, turned the corner and stood impatiently waiting for the lights to change. She had made up her mind: it was time they discussed things properly. Mark had been promising to leave his wife for years, but nothing ever happened. He spent his time flitting between the two of them. And there had been other women, she was sure of that. Now it was time for him to decide: it was either his wife or her. And his affairs would have to stop. She did not want to share him with anyone else.

The lights changed and she rushed quickly across the road, her shoes biting at her feet. A smile flitted across her face as she thought of the night that lay ahead of them. Hamilton was always at his best in his London home. With his wife safely tucked away in the constituency, the door locked and the phone off the hook, he was able to relax. And Mark Hamilton was a passionate man. Emily had known other lovers, but none of them like Mark. They had been boys in comparison, hopeless, bumbling, selfish men who had used her as they might use a new toy: for five minutes she had claimed all their attention and then they became bored and turned their attention elsewhere to newer, more flashy models.

Mark was different. He might have other affairs, but he always treated her as something special, never used and discarded her. He was always there for her in a way no other man had been. And now she sensed he was in trouble, he was becoming ever more dependent on her. She sensed the time was coming when he would finally make the break with his wife.

She turned down the narrow road of small terraced cottages. She did not notice the unmarked grey transit van that moved slowly away from the curb opposite Hamilton's house and passed her as she fumbled in her handbag for the house keys. The gate was open and a moment later she was at the front door. She pushed the bell briefly to let Mark know she had arrived and then opened the door.

'Mark!' she called. 'It's me.'

There was silence. Somewhere in the kitchen she could hear a radio. She smiled and put down her document case and removed her raincoat. Beneath it she was wearing a mini skirt and a tight top that emphasised her breasts and revealed a stretch of tightly muscled abdomen. In the hall mirror, she adjusted her make up, brushed back her hair the way she knew Mark liked it.

And then she walked into the kitchen and screamed.

The Jewish spy was not proving as easy to break as Rami had anticipated. His cover had been good, but there had been little mistakes. He had asked too many questions, been far too inquisitive about their operations and what their future plans would be. Rami had begun to take a close interest in the Mossad's man soon after his arrival. At first he had taken the man at face value, accepted Stronik's assurances that he was one of the best, a man they could depend upon. But the story had been a little too perfect, the man's comments a little too polished.

Finally Rami had searched his room. He found nothing, but the man had returned before he was finished. There had been a scene. The man had attacked him and Rami had lashed out. Stronik had been furious, but when Rami convinced him of the need to check the man's true identity, Stronik had agreed. Rami took the man into the basement cells. At first he had tried persuasion, but the man refused to talk. They discovered a cyanide pill in the man's clothing and removed it before he could take it.

When persuasion failed, Rami turned instead to other methods.

'You will talk eventually,' he whispered into the man's ear. 'Everyone does.'

The man smiled at him. 'You will learn nothing. You will have to kill me.'

Rami had smiled. 'Indeed I shall,' he replied. 'But not yet. First you will talk.'

He turned and reached for the stick. The sooner he started, the sooner the man would talk. And the sooner he could be removed.

Monroe was surprised when he received the call from Brewer. 'What package?' he asked.

Brewer resisted the temptation to scream at him down the phone.

'Stop messing about, Monroe. This is urgent.'

'Who's messing?' Monroe's calmness was infuriating. 'I told you, Peter. I never received any package from you. Whatever was in it?'

Brewer slammed down the phone. Either the post office had lost the package, or someone had intercepted the copy of the GDM documents he had sent to Monroe for safe-keeping. And that would mean someone inside the Firm. But who? Pendleton? But if it was Pendleton, he would hardly admit it to Brewer. And if it was not, it might place Pendleton in an awkward position. If someone was working against them from inside the Firm, it might begin to explain some of the problems he had encountered. It would also explain some of Mark Hamilton's comments.

Brewer left the phone box and walked into a newsagents. He stopped as he caught sight of the headlines in the papers.

MP in Kinky Death Scandal!!

It was the picture that shocked him. It was not just any MP: it was Mark Hamilton.

Brewer fumbled with his loose change and bought several tabloids together with a copy of *The Independent*. He hurried back towards Jane's flat, impatiently fumbling through the papers. The story was a journalist's dream. Hamilton had been found dead in his kitchen by his Parliamentary secretary when she called on him to ask him to sign some urgent papers. Worse was to follow.

When he was found, Hamilton had been dressed only in a pair of women's stockings. A small rope was tied around his neck and in his mouth was a piece of orange. The papers explained that it was an example of an autoerotic sex experiment that had seriously misfired. Experts pontificated about the phenomenon. Hamilton was known for his sexual indulgences and somehow, the papers implied, his death in such a manner was not so surprising as it might seem. In the privacy of his flat, he had been indulging himself in a form of sexual fulfilment that apparently caused immense satisfaction, but also ran the huge risk of misjudgement—and death.

Brewer was not convinced by the newspapers' easy acceptance of a method of death they had never mentioned or known about before. Like so many stories, suddenly the media were instant experts—on a subject about which someone else had provided the steer and the material to back it up. The technique was not unknown to him: faking deaths from sexual deviation was a standard method of removal by both the Security Service and the Firm. It was far more convenient and far less suspicious than a bullet in the back of the head. Deaths from perverted sexual indiscretions always ensure that no-one probes too deeply: it was too embarrassing, too sordid and ultimately too ridiculous for anyone to dig deeper, or maintain that something more suspicious might lie behind the death. It was a bluntly effective way of silencing a problem and eliminating the possibility of a proper investigation. But the timing of Hamilton's death was too convenient for it to be anything other than a deliberate death.

Someone had eliminated him. And the trademark fingerprints of the Firm or the Security Service were there for anyone who knew how to read the evidence.

As Brewer pushed open the crudely mended door to Jane's flat, he knew one thing was for certain: he had to be very careful. It was all beginning to unravel.

When Parke and Cham met later that day, Hamilton's death and the stolen GDM papers were at the forefront of their thoughts. Cham was abrupt and not for the first time, Parke wondered what was going through his mind.

'Forget the missing papers, Parke. They will be retrieved. And as for Hamilton, he was merely careless,' Cham commented as he ordered tea for two from the Ritz waiter. 'His sexual indiscretions were a risk we could do without. We always knew that.'

Parke did not reply immediately. He had known of Hamilton's affair with his secretary, as did most of Hamilton's close colleagues and associates. But there had never been even the slightest hint in any of the Press. Unlike the other stories that populated the daily and Sunday papers, Hamilton's peccadilloes had passed without so much as an ironic or cryptic reference. Newspaper journalists are never too quick to accuse and expose those politicians with whom they work most closely: their existence relies too much on mutual back scratching. And in any case, former Defence Secretaries have too many highly placed friends. One wrong word and a promising Fleet Street career can be extinguished under foot with as little concern as that of a child stepping on an ant.

What concerned Parke most was Cham's apparent lack of concern. Hamilton had been at the centre of their plans: his loss would surely change everything. Yet Parke sensed that Hamilton's loss had not touched him. In fact, Cham almost appeared relieved by the news of Hamilton's death.

'It must have been dreadful,' Parke commented, watching as the waiter brought their tea. 'I mean, for his secretary. Fancy finding anyone like that. Awful.'

'She can't complain,' Cham commented bluntly. 'She danced near the flame and got burnt. Anyone who has an affair with someone like Hamilton deserves what they get.' He glared at the waiter, who had made the mistake of taking too much interest in their conversation. 'If you must insist on feeling sorry for someone then think of his wife. She did not even know he was having an affair. Had her suspicions of course. Next thing she knows, her husband's mistress finds him wearing the sort of outfit that even Amsterdam would find somewhat risqué.'

'You believe the papers then, do you?'

Cham stopped stirring the tea in the pot. 'Are you saying you don't?'

Parke shrugged. 'I know Hamilton was highly sexed, but a sexual perversion like this is something else entirely.'

'You speak from personal experience do you?' Cham asked quietly.

'Of course not,' Parke flushed bright red.

Cham leaned towards him. 'Then stop your speculation. It's what has destroyed this country. Constant negative thought, constant attacks on everything, endless waves of cynicism. One thing you learn about cynics: they always sit on the sidelines running down everyone else, but they're never prepared to stand up and be counted. It's always so much easier to knock and destroy than to create.'

'But Emily and Hamilton were close,' Parke persisted. 'I just find it unbelievable.'

Cham shrugged. 'It happened, I believe it. Ergo, it is believable.'

'You don't suspect foul play?' Park enquired.

'Come, come Parke. Listen to yourself, will you? Now you're talking like a cheap airport paperback,' Cham laughed. 'Foul play? With Hamilton and his minders? Just face the facts, Parke. Unpleasant they may be, but Hamilton took his own life. You might not believe it now, but that will be the verdict. Trust my word. An independent coroner's report will find precisely that, you mark my words. A sad, perverted man.'

Parke chewed thoughtfully on a sandwich. 'And how does this affect us?'

'It doesn't,' Cham commented. 'Hamilton had played his part.'

'Then what about me?' Parke enquired softly. 'When I've played my part, will I be found like Hamilton?'

Cham laughed, but it struck Parke as a false, hollow laugh. 'Of course not. You should have been a scriptwriter, Parke. You have such a false sense of the dramatic. Hamilton was an exception. Our plans continue as they were. It's merely unfortunate that Hamilton has left us before he could reap the benefits.'

'And what about the Press? You think their theories are crazy too?'

Cham smiled and sipped at his tea. 'The papers see conspiracies where in reality there is only cock-up and personal despair. Hamilton was a sad man, past his peak. It was all going to be downhill from here for a man like that.'

'And so he committed hari kari?' Parke enquired, wishing the Ritz had left the crust on the bread. Crustless sandwiches reminded him of the sticky Marmite sandwiches his childhood nanny had made him. 'Not like Hamilton. In any case, he was looking forward to the results of our work. It meant a great deal to him.'

'Who knows what goes through another man's thoughts in the privacy of his own bedroom?'

'It was the kitchen,' Parke said. 'And I still don't believe it.'

'You must,' Cham insisted, pinning Parke in his gaze. 'Believe me, you must.'

18

Brewer arrived at Pendleton's house shortly after six p.m. It was a large three-storey terraced house in Notting Hill, tucked away in one of those exclusive tree-lined roads blocked by rows of double-parked BMW's and Mercedes. Pendleton had owned it since the 1960's, long before Notting Hill became fashionable. Brewer rarely visited Pendleton outside of work. He could only recall two previous occasions. Once for a party to celebrate the retirement of the one of the other controllers, and once for the funeral of Pendleton's wife. Neither had been enjoyable occasions.

Third time lucky he thought as he knocked on the door and waited. He had been surprised by the royal summons that he had found waiting for him on his answer phone: if Pendleton wanted to see him outside of work, something serious must have happened.

'Come in.'

Pendleton was wearing a shiny plastic apron, his hands coated with flour. There was another smudge of flour on the side of his nose. Brewer stepped forwards and followed Pendleton through to the kitchen. A fruity, alcoholic, garlic-rich smell came from the oven where something was cooking. The surfaces were cluttered with bowls and fresh foodstuffs, a reminder of Pendleton's penchant for fine cooking.

'Please excuse me while I cook, won't you?' Pendleton asked. 'Sherry?'

Brewer nodded and accepted the glass, wiping the flour from its brim.

'Don't worry, it's not that cheap stuff some people call cooking sherry,' Pendleton remarked. 'Even for cooking, I use only the best.'

'I never doubted it,' Brewer replied. He pulled himself up onto a stool and watched while Pendleton whipped eggs into a flour base.

'I presume you've seen the news?' Pendleton enquired.

'Hamilton's erotic demise, you mean?' Brewer nodded. 'I take it you don't believe the verdict either.'

'Of course not,' he replied shortly. 'We've seen it before of course. Although Jung would argue it as mere synchronicity,' Pendleton suggested, concentrating his attention on his cooking.

'I didn't think you went in for all that psycho-babble, sir,' Brewer said, sipping at the sherry, which was more like a port than anything else.

'I don't,' Pendleton replied. 'And in case you were wondering, I didn't call you here today merely to observe my cooking. You might be interested to note that I'm on gardening leave. Or in my case, perhaps gardening and cooking leave.'

'On leave?' Brewer was surprised: Pendleton never took leave. It could mean only one thing. 'Don't tell me they're gunning for you too?'

'I think it may be more than that,' Pendleton replied. 'This Hamilton business is getting out of hand. The powers that be want me well out of the picture. There's something far bigger going on. Including an American connection.'

'American? What makes you think that?'

Pendleton smiled and touched his nose, leaving another white smudge of flour. 'Contacts,' he said. 'Monroe has kept me fully informed of your discussions.'

'Two-timing bastard.'

'Oh, don't blame him. He was only obeying orders. My orders. Anyway, you should be grateful. We did some checking on your information. Came up with one or two useful titbits.'

'Such as?'

'The FBI are working on a case that I have very strong

suspicions overlaps with ours. From what I gather, some time ago they received a tip-off some about a German scientist who was involved during the 1980s in helping build poison gas factories in Libya and Iraq.'

'Sounds like a really nice guy,' Brewer whispered. 'But the 1980s is a long time ago by international standards. Since then Libya seems to have come in from the cold and Iraq's changing following Saddam's downfall, so why the interest now?'

'What really rattled the Bureau is that now this chap's somewhere in the States. But what's more important, that other name you came up with, Thielstrom. He's there too.'

'In the States? No wonder I couldn't find him.' Brewer finished his sherry. 'So what do you think is going on?'

'I don't have a clue,' Pendleton responded. 'And the way things are going, I'm not going to.'

'What about Cham? Isn't he going to back you on all this?'

Pendleton hesitated and shook his head, adding a slab of butter into the bowl. 'Cham was distinctly unhelpful. Said we had spent too much time on the other lot's territory. Quite sniffy he was about the whole thing. In fact, he was involved in my enforced leave. I'm sure of that.'

'Great. So now we're both out in the cold,' Brewer observed. 'Perhaps we should just take early retirement and set up a knitting circle.'

Pendleton glared at him. 'You can do what you like, but I'm going to see these new bastards out if it's the last thing I do.' He resumed his preparations. 'Anyway, I'm not completely out in the cold. I'm still maintaining informal contacts.' He stopped and wiped his hands on the apron. 'That envelope over there.'

'This?' Brewer picked it up.

'It should keep you going.'

'What does that mean?'

'I want you to follow up this American lead. If there's something rotten inside the Firm, our cousins are the best friends we could have.'

Brewer smiled. 'You're doing it again, Pendleton. Sending me out of territory. That's well outside your control area.'

'It's not my fault,' Pendleton replied patiently. 'If the Firm runs itself on such ridiculous lines. Anyway, I'm on leave. This conversation isn't taking place.'

Brewer thought for a moment. 'Do you have a contact?'

'There's a special agent called Paul Yellow Hawk in charge of their op. You'll find him working out of a temporary Bureau facility in Lincoln. That's where they're running their surveillance.'

'What surveillance?'

'I believe in part it's to monitor this elusive GDM director chap Thielstrom you were after. But he's not their main target. They're more interested in this Schengel fellow. I'm not sure they know much about Thielstrom.' Pendleton tasted the mix and pulled a face. 'Too bitter.' He stirred in some castor sugar.

'And what's their angle? Do they know what's been happening at this end?'

'That's up to you to discover,' Pendleton responded. 'Do help yourself to more sherry. GDM's certainly been trading illegally, but it looks like there's something bigger than that. GDM itself may have been used by a third party as yet unknown to us.'

'And where does Hamilton fit into all this?'

'Difficult to say. Certainly his contacts would have been useful.'

'I don't understand it. Hamilton must have been under the care and protection of Special Branch. You can't tell me he was conducting a business like this right under their noses without them spotting something suspicious.' Brewer helped himself to more sherry and topped up Pendleton's glass.

'Brewer. You have a very irritating habit of putting your finger right on the hot spot,' Pendleton complained. 'My sources indicate Special Branch is already investigating GDM and the Hamilton business.'

'And what about the Security Service?'

'As far as I know, they don't appear to know a thing. Neither SB nor the Firm has tipped them off about our current enquiries and they don't appear to have picked up on anything themselves.'

'I didn't suppose the Yard would co-operate, but I thought Cham might have communicated the information. Particularly if, as you say, he thinks we've been wasting too much time on a case that should be theirs.'

Pendleton shook his head. 'Cham's being very mysterious about this whole thing.'

'You don't suppose he's already running somebody under deep cover?'

'It's possible.' Pendleton moved the bowl under the electric mixer. For a minute it was impossible to talk while the shriek and whine of the motor obliterated all other sound. Finally it groaned into silence.

'On the other hand,' Pendleton said thoughtfully, dipping his finger into the mix to taste it. 'Perhaps he has other objectives.'

'What other objectives?'

For the first time Pendleton stopped his preparations and looked directly at Brewer. 'It was Cham who intercepted that package you sent Monroe.'

Brewer frowned. 'Are you sure?'

Pendleton nodded.

'So what does that mean?'

'It means,' Pendleton said slowly. 'That Cham's playing his own game. And I think we need to be very careful. After much persuasion, I also found out from Monroe that it was Cham who told him about the safe house where Anastasia was being held.'

'So Cham's more involved with this case than any of us realised,' Brewer remarked. 'Have you spoken with C?'

Pendleton shook his head. 'Not yet. Cham might be working on his instructions.'

As a Deputy Chief, Cham reported directly to C, the head of the Service. Pendleton's reporting line was normally direct to the Assistant Chief of Operations, but at present the post was vacant and his reporting line had moved up a tier, directly to Cham. It was only in exceptional circumstances that Pendleton would expect to approach C directly. When a Controller like Pendleton runs into operational problems, it is more customary for them to discuss options with their fellow Controllers. As well as Pendleton, the European Controller, there were Controllers for the Western Hemisphere, the Soviet Bloc (which comprised those countries that now called themselves the CIS, or Confederation of Independent States), Africa, Mid-East, Australasia and Liaison, which attempts to co-ordinate activities across the arbitrary Control areas.

The vacant Assistant Chief of Operations post would normally report into one of the Deputy Chiefs of the Service, such as Cham. They would also work alongside the other Assistant Chiefs, who were responsible for the other four divisions: Intelligence (responsible for the analysis of information), Technical (which furnishes technical gadgets and false papers), Administration (which looks after salaries, pensions and other items related to the routine running of the Service) and Counter-Intelligence (which checks and vets those employed in the Service).

It was unusual for a Deputy Chief such as Cham to involve himself so directly in an operational case. Most of the work of the Service is managed and directed through committees, rather than through individual action. Brewer wondered why Cham had involved himself so closely and what purpose there had been in his removal of the files sent to Monroe and the information about Anastasia and the safe house. Was Cham laying a cover as part of an official operation of which neither Brewer nor Pendleton were aware? Or did he have a different agenda?

Brewer watched Pendleton busying himself with his preparations. If Cham was not working on an official operation, that left only one other option.

An option that left Brewer highly vulnerable and isolated.

Yellow Hawk was surprised to receive instructions to expect a visitor from London. The news that an agent from the United Kingdom was interested in their operation puzzled him. He had considered their surveillance and the interest in Schengel as purely a Bureau task with an American, and possibly a middle-Eastern, aspect. If there was a European connection, it was the first he knew of it.

Doubts flitted through his mind. It would not be the first time he had been briefed to lead an operation without all the information being made available to him. He was under no illusions. If this operation went wrong, he knew who would be left to carry the can.

Of course, the Bureau has not been without its mistakes: no Government agency of its size and scope has not. There have been rogue operations, often influenced by the disastrous legacy Hoover left behind, with its absurd and impossible belief that the Bureau is incapable of mistakes and worse, that it is incapable of admitting to such mistakes when they occur. The reality that mistakes are important, that they provide the key means to learn and develop, was anathema to the legacy left behind by Hoover. Luckily that legacy was changing.

Yellow Hawk ordered another beer in the downtown Lincoln bar and wondered what the Englishman would be like. He knew little about the British intelligence services, or even whether they had an FBI of their own. But most of all he was curious about the connection: they had seen no evidence of a European angle. How could they have missed something so obvious? He would contact the FBI legat in London, see whether they could shed any light on possible links between those identified in the compound and developments on the European continent. Schengel was a German national, but he was rarely in Germany itself: his work kept him almost permanently abroad.

When his new beer arrived, he drank it straight from the bottle and nearly finished it in one.

'You're a thirsty man, mister,' the waitress commented.

Yellow Hawk looked at her. 'Fancy one yourself?'

She looked around. The bar was quiet. It was still early evening, in that slack time before the evening crowd emerge. 'Sure. I'll join you.'

She fetched another bottle and came round the bar counter to sit on the stool beside him. Yellow Hawk leaned back. Tonight he was going to put work from his mind. Tonight he was going to relax.

He had the nasty feeling nagging him at the back of his mind that it might be his last opportunity.

It was Stronik's idea to use Schengel to assist with the interrogation of the Jew. Rami had not been convinced by the idea at first, but then Stronik had shown him pictures of the effects of Schengel's concoctions. Even Rami, who had more experience than most in the unpleasant nature of death, was taken aback by some of the images he was shown.

Schengel was like a child as he prepared his syringe, his breath coming in short, excited bursts. The Israeli agent had resisted, tried to pull away from the needle, but his struggles were in vain. Schengel had injected the full syringe and then stood back and smiled.

Within hours, Rami had been shaken by the transformation. By the second day the hair had started to fall from the prisoner's body. Then the skin itself started to flake, dissolving like wax in front of a flame. The Israeli screamed, his sight failing, his voice no more than a crude rasping noise. He pleaded to be killed, for Rami to end his life, to show a shred of humanity.

But Rami stood and watched, fascinated by the effect of the biological agent. Schengel had joined him.

'It is good, yes?' he enquired, a schoolboy proud of his artwork.

'It is achieving its purpose, yes,' Rami agreed quietly.

'This is nothing,' Schengel replied. 'I have better than this. Whatever you would like. Slow death, quick death. All can be arranged. All have been tried and tested.'

Rami turned to look at the man and his bulging eyes behind his thick-lensed glasses. Schengel was mad, the sort of inspired madman that served the Reich so well during the Second World War. It was impossible to imagine how this man would have used his talents if the opportunities shown to him by terrorist regimes and the NSDAP-AO had not been available. Probably he would have spent his life tucked away in a leafy suburb of an anonymous town and become a serial killer, venturing out only to select the latest victim for his sick experiments. But under the Nazi's tutelage, such people find another platform, find respect and wealth. There is no soul too dark to be exploited in the furtherance of the Nazi cause, no thought or action, however sick, that cannot be explored and noted. Under the third Reich, night truly became day, and day night. And now others carried that cloak, disparate groups from the heretics of Al Qaeda to crackpot militia, all with a common agenda to seek power, to control and destroy others.

Schengel reminded Rami of many of the wartime scientists who had served the Nazi cause. It was interesting that those who were most on the side of the angels, the doctors, were amongst the first to sign up to the Nazi party. Long before it was necessary to do so, more than forty-five percent of doctors belonged to the Nazi party, the highest ratio of any profession. Their worst excesses can be seen in the work of men like Mengele: the Nazis applied a pure science that appealed to many, a science devoid of morality. And Schengel had followed their example. Radical, pioneering scientists will often seek extreme governments or regimes: democracy impedes their work.

Twenty-four hours later the Israeli agent broke. He rambled and talked, stammering and stuttering, many of his words barely audible, barely intelligible. He told them everything about the surveillance operation, everything that was known about the NSDAP-AO's plans.

When Rami took the information to Stronik, he was visibly shaken.

'They know all this?' he asked. 'We have to evacuate quickly.'

Rami nodded. 'And what about the prisoner?'

'You need to ask?' Stronik said with surprise. 'Deal with him yourself, or if you prefer, give him to Schengel.'

Rami dealt with the Mossad man himself. A single, merciful shot to the head. Rami did not enjoy suffering for its own sake, as Schengel clearly did. For him it had to have a purpose. That purpose had now been served and, as a professional, he wanted to finish the job professionally too.

When Brewer reached his hotel room in downtown Lincoln

he stripped off and stood under a boiling hot shower. The flight had left him dusty and tired, a reaction assisted by his almost continuous consumption of complimentary beers since leaving London. After ten minutes of subjecting himself to a fierce torrent of steaming water, he wrapped himself in a towel, sat in front of the air-conditioning vent and looked out over Lincoln. It looked to him like so many other US cities: a mix of newish high rises downtown surrounded by older, lower buildings with a snake of traffic moving constantly through its midst.

As he sat watching over the city, his thoughts turned to Jane and the night before his departure. She had met him at the American Bar in the Savoy for cocktails. Although still bruised from her violent assault, she had never looked better. There was a glow about her that he had not seen before, a feeling of calmness, sensuality and confidence. Her long, elegant dress had hugged her in all the right places, flattered her slim shapely legs and the shape of her breasts. He noticed the straying eyes of the other men—and women—turning to examine her. She had highlighted her high cheekbones with a subtle dash of rouge, blown and layered her dyed hair. Those who say that men age well while women decline with age should open their eyes: some women's beauty matures with age.

They moved on, dined at the Wig and Pen Club and afterwards took a taxi to Jane's flat. What had already been a good evening improved. They shared a steaming hot bath and massaged each other with rich body oil, Brewer skilfully avoiding the deep blue-violet remnants of her bruises. They had made love together on the rug in front of the fire, not once, not twice, but throughout the night until by dawn they were both drained and satisfied.

'Take care, Peter,' she had whispered. 'Promise me.'

And he had hugged her tight and promised.

The thought of her was enough to arouse him and he dressed quickly, putting her from his mind. He called room service for a pizza and several bottles of Coke. Since his meeting with Pendleton, everything had moved too quickly. Brewer liked time to breathe, to reflect on developments, but time was in short supply. Despite the problems at the Firm and his run-in with Cham, Pendleton had continued to operate. Additional information about the FBI's surveillance of the neo-Nazis in Lincoln had come via the FBI's legal attaché in London. A meeting had been held between Pendleton and the Bureau's representatives at the American embassy, where the FBI run their London operation.

Large legats, such as London, Paris and Bonn, operate as many as five agents, the smaller ones perhaps just one or two. Since 1989, the FBI has had the right to seize fugitives from overseas without seeking permission from the country involved. Anxious not to upset host nations, however, the Bureau generally operates in more overt ways and even makes sure that it holds annual parties for 'friendly' agencies in those countries where it operates. The late Winter London parties have proved popular amongst Britain's Security Service, Secret Intelligence Service and Special Branch.

The pizza and drinks arrived and Brewer ripped open the packet of chilli seeds and scattered them generously over the cheese topping. He took his first bite just as the telephone rang.

'Hello?' his voice was muffled as he chewed slowly on the pizza bread.

'Brewer?'

'Speaking.'

'Ten a.m.'

The phone went dead. Brewer replaced the receiver, ripped the top from a can of Coke and sat back to watch TV. The message was clear—and misleading to the casual eavesdropper. It had been agreed that whatever time the Bureau indicated they would collect him, he would need to subtract two hours. So they were coming for him at eight the following morning. That would give him time for a good rest. A rest he badly needed.

Jane opened the door on the second ring, the door restricted by a security chain. After the previous incident with intruders, she was taking no chances. She found herself looking out at a well-dressed man of around forty.

'I'm sorry to disturb you. I'm looking for a Mr Peter Brewer.'
Jane did not react. 'I've never heard of him.'

The man smiled. 'I'm sorry. I should have introduced myself.'
He took a card from his pocket and showed it to her in the narrow
gap between the door and the frame. She examined it closely,
suspecting a trick. It claimed to be a card identifying a Detective
Inspector David Howarth of Scotland Yard's Special Branch. The
man in the photo was the same man who stood on her doorstep.

'Can I come in?'

She hesitated a moment and then pushed the door closed,
slipped off the chain and opened it wider, signs of the recent
damage still visible. They went upstairs to the flat where they
both stood awkwardly in the front room.

'Would you like a tea or something?' she asked, standing
with her arms folded across her chest. Memories of her recent
assault were too vivid for her to trust anyone. Peter had given her
a number to call in the event of an emergency. But she knew
from the previous assault that she would not have the luxury of
time to make a call.

Howarth shook his head.

'I won't be staying. It's important that I speak with Mr Brewer.'

'He's not here.'

'So I gathered.' Howarth smiled. 'Can you get a message to
him? I think it would be useful for us both to talk.'

'Can you tell me what about?'

Howarth shook his head. 'I'm afraid not. It's very, let me say,
sensitive.'

'Is it?' Jane examined him closely. 'It's something to do with
this Hamilton business isn't it?'

Surprise showed on Howarth's face. 'What do you know about
it?'

'Are you covering up? Is that it?'

'I'm not covering anything up,' Howarth said softly. 'Exactly
the contrary.'

'You've been watching me, haven't you?' Jane asked
suddenly. 'How else would you know he'd been here?'

'I'm not at liberty to divulge that information,' Howarth responded. 'All I can tell you is that it is very important that we talk. Please listen to me.'

'If he calls me, I'll inform him of your visit,' Jane said.

They stood in silence. For a moment, Howarth toyed with the idea of taking her in for further questioning. But there were too many problems. One, he was not sure how much she knew, how closely she was involved and what her role was. If she was in fact working for one of the intelligence agencies, he would not be thanked for his action. Second, he was aware of her recent assault. She was still uncomfortable: he did not need to be a counsellor to see that.

'Is there anyone else I can talk to? Someone instead of Brewer? It really is important.'

Jane bit her lip. 'There's a man called Pendleton,' she said. 'I think you'll be able to find out how to contact him yourself.'

'Pendleton? I'll see what I can do.' Howarth turned away and then stopped for a moment. 'Thanks.'

Jane watched as he left and wished that Peter was home. A voice whispered uncomfortably in the back of her mind, reminded her that she had once hoped and waited in vain for Gary. It could happen again. And something deep inside told her it would. She prayed she was wrong.

It was a bright, blue-skied morning, a welcome contrast with the grey and damp of London. As Brewer stepped from the hotel into the crisp air of the dawn, a car pulled to a halt and a tall man stepped out. Brewer needed no introduction. The car had enough aerial technology attached to its boot to have been a mobile radio station and the man who had climbed out was unmistakably a Native American.

'Paul Yellow Hawk?' he said, holding out a hand of greeting. 'Peter Brewer.'

The man nodded and briefly crushed his hand in an arm-wrestler's grip. They climbed into the car and drove away from the kerb. Brewer did his best to ignore the arsenal of weaponry and communications equipment surrounding him. Above his head two shotguns were strapped into a quick release rack, in easy reach of Yellow Hawk. Clearly the FBI did not believe in taking unnecessary risks.

'Good hotel?' Yellow Hawk enquired.

'They should put a sign in the rooms of these places to tell you what city you're in. Maybe even what country. Sometimes I wake up in these places and don't have a clue where I am.'

Yellow Hawk grunted in agreement and cut through a series of side streets that left Brewer wondering which way they were heading.

'You don't have any idea who else might be muscling in on this show, do you?' Yellow Hawk asked. 'See, we have company at our surveillance.'

'I thought it was just you and me,' Brewer commented. 'Any clues?'

'Just that they're good. Thought they might be some of yours.'

'If they are, it's the first I've heard of it,' Brewer said.

The radio crackled and a snatched voice came through in disjointed segments.

'What's that?' Brewer asked.

'Shift change,' Yellow Hawk replied. 'Graveyard crew coming off duty down at the compound.'

'Anything happening?'

Yellow Hawk shook his head and shot across a major intersection in front of a police car.

'Same movements every day. Provisions, unmarked lorries. They look after themselves well, food and drink wise. Some of the other shipments are weapons. Semi-automatic and automatics. Nothing illegal of course. It's all done by the book.'

'Nothing unusual?'

'Yeah. Large shipments of chemicals.'

'Chemicals? What sort of chemicals?'

'Not my field I'm afraid. You'll have to ask our eggheads. With this guy Schengel around, it don't look good. The stuff comes in, various chemicals, and then they ship stuff out. Looks like they're making something in there. We're tracing where the shipments are going. Usual thing for now, just monitoring and observing, building up the case file.' Yellow Hawk cast him a sideways looks. 'So remind me, what's your interest?'

'A man called Thielstrom,' Brewer replied. 'He's connected to a defence consultancy company in the UK. They've been handling dodgy shipments of arms and matériel.'

'That all?' Yellow Hawk asked with surprise. 'Hell, we have hundreds of them over here. Take your pick. It's a national pastime.'

'It's not quite all,' Brewer continued softly. 'There's a political connection.'

'Ah.' Yellow Hawk's attitude changed. 'Big shit?'

'Big shit,' Brewer confirmed. 'Does the name Hamilton mean anything to you?'

'Hamilton?' Yellow Hawk shook his head. 'Can't say it does.'

'He was Minister for Defence in the last administration. And he was involved with this arms company I mentioned. I emphasise 'was'. Last week he was found dead. Wearing stockings and little else.'

'Kinky.'

'Looks like a deliberate diversion,' Brewer replied. 'Removal of someone who had become too hot. They knew we were onto him. This has to be more than just an illegal arms-trading case. I always think murder's an extreme way to cover up.'

'Yeah, we've got it figured as more than just the usual nutcases,' Yellow Hawk agreed. 'They're working on something and they're better organised than anyone else we've come across, except maybe the casa nostra. Question is, what the hell are they doing? None of our sigint has come up with anything. They know how to block everything we've thrown at them. And they have got some pretty heavy cipher technology. We really need some good humint.'

'You don't have anyone inside?'

'Fat chance,' Yellow Hawk shook his head. 'And the guys they employ inside aren't the type you buy with money. They're fanatics. Some of them known to us, some of them not. Right-wing rednecks of the worst kind.'

The car hammered to a halt. Yellow Hawk cut the engine.

'Welcome to home base, Lincoln's regional office. We've reporting lines into here, Omaha and New York.'

'New York?' Brewer was surprised. 'I thought you lot were based in Washington.'

'Anything this big involves New York. That's where we run our Operations and Command Centre. Anything with a major political dimension. We'll give you an update.'

They stepped out of the car and entered the building, a squat office block set back from the road and dominated by the surrounding skyscrapers. The entrance had bare concrete walls and a short walkway leading to an elevator. Several video cameras swivelled to watch their progress.

When the elevator doors opened on the next floor, all that faced them was a pair of closed metal doors. Yellow Hawk entered a security code into a punch pad and put his eye against a scanner.

'Retina scan?' Brewer enquired, surprised by the sophisticated arrangements.

Yellow Hawk nodded. A second later, the door clicked. Yellow Hawk straightened and walked through. A receptionist behind a bulletproof panel looked up and smiled at Yellow Hawk. She handed Brewer a pass that already had his photo embossed.

'They snatch them from the video image on the CCTV,' Yellow Hawk explained. 'We already ran a check on your fingerprints from a glass at the hotel. We know you're the right guy.'

They went through another door and along a plain green corridor with closed, unmarked doors on either side and bright, high wattage lighting. Yellow Hawk opened a door into one of the offices to reveal several desks laden with papers and photos. On one wall was a large photograph of a heavily guarded complex. On another, an aerial shot of the same complex with arrows and text appended explaining the purpose of each building.

Yellow Hawk nodded at the two agents busy working at the desks and introduced Brewer.

'This is Wolf and Minor,' Yellow Hawk explained.

Wolf was a middle-aged man who, with his short clipped hair and white shirt and tie, looked like he was aiming to emulate Hoover's idea of a true G-man. Minor was a younger, power-dressed woman who specialised in intelligence operations. She would have looked at home in a lawyer's office.

They sat around Yellow Hawk's desk.

'Brewer needs an update. Particularly anything we have on Thielstrom.'

Wolf and Minor exchanged a look.

'Hey, what does that mean?' Yellow Hawk asked.

'Thielstrom left last night. Destination London.'

'London?' Brewer was unable to hide his disappointment.

'From what we know,' Minor continued. 'They had some sort of big meeting yesterday. There were a whole load of new faces.'

Wolf reached over to his desk and pulled over a stack of photos.

'Can I see those?' Brewer asked.

Wolf looked uncertainly at Yellow Hawk. Yellow Hawk nodded. 'Sure. If we're going to co-operate, we're gonna have to trust each other.'

Brewer took the photos and started to leaf through them. 'Have you identified any of these?'

'We're working on it,' Wolf said. 'We know where most of them flew in from. We've put word out to the other field offices we need positive ID and quick.'

The photos varied in quality. Some were fuzzy, taken in low light. Others were sharp and clear enough to accompany a magazine article in *Time*. Most of them showed anonymous middle-aged men in suits. They could have been anyone: a convention of bankers, a meeting of shareholders or businessmen. From what Brewer knew of the operation, and what Lord Northwood had told him about the Nazi financiers, they probably were.

Brewer stopped. 'I know these two.'

He handed the photos round.

'Interesting pair. They've been inside the compound for some time,' Minor commented. 'They arrived before Rami and Thielstrom. They seem to be more closely involved than some of the others, right at the heart of the operation.'

'They were calling themselves Straker and Hümmler last time I met them,' Brewer added. 'Hümmler shot a man in Denmark. Both of them were involved in the theft of some papers.'

'What sort of papers?' Yellow Hawk asked.

Brewer shrugged. 'I never did find out. One set came from a Second World War U-Boat. Another from the KGB archives in Moscow. Possibly both sets of papers contained the same information. We suspect they were also implicated in the death of a British academic in Moscow and his Russian assistant.'

'Papers from a U-Boat? I don't understand.'

Brewer filled them in as quickly as he could. The information left them looking as blank as he felt.

'You think there's some kind of link between these old papers and this bunch of neo-Nazis?' Yellow Hawk asked.

'I'm not so sure that Straker is a neo-Nazi,' Brewer replied. 'He's just about old enough to be the real thing. Like Thielstrom.'

'And Stronik,' whispered Wolf.

'Stronik?' Brewer had not heard the name before.

'He's the person in charge. Leastways, far as we can tell. But your guess is as good as mine whether he's the real guy at the top of the tree. They're very good at covering their tracks these guys.'

Yellow Hawk leaned back in his chair. 'Okay, okay. This is getting complex. I get the feeling that all of us here should share everything we know. I think we may discover we can fill in some of the missing pieces. Agreed?'

The others nodded.

'Let's get cracking.'

Howarth was surprised by Pendleton's suggestion they should meet at Howarth's office in New Scotland Yard. He had presumed the intelligence man would want to meet on home ground at Vauxhall Cross, but Pendleton was insistent they meet at the Yard.

It was shortly after three when his secretary showed Pendleton into the room. Howarth was amused to discover that Pendleton looked exactly how he had imagined him from his voice: a portly, bank manager figure of a man who would have looked at home in a bowler hat striding down 1950's Whitehall. He was the spitting image of one of the Thompson twins from the *Tintin* books, if somewhat balder.

Howarth waited while his secretary poured them both a coffee and then asked her to ensure they were not disturbed by anyone—visitors or phone calls.

'Let's cut the formalities,' Pendleton started. 'How much do you know?'

'I'm not sure how much I know for sure and how much is just suspicion,' Howarth replied carefully, surprised by the directness of the question. His previous dealings with intelligence officers had involved conversations containing vague terms and concepts: nothing had been referred to directly. 'We've been maintaining a surveillance on Hamilton, the MP, and those concerned with his company, GDM. I also know that one of your men burgled their offices.'

'Apparently,' Pendleton said, without any indication of whether he had approved of the action or not. 'And do you have a clear picture yet?'

'It looks to me like GDM is in breach of government guidelines on the trading of arms.'

'Anything else?'

Howarth frowned and hesitated before replying. This was not how he had imagined the conversation. He had wanted to meet Pendleton to acquire information from him, not the other way around. 'I don't understand why you lot are operating on home turf. I thought this would be native Thames House territory.'

'It's not so clear-cut,' Pendleton replied noncommittally. 'There are various international dimensions. Is your surveillance still in place?'

'As much as it is possible to be when our main target is dead.'

'Yes, I was wondering how that happened. You had his house under observation didn't you?'

Howarth sighed. 'You know how it is. Everyone eager to work long hours, earn the overtime. But they forget they can't survive without sleep indefinitely even with artificial stimulants.'

'Are you telling me they slept through whatever happened? That you don't have any evidence that may help?'

'It was a suicide wasn't it?' Howarth asked innocently, with a gleam in his eye that suggested he knew, or thought, something else.

'I can see you don't believe that either. Far too convenient for everyone. No, someone had him removed in such a way as to ensure there would be no further digging. Maximum embarrassment.'

'Any idea who?'

Pendleton sucked in his cheeks and then exhaled noisily. 'I think Hamilton was in deeper than he knew. I don't doubt that he was involved in the illegal trading, but I don't think he ever understood what really lay behind it.'

'And what exactly does lie behind it?' Howarth leaned forwards across his desk. 'Who was using GDM?'

'Possibly his fellow directors. There is a name we have run into several times. Thielstrom.'

'Yes, I know the name,' Howarth replied.

'He seems to be the real driving force. Hamilton was useful for his contacts and his political knowledge. We think Thielstrom was using him. Possibly he's using the other director as well.'

'Parke?'

'Or they could both be in on it.'

'Now I understand,' Howarth commented. 'Your man, the one who flew out to Nebraska.'

'My, my. You are keeping close watch, aren't you?' Pendleton commented sharply.

'I take it he's followed Thielstrom. Do you know what the American angle is?'

'Not at all,' Pendleton admitted. 'But it turns out our American friends have been taking an interest.'

'The Bureau?'

'They have an active surveillance operation that's almost a mirror of your own.'

Howarth looked thoughtful. 'I think it's time we had a longer talk, don't you?'

Brewer was surprised to receive the call, but he agreed to the rendezvous. He was at Dunkin Donuts fifteen minutes early and sat reading through a two-day-old copy of the *Financial Times* taken from the hotel. He ordered two large coffees and sat working his way through them. At the agreed time, a man slipped into the seat opposite him and sat sipping at a Coke.

'Mr Brewer. Thank you for coming.'

Brewer folded the paper and stirred his coffee. 'It's been a long time.'

The man smiled. 'Indeed it has, Mr Brewer.'

Brewer had last met Simon Gilbert in Paris in the late 1980's as part of an action that the Direction de la Surveillance du Territoire (DST) in France had been conducting against Islamic terrorists infiltrating from North Africa. The French had never realised that the Mossad were also watching their every move, but Brewer had. He had seen their methods before.

A few years earlier, in the old West Germany, an assignment had overlapped. Brewer had been involved in uncovering a senior army officer working for the KGB. The Mossad were targeting the same officer, but for another reason. Their information related to the officer's true wartime record: it diverged widely from his official record and involved a spell in Warsaw when the ghetto had been liquidated. The officer was later found dead in a mysterious road accident. That had been the first time Brewer met Simon Gilbert. Only at that time Simon Gilbert had been Leon Axel. In Paris he had been Martin Janner. It was at Charles de Gaulle airport that Gilbert had broken all the rules and introduced himself.

'What brings you here, Mr Gilbert?' Brewer asked.

Gilbert smiled. 'As ever, Mr Brewer, our paths seem to cross.'

For a moment Gilbert contemplated telling Brewer about how he had saved his life in Moscow, how he had protected him from the

Nazi assassin. It was with reluctance he resisted the urge. Pride has no place in an effective agent: it is a fatal weakness. 'I suspect you have the same interests here as ourselves.'

'I expect so,' Brewer replied noncommittally. 'And what might that be?'

'The NSDAP-AO compound?'

Brewer nodded. 'My only interest is the British connection.'

'You are working with the Bureau?'

'On the British connection, yes.'

Gilbert shook his head. 'You know that the Agency were handed information about this months ago?'

Brewer stared at him. 'Months?' If the CIA had known about this months ago, why hadn't they contacted the SIS? There were certain agreed procedures between the services. Something as significant as this should have been relayed to London as soon as the Agency had learned of its existence.

'Months.' Gilbert leaned closer. 'Mr Brewer, there is more happening here than you understand. Everything is not as it should be.'

Brewer sighed. 'Tell me about it. It's been like unravelling a spider's web. Bring back the cold war, the black and the white.'

Gilbert laughed. 'Those days have gone. You have raised the iron curtain.' He leaned closer. 'And now the enemy is within.'

'What would you say,' Brewer asked. 'If I told you that a plain black limousine with smoked glass windows has cruised past this café twice?'

'I would say that you are as observant as I remember,' Gilbert replied slowly. 'And it has an out of state licence plate does it not?'

Brewer smiled. So Gilbert had noticed it too.

Gilbert nodded. 'I know it. It's from the compound. There's a door in the counter ten feet behind you. It looks like the—'

'Dive!'

Brewer threw the table to the floor. Drinks, chairs and Gilbert crashed to the ground. A wall of noise shot through the café. A thousand sparkling diamonds cut through the air like miniature daggers as the glass shattered, ripping murderously through clothing and flesh. A hailstorm of bullets cut through the rear wall, showering the café with plaster and a dry, choking dust. The plastic display of donuts and prices split and fractured. Lights shattered in a blaze of electric sparks and fell to the floor.

Brewer kept his head masked with his arms, his eyes protected as he squinted out. He needed to know whether they were going to come for them on foot or whether it was a drive-past. The last thing he wanted was a bullet in the back of his head while he lay there sheltering from the glass. A moment later it was over. Silence.

'Let's go,' Brewer said.

He grabbed at Gilbert and pulled him to his feet. They shook the glass from them, ignored the moans of shock and surprise from the injured and dying and were out on the street in seconds. An emergency siren was already wailing.

'Was that you or me?' Gilbert asked, his breath coming in short bursts as they hurried down the street.

'Not me,' Brewer replied. 'I was clean.'

'I thought I was too,' Gilbert replied. 'Never saw anyone on my tail.'

They reached a corner and ducked into a McDonalds, drawing stares of surprise at their dust-covered appearance.

'What I wanted to tell you,' Gilbert said, catching his breath and brushing the worst of the dust from his hair and clothing. 'Is that we have someone inside.'

'Inside the compound?' Brewer was surprised.

'At least, we did,' Gilbert continued. 'But we haven't heard anything. I thought the Bureau might be thinking about moving in.'

Brewer shook his head. 'Not yet. They're still building their case. None of us are quite sure what we've got yet.'

'It's more than just this compound,' Gilbert replied. 'If you hear they're going to move in, get a message to me. We'd like to get our man out alive if we can. If that is,' he said softly. 'He is still alive.'

It was nearly three a.m. when Yellow Hawk stopped outside the Lincoln apartment he was renting and rooted in his pocket for the keys. He had spent a wearisome day checking Bureau records, examining details of everyone they had identified inside the compound. He was looking for a weakness, someone with a previous record of alcoholism or drugs dependency—or an embarrassment they could use. He wanted someone they could turn, someone who could work for them on the inside.

It had been a waste of time.

Yellow Hawk heard the telephone ringing inside the apartment. He pulled out the keys, caught them in his jacket and sent coins rattling onto the floor.

'Shit.'

He had nearly reached the phone when it stopped ringing. He wondered who would be calling at this time of night. When the phone rang again, Yellow Hawk was drifting off to sleep.

'Hello?'

'Mr Yellow Hawk?'

'Who is this?'

'You don't need to know, Mr Yellow Hawk. Just listen.'

Yellow Hawk fumbled at the answer phone.

'I'm listening.'

Success. The tape started, the record light blinking in the gloom of the room.

'Tell your friends to back off.' The voice was firmer now, more confident. 'Leave us alone, you hear me? You don't know what you're into.'

'And what are we into?'

'Let me tell you. Waco'll look like a picnic if you continue. You won't take us like you took them. We're everywhere, Mr Yellow Hawk. Call your men off.'

'You know I can't do that.'

'Listen to me, Yellow Hawk!' The voice was angry now. 'You're out of your depth. And you're too late. Back-off. This is your first and last warning.'

The line went dead. Yellow Hawk switched on the light and took the tape out the answer phone.

You're out of your depth. And you're too late.

What did that mean? An idle boast? Or just a statement of the truth?

19

Parke was in the office early. He wanted to tackle the confidential paperwork before the secretary arrived. She was far too efficient and seemed to be becoming increasingly suspicious—ever since Brewer's visit in fact. And then there was the mysterious break-in. The theft of papers and photos. Without reassurances from Cham that the matter would not cause difficulties, Parke would have been out of the country within twenty-four hours. Things were becoming too hot for comfort.

No matter. He had always known it would become more difficult at this stage in the project. In a few weeks he would dismiss the staff, close down GDM and set up a new shadow company. It would not be the first time he had been forced to take such measures. Despite Cham's easy reassurances, he was not happy that the company was attracting the attention of the intelligence services. The Hamilton affair had been clumsy. Whatever Cham and the general news media might say about it, Parke recognised the fingerprints of a deliberate removal when he saw them: he did not intend to be next. He would stay ahead of the game, keep Cham at arm's length. Cham was no longer to be trusted.

The confidential papers were in order. The shipments of biological and chemical weapons had been made without incident—all except one, a shipment lost in the channel during a storm. The captain had been forced to jettison the load. With its specially weighted containers, the shipment sank without trace. By the time the Coastguards arrived to rescue the crew, the stricken boat contained nothing but its legitimate cargo. The loss of the shipment was not a problem: Parke always over-ordered. The shipments were now waiting in a warehouse on the continent, ready for distribution to key locations throughout Europe.

The financing had worked well, courtesy of the MEPs. They had responded generously to the idea that possession and control of the illegal weapons would enable Europe to protect itself against the sort of chemical attack that Tokyo had already witnessed on its underground system. And the other promise—of large financial returns—had no doubt also played its part, of course.

Thielstrom contacted Cham within hours of his arrival in London. They met in their usual rooms at the House of Commons, tucked downstairs in the Ministerial rooms near to Speaker's Court. Before Thielstrom's arrival, Cham took a small device from his pocket and activated it. As long as it remained live, the listening devices implanted in the wall panels would be disabled. Their discussion would be secure from prying ears.

Thielstrom arrived a few minutes later and wasted no time on pleasantries.

'It's time to move.'

Cham did not react to Thielstrom's announcement. He held out his hand and took the envelope Thielstrom was holding.

'The Bureau is watching,' Thielstrom continued. 'And the Jews.'

For the first time Cham responded. 'The Mossad you mean?'

Thielstrom nodded. 'Stronik is taking care of the matter.'

'I'm sure he is,' Cham commented. He opened the envelope and flipped briefly through its contents.

'What is it?' Thielstrom asked.

Cham smiled. 'Instructions. On the matter of moving quickly, everything is ready. We await only the starting pistol.' He slipped the envelope and its contents into his pocket.

'Good,' Thielstrom sighed. 'Finally, after all of these years of waiting, we are nearly there.'

'Yes,' Cham replied with a strange expression that made Thielstrom feel uneasy. 'We are, aren't we?'

The call woke Brewer from a deep sleep. For a moment he thought it was his morning alarm call and then he saw the time: three-thirty a.m. He snatched up the receiver.

'Wrong number,' he said impatiently.

'I beg to differ.'

He recognised the voice: Pendleton.

'What the hell do you want at this hour? Do you have any idea what time it is over here?'

'And I hope you're well too,' Pendleton replied. 'I have news that may interest you.'

'I'm listening.' Brewer was already wide awake. Pendleton would not call unless it was important.

'Is this line secure?' Pendleton asked.

'It should be. The Bureau checked and cleaned it and I've got Daisy sitting on it at this end.'

'And Daisy's awake?'

Daisy was the incongruous code name for the Firm's latest field encryption device.

'Twenty-four hours a day.'

'Good. Parke's dead.'

'Not another shocking stocking incident I hope?' Brewer asked.

'No. Hit and run. He was leaving GDM's offices. A motorbike courier knocked him down. He died in the ambulance on the way to hospital.'

'How unfortunate. A traffic accident. There must be something very unlucky about working for GDM.'

'And unless you're careful, I have the distinct impression that the same fate may await you too,' Pendleton responded. 'Something's definitely moving this end. And it looks like you've wasted your time going over there. Thielstrom was back in the country.'

'Was?'

'Yes, was. We lost him for a time. He's turned up in Strasbourg now.'

'Strasbourg? Regular little commuter, isn't he? Any information on what's happening there?'

'Not yet,' Pendleton admitted. 'The DST are co-operating. Looks like this is another one that cuts right across national borders.'

'Any idea whether it's being run from here or Europe?' Brewer asked. 'I don't want to waste my time bird-watching here if all the action's over there.'

'Nebraska seems to be the key, but maybe just for the US part of their operation. There has to be a European centre too. I thought it was GDM, but it isn't. It was just one of their fronts. Now they've finished using it, it looks like they're eradicating it. First Hamilton, now Parke.'

'While we're swapping stories, I have some news for you too. I had a meeting with our Israeli friends.'

Brewer sensed Pendleton stiffening at the other end of the line: informal contacts with other agencies were not encouraged.

'And what on earth would you find to talk about with the Israelis?'

Brewer smiled. 'They tipped off the Agency at least a few months ago about this. From what I understand from the Bureau, the Agency passed it over to the Bureau quick as a shot. Wanted to keep well clear of it by the look of things.'

'Interesting. Not their usual MO. It must have a wider political angle. I'll check out whether the Agency ever communicated the information to us. Looks like there may have been a significant communications failure.'

'And another thing. They have a man inside the compound.'

There was silence. 'Do they?' Pendleton paused. 'Then they're not the only ones.'

'What?' Brewer frowned. 'What do you mean?'

'That's the other thing I needed to tell you. We have someone deep undercover as well.'

'What! Inside the compound?' Brewer sat up on the bed. 'Since when?'

'He's well established. Years rather than months.'

'Years! Jesus! Why don't people tell me these things?'

Pendleton coughed. 'I only found out a short time ago myself. It's very hush-hush. Not one of our ops.'

'Not one of ours?' Brewer frowned. 'So who the hell is it?'

'SAS. Working on the direct instructions of the Joint Intelligence Committee.'

'Christ, what a bloody mess. So what do the JIC know about this?'

'They're not saying. They think there's a leak in the Firm.'

'When hasn't there been?' Brewer replied sharply. 'But they trust you do they?'

'So it would appear.'

Brewer hesitated. 'And should I trust you?'

There was a pause. 'What do you think, Brewer?'

'I don't know right now Pendleton. You could be the leak, you could be selling me a set of grandmother's rosy-tints. This guy inside. Can we contact him?'

'Ah. Now you've put your finger on it. That's the problem,' Pendleton replied. 'All contact has been lost.'

'Same story as our Israeli friends and their sleeper,' Brewer replied.

'Then it's probably true,' Pendleton commented. 'There has been a leak. The operation is compromised. If you do get someone inside, or establish links, and find our man there, you'll need to identify yourself.'

Pendleton gave him a password and contact recognition sequence.

'Pendleton. Shall I share this with the Bureau?'

Pendleton hesitated. 'I can't tell you that, Brewer. You're the one in the field. Use your discretion. Whatever you think necessary.'

'What have you got me into Pendleton?'

'I wish I knew, Brewer. I wish I knew.'

Simon Gilbert did not take the call himself. It was one of the other men.

'He's on his way up.'

Gilbert was annoyed by the development: it was not like Brewer to be so obvious. Surely he understood the necessity to keep their operation as quiet as possible? Why had he come to their hotel in the open like this and invited himself up to see them? It was unusual behaviour, out of character. Not the Brewer he remembered. Perhaps he had made a bad error of judgement about him.

'You're sure it was him?' Gilbert checked.

'Sure,' the man nodded. 'Gave the codeword and everything.'

'Fine,' Gilbert said slowly. He was still suspicious. 'Send him through when he gets here.'

He entered the bedroom that doubled as their surveillance centre. Several DVD recorders in racks worked silently, their lights the only sign of activity. A man sat listening with headphones, his face blank, a pencil in his left hand doodling idly on scrap paper in front of him. Near to his right hand was an Uzi submachine gun: one thing the Mossad's field agents soon learned was to remain vigilant. One moment of idleness, one moment of carelessness is often all it takes for an operation to be compromised and fail.

Photographs were pinned around the walls, many taken from long range and poorly defined. So far they had identified only a few of the main figures inside the compound. It would be useful to co-operate with the Bureau. With nearly eighty million records on its computer system, it has one of the most sophisticated identification systems of any law enforcement agency in the world. Even the Mossad could not match that. And time was running against them. Brewer's help would be essential.

Gilbert heard the door to the main room open behind him and the murmur of voices.

'In here Brewer,' he called.

As he flicked through the folio of pictures on the desk, there was the quiet and unmistakable *sntch-sntch* of a silencer. Gilbert dropped to the floor without turning, his hand sweeping the Uzi from the desk and into his grip. Before the agent with the headphones could react, his head exploded violently in a spray of blood, his body jerked from the chair and onto the floor.

Who was it? How many of them were there? He caught a movement in the main room and unleashed a burst from the Uzi. The noise from the gun in the confined quarters was explosive. Plaster dust showered the room.

He missed. But he had seen and recognised the gunman: Ahmed Rami. Rami! How could his men have been so careless? They knew the dangers. He could see their bloody corpses in the room outside. There was no time to wait. Rami would be working alone. He always worked alone.

Gilbert sprinted forwards and as he reached the door, he rolled forwards and hurtled across the room outside in a tight ball, the Uzi tucked in close to his chest.

Sntch-sntch. Two bullets struck him, one in his arm, one in his chest. He unleashed another volley, but Rami was already moving, was nearly at the door. Gilbert dragged himself to his feet ignoring the pain and the blood and shot again. Dust scattered around the doorframe enveloping Rami as he hesitated and turned. *Sntch.* Gilbert was struck again, the bullet scorching the side of his neck. He staggered forwards and nearly dropped the Uzi.

At the doorway, Gilbert collapsed sideways against the frame and looked down the hallway. Rami was moving quickly. Gilbert raised the Uzi and fired again, his finger squeezing the trigger until the gun emptied. Rounds ricocheted around the hallway, tearing light fittings and wallpaper. Too late, too late. Rami was gone.

Gilbert turned, trying hard to mask out the pain and think clearly. There was no time to waste. He had to clear down the operation and move everyone out before the police arrived. He moved across the room almost in a dream, his head faint from blood loss. The radio was in the surveillance room. It would only take the transmission of a few emergency codes to summon assistance.

And then, through his pain, he noticed for the first time an unfamiliar suitcase on the floor. He stopped and reached out a hand towards it.

It was at precisely that moment the Semtex exploded.

Brewer heard the explosion as he was climbing into Yellow Hawk's car. Neither of them said a word. They both recognised the *thump* of high explosives. Yellow Hawk spun the car round and drove at high speed towards the sound and the plume of ugly dark smoke that was already reaching its fingers into the sky. A chorus of sirens could be heard converging on the scene and when Yellow Hawk turned the corner, neither of them were prepared for the sight that faced them. Several floors of the hotel had been completely obliterated, the front fascia torn away with as little apparent effort as a curtain snatched from a window.

'Jesus,' Brewer muttered under his breath.

By the time they arrived, injured people were already being helped into the first ambulances on the scene and the usual crowd of ghouls were circling ready to soak in the atmosphere of misery and pain. Brewer stood staring up at the building. He already knew its significance. Someone had taken out the entire Mossad operation and they had not been concerned with doing it subtly. This was intended to send a clear message that they were not to be messed with.

Yellow Hawk finished talking to the fire chief and came back over.

'No doubt about it. Definitely a bomb, likely to be Semtex or something similar,' he confirmed. 'There are some reports that shooting was heard shortly beforehand.'

Brewer forced a smile. 'You don't surprise me,' he commented. 'Yellow Hawk. Can I have a word? In private.'

Yellow Hawk looked at him closely and then waved Brewer back into the car. They climbed inside and shut the doors.

'So what do you know?'

'There was a Mossad operation being run from this hotel,' Brewer responded. 'You asked who the shadows were. Now you know. They were doing exactly what you are. Keeping an eye on the compound.'

'Hell Brewer. Why the hell didn't you tell me this before?'

'I only found out yesterday. But I think you ought to start thinking about your own guys. If they're prepared to do this to the Mossad, they won't hesitate to do it against the Bureau.'

'Impossible,' Yellow Hawk exclaimed. 'Nobody's ever taken on the Bureau like that. They know they wouldn't stand a chance.'

'Yellow Hawk,' Brewer said, taking a firm grip on his arm. 'I don't think you understand what you're up against. Remember Oklahoma, remember New York. This is something bigger than you or I have ever seen. This isn't the same game we played in the cold war. This is a whole new war with a whole new set of ground rules.'

'No way,' Yellow Hawk shook his head in disbelief. 'They're just another bunch of Waco's.'

'Not these ones,' Brewer said. 'I knew the man in charge of the Mossad operation. And you know what? That's what worries me most. If they could get him, they can get any of us. He didn't make mistakes. He was like me: a survivor. Only he couldn't survive this. They're playing by different rules. This is a different game to the one we know. If the lot in that compound are prepared to behave like this, it means they're getting ready to move.'

'So how do you figure that? I don't follow your thinking.'

'They wouldn't have run the risk earlier. I'm telling you, Yellow Hawk. Get a warning to your men. Maybe even pull them off for a time, or put in a different team in a different location. We need to run fast to keep ahead of this lot.'

Yellow Hawk sat and thought for a while.

'I can call in whoever and whatever I need,' he said quietly. 'If I can convince them about what's happening inside the compound, we can demolish it, wipe it off the face of the earth. I can call in an air strike right now and have that whole damn cesspit blown sky high.'

'That's bullshit Yellow Hawk. Even now, even after September 11, no-one in the Bureau's going to stick their neck out and make an executive call like that. They'd be worried it's just another Waco waiting to happen. And we don't have enough to go on, do we? We've only identified a handful of people inside, none of the details of what they're up to. Sure, we can guess they're producing some pretty nasty chemical and biological weapons in there. But it's all circumstantial, suspicions not proof. Even this bombing we can't tie directly into them.'

The Bureau radio crackled in the silence.

'We need someone inside,' Yellow Hawk whispered.

'Well guess what Yellow Hawk? We already have someone inside,' Brewer replied slowly. 'Or we did have. Contact has been lost. The Mossad had someone in there too. Same problem.'

Yellow Hawk stared at him. 'Are you serious? Where the hell's all this coming from all of a sudden? You're not taking some kind of funny substances are you?'

'You have to believe me when I say I'm as surprised as you. I only found out yesterday.'

'Seems like there was a heck of a lot that you only found out yesterday,' Yellow Hawk reflected gloomily.

Thielstrom had moved rapidly on to Strasbourg, taking the first flight out of London. His meeting with Cham had left a bad taste. He kept replaying it in his mind to uncover the cause, but nothing came of it. Cham remained an unknown element, his motives uncertain. Thielstrom was surprised that after Hamilton's and Parke's removal, Cham had also not been removed. Special Branch were still probing and the situation in Britain was rapidly getting too warm for comfort. Their initial planning and organisation had worked well. But recent events indicated that time was running against them. There had been too many mistakes, too many incidents that had brought the law enforcement agencies sniffing around. Brewer should have been removed early on. His survival remained the main cause of their problems, compounded by the persistent and awkward questions coming from Howarth.

Thielstrom's limousine was waiting to meet him at the airport.

By the time he arrived at the large apartment on the outskirts of Strasbourg, his guests had already assembled. He kept them waiting while he showered and changed. Finally he walked into the dining room where they were gathered and motioned for them to remain seated.

He found himself facing the same group of Euro-MPs that Hamilton had addressed only a few weeks before. A lot had changed in those few weeks. For one, Hamilton and the Spanish Euro-MP who had questioned his motives were both dead. For another, whether they liked it or not, the Euro-MP's were now drawn closely into the web. They would either have to co-operate or they would be killed. The meeting would make the options clear to them. But for the moment there was no need for such unpleasantness. Thielstrom made sure they were all supplied with coffee and light snacks before starting his talk.

'Gentlemen,' he started. 'Thank you for coming here today. I think you will find it more than worthwhile, for today you are going to have the chance to take part in history. Europe is about to be reborn.'

He had their attention. Now all he needed was their support.

20

The suggestion was plain enough: Brewer would go inside the compound. Although from Brewer's personal and somewhat selfish perspective it did not look like a particularly life-enhancing option. The high-risk strategy emerged during discussions with Yellow Hawk and the Bureau's Special Agent in Charge, Norman Desuza. It grew out of exploiting the knowledge that various British fascist groups had well-established links with the NSDAP-AO. The Bureau's vigilant surveillance had already identified several English and Scottish neo-fascists who had visited the base. They had been well received. So another visitor also claiming to be from one of these groups would not arouse suspicion. That was the theory: it remained to be proven, with Brewer as the guinea pig. The main obstacle was to furnish Brewer with a credible identity and ensure that any checks into his background would stand up to close scrutiny. Brewer's credibility would be increased by casually dropping into his initial approach the names of the other recent visitors to the compound.

Brewer had not been the SAC's first choice. Logged into the Bureau's database are details of all their agents and any particular skills or interesting background they may have. But searching for someone with the right skills to go undercover and transferring them to Nebraska and briefing them would take days, maybe even weeks. They did not have the time.

'Besides,' Brewer commented. 'I'm not authorised to reveal the recognition code and password to anyone else. I'm the only one who can establish contact with our man.'

It was bullshit and they knew it, but they had the decency to pretend to buy it. If anyone was going in, Brewer was resigned to the fact that it would have to be himself. As well as finding their own man, he wanted to find out what had happened to the Mossad agent. He owed Gilbert that much.

'It's the only chance we have,' Yellow Hawk confirmed. 'Whatever the outcome, it'll give us the excuse we need to go inside.'

'And there's a chance that if I can make contact with our man inside, it should give us the proof we need.'

'That's if they don't blow your cover,' Yellow Hawk observed. 'A very big if.'

'Thanks for the confidence boost.' Brewer shrugged. 'I reckon I have a day or two at most once I'm inside. Once they start digging they're going to find out my cover story doesn't hold.'

'We're pretty certain now that this guy Rami who's inside was the one who took out the Mossad operation. He left the compound at around the right time, came back at the right time. It all fits.'

'You managed to hush it up okay,' Brewer commented.

'Sure,' the SAC replied. 'Faulty gas appliance. We know how to handle publicity when we've got something big like this. More terrorist attacks are the last thing anyone needs to hear about right now. But it's only so much longer we can keep the media vultures from the door. One or two are already suspicious. They know we don't normally run this size of operation in Lincoln.'

'We can't risk wiring you,' Yellow Hawk said. 'You're going to have to go in cold.'

Brewer nodded. It wouldn't be the first time he'd gone undercover without any means of defence or the ability to summon help. It was not a situation he welcomed. But this was no ordinary operation.

'So when do I go in?' he asked.

Yellow Hawk grinned. 'How about tonight?'

For a time, Brewer thought no-one would answer his knock. Finally a small eye-level grill swung open and a face stared out.

'Hello there. My name's Eric, Eric Shawm. I'd like to come in. I've come from London. English Nationalists, Isle of Dogs division.'

Brewer emphasised his London accent. The man stared at him for a time. The grill shut. A moment later the large metal door shuddered and a smaller door set within it opened. The man waved him inside. Brewer stepped forward and into the compound. The man shut the door behind him. For the first time Brewer saw that the man was wearing a full SS uniform. It was too late to turn back now.

'Nice,' he said, nodding at the uniform.

The man grunted and waved him forwards. The lighting inside the compound was low. Brewer knew from the Bureau's surveillance photos the approximate layout. He was being escorted to the guard building. To his left lay the complex where the deliveries of chemicals were made. To his right, the office and administration block.

They reached the guardroom and the man thrust him forward and into a blaze of light. Another guard turned to face him.

'Who are you? What do you want?'

Brewer explained why he had come, that it was a fraternal visit from the English Nationalists. He mentioned the names of the members who had already visited. There was no reaction.

'This is not a good time,' the man commented and picked up a telephone almost before it had rung.

He spoke for a time in short, clipped sentences and then replaced the receiver.

'You are in luck. You will have an audience. And smile, you're on camera.'

The guard nodded towards the video camera in the corner. Brewer tried to look suitably awed: but since his arrival in the compound he had noted a series of cameras monitoring his progress. Whoever was financing this operation certainly wasn't tight with the purse strings.

The guard led him along a corridor and up a flight of stairs. They were entering the main administration building. Brewer kept careful note of where they had been, the route they took, the doors they passed. He would need to know his way around in darkness: it would be the only way to move around and avoid the scrutiny of the security cameras.

They reached the second floor. His escort nodded briefly at a uniformed armed guard outside the door and then they entered an elegant wooden office. A uniformed man worked behind a desk, his lapels decorated with a small silver skull and crossbones. He looked up as Brewer and the guard entered, his face immobile. Brewer guessed the man was somewhere in his seventies, maybe his eighties. He recognised the face from the Bureau's photos. He had been identified as Walter Stronik, but detailed searching had revealed discrepancies in the man's past. The Bureau were not convinced he was who he said he was: his history showed all the trademarks of a new identity given to him by someone else, possibly the CIA.

Brewer took the opportunity to examine the room. The walls were covered with swastikas, third Reich memorabilia and photos and paintings of Adolf Hitler. A rack against one wall held a series of booklets and posters with titles like *Did Six Million Really Die?* and *Our Nordic Race.*

Stronik dismissed the guard and waited for him to leave before standing and walking round the desk.

'Mr Shawm.' He extended a hand.

They shook.

'Or more accurately I should of course say Mr Brewer,' Stronik continued, a thin smile playing briefly across his lips.

Brewer felt cold. He had relied on his cover lasting at least twenty-four hours. It had not even lasted twenty-four minutes. For the first time he regretted coming unarmed and unwired. Right now it felt like a really bad decision.

'Cigarette?' Stronik held out a box towards him.

Brewer shook his head.

'Very wise,' Stronik replied, taking and lighting one for himself. 'I understand they cause premature death.'

He placed undue emphasis on the last two words. There was

a sound at the door. Brewer turned and saw Rami enter the room behind him. Rami displayed no reaction to his presence and moved to stand beside the desk. Stronik puffed thoughtfully at his cigarette before returning to his seat from where he examined Brewer.

'Well? Would you care to tell us the reason for your visit?'

'You are Ahmed Rami, aren't you?' Brewer asked.

Rami did not react. His eyes remained cold, his gaze fixed unblinking on Brewer.

'You are a very reckless man, Mr Brewer,' Stronik commented. 'Did you really think you were unknown to us?'

'A small delusion on my part,' Brewer said. He moved over to one of the leather armchairs and lowered himself into it, affecting an air of disinterest.

'And what had you hoped to gain? Information about our plans? Inside secrets? Or perhaps you came inside to destroy things.'

'You planted the bomb, didn't you?' Brewer directed the question at Rami. 'And what about Hamilton? Was that your handiwork too?'

Rami looked briefly at Stronik, who nodded as if in answer to a question.

'Mr Brewer. The arrangements are quite simple. We both have our professions, our own work to complete.' Rami spoke gently and for the first time the frostiness of his face was broken by a smile and a deceptively warm expression.

'Only Rami does his work rather better than you,' Stronik observed, a note of humour in his voice. 'I don't think you would walk into a trap wearing nothing but the clothes you stood up in, would you Rami?'

Rami shook his head. 'Of course not.'

'A trap?' Brewer enquired. 'What do you mean by that?'

'Information about a man on the inside, perhaps?' Stronik asked. 'And I presume you came inside to make contact, did you?' Stronik turned to Rami. 'See? You were right. Throw out the right bait and the little fishes bite.'

'And what do you plan to do with me?' Brewer asked. His mind was racing. Someone had deliberately told Pendleton there was a man inside. And like a fool, Brewer had swallowed the bait. Hook, line and sinker. It was another mistake in a recent pattern of mistakes he had made. The only difference was that this time it was possible the mistake would be his last.

Stronik considered him for a time. 'We shall be moving on very soon. This compound has fulfilled its function. I think you will find it a suitably permanent home.'

'I'm surprised you still think your plans will succeed, after everything that's happened,' Brewer stated. He was thinking quickly now, trying to out-guess them, to plant seeds of doubt in their mind. He had to undermine their confidence. 'And with poor old Thielstrom leaking like a sieve.'

It was a gamble. And it failed.

'An irrelevance. Thielstrom's function is nearly complete,' Stronik commented. He looked at his watch. 'Only a few more hours now and that particular leak will be fixed.'

'Ah. Another accident? I'm surprised you have anyone left in your organisation. You seem to dispense with their services so easily.'

'We keep those we need. All generals understand that foot soldiers are expendable,' Stronik replied. 'Take him to the cells will you Rami? I need to decide what we shall do with him.'

Rami nodded and stepped forwards. Brewer remained seated. He had no intention of making things easy for them. He waited until Rami was in striking distance and then jumped from his seat. His fist landed just below Rami's chin. Or would have done. But Rami had already moved. Brewer overbalanced. His right hook sent him sweeping round. He grabbed at the desk, gripped it and turned just in time to take Rami's blow full force on his nose. Something cracked and he could taste blood streaming from his nose. He ducked, punching Rami hard in the groin. Rami doubled over. Brewer reached out and spun him, feeling in his jacket pocket for a gun, a knife, anything to arm himself. Nothing.

There was a click. Brewer turned, Rami pinned immobile in his arms. Stronik stood with a small automatic pointed at them both.

'If you shoot, you'll kill Rami,' Brewer hissed.

'It would also kill you,' Stronik replied and raised the gun.

It was true. And Stronik was capable of it. For a moment Brewer assessed his chances. But the door was too far away, the guard outside it impossible without a weapon. He let Rami go.

Rami spun and stared at him, his eyes dark with anger.

'You are a fool,' he hissed.

'Quite possibly,' Brewer replied. 'Rather a fool than a madman's lapdog.'

'Take him down,' Stronik commanded. 'Your time will come Rami. For the moment I want to keep him. He could be useful if we should need to negotiate with the Bureau to prevent them doing something rash.'

Rami grabbed hold of Brewer's arm and shoved him out of the room and down the stairs. Brewer guessed that Rami was trying to goad him, to make him break free, to give Rami the excuse he needed to kill him. They reached a basement and passed through a heavy metal door into a long chamber. On either side was a row of solid doors with eye slots: a simple prison. If the Mossad's man was still alive, this is where he would be. Brewer tried to listen as they went past the first few doors, but it was impossible to hear anything above the sound of their shoes scraping against the cold ground.

'One moment.'

Rami pulled him to a halt outside a cell door. He looked at Brewer with a strange expression. 'There is something I would like you to see. You should know the kind of people you are dealing with.'

He took some keys from his pocket and opened the door.

'Go on. Closer. See for yourself.'

He waved Brewer towards the door. Brewer hesitated. Was this a trick? There was a pungent, unpleasant smell emanating from the cell. He stepped forwards uncertainly.

'Go on, take a good look,' Rami encouraged him.

Brewer looked inside the small, dank cell. In the dim light it took him a moment to understand what he was looking at. Fixed to the wall was some kind of sack, a papier mache figure in the shape of Christ on the cross. The smell was becoming stronger. He moved a little closer and stopped.

'Oh my god,' he whispered.

He felt sick. He wanted to shout, to run, to hit out at someone. Anything rather than standing there. It was not a papier mache figure fixed to the wall: it was a man. Or what had once been a man. Only where there should have been skin there were only veins and muscle. Where there should have been eyes were only sunken sockets. Brewer swallowed hard. Who had this been? The Mossad agent? And who, or what, had done this to him?

He turned back towards Rami, unable to talk. Rami lead him from the cell and pushed him further along the corridor.

'Here.'

Rami stopped, opened a door and pushed him into a cell with enough force to crack him against the opposite wall. And then Rami was gone, the door locked with the metallic rasp of a key. Brewer shook himself, wiped the worst of the dried blood from his nose and listened to Rami's retreating footsteps. He still felt sick.

The room was about four by four and around six feet tall. Just tall enough for Brewer to stand. In one corner was a drainage hole and beside it a bucket. The bucket was empty. There were no windows. Light came from a dull bulb recessed into a small hole in one wall.

Brewer turned round and kicked furiously at the door, venting his anger and frustration and repulsion. So this was it. All those years of running behind the Iron Curtain, of expecting to end his days in a basement of the Lubyanka, and now here he was trapped in a compound in America. The irony was not lost on him. He squatted down on the floor. Whatever had been done to the man in the other cell, it was like nothing he had ever seen before. He wondered whether the same fate now awaited him.

It was some time before he noticed the distant tapping. When he heard it he wondered how he could have missed it for so long. He had no problem identifying the characteristic Morse patterns: . . . — . . . SOS. He responded, tapping on the cell door. There was silence and then the Morse started again, only stronger this time. Brewer was cautious. This could be a trap. If they had cracked previous undercover agents, they could know everything. And now they would be trying to discover how much he knew too. The tough routine with Rami could have been a setup, something to make him ready to accept the idea of a friend down here in the cells.

When the message requested him to identify himself, he sent back his name: after all, Stronik knew his true identity. Suddenly the messages stopped. As soon as he had sent his name there was only silence. Brewer waited. Finally the Morse started again, slower and more careful. It asked him to repeat his name. Puzzled, Brewer did so. This time the reply came more quickly.

The message surprised him. It was in code: a code known only to operatives inside the Firm.

He translated it and stopped. He checked it again, translated it again, going over and over it in his head. The message was the same. But he could not believe it:

Hello Pete. This is Gary. What the hell are you doing here?

Brewer felt cold. Was he going mad? Had he already gone insane? Either this was a very sick trick, or something was seriously wrong. There was only one way to find out for certain. Brewer tapped out the recognition code and password that Pendleton had given him and waited for a response. Finally the answer came: it matched.

Brewer sat back against the wall and drew in his breath. It couldn't be Gary. Gary was dead. He had seen the photos, seen the official report. For god's sake, he even had a memorial in the

SAS cemetery at Hereford. But what the hell was it that Pendleton had said?

He's well established. Years rather than months.

Years? An agent that deep undercover? It was possible. But such deep undercover roles were uncommon. If it was Gary and he had been so successfully put into place so long ago, that meant someone had known about this years ago. In which case, why hadn't they acted before now? And how had Gary's true role been uncovered?

He needed to talk with Gary and soon: if the unseen man was Gary, he needed to get word out before it was too late.

21

Yellow Hawk skimmed through the briefing without saying a word. His expression was negative.

'Dammit. They're preparing to move out,' he commented and handed the note to his SAC. 'We can't sit this out any longer. It's time to move in.'

The SAC sucked his teeth. 'Hold on, let's tread carefully here shall we? I just don't think we can be so certain. And that's the view New York has expressed.'

'Damn New York,' Yellow Hawk responded. 'The ghost of Waco neutered them long ago. They wouldn't move in if the Devil himself set up camp on Capitol Hill.'

The SAC looked at him and smiled briefly. 'You so sure he hasn't?' he joked. 'And Yellow Hawk. You should know me well enough by now. When it comes down to the wire like this, I'm with you, not the suits on the East Coast. The moment we see this last set of transporters leaving, we go in. Is that good enough for you?'

'No. I say we go in now.'

'We don't have enough. Once they start shipping out whatever they still have in there, we can find an excuse to take them. The SWAT team's on standby. Everything's in place.'

'And what if they torch the place as they go?' Yellow Hawk enquired softly.

'You think that's likely?'

'Bunch of crazies like this,' Yellow Hawk said. 'Who knows what goes through their minds? Worse, they could booby-trap the place.'

'Right now I don't fancy our chances of taken them on in the open, looking at the arsenal they've got. And I sure wouldn't fancy trying it inside the compound. But you're right—they could have rigged the place. We go in, they blow it.'

Yellow Hawk was frustrated by the delay. 'We need to find out from Brewer just what the hell it is they're up to. They ain't just playing games.'

'Yellow Hawk,' the SAC replied. 'We have to face the fact that Brewer is probably dead.'

'Sure,' Yellow Hawk nodded slowly. 'And that's another reason to act now, not later.'

He spun on his heel and walked away, angry with the SAC's reluctance to act. One day, he thought, one day when he was an SAC he would show no such weakness. Law and order came through strength and discipline, not hesitation. Hesitation cost lives: and what really hurt was that the SAC's continuing hesitation could well cost Brewer his life. Too many of this type—the pleasant, well-meaning set of middle managers—just didn't get it: and if they didn't get it now, after 9/11 and all the fall-out from that, he wondered when they would. The rules had changed: this was not a game any longer. This was a war: and right now he felt like they were running this war with one arm tied behind their back. It was not a good feeling.

Thielstrom's briefing to the MEPs provoked a mixture of alarm and fear amongst his audience: precisely the result he intended. At first there was only a shocked silence around the table. But then the situation sank in: they had no choice but to co-operate. The deal they had signed with Hamilton no longer appeared the benevolent and forward-looking act that they had convinced themselves of at the time. Instead, based on the scenario Thielstrom had described to them, they would appear as co-conspirators in a plot to attack Europe with sarin gas.

The choice in front of them was both stark and clear. The following day, the European Parliament would debate legislation on Europe-wide emergency security powers, powers intended to be adopted in the event of a significant external, or internal, threat to pan-European security. The legislation would for the first time enable power to be exercised exclusively from the centre, rather than involving each of the nation states. After all, its supporters argued, it would be impossible to counter a major threat to the internal or external security of Europe with the speed and efficiency required if it meant consulting all the nation states: the debacle, muddle and weakness of the EU's handling of the ugly war in the former Yugoslavia had demonstrated that.

Thielstrom's request was simple: he sought the MEPs support to ensure the smooth passage of the legislation through the Parliament. Until now, there had been little prospect of it becoming law. Each of the EU nations saw it as a threat to their own sovereignty. But the group of Euro-MPs had been carefully selected. They were key influencers, men whose word was listened to and respected. They represented sufficiently powerful blocs within the European Parliament to influence events. It seemed little enough price to pay to ensure that Thielstrom did not reveal their complicity with the Hamilton sarin agreement.

As Thielstrom explained to them, there was nothing to worry about: what chance would there be of the new legislation being used? None, of course. Who, he joked, would be in a position to threaten the European Union to the extent that such emergency powers could be enacted and martial law imposed?

And who in their right mind would want to see such a transformation, a European super-state with all the power across Europe of the old, disgraced German Third Reich?

Who indeed?

Pendleton analysed the report from France and frowned at its contents. It made references to previous intelligence reports. But Pendleton had not seen any earlier reports. One quick call to his contact at the DST was enough to convince him that previous reports *had* been made: and they had been made direct to Cham. And yet no-one else had seen them. It did not make sense. Pendleton would speak with Cham later to sort things out. There had to be a simple explanation.

In the meantime, he actioned the report. It contained detailed notes and transcripts of Thielstrom's meeting with the Euro-MPs. For the first time, the DST had succeeded in taping the meeting. It was not perfect, but the transcript was as puzzling as it was revealing. Why would Thielstrom have such a strong interest in seeing controversial new security legislation passed by the European Parliament? And what were these obscure references to 'the Hamilton agreement'? From the context, it was clear that Hamilton had met previously with the Euro-MPs, but what had they discussed and why were they now in the weak negotiating position that Thielstrom was able to exploit?

There was one reference that made him sit up and take notice: *Tokyo*. Several times during the meeting it was mentioned as if it had a special significance. Yet surely the only significance it could have was by way of reference to the sarin attack on the Tokyo underground system. Sarin. Mention of chemical weapons in the transcript. And GDM had been dealing in such weapons. The links were slowly falling into place. But there was still no clarity about what was happening, what their plan might be, what level of threat these collection of worrying facts might pose to UK and European security.

He reached for the phone intending to call Cham and arrange a meeting. They needed to act on this and act on it quickly. But the phone rang just before he could make the call. It was DI Howarth from Special Branch.

'We need to meet,' Howarth said. 'And soon. There's something I think you should know about Cham.'

Howarth ushered Pendleton into a room on the top floor. Several casually dressed men sat listening to monitoring equipment. Pendleton raised his eyebrows and Howarth pointed at a spare headset. By Pendleton's rough assessment they were in a room in the building adjacent to GDM's offices. Pendleton was impressed by the professionalism of Howarth's surveillance operation. It was a long time since Pendleton had been directly involved in field work. He was still not sure what Howarth wanted him to hear, but did as he was instructed and put on the headphones.

It took a moment for him to adjust. There was a voice he did not recognise. And then one he did: it was Cham. But what was he saying? Something about mobilisation, the plan being ready. He mentioned the other man's name: Thielstrom. *Thielstrom!* It did not make sense. Why would Cham be meeting with someone like Thielstrom? He leant forward and listened more closely:

'Thielstrom.' Cham's voice sounded muffled and remote through the monitoring devices. 'You have been most useful. Both to me and the movement.'

'Of course.' Thielstrom spoke English with an accent Pendleton couldn't place. 'It is a privilege to work again for the cause.'

'Indeed. But you do understand that some of us in reality are only foot soldiers? And that when we face threats from outside, when such a foot soldier has become a focus of unwanted attention by our enemies, then we must do something about that? For the benefit of the cause?'

A beat. And then a muffled crash and a shout. And the unmistakable sound of a silenced gun. Two shots, evenly paced, not hurried. The hallmark sound of a planned shooting: an execution.

Pendleton looked at Howarth. Howarth waved his hand to indicate he should stay where he was. They stood in silence and listened.

'Thank you Thielstrom. Your help was invaluable.'

The words were a barely audible whisper. And then there was the sound of fading footsteps through the headphones. Howarth looked at Pendleton and motioned him to remove his headset.

'You want us to arrest him?'

Pendleton was shaking his head. He could barely believe it. What was Cham doing? Had he gone mad? Was he playing some kind of undercover game—or was he betraying them? He needed to tread carefully. If this after all a planned, inside job, if he moved in now hard and fast there was the danger he would wreck an intelligence operation of great significance. On the other hand, if Cham had turned bad and he did nothing . . .

'I think I'm beginning to make sense of some of this,' he said quietly, thinking aloud. 'There are files missing. Intelligence information about this group.' He looked at Howarth. 'Cham was the only one to see them.'

'Then we have to reel him in.'

Pendleton shook his head. 'No, not yet. We still don't know what or who we're dealing with.'

'We know enough,' Howarth responded. 'Arms trading, murder, political conspiracy.'

'I regret to say this, but I think there's more. Much more,' Pendleton said. 'We're just seeing scattered parts of the operation. I can't see the whole picture yet.'

'Can we afford to wait?' Howarth asked slowly.

Pendleton looked at him with alarm. 'Oh God I hope so. I really hope so.'

When it came, the FBI attack on the compound was swift and efficient.

The FBI SWAT team were backed up by elite specialists from the Hostage Rescue Team, flown in directly from Quantico. They moved in as the first juggernauts pulled out of the compound. Before the first vehicle had left the gateway, Bureau men were everywhere. One thing the Bureau has always ensured is that it has enough backup for its operations. If anything, it is usually accused of overkill. It is one of the reasons it has lost so few personnel on active service compared to similar organisations.

But this operation was of a type and a scale that few internal security organisations have ever had to confront. They met fierce resistance. Uniformed guards jumped down from the cabs of the vehicles, but by the time they levelled their guns they were already falling to the ground, punctured by multiple shots from Bureau agents. The timing was tight. Two unmarked helicopters climbed rapidly out of the compound and moved away at high speed, three Bureau choppers in hot pursuit, machine guns firing. A call went out for Air Force assistance.

An explosion ripped through the compound as the second wave of agents moved in, Yellow Hawk amongst them. The SWAT and HRT teams provided the advance guard, while other agents tucked in close behind them conducting the mopping up operation. The noise was shattering. The Nazi guards inside the base were under instructions to resist to the death: and they were following orders to the letter.

The sound of gunfire rattled from Yellow Hawk's left. He turned and unleashed a barrage of shots at a guard positioned on one of the watch towers. The guard jerked and toppled, his head and limbs suddenly a lifeless shower of flesh and blood. Before his body reached the ground, Yellow Hawk had turned and moved on. He had only one thought on his mind: to find Brewer, to find out what the hell was happening.

'Gas!'

The shout went up amongst the agents. In seconds they had snapped masks into place. So long as it was only ordinary CS gas, Yellow Hawk prayed. In their backup trucks were NBC suits, but they were impossible to use. There would have been no element of surprise if the SWAT team had been forced to wear them: they would have been cut down like cattle. The risk had been taken: so far it had paid off. There was another, larger explosion, the heat from the blast fanning his face.

He moved and pushed through into the nearest building. He had run through this operation countless times in his head. Somewhere—he guessed below ground—had to be some kind of containment area. As he hammered down the corridor he became careless. Suddenly a man lunged at him with a knife. It sank deep into his left arm. The pain was intense. Yellow Hawk dropped his gun. The man swung the knife again. This time Yellow Hawk caught his arm and unbalanced him. He pulled back sharply, forcing the man down onto the knife. The man kicked a few times like an unbroken horse and then lay still. Yellow Hawk ripped off his gas mask and threw it away, breathing in deep gulps of fresh air. He looked at the blood gushing from his arm as if it belonged to another person and then ripped a strip of cloth from the dead guard's uniform and bound it tight. He grabbed his gun from the floor and hurried on.

Ahead of him was an open door. Beyond it he could see a large swastika flag and a portrait of Hitler. He stopped for a moment and stared at it, unwilling to believe what he saw. And then he unleashed an angry magazine into the flag and the bust, sending it shattering into a thousand pieces. He reloaded and moved on, finding a staircase and heading down.

There was a heavy locked door at the bottom and no sign of a key. He fired a few test shots, but they ricocheted, nearly catching him on the rebound. He jumped back up the stairs two at a time. On the landing two flights above he ripped a low-impact grenade from his tunic and hurled it downwards at the locked door. He ducked, shielding himself from the detonation. A cloud of stinging, pungent dust rose up the stairs as he hurtled down even before the sound of the explosion had died away. The door was still holding, but it was buckled and twisted enough to squeeze past. Beyond it was another flight of narrow stairs and then what he had been looking for: a long corridor with sealed doors.

'Brewer! Brewer! Are you down here?'

There was an immediate muffled response from behind one of the doors.

'Stand back! I'm going to shoot out the lock!' Yellow Hawk pumped half a dozen rounds into the lock. The door held. He tried again. This time it gave. He shoved the door open and pulled a dazed Brewer from the dark, stinking hole inside.

'Jesus! You stink!' Yellow Hawk shouted at him. 'And what the heck have you done to your nose?'

'What the hell's happening?' Brewer shouted back, trying to be heard above the explosions from upstairs.

'D-Day,' Yellow Hawk grinned. 'We got a little impatient waiting for you to get out of here. Let's go.'

Yellow Hawk turned to leave. Brewer grabbed at him.

'Hold it!'

'Huh?' Yellow Hawk looked at him as if he was crazy.

'We need to fetch someone else.'

'What you talking about? You gone stir-crazy down here or something?'

'Our man,' Brewer replied, barely able to believe it himself as he said the words.

'No way,' Yellow Hawk looked at him in disbelief. 'Where?'

As if in answer, a frantic tapping came from one of the other doors. Yellow Hawk looked at it and then back at Brewer.

'Jesus.' He turned to the door and raised his gun. 'Stand clear.'

Three rounds shattered the lock. Yellow Hawk and Brewer stood in silence and watched as the door was pulled open. For a moment no-one appeared. And then a man stepped forwards. Brewer did not recognise him. The man was unshaven with long hair and damp stinking clothes. His face was drawn and thin: the living picture of a concentration camp victim. This man had been down here for weeks, maybe months.

'Gary?' Brewer asked, barely a whisper. It was impossible. He moved closer, peering closely at his eyes. 'Gary! It is you, you bastard!'

He stepped forwards and hugged him in his arms.

'I don't know which of you smells worse,' Yellow Hawk commented. 'You Brits. Don't you ever wash?'

'Pete, Peter. It is you. I thought I was going mad.' Gary's voice was almost a whisper, a stranger to speaking.

'*You* can't believe it! Everyone thought you were dead. Even poor old Jane.'

A shadow flickered across Gary's face. 'Jane,' was all he managed to say.

'Come on you two, will you? You can do all that male bonding stuff later,' Yellow Hawk shouted. 'We need to get out of here, like now if it's not too much trouble?'

A loud explosion overhead emphasised his words. They started to move towards the door. Gary grabbed hold of Brewer.

'Pete. She is all right, isn't she? You did look after her for me?'

'I looked after her just fine,' Brewer replied.

Gary leant closer and looked into his face. 'You dirty bastard,' he said finally and took a punch at him.

Brewer caught him in his arms.

'What the hell's going on?' Yellow Hawk shouted at them.

'He's fainted,' Brewer replied. 'Give me a hand will you?'

'Jesus!'

Yellow Hawk handed Brewer his gun and heaved Gary onto his back as if he were no more than a paperback book.

'Let's go.'

22

Yellow Hawk and Brewer emerged into a vision of hell. It took several unsettling seconds before they could make any sense of what they were seeing. Discoloured smoke in eerie shades of green and orange floated listlessly around the burning buildings. Vehicles, bloody uniformed bodies, and body parts littered the walkways and stairwells. Somewhere overhead, masked by the smoke, came the sound of a chopper. Voices could be heard shouting above the occasional shot and explosion. A couple of indistinct figures ran past them, their faces unseen.

'This way,' Yellow Hawk headed left toward the compound entrance, Gary limp over his shoulder, unconscious to the events around him.

'Stop right there!'

The order froze them to the spot. For a moment they could not see where it came from. And then the truth dawned. In front of them was a row of FBI SWAT and HRT agents, their hands tied behind their backs, their weapons stockpiled on the ground in front of them. Guarding them was a group of men in dark black paramilitary clothing. One of those men also had a gun pointed towards Brewer and Yellow Hawk.

'Hey, what's going down?' Yellow Hawk demanded.

'CIA. Put down your weapons. We're taking over this operation.'

'CIA!' Yellow Hawk nearly exploded. 'What the shit do you think you're doing? Have you gone crazy?'

The man came closer and jabbed the gun into Yellow Hawk's ribs.

'I said put down your weapons. We're in charge here now. Operating under the authority of the Department of Homeland Security. And you can drop the stiff too.'

Brewer slowly let his gun slide to the ground. Yellow Hawk shifted and moved Gary from his shoulder, placing him gently beside Brewer's discarded weapon. The man leaned forward and took the automatic from the holster on Yellow Hawk's belt.

'Get over there.'

He waved them towards the Bureau agents. A rattle of machine-gun fire came from the far side of the compound. Reluctantly, Yellow Hawk and Brewer obeyed the instruction. Two of the other paramilitaries stepped forward and roughly tied their hands behind them, shoving them into line beside the members of the SWAT squad.

'Just do as you're told and nothing's going to happen. We're just going to hold you here a while.'

Brewer glanced around the compound, trying to estimate numbers. He could see about a dozen of the dark-clad men. How many more there were beyond that was impossible to say. Visibility was too bad. Another group emerged from the smoke, leading more SWAT agents in handcuffs.

'This is crazy,' Yellow Hawk muttered. 'What the hell do they think they're playing at?'

An alarm rang in the back of Brewer's head. What was it Simon Gilbert had told him: *You know that the Agency were handed information about this months ago? Beware the Agency. Everything is not as it should be.*

'Someone's blocking us,' Brewer whispered to Yellow Hawk.

'I can see that. Only thing I don't understand is why. This is nuts.'

Brewer spoke in short sentences, stopping whenever one of their guards came too close or watched them too closely. He told Yellow Hawk about his meeting with Gilbert, his suspicions about the CIA. Over the next hour, more of the Bureau agents were brought to join them. Shortly after midday the compound finally cleared of the worst smoke and dust. From what Brewer could see, all of the FBI agents had been rounded up. Approximately twenty CIA men—if that was who they really were—stood guard.

On the far side of the compound, one of the concrete buildings trailed smoke from its roof. The others lay silent, their walls cracked and broken. Burnt out lorries and jeeps littered the roadway. Uniformed SS men lay silent around the compound, some looking barely marked, others torn apart by bullets and explosions. A few Bureau agents were dead beside them. Whatever else might have failed, the Bureau had put an end to the compound's operation.

'How long you keeping us here?' Yellow Hawk demanded.

One of the men turned. 'As long as we need to.'

'You're out of order. You're out of territory and you know it. I want to know who authorised this operation.'

'You'll find out,' the man responded.

'They're buying time,' Brewer said.

'But for what?'

'Someone wants this bunch of Waco-heads to succeed. Whatever it is they've been planning, it's about to happen. They're holding us here to keep us out the picture.'

'You really think that?' Yellow Hawk looked at him with surprise. 'But why would the Agency want to help a bunch of hoods?'

'I'll bet you one thing. This lot guarding us don't have a clue what's going on. It's someone higher up. One thing we've known for some time, the NSDAP-AO may be crazy but they have the right contacts.'

'You're telling me,' Yellow Hawk muttered. 'And if they're buying time, we have to get out of this.'

Brewer smiled. 'Sure we do. Just tell me how.'

Yellow Hawk looked around the compound. The CIA agents carried enough weaponry to start a civil war. They had already taken the precaution of removing the Bureau's weapons and storing them in the back of an unmarked truck. With no weapons, his hands tied behind his back and surrounded by heavily tooled guards, even Yellow Hawk had to admit things were not looking rosy.

A chopper approached, sweeping in low over the compound

and sending billowing clouds of dust over the prisoners and their guards. It circled twice before settling on the far side. The blades whirred into silence and three suited men descended from it, flanked by two larger men who even from this distance Brewer could see were discreetly, but heavily, armed. The pilot climbed down and loitered a little distance from the cabin, lighting and smoking a cigarette.

As the men came closer, Brewer sat up in alarm. He recognised two of the figures.

'Shit.'

'You know those guys?'

Brewer nodded.

'Those two on the left.'

'That's cool. I know the guy on the right. Trade you for mine. Vogel.'

'What?'

'Vogel. Head of the CIA.'

'Chrissake!'

'So who are the other two?'

Brewer watched them come closer. 'They go by the names of Straker and Hümmler. Remember, I pointed them out in your photos. I don't want them to see me.'

'Too late baby,' Yellow Hawk commented.

The group from the helicopter had reached the guards at the front and exchanged a few words with them. While they were talking, Hümmler's eyes had been passing casually over the assembled ranks of FBI agents. They had come to a stop on Brewer. While Brewer watched, he saw Hümmler turn to Straker. They both turned to look at him. Straker nodded and Hümmler moved away from the group and headed towards him, pushing the other prisoners out of his way.

'Good morning, Mr Brewer. Long time no see, as you say.'

Hümmler reached down and jerked Brewer to his feet.

'Time to talk.'

'Hey! Leave him alone, he's working for the Bureau,' Yellow Hawk protested.

Hümmler looked down at him as if he had just trodden in something a sick dog had left behind.

'Shut your mouth, aborigine.' Hümmler lashed out with his foot and caught Yellow Hawk a powerful blow on the temple that spun him sideways.

Hümmler pulled Brewer through the prisoners towards Straker. 'Well Mr Brewer. Looks like the fun's only just beginning,' he whispered close to his ear.

Vogel and Straker turned at their approach.

'Ah, Mr Brewer. We meet again.'

Straker extended his hand and then saw Brewer's predicament.

'I'm sorry,' he said, almost sounding as if he meant it. 'I would suggest that Hümmler cut you free, but something warns me not to. I seem to remember you escaping once before.' Straker glared at Hümmler. 'But we all make mistakes, don't we?'

Brewer said nothing.

'Allow me to introduce you,' Straker continued, as if he were a host at a cocktail party. 'Mr Vogel, Mr Brewer. Mr Brewer, Mr Vogel.'

'I gather you have caused us a great deal of trouble, Mr Brewer,' Vogel commented.

Brewer did not take to Vogel. He was a thin, gaunt man with the look of hunted animal about him. Brewer had seen his kind before. On the outside they were all affable and pleasant. But they rode on the shirt tails of others and always turned into nasty, selfish little shits when the going got tough.

'That all depends how you define 'us', doesn't it?' Brewer asked. 'I can't believe you are helping these people.'

'*These*' people, Mr Brewer?' Vogel laughed, a thin, humourless laugh. 'These people, as you put it, are *my* people, Brewer. Their ideals, their aspirations. Decent, white, wholesome. They are ones we should all share.'

'I didn't realise you regarded Hümmler so highly,' Brewer responded.

A look of irritation crossed Vogel's face. 'Hümmler's type are needed from time to time. Every political movement has its foot soldiers.'

'How long do you think you can get away with holding Bureau agents prisoner?'

'But they are not prisoners,' Vogel replied. 'We are conducting an interesting inter-agency collaboration under the authority of the Department of Homeland Security. Testing the Bureau's ability to respond to a large scale problem. My men will be holding the Bureau's men for a few days more. Then the exercise will be concluded.'

'And when the truth comes out later?' Brewer asked.

'Whose truth, Brewer?' Straker asked. 'In a few days everything will be concluded. My friend Vogel here will be rewarded for his foresight.'

'What will be concluded?'

Straker smiled. 'You still don't know, do you? You've chased us from Moscow to Denmark, from Denmark to London and from London to Nebraska. And you still don't have a clue.' Straker laughed. 'And after all the trouble you've caused us.' Suddenly he leaned closer, all hint of humour drained from his face. 'Or are you playing with us?'

Brewer remained silent.

'I think he's too dangerous,' Vogel said. But it was not a comment. It was a command, an instruction.

Straker stared at Brewer and then slowly nodded.

'I agree. Hümmler. Sort him out for us, will you?'

Hümmler nodded and took hold of Brewer's arms.

'Now the fun really starts,' he said.

He pulled Brewer roughly away, towards one of the derelict buildings at the edge of the compound. Brewer stumbled as he walked, Hümmler enjoying every moment as he pushed and shoved at him, slapping him around the head.

There was a single shot. In the silence of the compound it sounded as loud as the earlier explosions. Everything froze. Hümmler turned, Brewer straining in his arms to see what had happened. For a moment it was as if time had been frozen, nothing seemed to move. Straker and Vogel were still standing with the guards. Their bodyguards stood beside them. The prisoners were seated on the ground, Yellow Hawk unconscious on his side.

'Nobody move!'

And then it happened. As if the strings of a marionette had been sliced through by a scythe, Vogel suddenly crumpled and fell. One moment he was standing beside Straker and the bodyguards and the next he was a corpse on the floor. And still no-one moved. For a moment Brewer thought that Straker had shot him. Then Straker turned, a look of alarm on his face.

'Start the chopper!!' he shouted.

The second shot sounded. Straker stumbled and started to run towards the chopper. The bodyguards squatted down on either side of Vogel and pulled out their guns, too late to save their boss, but disguising their failure with a volley of shots at the unseen sniper. The pilot dropped his cigarette and jumped inside the cockpit. The whine of the helicopter starting filled the compound, the blades limping slowly into life. Hümmler's grip weakened on Brewer's arm. He started to move away.

Brewer leapt after him, jumped and brought his forehead cracking down onto the back of Hümmler's head. It was a good idea, but Hümmler's head was as hard as marble. They both fell crashing to the floor, Brewer nearly unconscious. A moment later, Hümmler was on his feet again, Brewer holding as best he could onto his ankles. Hümmler lashed out viciously, his escape a stumbling, frantic dash with Brewer like the carcass of a hunted dear strapped to his ankles. The pain clouded Brewer's vision, but still he held on. Another kick from Hümmler and then another shot. He felt rather than saw Hümmler hesitate.

Brewer blinked to clear his vision, saw Straker limp aboard the chopper. Hümmler was now only feet away. Another shot and this time Hümmler came to a halt and swayed, like a tree in the moment before it falls.

'Hümmler!' Straker was desperate.

Another shot. This time it hit the chopper. That was it. Without a word of instruction from Straker, the chopper lurched from the compound. Brewer jumped towards it, but Hümmler finally fell and crushed him to the ground. He scrambled to be free, but it was too late. Already the chopper was airborne. It circled once over the compound, another shot rang out. It swerved and for a moment looked like it might fall. And then it was off, lifting skywards and disappearing from view over the perimeter fence.

Brewer crawled from under Hümmler's dead weight and discovered he was exactly that: dead. He lay panting on his back, tired and bruised.

'Now, now folks. I did say nobody move.'

The voice came again. There was something familiar about it. Brewer shuffled himself onto his elbows. The prisoners were standing, the guards around them holding their weapons uncertainly, scanning the compound for the hidden voice, the hidden gunman.

'Lay down your guns.'

The guards looked at each other, uncertain. A shot rang out and kicked dust beside the foot of one of the guards.

'I can pick you all off if that's what you want. One by one if I have to. I'm not in any hurry. You've already seen the evidence I can do it.'

The guards hesitated a moment longer and then put down their weapons. Vogel's bodyguards did likewise.

'Good. Now untie the Bureau agents.'

Again there was hesitation and uncertainty. But then they did as they were told. The Bureau agents needed no instructions. As soon as their hands were free, they retrieved their weapons and rounded up the men who a few moments ago had been their guards. Others moved to their vehicles and radioed for assistance.

It was only then that a figure appeared at the window of one of the derelict buildings and threw a gun to the floor.

'I'll be right with you, guys,' the owner said and disappeared from view.

'Gary,' Brewer whispered under his breath. 'You jammy, jammy bastard.'

23

They sat in Brewer's hotel room, empty beer bottles spread around them like the forgotten debris of a party. A discarded magnum of champagne rested upside down in a silver bucket, the ice around it long since turned to water. Yellow Hawk had left just a few minutes before, exhausted from the activities of the previous weeks and the effects of drink. Now, left alone, Gary and Brewer could finally talk.

Gary walked over to the window and stood looking out over Lincoln.

'This is such a great feeling,' he said, his words slightly slurred from the drink.

He had spent two days in hospital under observation. Apart from malnutrition, the doctors had been astonished by how well he had survived the degradation and torture of the compound. During that time, like other visitors, Brewer was not allowed to see him. But after several days Gary insisted that he wanted to leave and, ignoring the protestations of the doctors, booked into the hotel in the room next to Brewer's. The hospital had compromised by agreeing a schedule with several visiting doctors and nurses who kept him under regular medication.

'My Colonel's arriving tomorrow,' Gary said flatly.

'Debrief?'

Gary nodded. 'I have the impression they don't want me back in Hereford. They've got something else up their sleeves, something else for me to do.'

'You'll be a crazy man to take it. You owe yourself some time. Cut yourself some slack and get out while you can Gary.'

Gary turned to look at Brewer and smiled. 'You think they'd let me? After I've been in this deep?'

Brewer did not reply: he could not find the words. Instead he lifted another bottle of beer, flipped the top and handed it over.

'What about Jane?'

Brewer had been trying to think of a subtle way to ask the question, but there wasn't one. Gary sighed, slugged at the bottle and sat down beside him.

'I should never have married her, Pete,' he said quietly. 'We both know the dangers of our work. It was a crazy, stupid thing to do.' He hesitated. 'You know, I still think of her. Most days when I was down in those dungeons, when they were trying to make me talk. It was her I thought of, her I swear I could see right in front of me.'

'Maybe you should call her, end her misery,' Brewer said quietly. 'She still has your pictures around the flat, still talks about you. It cut her really deep when you didn't come back.'

'Shit.' Gary rested his head in his hands. 'I can't get out. Not now, Pete. You must see that. Everything I know, they'd never trust me. I can never go back to the way things were. You make your choices in this world and mine is made. It's not the life I would choose, but it's a good one.'

'Good? What, to live like this?'

'You know what I mean, Pete,' Gary responded quietly. 'It's the best job, everything for the right cause.'

'Let me have a word with my people. They could put on pressure. This isn't right, Gary. They can't put you through something like this and expect you to carry on. There must be rehabilitation programmes that could get you back into a civilian life.'

Gary smiled a hard, humourless smile. 'Thanks for the thought, but it won't work. Not knowing what I do.' He sat up and stared long and hard into Brewer's eyes. 'Do you know what happened in the Gulf, how I got into this thing?'

Brewer shook his head and sipped slowly at his beer. His nose still ached, but the doctors at the hospital had assured him it would set straight. He just needed to give it time.

Gary paused to take another drink from his bottle. 'We took several teams deep behind Iraqi lines. You can guess the details. Subversion, disruption of communications, transport. God knows, there's enough books on it all now. Crazy. What none of us realised was the extent of Saddam's biochemical industry. Deep in enemy territory we hit a lucky streak: we intercepted communications between Baghdad and an unidentified plant, disguised as a milk processing plant. Details of formulae, specifics of shipments. For the first time we discovered that some of the Scud missiles were being fired with experimental biochemical warheads. We mounted a surveillance of the plant, hoping to identify who was behind the programme. Photos were wired to Cyprus and on to Cheltenham and the States.' He stood and moved back over to the window. 'That's when we identified Schengel.'

'Interesting. So he'd moved from Libya to Iraq. We should have picked up on that.'

'And from Iraq we found him moving on to Japan. By that time, London had decided it was time to run somebody undercover.'

'Those photos,' Brewer asked quietly, shuddering as he remembered the bloody images of the severed head, the bloody body that for the last few years they had thought was Gary.

'No-one knows exactly who he was. Some poor American or British doughboy that fell into the wrong hands. They did worse to some of our guys.' He paused. 'I didn't know they would send them to Jane. I would never have agreed to it.'

'It nearly broke her,' Brewer whispered.

'I never wanted that, I never meant to hurt her.' There was a break in Gary's voice, his breathing uncertain. He turned to Brewer, his eyes moist with tears. 'Look after her for me Pete. Promise?'

'I promise,' Brewer nodded.

Gary took a while to compose himself and then: 'We started to build up a picture of Schengel's movements and his contacts. And then this group, the NSDAP-AO, became bigger and bigger in the picture. And I moved in on that too. You should have seen me, Pete. Dressed in black Nazi uniform, pulling fascist salutes.' He smiled. 'They were crazy, living in the past. But they were dangerous too. We knew they were planning something big, but never guessed it would be on this scale. What I don't understand is where the money comes from. There's so much of it.' He sighed. 'I was beginning to get somewhere, had their trust. I was close to unravelling their crazy plans to return to power, when they uncovered me. Of course, now I know Vogel was involved it makes sense. Somehow he got to know about the operation. He must have betrayed me.'

Brewer stood and cleared the debris of bottles into the bin. There were many details that Gary had skipped over that he wanted to know more about. Details of operations in Iraq during the first Gulf War, his penetration of the neo-Nazis and his suffering after his exposure. But he knew Gary would never talk about them. Possibly he might tell his Colonel, might include all the details in his debriefing. But somehow Brewer doubted it. Men like Gary, who risk and often lose their lives, can never explain to others exactly what they have suffered, exactly what they have been through. They inhabit another world, a world of death and treachery, of coldness and betrayal. There is no common language between their world and ours. And hence no way of communicating their experiences. They live—and die—alone.

He turned to look at Gary and wondered whether he would ever see him again.

24

Yellow Hawk took the samples discovered at the compound to Washington himself. Special metal cases with carefully segmented compartments were supplied, together with a specialist who flew in to assist with moving the substances from their storage and development tanks into the sample bottles. A chartered helicopter took them directly to the Bureau's head office, while Yellow Hawk kept a nervous eye on the container and its deadly contents.

The FBI's laboratory occupies nearly 150,000 square feet on the first basement level and third floor of the Hoover building. The lab staff are a mix of agents and external scientists brought in for special assignments who conduct around one million examinations a year and handle around 20,000 caseloads. As well as its forensic and investigative functions, the lab also handles false documentation and prepares specialist materials for its agents. It was the Washington lab that provided the model of the Lincoln compound to enable the SWAT and HRT to familiarise themselves fully with its layout prior to its storming. And it was also the FBI's lab that pioneered DNA fingerprinting, a tool which has now become as important in criminal investigation as fingerprinting itself. It is generally accepted that the Bureau's lab is the best equipped and most objective forensic sciences facility in the world.

Yellow Hawk and the specialist went to a hurriedly prepared facility on the third floor of the headquarters building. A small group of scientists were already assembled and stood waiting in white lab coats. They took the packages from Yellow Hawk, and without a word removed the canisters and started to prepare for their work. Yellow Hawk stood and watched for a while. When the scientists started to dress themselves in NBC suits, he decided it was time to leave.

He retreated to the corridor outside, passing through the air-locked double doors, and discovered a guard fitting a biohazard sign. He looked up at Yellow Hawk as he emerged.

'Just as well you came out, buddy. You'd have got sealed inside.'

As they spoke, he turned a large cylinder on the door. There was the sound of bolts slamming home.

'That should hold them.'

'And what if something goes wrong in there?' Yellow Hawk enquired.

The guard pulled a face. 'Then I guess this door stays shut at least until you and me are drawing our pensions,' he replied.

Brewer held a meeting with Pendleton as soon as he returned to London. His journey had been one of the most unpleasant he could remember. Shortly before his departure, Yellow Hawk had arrived and handed him a large item of hand luggage.

'What is it?' he asked.

Yellow Hawk smiled. When he explained that it contained sealed samples of the contents found in the Lincoln labs, Brewer refused to believe it. But Yellow Hawk insisted that London had requested it. It wanted to conduct tests to identify the biological and chemical agents that had been used. And because of the urgency, normal handling procedures had been over-ridden. Brewer had permission to take it onto a normal commercial flight rather than a special military flight as was normally required.

'Why can't you test it yourself?' Brewer had complained.

'We will, don't worry. Think of your tests as a second opinion,' Yellow Hawk responded.

During the journey Brewer found it difficult to stop thinking about the case lodged in the rack above him. If what he had seen of the remains of the Mossad agent was any indication of its potency, the last place Brewer wanted it was in an overhead locker adjacent to his head.

Pendleton arranged for a limo to meet him at Heathrow and by half past eight he was already sitting in his office.

'What's the matter with your nose?' Pendleton asked, peering at Brewer's face.

'I ran into another brick wall,' Brewer said, smiling.

'Will you never learn? Anyway, enough of this small talk. We're running out of time.'

'Does that mean we don't get our chocolates and medals yet?' Brewer asked, looking across to where he had left the case on the far side of the room.

'Hardly,' said Pendleton. 'Not when the job's still half done.'

'Half done!' Brewer felt tired and emotional after another long flight spent sampling the complimentary alcohol. 'Now I know you're joking.'

'Not at all.' Pendleton looked at him sternly. Brewer's spell in the States had certainly done nothing for his discipline. 'You might have removed their compound, but it was too late. They had already removed the stocks they need. The compound was already closing down when you moved in. I take it you have the samples in that case?'

'That's what I was told.'

'Good. As soon as we finish here, I want you to take them personally to Porton Down. They have people standing by.'

'There isn't time. If what you've told me is true, we have to prevent the rest of their plan coming to fruition.'

'Then you'll have to find the time,' Pendleton snapped. 'If we don't know what we're up against how on earth are we going to fight it?'

Pendleton's logic was as faultless as usual. Brewer nodded reluctantly. 'Okay, okay, I can see that.'

'I gather from the debriefing of agent Gary Sheehan that some of the key organisers evaded capture.'

'That wasn't our fault,' Brewer interrupted. 'The Company can take the blame for that.'

'Not entirely,' Pendleton contradicted. 'I gather they departed in two unmarked helicopters at the start of your raid.'

'Maybe,' Brewer shrugged. 'But the Bureau put out a call to the air force to intercept them, blow them out the air if necessary. The Agency called them off.'

'Incredible.' Pendleton shook his head in amazement. 'How many people were working with Vogel?'

'You won't believe this,' Brewer replied, shifting uneasily in his chair. 'But it looks like it was just him and the Deputy Director of Intelligence. The Bureau has been called in to see just how far it goes. It's possible there was also some contamination in the Science and Technology Directorate.'

Pendleton arched his eyebrows in an expression that Brewer had seen before. 'What I don't understand is how they managed to organise so many key people. Mind you,' he moved uncomfortably in his chair. 'Let's not throw any stones. We have the same problem here, if you haven't heard already. Cham.'

'Cham?' Brewer frowned. 'Are you suggesting he's involved?'

'No. I'm not just suggesting,' Pendleton replied. 'We have more than adequate proof. I went over his head to the Chief. Cham doesn't know it, but I've been authorised to act in his job. He won't be getting any more sensitive reports. Of course, none of this would have been possible without the legwork done by that Special Branch chap Howarth. We've even identified calls between Vogel and Cham. It would appear they were working together to ensure that the whole underhand operation was kept out of the limelight. He's in it up to his neck.'

'Where is he?' Brewer asked.

'Mainland Europe,' Pendleton replied. 'And I want him dealt with.'

'Same thing as Vogel?' Brewer joked.

'I leave that to you. Once you've dealt with Porton Down, what you do with Cham is your own affair.'

For once, Pendleton was not joking.

Cham had arrived in Eindhoven two evenings before, still

unaware of the events unravelling behind him in London. He rented a small house on the outskirts of the town from where the final parts of the operation would be supervised. At six a.m. the following morning, lorries would leave the Eindhoven warehouse to distribute their lethal cargos across Europe. Every member country of the EU would receive its own delivery. The day after that, the new security legislation would become law. And the morning after, Europe would wake up to a day of disaster and despair. The new law would be swiftly acted upon. Power would be assumed by the centre. And at the centre was their man, the man whose identity had remained the most closely guarded secret of the entire Nazi organisation.

Straker and Stronik had arrived the night after Cham. But there was no sign of Schengel. Dinner was a subdued affair. Straker was in sombre mood, his arm in a sling. Luckily the bullet had passed through him cleanly, without damage to any internal organs. Hümmler had been less fortunate. His loss was a disappointment, but he was replaceable. Foot soldiers always are. Stronik looked tired, unaccustomed to travel. He had rarely been outside of America since his arrival there in the fifties, partly from fear: there were too many in Europe who might have recognised him, might have denounced or attacked him in the street. But now most of that generation had passed. And power was once more on his side. Finally the ideas and beliefs that had shaped his childhood, that came to fruition in the glorious years of the 1930's, were preparing to return.

After eating, they moved into the small living room and sat around the table. Maps and papers littered its surface.

'It has gone well,' Cham observed. 'A few setbacks, but they were to be expected.'

'Indeed,' Stronik agreed. 'Just a few more days. The history books tell us they destroyed the Third Reich.' He thumped the table. 'Not so, my friends. It was merely sleeping.'

Straker shook his head slowly. 'There have been too many mistakes. In a few days, anything can happen. The whole situation can be reversed. We should have been harder, quicker to react.'

'What do you mean?' Stronik looked at him uneasily.

'First there was Brewer,' Straker glanced at Cham. 'He should have been removed a long time ago.'

'I left that to you,' Cham commented.

Straker did not rise to the bait. 'And then the leak to the Bureau, the constant interference from the Mossad. That,' he said loudly. 'Was inexcusable.'

Cham thought for a moment before responding. 'I thought we had it buried. With Vogel in the States and myself in the UK, I thought we killed it.'

'Thinking wasn't good enough. We needed action. Rami could have sorted the Mossad sooner. He could have dealt with Brewer, the Bureau. If need be, we could have removed the Hadar Dafna Building itself. '

'The Mossad headquarters?' Cham asked with surprise.

'A simple matter,' Straker said with an offhand manner. 'Rami has the contacts. Gullible suicide bombers are easy to find. Tell them it's part of the Holy War against the Jewish invaders.'

'Anyway,' Cham replied. 'It's too late now. We've lost Schengel. I checked with the airline. He definitely caught his flight. But he's always been a law unto himself.' He hesitated. 'And where is Rami?'

Straker smiled. 'I have given him a little assignment to attend to. Some preparations, let me say.'

'Preparations?' Stronik asked. 'Preparations for what?'

'Time will show you,' Straker replied. 'But tonight I think we should turn our attention to more immediate things. Our man is ready. He knows when he is to move, what he is to say. And the units?'

'The units are ready,' Cham confirmed. 'Each cell has been separately trained and briefed. Even if one or two of them should be compromised before the designated day, the overall operation will not be jeopardised.'

'Good. Then Schengel's disappearance is insignificant. He has done his work. The materials are ready. Unfortunately we shall have no reserves as a result of the raid on Lincoln,' Stronik added. 'But the cells will be more than adequately provided for. Tokyo was a tiny sample compared to what we have prepared.'

'Right across Europe,' Straker said quietly. 'We shall see fear like we have not seen fear since the last war. Europe will cry out for strong and determined leadership. It will be shaken from its apathy and decline. The liberals have had their day. Their methods have not worked. Crime is high. Violence, depravity is rife. Foreign terrorist infiltrators are in our midst. A strong hand is needed. Our man will provide it. People will welcome him with relief, worship him as the German people once worshipped the Führer. Let us drink to tomorrow.'

'To tomorrow,' the other men concurred.

Despite the moves to openness in recent years, not all of Britain's covert operations have been placed in the public domain. One of the most significant of the operations to remain undercover is the government's research centre at Porton Down. Located in Wiltshire, as part of the Ministry of Defence it is involved in the investigation of biological and chemical warfare. Its official remit is to assess the risk to British people and the armed forces of CBW attacks and to devise means of protecting against such attacks. Most experimentation has taken place on animals. Allington Farm forms part of the Porton Down complex and its main function is as an animal breeding centre.

Despite elaborate security precautions, mistakes and accidents have taken place. Several dangerously contaminated animals have escaped in the past and had to be shot on sight. And during the 1960's a research scientist died of a plague infection. There have also been several explosions. Porton Down was originally established in 1916 during the middle of the First World War, a war in which chemical weapons were used with devastating effect. Its role was later extended into biological weapons during the Second World War to counter the perceived Nazi threat.

The same limousine that collected Brewer from the airport transferred him and his deadly cargo to Porton Down's premises in South Wiltshire. The journey was swift and uneventful, taking a little under two and a half hours, despite heavy traffic on the M4 in West London. As they approached the establishment along the A30, large signs warned that it was a restricted premises under the meaning of the Official Secrets Act. They turned right and reached a security checkpoint, identified themselves to an armed guard and proceeded beyond a metal chain link fence and into a compound screened by a towering brick wall that would have looked more at home around a prison. Security cameras and scissor wire decorated the top of the wall.

A casually dressed young man came out to greet him, taking the case from Brewer with great enthusiasm.

'Is this them?' he asked. 'Smashing.'

He led Brewer into a long, low building with the look and feel of a World War II barracks. But inside it was expensively equipped and divided into a series of labs, a long corridor stretching from one end to the other and large viewing windows cut into the side overlooking each of the labs. As they entered Brewer realised they had passed through an air lock. Men and women in white lab coats were busy. The building was very quiet, an indication that the viewing glass was soundproof. Brewer had the unnerving sensation of being under water. Several of the labs contained animals in cages, some small rodents, others larger animals like monkeys. Brewer recalled that several of the establishment's top scientists had been killed in acts of terrorism by animal rights fanatics.

'Here we are.' The man waved Brewer into a larger lab towards one end and then followed him in. Two women and a man in a lab coat stood waiting for them. There were brief introductions, but it was not Brewer they were interested in. It was his case. They opened it and looked at the canisters inside.

'Any idea at all what we're looking at?' the young man asked Brewer.

Brewer shrugged. 'At a guess, I'd say some of it must be sarin.' He hesitated. The image of the dead Mossad agent had come back into his mind. 'There is something else.' He described what he had seen.

Their reaction was calm. He realised they were not listening to it as an anecdote of a fellow man, but as a scientific problem. They probed at him, asking questions about the man's skin, the appearance of his eye sockets. There was a consensus amongst them that a biological agent was responsible. But they could not agree on which.

Finally he left them and went outside for a walk. There was a chill, damp edge in the air and in the distance he could hear the rumble of thunder. He lit a *Romeo y Julieta* cigar and wandered slowly around the collection of huts and buildings. Several of the premises had additional security warnings on the outside, some of them biohazard, others just threats of prosecution and reminders of the Official Secrets Act.

It was a god-forsaken place and Brewer wanted nothing more than to get as far away as fast as he could.

The lorries left the Eindhoven warehouse shortly before six a.m. the following morning. In the cold grey light of dawn, a ceaseless line of juggernauts came slowly from its gates and moved in convoy through the surrounding roads. As they approached the motorway junctions, some headed north, some south, some east, some west. Their deadly cargo crept outwards across the waking Europe like the spinning web of a spider.

Brewer looked through the glass at the scientists busy with their work. They wore enveloping NBC suits complete with hoods. Clearly they were taking no chances. He heard a sound at his elbow and turned. It was the young man who had greeted his arrival.

'Any success?' Brewer asked.

'A right cocktail of chemical and bacteriological agents you've brought us, haven't you? You were right about the sarin,' the man observed. 'And we've identified its two relatives as well, tabun and soman. It's the others that are more a problem. One of them is definitely a mustard gas derivative, another possibly anthrax. It's certainly close to the *bacillus anthracis*.' He turned to look back through the window. 'And one of them is very close to the plague-type virus that the Russians were developing. Another possibly *pseudomonas pseudomallei*, or meliodosis. Like anthrax, it's nearly one hundred percent lethal.'

'I didn't think any of the major powers were working on biological and chemical weapons.'

'Think again,' the man responded. 'That's just for public consumption. They're cheaper, easier to produce and more effective than nuclear weapons. And they're much more difficult to detect during production. Interesting thing about the sarin gas. It's exactly the same fingerprint as the stuff that went off in Tokyo.'

'That is interesting,' Brewer said thoughtfully.

'Now all we have to do is identify the rest and start looking into ways of neutralising them.'

'How long will that take?'

The young man turned and raised his eyebrows. 'How long? Months, possibly years. Some of these are complex agents. I take it you're in a hurry?'

'That,' Brewer smiled weakly. 'Would be an understatement.'

Pendleton was not going to be impressed.

Yellow Hawk asked for Brewer when he called, but in his absence was switched through to Pendleton instead.

'It's about these chemicals,' he started.

The Bureau was able to confirm the results of their own lab work. And Pendleton shared the news from Porton Down that sarin, mustard gas and anthrax had been identified. It was then that Yellow Hawk dropped his bombshell.

'We also identified two of the others, one a chemical agent and one biological. The chemical's VX. The other one's a virulent strain of superplague.'

This was not the news that Pendleton wanted to hear. 'How serious are they?'

'Let's just say the guys here estimate both of them to be the most lethal agents currently capable of production. The plague virus is around ten times the lethality of the basic plague virus.'

'Ten times! Are they certain?'

'As certain as they can be. You know these scientist types. Always cautious, never like to guess. Because of that, their warnings alarm me even more.'

'And what chance do we have against it? Do they have any neutralising agents?'

There was a silence and then: 'They tell me there's something called atropine that can help against some of the chemicals. Vaccines against the biological weapons sound even less hopeful.'

Pendleton let out a long strained sigh. 'It's not looking good is it Yellow Hawk?'

'You'd better tell your man Brewer to be careful. Do you know if the supplies of this stuff are still holed up in Europe? Or are they already out there in the wild?'

'We're working on it,' Pendleton replied, realising the inadequacy of the reply.

Europe stood on the threshold of a biochemical holocaust with no means of preventing it. What had the defence establishment been doing for all these years? This failure of defence policy and intelligence product was going to make September 11 look like a minor oversight.

As soon as his call with Yellow Hawk was over, Pendleton called Howarth and asked him to escalate their response through Interpol. Not for the first time, both Howarth and Pendleton regretted the absence of a unified security structure in Europe, a means of tackling a problem that transcended boundaries. The terrorists understood these weaknesses, had played them to their advantage. Now Europe would pay a heavy price—unless they got lucky.

Pendleton fiddled uneasily with a rubber band on his desk. He had the nasty impression that they were too late, that whatever they did they could not change anything. He hoped that Brewer would prove him wrong, that the police would prove him wrong. In fact, he would be happy for anyone to prove him wrong.

The limousine driver dropped Brewer off outside the small office building near the Cenotaph in Whitehall. Brewer ducked past the uniformed guard and into a small meeting room inside. The contact was sitting patiently in the room, reading a newspaper in an armchair drawn up in front of an unlit fire.

'Ah, Mr Brewer.'

Brewer slipped into the armchair opposite.

'I understand you were one of the last to see our people in Lincoln,' the man asked.

Brewer nodded. 'Gilbert and I had met before.'

The Mossad man looked around uneasily. 'We prefer not to use actual names,' he whispered.

'He's dead,' Brewer replied. 'And I'm sorry about that. I don't think mentioning his name is going to hurt anyone now. Certainly not Gilbert.'

The man shrugged. 'I accept you are probably right. He was a good man. His loss has touched us all. It was also unnecessary. If action had been taken sooner, we should not be in this position.'

'I don't think any of us knew the true extent of this operation,' Brewer replied. 'Or did you?'

'We knew about the operation, but no, not the extent of the organisation they had in place. It has been a surprise to us all, what we have always feared.'

'I don't think any of us realised the scale of the problem,' Brewer conceded.

'And I do not suppose that you brought me here merely for idle chatter,' the Mossad man observed, his eyes watching Brewer closely. 'Are you on official or unofficial business? And,' he waved a finger. 'I should explain, Mr Brewer, that before you say anything else that we do have a file on you.'

'You do? And what does it say?' Brewer was not sure if he was surprised or flattered.

'Everything you ever told Gilbert,' the man replied. 'I told you he was a good man.'

'Then you must know you can trust me?'

The man hesitated and then nodded. 'Yes, I would say that is true. But you must understand I am wary. It is difficult to know now who may be working for them and who may not.'

'Isn't that always the way these people work? They make everyone distrust each other. Divide and rule.'

'True. That is one of their techniques. Now how may I be of assistance?'

Brewer cleared his throat. 'Someone has become an embarrassment to us. Normally as you know we take care of our own dirty laundry. But this is different. It might be misunderstood if we took action ourselves.'

'Misunderstood?' The man frowned. 'It would help if you told me who this mysterious person is.'

Now it was Brewer's turn to hesitate. 'Cham,' he whispered.

'Ah.' The Mossad man sat back in his chair. 'Now I understand. We cannot have members of the Firm removing each other can we? Particularly not one of the bosses.'

'It wouldn't look good,' Brewer conceded. 'I wondered if you might assist us in our hour of need.'

The Mossad man smiled. 'And why should we wish to do this?'

'You know what he stands for. I'm giving you the green light. You do it, there'll be no comebacks. Some hypocrisy on our part, maybe. An obituary in *The Times*. The best potential leader of the SIS we ever had, etcetera, etcetera. I'm sure you could live with that.'

'More easily than I can live with the idea of a man like Cham, yes,' the Mossad man conceded. 'So you wish us to remove him like your man removed Vogel?'

'Something like that, yes,' Brewer agreed. 'And I expect you already have plans for Straker and Stronik as well.'

The man did not react. 'You may guess whatever you like, Mr Brewer. But tell me this: just where is your Mr Cham?'

Brewer looked surprised. 'Ah. You mean you don't know?'

'The loss of our team in Lincoln has left a small hole. We are busy repairing it, but in the meantime, some things are falling through.'

'Eindhoven, to the best of our knowledge,' Brewer said. 'And he has company. Straker and Stronik. It looks like they're still planning to carry their operation through to its conclusion.'

Brewer slipped him an envelope containing details. It was in a cipher that he knew the Mossad would have no trouble breaking.

'I am impressed,' the Mossad man commented, slipping the envelope into an inside pocket. 'The Firm must be improving.'

'Not us,' Brewer shook his head. 'Special Branch.'

'Special Branch?' The man frowned. 'Since when did they operate abroad?'

'They don't, not directly. But they do liaise, of course. We only know half of what we do about this operation because of their work. They exposed Hamilton.'

'Correction,' the man said. 'We exposed Hamilton. We told you about everything.'

'Correction,' Brewer mocked. 'You told Cham. And you probably cost Gilbert his life.'

The man from the Mossad sat silently for a while.

'I regret to say so, but you are probably right.' He stood. 'It was nice to meet you Mr Brewer. Perhaps we may we meet again in less troubled times.' He turned to leave.

Brewer stood. 'Are you doing anything about the chemical stores? We need to work together on this. If just one of those weapons consignments is used in Europe, it's going to make Hiroshima look like a minor incident. What are you planning to do?'

The Mossad man raised his eyebrows. 'You shall have to wait and see, won't you?'

Brewer followed him towards the door. 'One moment. That business in Moscow. And in Hirtshals in Denmark. What was all that about? Who did kill the Professor? And his assistant?'

The Mossad man turned to look at him.

'For an SIS agent, you do seem remarkably ill-informed,' he commented. 'I tell you this only out of respect for Gilbert. He thought very highly of you. We were after the Moscow files at first. If only the Professor had done as we asked, maybe none of this would have happened. But he drank too much and so he spoke too much. And so did his assistant.'

'So you killed them? What the hell was in those files?'

'Of course we didn't kill him,' the man retorted angrily. 'It was Straker's friend.'

'Hümmler?'

'The Professor and the woman knew too much, I suppose you could say. The files contained details of the Nazis' spy network. All the names, all the contacts, all the addresses.'

'But what possible use was that to anyone?' Brewer asked. 'A list from what, 1945?'

'It was of every use,' the Mossad man commented. 'Stronik was on it. And many other names. Names you would be surprised to see, names that you would know. There was also a copy of the same document in the U-boat, ready for use after the war.' He turned away. 'And now, if you will excuse me, I really must be going. So nice to make your acquaintance.'

And then he was gone, leaving Brewer alone to nurse his thoughts.

25

It was Straker who first detected the surveillance operation outside the rented house. He woke during the night, his throat dry and his head heavy from too much wine the night before. In the kitchen he ran some cool, fresh water from the tap. As he stood beside the sink in the moonlight, something flashed in the night sky outside. He froze and watched. A moment later there was movement, dark shadows in the gloom. There was the flare of moonlight on metal and then darkness again.

They were careless. Even during the night—sometimes especially at night—a surveillance team must remain vigilant, assume nothing. If Straker had not been thirsty, their lapse might have passed unnoticed. But he had been thirsty. And now they would pay for their mistake.

He returned to his room and dressed silently in the dark, slowed down by his injured arm. He gave no thought to waking the others. The noose had been tightening around them for weeks. At times of danger, the only way to survive is by ruthless self-preservation. It was a lesson he had learned before. He was no longer prepared to take risks: they could look after themselves. The disaster at the compound demonstrated how dangerous the situation had become. And now they were surrounded once again: it was beginning to look like someone had talked. That worried him. How much did they know? Did they know about the lorries that had departed the previous day? Did they know about the deliveries that were even now being made, the cells that were preparing for action? And did they know that today was the key day, the day when the legislation would be passed: the signal that would trigger the start of their return?

Stronik and Cham slept soundly in their rooms. No matter. They had served their purpose. Straker moved past them and through to the back of the building. He prised open a window and climbed out and into the garden. Midway through, he caught his injured arm on the catch. Sharp arrow points of pain jabbed into his arm and clouded his vision. He closed his eyes, trying to block the agony. It was a few minutes before he could move again. This time he was more careful. He reached the garden and ducked down low. The ground was hard underfoot, his shoes too noisy. He bent down and removed them, carrying them in his good hand.

The moon was hidden by cloud. He detected at least two observers. And there were probably more at the front. The slightest sound, the slightest wrong move would give him away. If they had night vision goggles, he was a dead man. He carried on regardless. Every step was considered, every movement cautious. He was not about to be caught, not now. Not after all these years of waiting and planning. He was going to escape, was going to make sure that the plans were carried through. Only a few more hours now and it would be too late to stop them.

The Dutch police were surprised to receive the instruction to abandon their surveillance operation in the middle hours of the night. But the six army officers who arrived to relieve them looked official. They had all the right papers, all the right documents and identification. And most importantly, they had the right rank. It was four a.m. and the police were tired. Who were they to argue about the instructions? Why should they care if the orders they had been given earlier, their strict orders not to leave the surveillance under any circumstances, had now been countermanded? A short drive away were homes and warm beds and families. It was a simple decision to take.

The army officers waited until the police had departed. As soon as they were gone their leader issued a single word of command. The soldiers moved quickly, removing their outer Dutch military uniforms to reveal plain camouflage clothing beneath. One of them wore a small Star of David and was clearly in charge. They took machine guns from the rear of their Jeep and fanned out around the building without any further discussion.

At four thirty precisely the silence of the night was broken by the sound of shattering glass.

The two men at the front moved rapidly through the front door, down the hallway and to the left. They had been over the plans of the building until they knew it as well as their own homes. They burst into Stronik's room and flicked on the light. He was sitting up in bed, a pillow gripped tightly between his fingers, holding it out in front of him like a shield.

'*Nyet, nyet!*' he pleaded, in his fear retreating to the Russian of his childhood.

The first volley of shots blasted his head into the wall behind him. Stronik, or as he had once been, Wasyl Stronicic, had never shown mercy to anyone in his life. The same discourtesy was now extended to him.

Moments later the men burst into Cham's room. The door frame splintered and shattered. But as they entered a shot killed the first soldier outright, sending him spinning to the floor. The second was struck in the chest by a rapid second shot and fell screaming to the floor, the dum-dum bullet ripping through his internal organs. By then Cham was out of the door and past them, his automatic ready. Behind him the screaming intensified. He looked left. There had to be more of them. He was sure of that. Four or six? If it was SAS it would be four. He caught sight of Stronik through the bedroom door. His stomach convulsed. One second's delay and that would have been him too.

But where was Straker? Had he already been taken out? He ducked into Straker's room. The clothes and bags scattered on the floor told him everything he need to know. Straker had already fled. But where and why? Was this his idea? Were these his assassins? Cham grew angry. This was a double-cross. It had to be.

There was a crash in the kitchen, loud enough to be heard above the men's screams. He spun in time to see two dark shadows closing on him fast. He fired, two quick shots. The shadows fell to the ground. A .45 dum-dum can stop a charging rhino: against men it does far more than stop them.

If they were SAS, that was all men down. But Cham had a feeling this wasn't SAS: their operation was a mess, they were ill-equipped and careless. He ran towards the front door, stopped and peered out. There was a jeep on the far side of the road. His own car was parked in the garage on the other side of the house. It was time to choose: he would stand no chance if he fled on foot. The choice was simple: he did not have the keys to his car, they were back in his room. It had to be the jeep.

He ducked down and zigzagged across the road. The men's screams faded behind him. A burst of close gunfire rang out, zinging off the tarmac with a sound like broken springs. Something jolted his left heel and the next moment he was in the cover of the bushes on the other side. Machine gun fire raked along the undergrowth, spitting leaves and dirt into his face. He peered back towards the house. The shots were coming from the right hand corner. He levelled his automatic. It was about thirty yards away: he would need to be more than a good shot, he would also have to be lucky. Or they would have to be careless.

The European Commissioner sat in his Brussels office and looked at the phone. The call was late. For the first time, doubts crossed his mind. What would happen if the plans went adrift? He pushed the thoughts from his mind. Nothing would go wrong. Not now.

The Commission is one of the key institutions of the European Union and its members amongst the most influential. For reasons obvious to anyone who understands the way politicians work, the member nations of Europe have not yet delegated full control to the democratically elected European Parliament. Instead, the government of each member state has maintained the idea of the Commission to ensure that they continue to control the real decision-making in Europe, rather than handing control to the democratically elected Members of the European Parliament. The Commission makes all proposals for new laws. It has twenty members who are appointed for five years and can only be removed by a special vote in the European Parliament. On appointment they become independent of their national governments and are intended to act only in the interests of the Union as a whole and not of their own country. Each Commissioner is responsible for a particular area, such as economic policy, social affairs, or foreign and security policy.

The stated goal of the European Union is to bring peace and prosperity through the co-operation of its member states. The process of integration started in the bloody aftermath of World War II with the pooling of heavy industry. On the back of this success, they started to create a single market in which goods, services, people and money could move about as freely as they can within one country. In a sense, the purpose was to create a united states of Europe, although some dispute this interpretation. A closer analogy may be the former political confederacy of States in America, which had a looser form of co-operation between its member states. The process in Europe has been slow: centuries of history and historical differences and grievances cannot be displaced overnight. The initial processes of integration took nearly forty years to incorporate political and social issues as well as economic and trade dimensions. The single market came into existence in January 1993 and was powerfully reinforced by the Maastricht Treaty on 1 November 1993.

Maastricht prepared the way for complete economic and monetary union and ultimately a single currency. Maastricht also gave significant extra powers to the European Parliament. Most notably, it added a common foreign and security policy together with co-operation on justice and police affairs. The man sitting nervously at his desk held the post of Commissioner for Security and Defence. It was he who in the event of a 'significant threat to Europe's wellbeing' would be empowered to impose emergency measures. If need be, he could impose martial law. Europe would come under his direct military control. He could take whatever measures were judged necessary. Locked away in his safe were precisely such plans. But they were not the ones that had been prepared for him by his Brussels civil servants and military advisors, in close co-operation with NATO and the Western European Union.

They were plans that had been developed by the NSDAP-AO.

The Commissioner impatiently checked his watch. Today the European Parliament would debate the new legislation. Today he would receive his final instructions. And tomorrow he would act. But the call he had expected at eight a.m. was late, the call that would confirm the deliveries were complete, the cells initiated.

It was another half an hour before the phone rang. He snatched it up. But it was not the call he had been expecting.

Two policemen had arrived to see him and were waiting in his secretary's office.

Straker rendezvoused with Rami at the pre-arranged location, a small estaminet bar tucked away in the sprawling alleys of central Brussels. Rami bought Straker a coffee from the bar and waited while Straker settled down.

'It's blown, isn't it?' Rami asked.

Straker shook his head. 'No, no. It relies on us. Everything else is in place.'

Rami examined the elderly German. For once, Straker looked his age. His pale blue eyes were tired and lined, his fading straw hair bedraggled across his scalp. His arm in the sling looked thin and pathetic. Rami wanted to reach out and touch him, this man who had lived through the 1930's, who as a child had met and talked with Hitler. He wanted to reach out and touch this example of living history, this link with the past, as if in some way by doing so he would be able to see through his eyes, share in his memories. The Nazis were an inhuman aberration he abhorred, but there was a power in their evil that fascinated him. He wanted to understand them, what could have fuelled such hate and such mindless total war. And more than that: it was their actions that had triggered the creation of the state of Israel. And without the creation of that country, Palestine would still exist, there would be no Israel. There would be peace—and true power—in the Middle East.

'Is there,' Rami started and then stopped. 'Is there any tidying up of loose ends you want me to do?'

Straker shook his head. 'I don't think so. By now, Stronik and Cham will have been taken out.'

'By who?'

'I don't know. We seem to have left too many trails behind us. I escaped, but only just. And I'm getting too old for this.'

Rami looked at his watch. 'Has anyone given the signal to our man at the Council?'

Straker stared at him. 'No. It was too risky earlier. Would you mind?'

Rami went to the phone. He was back in five minutes. Straker looked up at him as he sat down.

'Well? Was he okay?'

Rami nodded. 'Everything's fine. No problems.'

Rami hoped that Straker would not guess he was lying. When he had made the call it had not been answered by the Commissioner. It had been a voice he did not know. He had hung up and tried again with the same result. Now all he wanted was to get out. Their plans were coming to pieces. Their crazy ideas had served their purpose. The longer he delayed his departure, the greater the risk of capture. Or worse.

'He hasn't been approached by anyone?' Straker was clearly on edge.

'No. Everything's going to plan. The cells have had their deliveries. He received the notification right on time. The Parliament looks set to pass the legislation later today.'

'Excellent,' Straker replied. 'Then your work is finished.'

'In which case,' Rami said. 'Payment is due.'

Straker looked at him sharply. 'Some of us do this for the love of the cause.'

'I know,' Rami replied. 'But some also do it for the love of the money. The modern world is a very expensive place to live. And many of us have ambitions of our own.'

'We can sort out the final arrangements tomorrow, once everything is concluded.'

Rami leaned forwards. 'That was not the agreement. I have done everything requested of me.'

'Is something bothering you, Rami?' Straker waited. 'Well? You told me only a moment ago that everything was going to plan. What difference will a day make?'

Rami tried to hide his resentment. He already had the ticket in his pocket. A short flight to Frankfurt and then on to Bangkok. He wanted his money and he wanted it quickly. Funding his ambitions was an expensive exercise and he needed these funds urgently for work elsewhere in the Middle East. The whole neo-Nazi plan was falling to pieces. Only Straker was too old, too lost in his dreams to see it.

'Come on,' Rami insisted. 'We're going to the bank now.'

Straker pulled back away from him. 'Stop it!'

Several customers turned to stare.

'I said come with me.'

Straker looked down at the discreet knife Rami held against his stomach.

'You are serious, aren't you?' Straker asked. 'I thought you were one of us.'

'I belong to no-one but myself. And I'm always serious about money,' Rami replied quietly. 'Now let's go.'

Brewer looked at Stronik's bloody remains with a feeling of indifference.

'I still don't understand how Cham and Straker escaped. Whoever did this wasn't messing about.'

He turned to the policeman. The policeman shrugged.

'There is a lot here I do not understand,' he admitted in a heavy Dutch accent. 'Who were the army soldiers?'

'Your guess is probably better than mine,' Brewer lied. He

had a pretty good idea who the fake army officers had been: Mossad agents. The only problem was they had clearly screwed up. And screwed up badly. From the blood on the carpets, several of them had either been killed or badly injured. The only corpse in the place was Stronik's. No sign of Cham, no sign of Straker. Very messy.

He could only guess what had happened. Straker and Cham must have been armed, must have been alerted to the raid in some way. They had fought back and escaped. The Israelis would not have taken them prisoner: too many political complications they could do without. And if Cham and Straker were on the loose and still working together, the situation was still highly volatile, highly dangerous. All the time that the command structure stayed in place, the chemical depots remained a threat. They had to cut off the head.

He phoned Pendleton on his mobile to break him the news.

'What a bloody mess,' Pendleton sighed. 'Just sort it out, will you?'

And then, thought Brewer, he would also part the waters of the Red Sea and turn grape juice into wine. Pendleton had an intensely irritating habit of passing simple-sounding directions that turned out to be impossible to deliver. For a moment Brewer thought about going to the airport, faxing his resignation and heading off to a remote Pacific island. One thing was certain: however this case might turn out, he was going to leave the Service. He had finally had enough: this had become an assignment too far.

Outside, the Dutch police were combing the scene for forensic evidence. He did not envy them their task. He climbed back inside his rented BMW and started the engine, thinking back over the day's events. Howarth at Special Branch had suggested to Pendleton a link with Brussels some time back. Calls had been traced from GDM's offices to a member of the European Commission. From what Pendleton told him, Howarth had a good track record. If he thought there was a link, then Brewer guessed it was worth investigating.

He checked his watch. It was nearly two p.m. Time was running against them. He gunned the motor and scorched away from the house. In the rear view mirror he saw several of the policemen staring after him. He headed south, towards the border with Belgium. The car handled well, its tyres holding tight as he pushed it to the limit around some of the tight country roads before he reached the motorway and could open up the throttle and cruise at speeds at least thirty miles an hour over the legal limit.

Gary's information had been good, but out of date. And out of date intelligence is about as much use as a pony and cart at Silverstone. All of the operational centres he had named had been systematically checked—and all of them were long since abandoned. The European distribution point was rumoured to be Rotterdam, but when the police raided the dockyard warehouse they found nothing. And now there was this incident near Eindhoven. The significance was clear enough. If Eindhoven specialises in anything, it is storage and distribution: certainly no tourist finds much to recommend in its bland and depressing surroundings. Already the police were checking records of all the storage and warehouse depots they could, but it would not be a quick job. If Gary's dates were right, the distribution had already been made. And if the cells already had access to the bio-chemical weapons, there was little they could do to stop them.

On top of which, Porton Down's provisional analysis did not make cheerful reading. Worse, a document came through from the FBI lab that really depressed him. The superplague they identified would make the medieval Black Death look as insignificant as a runny nose in comparison. As soon as it was released, it would have to be allowed to run its course. It would kill millions within weeks. The only way to stop it spreading was to prevent its release: another challenge worthy of Pendleton. There was still too much of the terrorist's European operation that had not yet been exposed. And it was beginning to worry Brewer that the command structure appeared to be loose, a set of largely autonomous cells. Like the structure of Al Qaeda, that would make it almost impossible to break even if they did track down the ringleaders.

Brewer was over the border before he knew it. In the sprawling outskirts of Brussels his journey slowed and he ditched the car in a side street near to a bar he knew well and went the rest of the way by tram.

He was alighting from the tram near to the Bourse when the phone rang in his pocket. It was the duty desk. But Brewer thought he recognised the voice.

'Monroe? That is you isn't it?'

'Sure it is Brewer. Guess what? They gave me the job they were going to give you. Don't go getting jealous on me.'

'You? On duty desk rota? I'd never have believed it.'

'And guess what? I'm about to make your day.'

'Don't mess about Monroe. What is it?'

'We've a reported sighting of Straker in Brussels.'

'Now I know you're winding me up,' Brewer responded. He moved over to the edge of the street and watched the movement of the trams and buses.

'An off-duty Belgian policeman recognised the photo-fit as soon as he got into work about half an hour ago. Apparently he was having a pre-work pick-me-up in a local bar and Straker was there with some other guy. Middle-eastern. They had some kind of fracas, made a scene. That's why he remembered him.'

'You have the name of this place?'

'Sure. It's the *Imaige de Nostre Dame* in the *Impasse des Cadeaux*.'

'I know it.'

'Brewer. I'd be disappointed if you said otherwise.'

'Get a watch on the airports, will you?

'Done. There's an APB.'

'Thanks Monroe. I owe you one.'

'By the time you see me next, I'll be back at my desk, Brewer. You can put money on it. Oh, and Brewer.'

'What is it?'

'Those documents you sent me. The ones I told you I never received.'

Brewer stiffened. 'Yes? What about them?'

'It was Cham. I'm sorry Brewer. He took them from me, assured me it was a high level undercover operation. I didn't know he was rotten.'

'None of us did,' Brewer said coldly.

The *Imaige de Nostre Dame* was a few streets away, tucked away at the end of an alley. Within two minutes he was inside and one look was enough. If Straker had ever been here, he wasn't now. And from the description, it was likely his companion was Rami. Brewer wanted them both. Straker for the death of Larsen Lak, and Rami for Simon Gilbert. He felt the comforting shape of the automatic through his jacket and spoke briefly with the barman. The barman remembered serving them, had heard them talking about a bank, so the policeman's report was right: good work.

Brewer checked the nearest banks, clutching at any straws he could. Nothing. What had seemed like a chance breakthrough was fading fast. With no other clues to follow-up, Brewer headed towards the offices of the Commissioner implicated in Howarth's information. The police had already spoken with him and got nowhere, but Brewer might be luckier. Or more persuasive.

It was as he was climbing onto the tram that he saw them. Rami and Straker were standing on a street corner and hailing a cab. For a moment Brewer could not believe what he was seeing. And then he spun on his heel and pushed his way back off the tram, ignoring the chorus of protests. Already a cab had stopped, the door was open. Fifty yards and closing. Brewer broke into a run. Forty yards. Straker was climbing inside, moving awkwardly with his damaged arm, Rami close behind him. Thirty yards. Rami was inside, the door was closing. Twenty yards. Brewer reached for his gun as the taxi started to move away from the kerb. Ten yards. The taxi was gathering speed. Brewer levelled his gun, his finger poised on the trigger. His eyes narrowed, his focus tightened. The rear window was in his sights. But it was too late and too dangerous. He slipped the gun away.

He turned and saw a taxi heading towards him. He hailed it

and clambered inside. Further down the street the other taxi was stopped at traffic lights. Brewer urged his taxi driver on, shoving a wad of Euros onto the front seat. It was enough to excite the driver. The lights ahead changed and the other taxi moved on, Brewer's car close behind. At the next junction they pulled alongside.

Brewer was out and opening the front passenger door of the other vehicle before Straker and Rami realised what was happening.

'Good afternoon,' he greeted them, turning to face the back seat and covering them with his gun. 'Where are we going?'

'*Banque National de Paris*, Sablon Branch,' the driver replied nonchalantly, as if he were used to men with guns leaping into his cab every day.

The car moved on.

'Making a collection? Or depositing, I wonder?' Brewer speculated.

'You're too late Brewer,' Straker told him. 'There's absolutely nothing you can do now. By this time tomorrow, Europe will be ours.'

'You think so?' Brewer asked. 'Do you agree with that, Rami?'

'It is no concern of mine,' Rami replied evenly.

'Rami's work is finished, isn't it Rami?'

Brewer noted the bitterness in Straker's voice.

'My, my,' Brewer taunted them. 'Don't tell me Tweedle-dum and Tweedle-even-dumber have fallen out have we?'

The two men fell silent. Brewer turned to the driver and gave him another address in the Sablon district.

'Where are you planning to take us?' For the first time Rami looked concerned.

'A little place I know in the beautiful district of Sablon,' Brewer replied. 'But I don't think you'll be so keen.'

'Look, Brewer. I don't have an argument with you. I'm sure we can come to some arrangement.'

'I wouldn't be so sure Rami.'

'I'm nothing to do with this. Straker told you, my work is over.

I was, let me put it like this, the hired help. We were going to the bank, he was going to pay my fee and I was going to leave. Why complicate things?'

Brewer looked at Rami in silence. Straker turned to look at him with surprise and loathing.

'I can pay you, Brewer. More than you can imagine.' Rami was clearly not going to give in easily.

Brewer was unmoved. 'How much is that, Rami? I have a very good imagination. I don't think you could afford me.'

Rami fell silent and looked out of the window. Brewer recognised where they were. Only a few more minutes and they would be arriving. Keeping the gun fixed firmly on the two men, he took the mobile phone from his pocket and tapped in a local number. When it was answered he said:

'Two-one-three. Tiger and Mammoth,' and ended the call.

They turned the corner into the street he knew so well. Ahead he could see the Firm's Brussels safe house, the door already ajar. The car began to slow. Suddenly Rami had the car door open and was out before Brewer could react. He shouted at the driver to stop. He was thrown forward as the cab screeched to a halt. A moment later Brewer was out, but Rami was already running fast. Twice Brewer fired and twice he missed. He started to give chase and then saw Straker easing himself out of the car behind him. He stopped and spun round.

'Don't even think about it,' he said.

Straker smiled. 'I'm not going anywhere, Mr Brewer. Tomorrow everything will change. Tomorrow everything will belong to—'

The shots threw Straker's body back over the taxi. His blood smeared its bright bodywork. Slowly he turned and dropped to the floor, a forgotten rag doll. Brewer ducked and spun behind the car, using it for cover. The taxi driver was out and beside him without any prompting.

The shots came from inside the safe house. He was sure of that. He turned and looked down the road. Rami was gone. Straker was not quite dead. Faint words came from his mouth. Another shot came from the house: this time Brewer saw the gunman. He responded without thinking. His arm flicked upwards, his gun kicking twice in his hand. The figure at the window flew backwards. This time he had not missed. He dived round the car and ran for the door.

'Stay where you are,' he shouted at the driver. It was probably an unnecessary instruction.

Brewer entered the house without pausing, the gun held firmly in both hands. In the back room downstairs he found two bodies. He recognised two of the Firm's Belgian agents. Both had been shot with a single bullet through the back of the head. There was no sign of a struggle: it had been a controlled execution—or someone they trusted.

He took the stairs three at a time and burst into the front room, ignoring recommended procedures. Cham was squirming on the floor, blood oozing from two wounds. One in his arm, the other his chest. His gun was below the window where it had fallen.

'You're too late, Brewer,' Cham hissed. 'You can't stop us now.'

Brewer squatted down beside him and prodded at Cham's wounds with his gun. Cham screamed.

'Talk to me, Cham,' he prompted. 'If you don't, I'll make sure you don't die and you don't get treatment. You have no idea how painful it will be.'

'Straker betrayed me,' he whispered. 'They tried to kill me.'

Brewer smiled. 'Is that what you think? You're paranoid. That wasn't Straker's friends who turned up to remove you. That was the Mossad.'

'What?' Cham nearly sat up with surprise. 'You're lying. It can't have been.'

'And we know all about your betrayal,' Brewer continued. 'You're going to stand trial, Cham. You're going to be bigger than Philby, Burgess and Maclean combined.'

'Betrayal!' Cham spat out the word. 'What would you know about that? Look at England, for god's sake. It's nothing. It's been destroyed by weak men. We have to change. Western democracy has failed. There's only one way forward.'

'Only one way?' Brewer mused. 'I don't think so. Your

alternative seems even more corrupt than what we have already. And that is saying something.'

Cham groaned and writhed on the floor. The pool of blood was growing larger. Brewer reached forward and felt his pulse.

'You're dying, Cham.'

'It doesn't matter. At least we have succeeded.'

'Oh, I don't think so Cham,' Brewer replied, standing and moving over the window. 'We know all about the new legislation. We have transcripts of Thielstrom's meetings with the MEPs. We're going to remove them, the legislation will be suspended.'

'You're bluffing,' Cham insisted.

'Not at all. Your signal, the trigger for your poisonous little cells will never go out.'

The taxi driver put his head around the door, caught sight of Cham's bloody presence and disappeared. A moment later the sound of vomiting came from the bathroom.

'Tut tut. I did tell him to stay where he was,' Brewer commented.

Cham sighed. 'You don't understand do you? Even if you remove the MEPs, stop the legislation, you won't stop us.'

'We know about the distribution from Eindhoven, the cells. We're closing in right now.'

'No, no,' Cham shook his head. 'You don't know what you're doing. We have a failsafe. You can't stop it, whatever you try. Don't you understand? I did this for England, for Britain. We're drifting Brewer. We need strength, we need unity.'

'I agree,' Brewer replied. 'But not fascism, not thugs, not this.' Brewer paused. 'Right analysis, wrong conclusion. Tell me, Cham. Did you order Hamilton's death? And Parke?'

'They served their purpose. Hamilton never knew a thing. Thought he was doing his bit for King and country. Which he was.'

'Have you always used people, Cham? Or was there a time when you had some remotely human feelings?'

Cham pulled a face. 'Hamilton wrote his books, didn't he? About Britain's intelligence services? Got all those lucrative TV and radio appearances as an expert. He didn't care whether what we gave him was junk, so why should I care about him? Who was using who, Brewer?'

'All those lies you fed him, all that crap he published and the public swallowed. The official history of the Service. Bullshit. You were using him, Cham. Spinning him a web of fiction. No doubt about it.'

Brewer needed to keep him talking. What did Cham mean: *we have a failsafe?* If that meant what Brewer feared, the cells would operate without their head. Removing Cham and his cronies would only delay their plans. But how long did they have, what was the failsafe and how could it be countered?

'So now what happens to me, Brewer? Secure ambulance to London?'

Brewer shook his head. 'You missed your first appointment with the executioners.'

A look of doubt flickered across Cham's face. '*You* sent the Mossad?'

'Not in so many words. We just happened to let them know where to find you.'

'You bastard, Brewer. Are you a Jew boy too?'

Brewer smiled. 'Everything's so black and white for you, isn't it Cham? Or perhaps I should say white and white. I really don't know where they find people like you. And if it matters so much to you, no. I'm not Jewish. Personally, I have a lot of sympathy for the Palestinian cause. But both Jews and Arabs have suffered enough. Not that you would care. Suffering's what you live for, isn't it?'

Brewer raised the gun and pointed it at Cham's head.

'Any last confessions, Cham? Any last-minute regrets or death-bed conversions?'

Cham forced a smile.

'You won't do it Brewer. Not you. You're too much of a liberal, too much of a grey suit. It's not the done thing, is it? Shooting someone in cold blood.'

The two shots blasted through Cham's skull.

'Now I don't mind being called a liberal,' Brewer whispered. 'But a grey suit? You really knew how to hurt a man, Cham.'

26

The MEPs who had endorsed and backed Hamilton's bio-
chemical defence initiative were early arrivals in the Strasbourg
Parliament building that morning. They had not been idle since
their tense meeting with Thielstrom on the outskirts of the city.
As soon as they returned to the Parliament building and the flats
and hotels nearby where most of their fellow MEPs stayed whilst
in Strasbourg, they had started intense lobbying. They found
their most fertile ground in the far right and far left wings of the
various parties and nationalities. Humiliated by the weakness
and indecision of the Union, right and left-wingers alike wanted
to see the Union move to a position of strength, to build the ability
to strike back quickly. To be an effective force on the world stage.
The MEP's arguments in favour of the new security legislation
flourished amongst such Members. A single defence and security
initiative, power removed from the weak, self-serving national
parliaments and their endless, decisionless committees, would
enable the Union to become as dominant on the world stage as
the United States. Such a view sat easy with the ideologies of
both far right and far left.

But their efforts to persuade did not work so easily with the
middle ground, with the liberals and libertarians who worried
themselves sleepless with the implications for civil rights, who
had the ability to foresee where the process might lead: to central
tyranny, to a truly single Europe devoid of effective democracy.
The MEPs trod carefully with such people, keen to avoid suspicion
and alarm. Although the blocs known as the Party of European

Socialists and the European People's Party made up the two largest single power influences in the Parliament, even within their ranks the MPs found uncertainty and division. Together with the support of the smaller, more extreme parties, for the first time since their meeting with Thielstrom, they began to believe they could succeed. Hurried calculations were made, figures added, subtracted and argued about: it was possible. The numbers could work. A new Europe could be given life.

Today would determine whether they could deliver Thielstrom his prize. Spurred on by their early successes, they redoubled their efforts, unaware that Thielstrom was dead, that the plan was already cracking open at the seams. Pandora's Box was open and its contents about to spew forth and contaminate the comfortable world in which they lived.

The Parliament building began to fill with MEPs, small groups discussing and debating the draft legislation. In the small meeting rooms situated around the main chamber, Members could be seen in heated debate, arguing the merits and problems of the proposals before them, the tabled amendments. The atmosphere was tense. Here was a chance for the Parliament to flex its new, post-Maastricht powers. The legislation before them at last presented the opportunity to stamp their authority on the new Europe and move it one step closer to the day when they, the Parliament, rather than the Council of Ministers and the Commission, would hold real power.

The huge semi-circular chamber was nearly full, the session about to begin. On the podiums, the national flags of the member states hung limply behind the Speaker, dwarfed by the much larger European flag. In their soundproofed booths the translators prepared themselves for the hard work that lay ahead of them. Members settled their papers on their desks, plugged in their headphones. The European Parliament does not use a common language, but accommodates all of the languages of its nation states. It makes proceedings slow and complex, promoting the translators to a key and influential role. On their turn of phrase, on their choice of words, the Members will decide to pass their verdicts. Every time a new country is admitted, a completely new set of bureaucrats and administrators is appointed—although it is a myth that the Union is overstaffed. Even the old Scottish Office in London's Whitehall, which dealt with the affairs of just one nation, had more civil servants to handle its affairs than the whole of the European Union. On the contrary, the EU's staffing has been kept deliberately too low to make it incapable of anything but the most insignificant activities: national politicians are not in the habit of relinquishing their perks and privileges voluntarily.

The chamber began to quieten for the new session. First there was minor business to be completed. Only then would the debate on the security legislation come forward. The five MEPs moved awkwardly in their seats, anxious for the business to be concluded and the day to end. Points of order were raised, the voices of the Members lost in the huge cavity of the chamber, headphones the only link with proceedings. The Italians and French were questioning the passage of new changes to the distribution of agricultural grants and subsidies. There was a question from the UK about privatised water companies who were still receiving public sector grants and distributing them directly into the pockets of shareholders.

Suddenly a new voice came over the headsets. The Members were asked to stay seated, to remain calm. Armed policemen and Gendarmes appeared at the doors. The Parliament stirred uneasily. Members looked at each other. What was happening? This was something new, something that did not appear on the Order of Business for the day.

'What's happening?'

The cry resounded round the chamber in a dozen languages. Fear mingled with anger. Some of the extreme left-wing Members stood up to shout abuse at the police, branding them fascists. The voice came again on the headphones. The chamber fell silent. Five men were named. Five Members were singled out and asked to leave the chamber. Five MEPs who found themselves looking at each other across the chamber with fear evident in their eyes. Now they knew the answer to the question: something was wrong, their worst fears had come true. They had been discovered.

They stood uneasily, the eyes of their colleagues fixed curiously upon them. As they stood, police and Gendarmes hurried towards them, hands hovering close to weapons. Four of the MEPs raised their hands, made clear they would not resist. The fifth decided to run. The chamber watched in silence as he scrambled along one of the aisles, attempting to dodge the police and Gendarmes who stood before him. He began to shout. Two Gendarmes reached him, there was a flurry of fists and batons and within moments he lay unconscious in their arms.

Now more Members started to stand, their sense of outrage growing. What was happening in this, their chamber? The Parliament building was sacrosanct. Entry was forbidden to even the security forces without a formal resolution from the floor of the chamber requesting their presence. It was a violation of everything the Parliament stood for. It was then that the Speaker's voice came over the headphones, the translators quickly shadowing his words. It was he who had given the French police permission to enter the chamber, he who had violated Parliamentary privilege. Many of the Members hardly heard his words, his sentences about 'Conspiracy' and 'Assault on Europe'. Their anger blinded and deafened them to what was happening. Several struggled to pull the captured men from the police and Gendarmes. Fights broke out.

In the TV control room upstairs, the production team, who had risen to their feet in disbelief at the activities on the floor of the chamber, reluctantly did as they were instructed and shut down the transmission.

Across Europe, small cells of dedicated men and women waited for the signal. The first indication that events were not proceeding to plan came from news reports on radio and TV stations. They heard of the arrests at the European Parliament, the suspension of proceedings and the delay to the new legislation. The cell commanders stood their teams down, retreating into their fallback plans. For forty-eight hours they would wait. And at the end of that time, if no instructions had been received to abort their missions, they would proceed with the plan.

The neo-Nazi movement had learned the lessons of the last world war. Never again would they retain all control at the centre. Instead they had devolved power to local commanders, provided enough initiative and independence to each cell to ensure that even should some of their operation be compromised, the other parts could continue to function without interference. Their bio-chemical assault would start in London, Paris, Berlin, Rome, Brussels, Lisbon, Madrid, Amsterdam, Copenhagen, Athens, Dublin, and Luxembourg. Before those cities had recovered, secondary attacks would take place on communications systems, transport infrastructures and military establishments. And if America tried to intervene, satellite cells would strike in New York and Washington. The Pentagon and Langley would follow. America had no stomach for such guerrilla warfare: their reaction to 9/11 had shown that, with their financial market in nervous freefall ever since. The message was clear: terrorism worked. The US would retreat once again into isolation if it was assaulted again on its home turf. Europe would be left to fend for itself. If America did not back down, it would be ripped apart by a civil war headed by highly trained and fanatical militia groups that would make the original civil war look like a tea party.

Within hours of the assaults on the European capitals, the shocking reality would dawn: no country could defend itself against bio-chemical attack. They had tested and proved it in Tokyo, had perfected the techniques with traditional bombings in America, Britain and France. The Western countries had ploughed billions of taxpayers' pounds into nuclear deterrents and modern armaments, a policy based on a belief that any future war would involve fighting traditional battles with a foe in clearly delineated territory, like Saddam in the two Gulf Wars. The political-military machine had ignored the true diversity of threats facing them and now they would pay for their mistake.

As the West's generals have always done, they had prepared for the last war they had fought. In the First World War, they fought the lessons learned in the Boer War: and found their horses and men cut down and butchered in their thousands by machine guns. In the Second World War, they had built huge defences like the Maginot Line, and found them by-passed or Blitzkrieged from the air. And now they had prepared elaborate air defence systems, satellite systems that could spot the smallest military movements and weapons deployments. But they were useless toys in a modern war, a defence against a style of attack that was rapidly passing into the history books. The new wars would be fought in the streets of the cities and the fields of the countryside. It was a lesson that had been there as plain as day in the conflicts of Korea, Vietnam and elsewhere: but it was a lesson no-one had yet learned. And now it would be too late.

The military had once again failed to anticipate, to see the new danger. Helmut Schengel and the neo-Nazi movement had out-thought them. With the backing of dictators and wealthy terrorist factions, Schengel had understood the need to think ahead, to conceive the inevitable, however unpleasant it might be. World War II had changed the agenda. What was it Churchill called it? Total War? Now the world would learn what Total War really meant.

Brewer searched Cham's bloody remains for clues without success. In London, Special Branch searched through Cham's personal papers, broke open his safe and security boxes, pulled his house apart. They too found nothing. Everyone they could link to the conspiracy was pulled in and interrogated, including Hamilton's secretary Emily. They too knew nothing.

The only breakthrough had been the identification of the MEP's. They were traced through references in the documents Brewer had taken from GDM's offices. Those, together with the evidence from the DST, had been enough, but the timing had been tight. No-one had wanted to arrest the MEPs under the full scrutiny of the European Parliament and the media, but they had no other option. It was the only chance. Delay would have meant the possible passage of the legislation, its endorsement by the Parliament. After that the approval of the Council of Ministers would have been a mere formality: on a qualified majority vote, it would have passed without comment. The trigger would have been pulled, the bullet fired.

In his Brussels hotel bedroom, Brewer watched the French President on TV, defending the action at the European Parliament as strongly as he had defended France's renewed unilateral testing of nuclear weapons in the Pacific at Mururoa Atoll. Despite the protestations of the other European countries, outraged that France had violated the integrity of the European assembly, the President was winning his case. Bit by bit the truth was beginning to emerge. The President was a convincing and robust figure, a throwback to the generation of Churchill and De Gaulle.

But the President did not tell the entire story. His confidence suggested the matter was closed, that the arrest of the MEPs was the end of the affair. If only. At any time Brewer expected to hear news of a wave of attacks across Europe. It was possible—probable even—that they were too late. Even as the President was talking of the developments, he knew that French intelligence was busy interrogating the MEPs. If they knew anything, they would talk, whether they wanted to or not. The President had given his personal authority for any measures to be taken against the MEPs—up to and including death if that proved necessary.

The phone rang. Brewer answered it before it could sound again. It was Pendleton.

'A senior Commissioner has gone missing from his Brussels office.'

Brewer sat up. 'Interesting.'

'It fits in with Howarth's information. This particular Commissioner was responsible for European security and defence. If the legislation had been passed today and a situation arisen where one man had to take control, he would have been that man. I should have seen it sooner. It's childishly simple.'

'Do we know where he is?'

'Of course we don't. All we know is that earlier today two policemen called to see him.'

'Let me guess,' interrupted Brewer. 'He disappeared along with the two policemen. He hasn't been seen since.'

Pendleton laughed. 'Why can you read me so easily?'

'It's not you,' Brewer replied. 'I can spot the Mossad's fingerprints without peering through a magnifying glass. They've been ahead of us right the way through this game.'

'You're sure it's them?'

'They're the most likely suspects,' Brewer replied. 'It's their method. But how did they get on to him?'

'Perhaps they already have somebody else. Rami. Schengel.'

'It can't be Rami. He wouldn't talk, not to the Mossad. He would rather die first. It must be Schengel.'

There was a silence. 'So why aren't they telling us what's happening?' Pendleton asked.

It was a good question. And now Brewer knew why Pendleton had called: he wanted him to find out what was happening. To get the Mossad to hand over their information and share the details of the conspiracy.

And of course, when he had done that he would tightrope walk backwards across Niagara Falls and swim the English Channel.

Helmut Schengel was a frightened man. He had arrived in Amsterdam expecting to attend the meeting with Cham, Straker and Stronik. Instead he was met at the airport by a luxury limousine which had taken him to a smart residential house beyond the *Leidesstraat*. There he had been bundled from the car and forced up several near-vertical flights of stairs to the top floor and thrust into a cell.

It was twenty-four hours before he understood what had happened. He had been caught by the Mossad. He could barely believe it. At first came anger, disbelief that they could have done this to him. Only afterwards had come the fear. What were they going to do with him? He would not talk. At least, he liked to think he would not talk.

He took comfort from the thought that they were too late.

Within days, hours even, the plan would come to fruition. Whatever they did to make him talk, the information would be useless. Events would already have overtaken them. If they did their worst, he would become a martyr to the cause, earn a place in the history of the movement. He consoled himself with that idea, although the thought of death disturbed him.

The door opened and he recognised one of his captors. The man placed a bowl of soup and several bread rolls on the floor beside him. Schengel spat contemptuously and turned his back. The man laughed.

'You had better eat, my friend. You have a long journey ahead of you.'

Schengel swung round. 'What does that mean?'

The man smiled. 'Like I say, you're going on a journey. You might as well eat.'

'A journey?' Schengel felt the hairs rising on the nape of his neck. 'Where?'

'The Holy Land. Lucky old you.'

Schengel felt faint. The man was joking. He had to be. They would not, could not, take him to Israel.

'What do you want with me?'

The man leaned closer, his smile gone.

'We want to know everything, Herr Schengel. What you have done and for whom. Where the weapons are, where they could be used. How we can prepare defences.' The man paused. 'You have very special abilities, Herr Schengel.'

Schengel sneered. 'You will get nothing from me, Jew.'

The man did not react, but a look of dark anger passed over his eyes. 'You don't deny you were a Nazi, do you Herr Schengel?'

Schengel pulled himself upright. 'I *am* a Nazi. Why should I deny it? I wouldn't want to be any other way.' He moved closer to his captor. 'And whatever you may think, wherever you may take me, I shall never work for vermin like you. Today Europe will change. Tomorrow Israel will be wiped from the face of the earth.'

He sensed the man losing his control for the first time, felt the anger and something else: fear. Yes, fear. Good. That was as it should be. These men might hate him, but they also feared him. Yes, that felt good. Very good.

Brewer took several hours to persuade the Mossad to agree a rendezvous. He contacted the agent he had met in London and played on Simon Gilbert's memory to the full. After initial resistance, finally he was told to go to the *Falstaff*, a restaurant opposite the Bourse in the heart of Brussels, to sit inside at the table by the window to the far right and to wait. He was there half an hour before the agreed time. First he checked the layout of the restaurant, making sure he knew where to find the exits. He wanted to be certain he could make a quick exit if the need arose.

The contact was late. She arrived shortly before midday and ordered a half-and-half from one of the waiters before taking her seat. She was in her early fifties, a buxom woman with dyed hair who looked more like most people's idea of a mother-in-law than a Mossad agent. She smiled briefly as they exchanged the agreed opening phrases. Brewer took a long sip from his Hoegaarden and lowered his voice. The woman knew what he wanted, but she shook her head.

'We have no-one,' she said. 'Eindhoven has caused us problems. Both the man Cham and Straker escaped.'

Brewer shook his head. 'You don't need to spend time looking for them. Cham and Straker are dead.'

He outlined developments since the failed Mossad assault on the house on the outskirts of Eindhoven. By the time Brewer had finished dealing with Cham at their safe house in Sablon, Straker was dead in the street outside, his body a small crumpled corpse.

'The problem is,' Brewer continued. 'Rami and Schengel are still on the loose. And the cells could move without them. We don't know enough about their structure.' He paused. Now was the moment. 'And there's also the disappearance of a Commissioner. We think he must have been theirs too. It would make sense.'

She was evasive and unhelpful. Brewer suspected she was lying, but this was not the place to press her. But why would she lie? If they had Rami or Schengel or the Commissioner, or possibly all three, why didn't they share the information? It was in no-one's interest for the assault on Europe to succeed, least of all Israel's. Not for the first time, Brewer regretted Gilbert's death. This woman either knew nothing, or was deliberately holding back. Brewer did not have time to waste.

He stood abruptly and finished his drink.

'You're wasting my time.'

The woman looked surprised.

Brewer said: 'I'll contact the Hadar Dafna myself. I'll speak to the General himself if necessary.'

He started to move away and she rose and placed a firm hand on his arm.

'Don't. Please sit down.'

They sat down again and for the first time he saw her unease.

'I will take you to meet Schengel.'

'Then you do have him?'

'Yes.' She looked uncomfortable. 'But we do not have much time.'

'I know that,' Brewer replied impatiently. 'It isn't me that's been playing delaying games.'

'No, no, you do not understand. We are taking him.'

'Taking him?' Brewer frowned. 'Where?' Then he understood. 'Of course. Tel Aviv.'

She nodded. 'For trial. It is the right thing to do. It will be like Eichmann. But you have to believe, we do not have Rami or the Commissioner.'

'Then who does?' Brewer responded.

'We believe Rami may have escaped, but who took the Commissioner? That we do not know.'

'Then I need to see Schengel. And quickly. We need information about their cells and their command structure. There must be some way of stopping them, of countermanding their instructions.'

She nodded and swept up her things. 'I have a car nearby. We can be there in a few hours.'

In a few hours, Brewer thought as they left, it might already be too late.

Once again it fell to Pendleton to take the call from Yellow Hawk.

'There's some information arrived here at the Bureau that may be of interest to you,' Yellow Hawk told him. He mentioned the name of the missing European Commissioner.

Pendleton sat up and started to take notes on the back of a recycled pad.

'From the latest information we have, the Company have taken him into custody.'

'What?' Pendleton could hardly believe what he was hearing. 'What on earth do they want with him?'

'Seems like Langley's been going back through its records, checking all the contacts Vogel made. This guy's name featured predominantly amongst them. Get this. It turns out the Company even monitors its so-called secure lines. There's a whole web of calls from Vogel. Took them until now to get around to reviewing them.'

'So what are they doing with the Commissioner?'

He could almost see Yellow Hawk shrugging. 'Pumping him for information, I would guess. The Company are running around like crazy trying to patch this one up. They're desperate to get something right before the whole thing spills over into the media.'

Pendleton nodded. He understood the political situation on Capitol Hill, the point scoring between the FBI and the CIA that was a mirror of the complex of relationships between Special Branch, the Security Service and the Firm.

Yellow Hawk had an address, the likely CIA holding-point. Pendleton would have to contact the Firm's resident agent in Luxembourg who was the nearest placed to cover the ground lost by Cham's costly elimination of their Belgian operation.

'How bad is it?' Yellow Hawk asked.

'Bad,' was Pendleton's simple reply. He looked at his watch. 'By my reckoning, we're already living on borrowed time. Literally.'

The Mossad agent drove with an expertise that revealed her true abilities. They made Amsterdam and reached the Mossad safe house in less than two hours, parking illegally in a narrow road near to a canal. She introduced Brewer to the men in the house, who regarded him with suspicion and whispered with her for several minutes at the far side of the room. When they had finished, she turned to him and smiled.

'They will look after you now. You have at most an hour. Then they will be leaving.'

She turned and left. Brewer heard her car screech away from the kerb and the hoot of another car in response.

The taller of the Mossad agents waved him to the staircase. 'This way.'

Brewer followed the man up several flights of almost vertical staircases until they reached the top floor. The man took a key from his pocket and indicated the reinforced door to a room in one corner.

'Be careful. He may react badly. And remember, we need him alive.'

He unlocked the door and waved Brewer forwards.

'Shout if you need me. If you're lucky, I'll be waiting outside.'

Brewer stepped into the room and heard the door being locked behind him. Schengel was seated on the edge of a narrow, metal-framed bed. He stood as Brewer entered, clearly trying to sum up this latest development. He guessed Schengel was in his early fifties, his thick-rimmed metal glasses emphasising his shortsighted eyes.

'Who are you?'

'The name's Brewer.'

Schengel smirked. 'Of course. I should know. We captured you.'

'Fat lot of good it did you,' Brewer commented lightly. He drew up a chair and sat down, taking a *Romeo y Julieta* number two from his pocket. 'We don't have much time.'

Schengel sat on the edge of the bed and crossed his legs. He looked far too easy, far too comfortable. It was almost as if he were the captor, Brewer his prisoner.

Schengel smiled. 'You are too late now. Nothing can stop us.'

Brewer cut the end of the cigar and lit up, dragging long and slow to ensure it was properly lit before turning his attention back to Schengel. 'You're full of shit, Schengel.'

Schengel's smile wavered. 'And you, Mr Brewer, are wasting your time.'

'Perhaps,' Brewer shrugged. 'I just thought you'd want to talk before they take you away.'

'They will not do it,' Schengel said confidently. 'They will not be able to.'

Brewer checked his watch. 'You have fifty minutes and then you're gone Schengel. And don't expect a friendly reception. I don't think the Israelis have very much affection for people involved in building poison gas plants.'

'You think so?' Schengel seemed unnaturally confident. 'I think they have other ideas.'

It was probably a bluff. But Schengel's confidence was unnerving. Brewer dragged thoughtfully on his cigar and blew a long trail towards the centre light. His mind was racing. What did Schengel know? However little it might be, he needed the information and he needed it fast. Even as Brewer sat watching him the neo-Nazi cells across Europe might already be moving, heading towards their targets. And then what? Once they had caused death and confusion across the continent, what would follow? And where was the Commissioner? Waiting in hiding ready to emerge to take control of the situation? Or had he been removed by persons unknown?

'You see,' Schengel continued. 'I have heard them talking.' He reached over and took a sip of water from a glass on a low table beside the bed. 'You think they want me for interrogation, don't you? And then for a public show trial.'

Brewer did not respond. If Schengel wanted to talk, that was fine. But he needed to direct him, to get him talking about the plans for Europe, to obtain details of the cells and how they could be neutralised. And if Schengel would not talk voluntarily, he would have to be forced to talk.

Ann Ferguson, the Firm's resident Luxembourg agent, reached the CIA's Brussels safe house within two hours of Pendleton's call. She had cleared her visit with the military attaché at the American embassy in Brussels. At first he denied any knowledge of the Commissioner being held in American custody, but her hard questioning, and particularly her threats to escalate the situation via the Prime Minister to the US President, had succeeded. Unknown to her, the position had also been assisted by a call made from the Bureau to the CIA's acting Director.

She was shown into the well-furnished house near to the Wolvendael Park. The Commissioner was seated on a low three-seater sofa with two American agents in suits seated nearby. Beside the door, a man armed with a small submachine gun kept watch on the proceedings. They looked up as she entered and nodded. There were brief introductions and then:

'What do you have?'

The two Americans looked at each other, surprised by the bluntness of her question. They indicated they wished to speak outside and once they were in the corridor, spoke in hushed tones.

'He's not talking, knows we have no jurisdiction here.'

'Jurisdiction?' She was surprised at their attitude, the polite way they were handling the situation while the last few minutes of European peace ticked away. 'It's not a question of jurisdiction, it's a question of getting answers. And fast.'

The shorter American pulled a face. 'You think you can do better?'

She swung to face him, disliking his condescending tone. 'As a matter of fact, yes.'

He smiled. 'Be my guest.'

She turned on her heel and moved swiftly back into the room. The guard and the Commissioner looked at her with surprise as she crossed the room alone and sat down on the sofa.

'Let's talk,' she said.

The Commissioner looked down at the small automatic held in her hands, small enough, he realised for the guard not to notice she had it. For the first time since the Americans had taken him, he experienced a sensation of real danger. There was a look in this woman's eyes that told him she was not bluffing, that she would shoot him dead if he gave her the slightest chance. Unknown to him, Pendleton's instructions had been clear and blunt: any action was permitted in their efforts to prevent the terrorist actions succeeding. It had not been easy to secure permission. Pendleton had cleared it with C, and C cleared it with an initially reluctant Prime Minister. It was only when the PM saw a summary of the Porton Down and FBI lab reports and saw pictures of the effects of the weapons that he came off the fence and decided in their favour.

'You see,' Schengel said, his confidence growing as he talked. 'They want me for my mind. For my knowledge. They intend to employ me.'

'Nonsense.' Brewer could barely disguise his impatience. The idea of a Nazi like Schengel working for the Israelis was absurd.

Schengel smiled. 'I don't think so. Think about it, Brewer. How will new wars be fought? Who suffered from chemical Scud attacks during the first Gulf War? Who has most to fear?' He leaned back on the bed. 'Who knows where Saddam buried his weapons, deep in the desert sands? I think they will pay me very well.'

'And what about your conscience?' Brewer snapped. 'You, the great Nazi hero working for your enemies?'

'Sometimes,' Schengel whispered. 'One must lose a battle in order to win a war.'

Brewer looked at his watch. Time was short. Within the next twenty minutes the Mossad guard would return. Any chance of breaking Schengel would be over.

'Tell me about the cells, Schengel. How they are organised, the chain of command. There's still time to stop this madness.'

Schengel sneered. 'You live in a dream world, Brewer. Nothing can stop us now.'

Brewer snapped. He shot from the chair and was across the room before Schengel could react. The drinking glass fell from his hands, his scream muffled as Brewer plunged the poker-hot cigar into his cheek. Schengel pulled violently away, dislodging Brewer's grip.

'Guard!'

His shout was cut short as Brewer punched a fist sharply into his chest and forced an arm behind his back, pulling it until he heard it crack. He bent Schengel's head forwards until it collided with the hard wooden floor. Schengel's glasses fell to the ground, the bottle-thick glass shattering. Brewer jerked him upright and thrust his face towards him until they almost touched.

'It's time to stop playing, Schengel. You're going to talk or you're going to be dead.'

Schengel cursed him, his words muffled by Brewer's firm hand across his mouth.

'One sound, Schengel.'

Brewer drew a hand across his throat. His meaning was clear. Schengel stopped his resistance and lay still, his large unfocused eyes blinking uncertainly back at him. Brewer removed his hand and took a shard of glass from the floor, pushing it close against Schengel's face.

'Now start talking.'

27

Ann Ferguson was with the Commissioner for less than half an hour. She lied. And she lied well. She told him they had taken his family, that he would never see them again. He was visibly shaken at the news. It was clear he had never even considered the idea. He was not a man accustomed to violence. His was the world of committees, of closed doors and meetings, of gentleman's agreements and double-dealing. For the first time he found himself thrust directly into the grubby, shabby work that his minions had always conducted for him. He did not enjoy the feeling. It was an environment he did not understand, a world he wanted to escape. Whatever it took. He had to play for time, to get this woman off his back. He could deal with the Americans, but not with her. For the moment, he would play along with her, tell her what she wanted to hear.

He pleaded for a deal: if he talked, he wanted an amnesty. He demanded to be free to leave in return for his information, for his family to be released. She gave him her word without hesitation. And he talked. He scribbled an address in her notebook, the location where copies of the plans had been stored, details of the cells, their operation, their command structures. She looked at the address: a security company with a reputation for precisely that: complete security. Within minutes she had left, brushing past the Americans and their protestations. She told them nothing about her deal. And it was just too bad she had forgotten to tell the Commissioner she had no sway over the Americans. So far as she was concerned her only priority was to retrieve the papers: in her mind there was no deal.

The Americans could do what they liked with the Commissioner.

Brewer looked down at the man beneath him. Schengel had broken like a balsawood toy. The man who had thought nothing of causing death and destruction to others was in fear of his life, pleading to be spared. One thing was clear: he knew nothing. Schengel had been the brainwave behind the biological and chemical weapons, but that was it. The detailed plans, the organisation of the cells, the transportation, the command structure. All that had been the responsibility of others, those at the tip of the pyramid. Brewer had interrogated him with the most persuasive methods he knew and still Schengel had repeated his story. Reluctant as he was to face defeat, he had to accept that Schengel could tell him nothing. He had failed. His only victory was a London address blurted out by Schengel. An address where, he claimed, the papers stolen in Moscow and Hirtshals could be found. But it all came too late. It was not good enough.

Brewer pulled himself upright and brushed down his clothes. Now the Mossad would take Schengel to Tel Aviv, to pick his secrets as the Americans and Russians had picked their way through the Nazi secrets and scientists at the end of World War II. But even as he thought about it, Brewer knew he could not allow it to happen.

He slipped a thin metal wire from the waist of his trousers and while Schengel was shaking his head and still complaining softly to himself, Brewer looped the wire over his head from behind and jerked it tight, slicing it into Schengel's neck. Schengel's hands scrambled wildly at Brewer, grabbing at his legs. The threat of death made Schengel fierce, gave him the strength of several men. But Brewer's grip held tight. He felt the wire biting, cutting, felt Schengel becoming weaker beneath him.

He waited until Schengel was dead and then placed him in the bed and arranged him to look like he was sleeping. He curled the wire back inside his pocket and tidied the room to look like nothing had happened. As he finished there was a sound at the door and the Mossad guard entered.

'It is time for you to go now,' he said. He looked suspiciously at the figure on the bed. 'What's the matter with him?'

'Dog tired,' Brewer explained. 'I gave him a hard time, but he knew nothing. I think he's dead to the world.'

The guard grunted and escorted Brewer from the room, locking it behind him. They clattered down the stairs in silence. The other guard looked up as they approached.

'Anything?'

Brewer shook his head. 'He's not going to talk.'

'I could have told you that,' the first guard said and the two of them laughed.

'Thanks all the same,' Brewer said. 'It was worth a try.'

He was out of the building and moving fast. As soon as they discovered Schengel's corpse they would turn nasty. Brewer did not intend to be anywhere near them when that happened.

The message from Ann Ferguson reached London at six p.m. It was on Pendleton's desk by five past. He read it quickly, spoke briefly with the Chief, and reacted.

The activation plans were retrieved from the security company in Brussels on direct authority of the Belgian Prime Minister, their details transmitted by Interpol to each of the EU member states. Within an hour, police forces across Europe and armed military response units were ready to move. NBC suits were tested, guns checked. After thirty-six hours on standby they were relieved at the chance to act.

Only now would they discover whether it was already too late.

Brewer found refuge in the anonymity of the centre of Amsterdam, took his phone from his pocket and waited for the waitress to bring a bottle of Chimay. Twenty minutes had passed since he fled the Mossad safe house.

It took two minutes to get through to Pendleton. Pendleton nearly exploded with rage.

'What the hell are you playing at, Brewer? The Mossad are running around like a randy dog with a burnt backside.'

So the old adage was true: bad news did travel fast.

Brewer stalled Pendleton with news of the London address given him by Schengel and details of the missing Nazi papers. But Pendleton was not impressed. The Mossad were on his back and giving everyone a very hard time.

Brewer tried another tack.

'They were going to use Schengel. I had to remove him.'

'The Mossad? Use Schengel? What the hell are you talking about?' And then there was silence while Pendleton absorbed Brewer's information—and the explanation of why he had no choice other than to terminate Schengel. Brewer could sense his mood changing.

'But the bad news is he wouldn't talk, I'm no nearer to cracking it.' Brewer could hardly bring himself to utter the words.

Now a note of satisfaction entered Pendleton's voice. 'Don't worry yourself, Brewer. It looks like we've already cracked it. One of our agents sweet-talked the Commissioner, tracked down the papers. She's very good you know. We believe we have details of all the cells, the targets. Can't be completely certain of course, but we're already moving on them.'

'Well, that's some good news at last. I'm going to find a hotel near here and freshen up. I'll check in again in about an hour or so.' He paused. 'One thing Pendleton. Are we in time?'

Pendleton hesitated. 'Unfortunately, that's the one bit of information I don't have.'

The cells prepared themselves for action, checking through their instructions one last time. The chemical weapons were no larger than big aerosol cans: a small detonation device attached to their side would release the contents one hour after they were primed. Each member of the cell took four of the canisters from their armoury officer, each of them checked their maps and their designated targets, although they already knew them from memory.

One last time the cell commanders took them through the procedure. One last time they tested the procedure on dummy canisters. They watched the clock while the hours counted down.

Still no word came to abort the operation. Soon they would be ready to move.

The Commissioner was alarmed, but not surprised, to learn of Ferguson's deception. When the two Americans returned after her departure, he listened with irritation to their plans to hold him. Now he had to think quickly. There was something he had held back from Ferguson, one more card that he had to play. And now was the time.

'Gentlemen,' he said and for the first time he felt calm. 'I believe we can reach an understanding of mutual benefit.'

'No deals,' the shorter American grunted. 'We told you that. Anyhow, you don't have anything we want. Not now. It's all over.'

'Fine. Your choice. But you should know—if you don't want to deal, you will die,' the Commissioner said quietly.

The two agents looked at each other.

'It ain't us that's gonna die, buddy,' the taller agent responded. 'It's you.'

The Commissioner shook his head and took a sip from the sherry that the agents had kindly provided. 'You don't understand. The operation is proceeding. It has a failsafe mechanism. It doesn't need orders to proceed, it proceeds anyway by default.' He paused. 'In order for it to be stopped, fresh instructions must be issued. Miss Fergusson has only half the plan, so what can she do now? Nothing. It is too late. The deadline has passed.' He shrugged. 'If you believe you have the resources to prevent several hundred autonomous cells carrying out their assignments across Europe, so be it. But I should tell you that Brussels is on the first contact list.' He leaned towards them. 'I'm sure you have friends, family. People you know in this city. Have you seen the effects of bio-chemical weapons?' He shook his head. 'Not pleasant, not pleasant at all.'

The two agents adjourned for a hurried discussion. One of them left the room. The other turned to him.

'Can you give me some sort of idea what kind of deal you're looking for?'

The Commissioner smiled. Now he had them.

28

With impeccable timing, Brewer stepped into the shower just as his mobile phone rang.

'Shit.'

Blinded by shampoo, he skidded across the bathroom floor and fell headfirst onto the bedroom carpet. His skin wet and scorched by the carpet, he finally reached the mobile and dragged it out, a pool of water forming at his feet.

'Brewer? It's Pendleton.'

'It would be,' Brewer replied breathlessly. 'What's the matter?'

'It's urgent, Brewer. Those files you mentioned, the ones you lost in Moscow and Denmark.'

Brewer let that pass. Suddenly he was alert. 'What about them? Did you find them?'

'Oh, we found them all right. The entire Nazi spy network in place at the end of the Second World War. Plenty of names to keep the historians busy. No wonder the Professor got so excited. It's certainly going to open some eyes.'

'Is that why you called me?'

'No.' Pendleton hesitated. 'We found another document with them.'

'Concerning what?' Brewer grabbed a pillow and did his best to towel himself down.

'We have a problem with the abort key our resident retrieved in Brussels.'

Brewer stopped drying himself, his grip tightening on the phone. 'What sort of problem? I thought you had it all under control?'

'Well, according to this second document, the abort command comprises two keys.'

'Two?'

'Both must be broadcast within half an hour of each other. If only one is given, the abort is ignored.'

'Shit. So what do you want from me? It's too late isn't it? We're just going to have to go reactive, handle the fallout as best we can.'

'Never say die, Brewer. You know that. I want you to have a go with the Commissioner. See if you can get him to reveal the second abort key.'

'He may not know it.'

'Quite possible, Brewer.' Pendleton sniffed. 'I'm sorry, have you something better to do?'

Brewer thought a moment and smiled. 'No, sir. I'll talk with the Commissioner.'

Across the European Union, the commanders of the terrorist cells checked the time. The hour had arrived. Part one of the plan was to commence. A few of the commanders puzzled about the partial abort instruction that had come a short time before, broadcast on all radio and TV media, terrestrial, cable and satellite. They had listened closely, waiting for the second key to come. But they listened in vain. The operation was to proceed.

Vehicles were checked, weapons tested. Secure armoury doors were opened and cell members issued with automatics and stun grenades for self-defence. Each took their four allocated canisters and checked them one last time, although it had long since ceased to be necessary. Their training had lasted months: they knew what they had to do.

They ran through the routine. Whatever the setbacks, they knew they would succeed. Once the canisters were primed, no-one could stop them. And they were prepared to sacrifice their own lives if necessary, a small price to pay for eventual victory. Finally order was going to be restored to the world. Finally they would be rid of the weakness and despair of the failed Europe. For that, they were prepared to pay any price.

They climbed into the back of their trucks. The same pattern would be followed in every country. The trucks would proceed to separate disembarkation points. One by one the cell members would disperse, make their own way to their targets using public transport. The designated targets were all very carefully selected: tourist centres, military centres, political centres. Dressed as tourists, the cell members would proceed easily to their destinations. The canisters would be placed and primed. Timing devices would ensure their detonation after placing. The members would need to move quickly. Two canisters at each location, one as backup. The backup canister was designed to detonate one hour after the first. Even if the first detonated successfully, the second would catch the rescuers and emergency services, causing further damage, death and despair. Each canister carried enough toxins to eradicate as many as 10,000 people in the right conditions. It would depend upon the target, upon the extent to which the location was enclosed or open, the climatic conditions. So far the weather was with them.

Each cell had thirty members. And there were twelve cells involved in the first wave. Even should some of them fail, the effects would be enormous. If each of the canisters worked, and killed just 10 targets, over seven thousand people would die across Europe that day alone. No political system could survive that level of assault, least of all weak Europe, riven by its divisive nationalities. Each day the onslaught would continue: new cells, new locations, new targets. There would be no pattern, the scale of the operation too great to counter. And once the chemical assault was rolling, then would come the biological assault. Wave after wave. America had faltered, its stock markets collapsed, after just 9/11: these actions would make people forget 9/11.

The Commissioner was satisfied with the deal agreed with the CIA. He would provide them with the names they needed to root out the entire underground organisation in the States. They in turn would arrange an amnesty. All charges against him would be dropped, no mention even made of his key role in the conspiracy. The story would be agreed and presented to the media: the Commissioner had penetrated the Nazi organisation and helped bring it down. His name would not only be left untarnished, his reputation would be considerably enhanced. His political aspirations could continue without interruption.

He trusted the Americans. Unlike the British woman, he believed they would keep their word. But even the Commissioner was not entirely convinced that a verbal agreement was enough. He wanted a written agreement: two copies, one for his retention, the other for the Americans. It would be a mutually assured guarantee: neither side would wish to go public, or betray the agreement. The two CIA guards consulted with their management. They told him to expect Mr Forster from their embassy. He would be with them within the hour. In the meantime, they said, he should make himself at home.

The Commissioner sat back in front of the open fireplace and smiled, looking forward to his meeting with Mr Forster. It was nearly over and still the fools did not understand the plan was proceeding. By the time they realised the extent of the European operation, it would be too late. He would have the agreement in safekeeping and be safely out of their reach. The Americans would not be able to touch him when the cells acted, when he stepped forwards to co-ordinate the European response. Indeed, it was possible the Americans would be forced into public support of his stance: they would not want to see their agreement become public. Whatever happened, he could not lose.

He checked his watch. Even now, he thought, the operation would be commencing. He hoped Mr Forster would not be long.

Brewer collected a copy of the Nazi papers from the British Embassy where they had been transmitted under secure cover from London. He flicked briefly through them and whistled. He recognised several of the names, men who had risen to senior positions in post-war Germany. Men who had risen to senior positions in other European countries. There were even several British names included, names he would never have suspected of Nazi involvement. But Brewer had always underestimated how much the British establishment had admired the Nazis. After all, a long queue of leading aristocrats and prominent figures had once publicly applauded Hitler's 'magnificent achievements'. There had even been a British regiment fighting alongside the Waffen SS. History, he thought angrily, truly is written by the victor.

He left moments later, aware that the embassy diplomats did not welcome his presence. It was not only that he was a spook, and did not fit into their neat world of diplomacy and guarded understatement. It was also that he was from a different class, did not share their values or aspirations. They had entered directly from college, passed the surreal irrelevance of the Civil Service fast-stream exams and been accelerated through the ranks and circulated amongst the pick of the Civil Service overseas postings. At the end of their bland, uneventful careers they would retire to large detached houses in the Surrey countryside, an index-linked pension and probably a CBE, or OBE, maybe even a knighthood or peerage. Brewer smiled, amused that anyone could find any sense of accomplishment in such dull, routine lifestyles. A lifetime squandered in pursuit of a good pension.

He reached the American safe house near to Wolvendael Park and flapped his pass. He was expected: Pendleton had done his job. As he spoke briefly with the two CIA men, he detected a certain unease, a degree of resentment. It was clear they did not want him there. It felt like he had walked in on a private party: he guessed some sort of deal was going on with the Commissioner—or perhaps had already been done. They delayed him for a time with irrelevant formalities and then finally waved him through to the room at the back of the house.

As he stepped into the room Brewer recognised the Commissioner. As a former Prime Minister of a European country, he had once graced the pages of newspapers and magazines. He had written books and even fronted a TV documentary on Europe's future. He was an eloquent and practical speaker: and he was respected and trusted. His face looked drawn and tired, but beneath was a middle-aged, prosperous man accustomed to good living.

As Brewer entered, the Commissioner rose from the armchair where he had been sitting and walked towards him.

'Mr Forster, I presume?'

Brewer shook his head and brushed past him, ignoring his extended hand of greeting. It was an elegant room, a large overmantel mirror above the fireplace and an open coal fire crackling against the damp of the day.

'So who are you?' the Commissioner asked. 'I was told to expect Mr Forster.'

'Mr Forster won't be coming,' Brewer replied. 'I'm Mr Brewer. Mr Forster has been detained.'

A look of uncertainty flickered across the Commissioner's face, but he covered it with anger.

'Detained? Look, the Americans told me that Mr Forster was coming to see me, that they would release me from here. We have a deal.'

'A deal? Really? It's a fast-moving world, isn't it?' Brewer took a decanter and poured himself what he hoped would be a decent Scotch. 'Drink?'

The Commissioner shook his head impatiently. 'This is wasting time. Am I being released or not?'

'It's not me that's been wasting time, Commissioner.'

'I have a deal,' the Commissioner repeated.

'I don't think so Commissioner. You see, I don't trust you. You may recall you met a colleague of mine. You provided her with information.' Brewer stepped towards him. 'The only problem is, you only told her half the story, didn't you?'

'I explained to the Americans,' the Commissioner insisted. 'If you want the rest of the information, the deal must be honoured.'

Brewer sipped thoughtfully at his Scotch. It was a blend: not what he would have chosen.

'Sit down. On the sofa, where I can keep an eye on you. And don't do anything foolish. I'm armed.'

The Commissioner's eyes narrowed, but he did as he was told.

'What is it you want, Brewer?'

'You know that. I want the other half of the key.'

'I have a deal—'

'No deals!' Brewer's anger cut through the room. 'Give me the other half of the key.'

The Commissioner managed a smile, his confidence returning.

'You're not in any position to dictate terms,' he said quietly. 'Whereas I am.'

Brewer threw his Scotch to the floor, smashing the glass. He stepped quickly forwards and grabbed hold of the Commissioner.

'Get this straight. I've had it up to here with you and your bunch of goose-stepping cronies. And if you don't think I'm in a position to dictate terms, you'd better think again. If I don't get the answers I want in the next ten minutes, you're dead Commissioner. Do you understand?'

'So.' The Commissioner pulled himself away from Brewer's grip and leaned back in the chair. 'You intend to kill me. Well, Mr Brewer. Go ahead.'

There was a silence broken only by the spit and crackle of the fire burning in the grate. Brewer checked his watch. Was he already too late? The Commissioner was not going to break, not now. He had gone beyond the point of caring, even about his own life. Threats were not going to succeed. If there had been time, he would have pumped the Commissioner full of sodium amytal or sodium brevital or one of the newer, more successful truth serums. And if that hadn't worked, he would have beaten him until he talked. And he would talk: Brewer was sure of that. But there wasn't time. Other methods were needed.

Instead, Brewer took a single photocopied sheet from his pocket and handed it to the Commissioner in silence. The Commissioner frowned and unfolded the paper. He examined it for a moment and then set it down.

He looked up at Brewer, his eyes intense. 'Where did you get this?'

Brewer smiled. 'I thought it might interest you.'

'I asked you where you got it.' The Commissioner was growing impatient, his voice dry and hoarse.

'So you did. But then,' Brewer replied. 'I asked you for the other part of the key.'

The Commissioner nodded briefly. 'I see. Are you proposing a new deal?'

'The idea repulses me.'

'But that is what you are proposing? Do I understand you correctly?'

Brewer stood in silence for a moment and then nodded.

'Good, good,' the Commissioner enthused, rising from his seat. 'Let me make the first suggestion. You provide all copies of this document, and I mean all copies, and I provide you with the other half of the abort key.'

'And how will I know that it is the real key, the complete key?' Brewer asked.

The Commissioner shrugged. 'You will not. Just as I shall not know whether you have provided all copies of this document. But I think gentlemen should trust each other's word, don't you?'

'But of course,' Brewer said. 'Gentlemen should.'

'Then we are agreed.' The Commissioner had regained his confidence.

'One moment.'

Brewer left the room for a few minutes and returned carrying a small brown, soft leather briefcase. He held it out in front of him, but as the Commissioner reached for it, he pulled it back.

'One moment, Commissioner. First I need the key.'

'Of course.' The Commissioner smiled. He moved over to the small Bureau and wrote briefly on a piece of paper. When he returned, he handed it to Brewer. 'Here.'

Brewer took the note and examined it. The Commissioner took the briefcase from him and moved over to the fire. He opened the case and looked carefully at its contents. For a moment Brewer feared he would smell a trick. But the moment passed and the

Commissioner started to remove the case's contents and place them on the fire.

Brewer watched in silence as the bright flames made short work of the document. How long ago it seemed that he had stood beside Larsen at the Hirtshals shipyard and looked through that very same document. And how much better off everyone would have been if it had stayed at the bottom of the Kattegat where it belonged.

The Commissioner stood and dusted his hands. He looked at Brewer and smiled. 'There. Now I think we can both be going our separate ways.'

Brewer had reached the door and turned to face him. 'Oh, I don't think so Commissioner.'

He opened the door and the Commissioner's two CIA guards entered. Doubt and a hint of anger flickered across the Commissioner's face.

'But we had a deal. A gentleman's agreement.'

'Firstly, you never asked for safe passage. You never even mentioned it. And secondly, didn't I tell you Commissioner? I'm not a gentleman.'

Brewer turned on his heel, ignoring the Commissioner's protestations. As he was moving away, he looked back and smiled.

'And in case you were wondering Commissioner, the papers you burned were worthless copies. The originals are in safe hands. Au revoir.'

29

London. A blustery, cold morning. Grey streaks of cloud stretched across the sky. Specks of rain caught in the air, picked at windows, brushed against pedestrians. In the windows of the shops, the Christmas decorations looked dull and out of place. The first commuter rush of the day was over. Now was the tourists' hour. Coaches of Japanese and Polish. Lines of Americans and New Zealanders. School tours with pupils laden with rucksacks and the primary colours of raincoats and kagouls. Children stared into the windows of Hamleys and Selfridges, their breath steaming the glass as they watched the animated Christmas displays of elfin workers and Disney classics.

Across Europe it was the same. In Paris and Berlin, Rome and Madrid, winter was in the air. But still the tourists came, still the streets were busy with locals and foreigners alike. Theme Park Europe was open for business. And business was booming.

The terrorist cells were already dispersing, their members moving by train, bus and boat. They wore the uniform of the tourist, could not be spotted. They smiled and laughed, smiled and nodded and took snapshots of each other: whatever was required to avoid suspicion. But inside they had one purpose, one objective. To reach their targets. Timing was critical. Strict co-ordination was essential to the effectiveness of their plan.

At the Tower of London, one loitered nearby, sipping at a coffee in McDonalds. Another stood in the queue at Madame Tussaud's. Near to Buckingham Palace, two cell members walked hand in hand like husband and wife. One watched where she would place the canister for the Palace while the other looked towards his own objective, the Wellington Barracks. Elsewhere in the capital, as cell members in Paris, Berlin, Rome, Brussels, Lisbon, Madrid, Amsterdam, Copenhagen, Athens, Dublin, and Luxembourg were doing, members moved closer to their targets, their canisters hidden in rucksacks and day bags. They checked their watches.

It was nearly time.

The two abort keys were broadcast at one minute past nine central European time. The two keys were broadcast together not once, not twice, but eight times. Puzzled listeners and viewers jammed TV stations' switchboards. What was happening? What did the strange messages mean? A special early edition of London's *Evening Standard* carried the two phrases on their front page: no explanation was given. Satellite TV stations carried the phrases on the tickertape at the bottom of their screens.

The streets of Europe's capitals were flooded with police and soldiers. Nothing had been seen like it since the armies of occupation and liberation of the second world wars. The official explanations were bland: a trans-European security exercise, nothing to worry about. Loudspeakers in public places repeated the two phrases of the abort keys.

Some cell members heard the abort keys. Confused, they wandered away from their targets. They did not understand. The abort message had come so late, was not meant to be communicated in this way. Some did not hear the abort, or chose to ignore it.

Then it started.

In Dublin, two cell members were gunned down outside the *Oireachtas*, the National Parliament, as they took their canisters out and prepared them for use.

In Berlin, a canister detonated outside the *Reichstag*. Fifty-three were killed, two hundred and thirty-nine badly affected by sarin. The cell member was shot by an alert policeman, who died moments later from the effects of the gas.

In Copenhagen, a canister failed, injuring the cell member. She was arrested, the canisters removed. A second canister exploded outside the Amalienborg Palace. A group of thirty school children and their teachers from Norway were killed instantly, their bodies dropping lifeless to the floor like rag dolls. Another seven tourists died in hospital, a further fifty-three were left badly affected.

Four canisters ripped through the streets near the Coliseum in Rome. Traffic slewed from the road. A lorry hurtled through a shop front and ignited. More died in the crashes and fires than from the effects of the gas.

On London's Northern Line, VX gas rippled through the tunnel from Tottenham Court Road station. Seven hundred and thirty-two were killed outright, another two thousand injured. As the rescue services moved in, more canisters detonated. Another sixty-seven died, another hundred and forty were injured. In the deep, dark tunnels of the Northern Line, the gas did not dissipate so easily: its deadly effects brought the entire system to a halt. Stations were evacuated, children brought screaming and crying from the system, kicking and hitting at their rescuers in their confusion and hysteria. Panic gripped the city.

At Westminster, Parliament was suspended, the Cabinet taken to their secure location deep underground. In government buildings, the near permanent state of black alert went instantly to red. In the chaos and confusion, riots broke out. A crowd of youths raced along Oxford Street, looting the shops. For once the response was not restrained: the army moved in, the army that had fought such battles for so many years on the streets of Northern Ireland and foreign theatres, finally turned its weapons onto mainland occupants. The youths were warned. And then they were shot, plastic bullets at first. And then live rounds. The government was in no mood for half measures. This was *Total War*.

Across Europe, governments appealed for calm. Some enacted emergency measures, others decided to wait. Panic gripped the streets. Europe was on the brink of collapse.

Generations unused to war and uncertainty were suddenly thrown into a dark, uncertain world. Offices closed, people clogged the streets, all trying to get home, to check on loved ones: husbands, wives, fathers, mothers, children. More canisters were detonated.

In the City of London, Liverpool Street station was obliterated by four gas attacks. Nearly two thousand dead.

In Paris, the Gare de Nord suffered the same fate and nearly as many dead and injured.

It was the single, bloodiest day of Europe's history since World War II.

In Italy, the government fell. Troops filled the streets, but there was no-one to attack, no-one to target and remove. Instead, they enforced law and order. After the first wave of initial crime, Europe had its first hours without crime that it has ever seen. Even the most hardened mugger did not risk their chances against armed troops and the risk of further gas attacks. Some pensioners pulled out gas masks from the Second World War, not knowing they would be useless against these new toxins.

The Commissioner looked in the mirror and smiled. He had heard the reports on the radio, seen early pictures on the TV and watched as the two CIA men had turned pale, unable to believe what was happening. Within half an hour of the first attacks, America had offered its support. An hour later, in direct consequence, five thousand died and eight thousand were injured by gas attacks on the New York Subway. America immediately came under intense media pressure to reconsider its pledge to help Europe. Two times before it had gone to war to help: this time it was no longer so keen. As predicted, the weak leaders of the West no longer had the stomach for war. Every time America came close to helping, it would be hit, harder and stronger. It would buckle and yield.

The CIA men received orders to return to the embassy. They turned to the Commissioner, hate evident for the first time in their faces. The Commissioner shrugged.

'You never asked whether the attacks would stop. I did my

best. I wanted to cut a deal sooner. It was not me who delayed, who played games with the lives of others.'

'And would you have told us the truth if we had asked?'

The Commissioner considered the question for a moment and then shook his head. 'No, I do not think so. It's time I was leaving. There is much work for me to be doing to sort and control this dreadful situation. Europe needs me. And we do have a deal, after all.'

He stood and moved towards the front door. No-one stopped him. As he walked outside the phone rang in the room behind him. He heard one of the agents answer it.

The grey autumnal sky was breaking to reveal streaks of blue. He breathed in deeply. He could not remember how long he had waited for this day. Once the initial shock had passed, he knew there would be anger. After generations of paying for defence, for nuclear weapons and other military toys, people would turn on their weak governments, governments that had so clearly failed them. They would want to see change, strong government, decisiveness and clarity. They would put liberal ideas and their freedoms to one side provided they were promised the chance to regain their security. Political disillusionment meant that it would be easy. Despite the setbacks, part one of the plan had proceeded. It was now up to him to implement part two. He would lead Europe towards its new future, a future of strength and purpose.

The Commissioner was only vaguely aware of the voices behind him. He moved slowly down the steps, careful to avoid the slippery leaves that lined them. He had reached the pavement and was stepping towards his car when the shots rang out. He spun, feeling the sharp pain spread through his back. He saw a CIA man at the door, his gun levelled.

'Wh . . . what?'

He tried to speak, to say *We had a deal*, but the man fired again. And again. He only stopped when the Commissioner had crashed to the ground in a bloody pool of blood, his car behind him riddled with holes.

The agent turned, tears streaming from his face. The voice on the phone had broken him the news. His wife, his father and mother and his two children were dead. Killed on the New York subway.

By sarin gas.

30

Six thirty-five a.m. Brewer walked swiftly along Great Peter Street past the Arts Council building and then turned sharply right at the top and along Millbank. The menu display case outside Number Four had been smashed, turning its glass into a silver spider's web. *Thirty Percent Off!* screamed a sign for the gymnasium, but Brewer resisted the invitation. Already his enforced week's leave, imposed on him at Pendleton's insistence, was no more than a pleasant memory.

A long week of panic and confusion had passed since the first day of the terrorist attacks. The death toll across Europe already exceeded fifty thousand: and continued to rise. Many civilians suffered such terrible injuries they now lay dying in hospital. A pause in the programme of assaults followed the initial attacks, a difficult time of waiting during which police and military raids continued on cell headquarters. Plans were taken. Canisters were seized, stocks of chemical and biological weapons destroyed. The countries of the European Union waited, fearing the second wave, the planned biological attack.

It had not come. With each day they became more confident, more sure the threat had been tackled and averted. Europe had rocked, governments had wavered, but the final assault had failed. Even in Italy, where the government had fallen, a new coalition of national salvation had already been formed. Now was the time for witch-hunting and post mortems, the intense media twenty-twenty vision of hindsight. Everyone was on the hunt for scapegoats. Politicians too sought someone to blame. They certainly did not wish to shoulder the burden of responsibility themselves. On the previous day the UK Prime Minister had announced the resignation of the combined Chiefs of Staff: resignations caused by the PM's threat to sack them with complete loss of pension for their gross incompetence. Across Europe, senior military figures were being purged. The politicians were anxious to vent the public's anger.

It would be months, possibly years, before Europe and the US, who had so quickly come to Europe's aid with such disastrous consequences for itself, fully recovered.

Brewer reached the Firm's building and took out his security card. He stopped. The entry system was missing. There was no sign of the night guard. He stepped back and looked up at the building. Everything looked quiet. Too quiet. He tensed, sensing that something was wrong.

The door opened. His hand moved instinctively towards the automatic hidden inside his jacket. A workman in a bright plastic helmet stood in front of him.

'You looking for someone?' the man asked, taking a cigarette from a crushed packet and lighting up.

'Who are you?' Brewer enquired.

'Ewan Murphy. Who are you?'

Brewer did not answer. Somewhere in the back of his mind cogs were working. Inside the building he could hear the sound of hammers and the whine of a drill.

'Tell me something, Ewan.'

'Sure,' the man nodded, drawing heavily on his cigarette.

'I work here. At least, I think I do.'

Ewan looked behind him at the building as if seeing it for the first time. He turned back and shook his head.

'Not any more you don't.' He stopped and leaned closer. 'Not unless you're a builder that is, and I don't think you are. Not dressed like that. You're one of the guys who works here, right?'

Brewer nodded.

'Ain't no-one told you?' Ewan asked.

'Told me what?'

'Your lot have moved. Last week it was. Over the river.'

He waved vaguely towards the Thames. Brewer turned to look. Now he understood. The move of his team into Vauxhall Cross. It had finally happened. And they had neglected to tell him. Brewer turned back to Ewan.

'Thank you,' he said with commendable self-control and turned to walk along Millbank.

'No problem,' the workman shouted after him. 'Let me know if you need any more help. You know, with intelligence work or anything like that. No job too small.'

Brewer was fuming. He had put up with the incompetent new management for long enough and now he was decided. It was time to resign and move on. As soon as he and Pendleton had completed their debriefing, he was going to leave. He had spent the last week discussing it with Jane and it was the only option open. Whatever civilian life brought him, it was better than the life he had with the Firm.

He crossed over Lambeth Bridge and reached Vauxhall Cross within ten minutes. He looked up briefly at its dated wedding cake design and bland concrete and glass facade and then stepped inside, waving his pass at the guard. The guard stopped him.

'That's no good, sir. You'll need a new pass.'

Brewer glared at him. 'The hell I do.'

Brewer stepped forwards and found his way blocked by electronic turnstiles. He slammed his card into the slot and watched as a bright red light blinked at him.

'Like I say, sir. You'll need a new card.'

'Okay, okay.' Brewer's patience was nearly exhausted. 'So where do I get it?'

The guard looked at his watch. 'Someone should be in at nine,' he said quietly.

'Nine!'

Brewer counted to ten. Twice. And then once more for luck. He turned on his heel and left, retreating to a small greasy spoon cafe where for the first time in years he ate a massive fried breakfast washed down with a bucket of tea. At nine sharp he was back in Vauxhall Cross. He was finally issued with a new pass half an hour later, after fingerprints, photos and an image of his retina had been sampled.

'Which floor for Europe?' he asked.

'Management or staff?' the guard enquired.

Nothing changed, thought Brewer. He checked his watch. Pendleton should be in by now.

'Management,' he responded. He moved away and then turned back, changing his mind. 'No, staff. And if it's not too much trouble, could you tell me which office is mine?'

He took the lift to the fifth floor and walked out into an anonymous corridor of doors, counting off the numbers as he walked along. He reached a door, pushed his card into the entry slot, tapped in his ID number after consulting the back page of his diary where he had written it and walked in. He stopped. The office was small, but serviceable. But what surprised him was that there was only one desk. He stepped back out into the corridor and checked the number on the door. It was definitely his office. He walked over to the desk and sat down, letting the door shut behind him. His hands ran over the empty desktop. It was the least cluttered it had ever been. A brand new Dell computer sat on the edge of the desk, connected into the data point in the wall. He wondered who had packed for him, what had happened to his case files. The drawers were empty, the filing cabinet was empty. The view from the window offered fine panoramas over scenic Vauxhall.

There was a knock at the door. Brewer crossed the room and opened it.

'Brewer! There you are!'

Monroe's bulk eased itself through the door. 'Not bad, not bad,' he said, wandering around the room and inspecting it like a colonel in a barracks.

'Is this really mine?' Brewer asked.

Monroe looked at him and laughed, 'Yes, crazy isn't it? I've just the same.'

'You Monroe? I thought they were sacking you.'

'Not me, boyo,' Monroe replied, easing himself onto the edge of the desk. 'It's all change again. This time it's the greysuits they're gunning for.'

'Now I know this is a figment of my imagination,' Brewer responded.

'I'm serious,' Monroe replied. 'Anyway, must dash. You know Pendleton's after you?'

Brewer nodded. 'I'm on my way.'

'See you later in the bar,' Monroe suggested, but by the time Brewer responded he was already gone.

Brewer took the lift to the fourth floor, where the Chief, deputies and assistants had their offices. Brewer wandered up and down the corridor, confronted by blank doors. Everything in the building had been designed to make it as difficult as possible for an intruder to find his way around. Unfortunately the same was true for the staff. Underfoot was a plain grey carpet and on the walls some of the least impressive paintings he had seen in a long time, splashes of red and yellow and a few of what appeared to be pyjama fabric designs in the style of Bridget Riley. The building was not ageing well despite its relative youth and the carpet and walls looked like they could do with a refresh.

A secretary emerged from one of the doors carrying a bundle of photocopying. She pointed at Pendleton's door in response to his question. He knocked and turned the handle. Nothing happened. A second later there was an electronic buzz and the door sprang open. He entered.

The large room disoriented Brewer for a moment until he saw Pendleton standing outside on the small terrace beyond the French doors. Brewer joined him in the brisk blue morning air. Unlike his own office, Pendleton's room had a superb view across the Thames.

'Ah, Brewer,' Pendleton said, turning to greet him.

'Sir.'

'Beautiful morning, don't you think?'

'Very pleasant, sir.'

It was the first really good day he could remember since before he went to Moscow. And that seemed like a lifetime ago. The sky was clear, the moody grey clouds had vanished and taken with them the miserable rain and drizzle. A slight breeze blew from the north-east and ruffled Brewer's thinning hair.

'You did a good job, Brewer. The Chief's very happy.'

'I don't know why. We should have done better. The whole thing's been a cock-up from start to finish.'

'You think so?' Pendleton examined him for a moment. 'Yes, perhaps you're right. But it could have been worse. Ultimately we succeeded.'

'Succeeded? Yes, I suppose. In a way.'

'Yes, yes. For the moment.' Pendleton moved over to the edge of the terrace and looked out across the river to the buildings opposite. 'There is one thing. In your report you mention the files that were stolen from Moscow. The problem is, you don't seem to have returned the copies we gave you.'

'Haven't I sir?'

Brewer knew perfectly well that he hadn't. He had placed them somewhere safe, somewhere the Firm would not find them. He wanted to keep a negotiating hand.

'I wondered if you had considered my request for early retirement, sir?'

'Don't change the subject, Brewer,' Pendleton snapped. He paused a moment. 'Or perhaps you're not? Yes, I see. The two subjects are related, are they?'

Brewer shrugged. 'Well, sir? What's the answer?'

'Request denied,' Pendleton responded. 'C doesn't want to lose agents like you. He's starting to turf out some of the grey-suits. The value of humint has finally been recognised. Hang around, Brewer. I think you're going to like the changes.'

'It's too late, sir.'

Pendleton turned and placed a firm hand on Brewer's arm. 'Look Brewer, whatever you decide, you have to return those papers. The consequences if you don't, I can assure you, will be most unpleasant. Nobody wishes to see the information in those documents brought into the light of day.'

'The way I see it, it's quite simple,' Brewer said quietly. 'Accept my request, the papers are yours.'

'Blackmail, Brewer? That's not like you.'

'Not blackmail, sir. Always negotiate from a position of strength. Isn't that what you're always saying sir?'

A hint of a smile played around the edges of Pendleton's mouth. 'Perhaps it is, Brewer. Perhaps it is.' He looked thoughtful for a while and then turned to walk inside. 'Come on, Brewer. I want to run through the contingency for the possible follow-up biological attacks.'

Brewer followed him back into the office. 'You don't think they're going to happen now, do you?'

Pendleton shook his head. 'I doubt it. But the PM's still anxious and the Chief Scientific Officer to the MOD's been worrying the Cabinet sick with tales of superplagues. Porton Down laid on a very unpleasant demo indeed. So now they want to know how we can head off any problem before it arises.'

'The superplague, sir? I don't think I'd want to handle that at all, would you sir?'

Pendleton looked back at him.

'Was that a joke, Brewer?'

Rami flew into Heathrow on a scheduled flight from Geneva. His instructions were precise and unambiguous: to tidy up loose ends. His fees for assisting the cause had finally been paid. Indeed, the backers of the Lincoln project had more than made up for his recent problems and the inconvenience caused to him with a bonus.

And they had offered him one more assignment. An assignment he had initially been reluctant to accept. But the price was right: and in times of war all things are possible and however unpleasant must be done. His bigger ambitions would not be allowed to fail because of minor disagreements on the journey. Compared to his other recent duties, this would be simple. He took a taxi from the airport and gave a London address. If all went to plan, his work would be completed within the next forty-eight hours and he would be out of the country.

During Brewer's leave he had stayed with Jane and they had behaved like a couple of teenage tourists, visiting London attractions and kissing in public like a couple of young lovers. But now, as Brewer sat and watched her putting on a new CD, he found himself thinking about Gary. Several times he had come close to telling her. Several times when they were laying in each others arms, naked on the bed, warm and relaxed after making love. And sometimes when they had been out, when the day had been too short and they had ended it drunk and content. But he could not bring himself to do it. His loyalties and emotions were split. Inside he wanted to pour out the truth, to share with her the reality, to take her weeping in his arms and let her know that Gary was all right, that he had survived. But his cold professional side nagged his conscience, reminding him that Gary was still continuing his role. That somewhere Gary was being briefed, being trained for a new deep undercover assignment. So what point was there in telling Jane, in raising her hopes? He might be alive now, but she could not see him, could not meet him. And if he told her Gary was alive and he then died on another assignment, what then? Her grief would be doubled, the wound that finally was beginning to heal wrenched cruelly back open.

She sat beside him and he slipped his arm around her. An old Eurhythmics track blared out from the stereo: *Women are doing it for themselves.*

'You're looking thoughtful,' she whispered, kissing him gently on the cheek.

'I'm being thoughtful,' he replied softly, squeezing her tight.

'And why's that?' she asked, amusement shining in her eyes.

'I was thinking.' He stopped.

'Yes?' she asked.

He cleared his throat and started again. 'I was thinking that we might, that is, that we could—'

She placed her forefinger on his lips. 'Let me try,' she suggested. 'You think we should get married?'

Brewer nodded. Now the words had been spoken they surprised even Brewer. They were words he had thought he would never hear. Not many field agents get married: it's not a marrying business. She removed her finger and lent forwards and kissed him. 'I'll think about it,' she whispered.

He pushed back her hair and started to gently caress her. She pulled at him, tugging him down onto the floor where they lay in a close embrace. He took off his glasses and they pulled at each other's clothing.

The room shook. There was a loud noise from downstairs. The sound of breaking glass, tearing wood. Footsteps running on the stairs.

'Wh—what?'

Jane's grip fell away. Brewer stumbled to his feet, his trousers caught around his ankles. He looked for his glasses. Where the hell where they? He could hardly see a damned thing. He had only one thought: his gun. He must get his gun.

But it was too late. Rami was through the door, his gun levelled. Jane screamed, jumping to her feet even as Rami fired the first two shots. Her body jerked, the scream suddenly silenced. Brewer felt her blood splash on his face. She fell to the floor, a tangle of flesh and clothing and blood.

Brewer stared at the blur of her body in disbelief.

'Jane!' Brewer screamed. He leant down and took Jane's body in his arms. 'It's all right,' he whispered. 'It's all right, everything'll be all right.'

Rami stepped forwards and struck him with the barrel of the gun. Brewer crashed away, a numbing pain cutting across his forehead.

'I just want you to know before you die,' Rami explained. 'That I have the Moscow papers.'

Brewer felt distant. The events around him were happening in another world, in a film. 'You can't have,' he whispered. He couldn't take his eyes from Jane. He still saw her as she had been moments before, alive and smiling. He wanted to see her move, to see her smile again. He stroked her hair, still wanting to see her eyes flicker open, to learn that it was all a joke, a bad dream.

'Security box 123E. Hatton Garden. That's right, isn't it?'

Brewer heard Rami's words from a long distance. Slowly they penetrated his pain and loss. *123E: Hatton Garden?* That was the security box, the Moscow papers: his future. Like Jane had been his future. He turned and looked up at the blurred image that was Rami.

'What?'

Rami repeated what he had said and then added: 'They are back with their rightful owners.'

Brewer sat on the floor in silence. In the space of two quick shots, this man had destroyed everything. Jane, the Moscow papers, his escape from the Firm. Instead of the vision he had seen stretching ahead of him there was only greyness and fog. There was nothing left to fight for, nothing left to live for.

'Get it over with will you,' Brewer whispered, his voice shaking and hoarse.

Rami raised the gun. 'Farewell, Mr Brewer.'

'Come on death, come on, take me,' he prayed to himself, all hope finally beaten from him.

Rami shot twice. The pain shot through his chest, snatched his breath away and jerked him onto the floor. It felt like he had been stabbed with a spear. The pain cut right through him.

And suddenly the shock was gone: suddenly his mind was moving faster than ever before. He was not going to die like this, a helpless dumb animal to be slaughtered. This man had killed Jane, killed his future. He continued the roll, ignoring the pain. His hand closed on the gun tucked beneath the small coffee table and as he turned, covering his movement with screaming, he had the gun in his hand, his finger tightening on the trigger. Rami was just a blur, an out of focus image.

But Rami had seen Brewer's gun and moved, his own trigger finger squeezing twice. Chips flew from the rug and table. Brewer's first shot missed. And his second. The third caught Rami in the temple, the fourth in the chest, the fifth in the arm. Rami's gun went flying. He slumped to the floor. Still the Eurhythmics sang.

Brewer lay panting, the gun falling limp from his hands. He felt his strength ebbing, felt the pain expanding through his chest. He fumbled for his mobile. Bloodstained fingers picked at the keys.

'Code 1,' he whispered. He hissed out Jane's address, heard the cool, matter of fact voice at the other end confirm his call and then blacked out, his body falling onto Jane's.

They lay like two intertwined lovers, their blood slowly mixing together as it spread across the rug in a large ugly Jackson Pollock stain.

Epilogue

The priest's words were over. The coffin was in the grave. The small group of mourners had long since turned away and left. But still Brewer stood there, ignoring the pain from his wounds. Two weeks later, they remained raw, bloody and painful. Pain made worse by the memory of their cause, the events of that pitiless, pointless day.

A cold wind blew from the north, cutting through him. He turned his back and shivered. It was as cold and bleak as it had ever been, as heartless as the darkest wintry days of the Cold War.

Brewer was not alone. One other person stood near him, one other person who had not found it so easy to leave with the crowd: Pendleton. And it was Pendleton who now placed a fatherly hand on his arm.

'Come on, Brewer. Come on.'

Brewer turned to follow him. And as he did, a movement in the trees near the graves caught his attention. He stopped and looked. Nothing. Had he imagined it? He watched and waited while Pendleton continued ahead of him, unaware that Brewer had stopped.

And then a figure stepped out from the trees and now Brewer could see him clearly. They stood staring at each other across the grave.

Gary.

And in that brief, flickering moment of shocked recognition, Gary nodded towards him—and was gone, leaving Brewer to wonder whether he had imagined the whole thing.

'Come on Brewer!'

Pendleton was waiting at the edge of the car park beside the church.

Brewer looked one last time at the grave and the trees.

'Goodbye Gary, goodbye Jane.'

The pain was intense, almost unbearable: two people he loved, two impossible, painful sacrifices.

And then he turned away and walked into the cold, damp gloom of the day.